DEFIANCE COUNTY

Also by Jay Brandon

Deadbolt
Tripwire
Predator's Waltz
Fade the Heat
Rules of Evidence
Loose Among the Lambs
Local Rules

Published by POCKET BOOKS

DEFIANCE COUNTY

JAY BRANDON

POCKET BOOKS

New York   London   Toronto   Sydney   Tokyo   Singapore

This book is a work of fiction. Names, characters, places and incidents are products of the author's imagination or are used fictitiously. Any resemblance to actual events or locales or persons, living or dead, is entirely coincidental.

POCKET BOOKS, a division of Simon & Schuster Inc.
1230 Avenue of the Americas, New York, NY 10020

Library of Congress Cataloging-in-Publication Data

Brandon, Jay.
    Defiance County / Jay Brandon.
        p.   cm.
    ISBN 0-671-53654-0
    1. Public prosecutors—Texas—Fiction.   2. Women lawyers—Texas—
Fiction.   I. Title.
PS3552.R315D44   1996
813'.54—dc20   96-3540
                                                                              CIP

First Pocket Books hardcover printing June 1996

10 9 8 7 6 5 4 3 2 1

Printed in the U.S.A.

in memory of Barbara Chasan, 1954–1995:
she had a gift for friendship

DEFIANCE COUNTY

1

"**S**o what's she like, this girl you're sending us?"

"Very bright, very quick," the attorney general said. "And let me just advise you that you will get off on the wrong foot with her if she hears you calling her a girl."

The district attorney didn't respond. It might be to his advantage, someday, somehow, to have the attorney general of Texas think him not very bright. If the time came to disabuse him of that notion, Morgan Fletcher could do so in a matter of moments.

"She'll probably listen to advice from you," the AG went on, "in fact she might welcome it, but you have to let her think she's making up her own mind. You know the kind?" The attorney general stopped abruptly, thinking he might have said too much. Morgan Fletcher heard a little cough come through the phone line. A little cough traveling all the way from Austin, carrying a tiny freight of the attorney general's uneasiness.

"Nothing wrong with that," the district attorney said easily. "What I want to know is, is she good? We've got a can of worms here."

"Sure she's good," the attorney general said halfheartedly. He moved papers around on his desk until he'd uncovered his calendar. His attention began to wander.

"She's not from your regular Assistance to Prosecutors division," Morgan Fletcher said without emphasis.

"No. Matter of fact, she hasn't tried a criminal case in a while. But make no mistake about it, she's good. Started in the Houston DA's office. She's damned good."

1

"Well, good. That's what we need."

After a few amenities the men hung up. The attorney general stared at his phone. *I've sent her to meet her maker*, he thought. Then he forgot about Kelsey.

Morgan Fletcher set his desk phone down lightly. "Well?" said the other man in the office.

"We'll be all right," the district attorney said. "I think the AG may even have done me a favor, sending someone who'll feel a little lost. We need to show her a nice welcome."

"I don't think I can get too many people out for a parade," Billy Fletcher said heavily.

The district attorney looked at him reassuringly. Billy sat in one of the semicomfortable wooden visitor's chairs, his hands up on the arms of the chair as if he were about to push himself up, but the lines of his body were slumped. His suit looked tired.

"Don't worry," Morgan said to his brother. "You didn't do it, Billy, you'll be all right."

The district attorney gave his brother a searching look that Billy didn't return. He sat there lost in thought. In memory.

It was the baby that had gotten the case statewide attention. That and the DA's brother being arrested for the murders. Otherwise it was just an ordinary family killing, the kind that happens every day. But the wide, futile search for the baby, reported daily in every newspaper in the state, and many in the rest of the country, had irretrievably stuck the case in people's minds. The sheriff of the county had become a recognizable TV figure as he'd daily announced, more and more glumly, the lack of clues. No one could have missed the story.

It was a big case, the biggest in the state, this week at least. The question had been startled out of Kelsey Thatch when the attorney general had handed her the assignment: "Why me?"

"Because my regular guys are up to their necks in alligators in other cases," the attorney general had said, then he'd looked at her with that wide, clear, untroubled expression, the one that appeared on his campaign posters. "You don't mind helping me out, do you, Kelsey?"

No, of course not. But Kelsey's suspicion, already awakened,

2

was put on full alert by the next exchange. "Which investigator is going with me?"

"Uh, actually, they're all tied up, too, right now. But don't worry, they're assigning you a Texas Ranger."

"Fine." But Kelsey didn't at all like that "they're." And she saw there was no more use asking her boss questions.

It was a wet morning, of course, in east Texas, a refreshing change from Austin, where rainstorms skirted the city or died passing over it. Kelsey had spent the night in Houston with an old friend from her days in the DA's office there. Kelsey had gone to work in the Harris County district attorney's office her first day out of law school, as green and wet as the lush grass of Houston, and by the time she was twenty-eight, nearly a hundred people in prison could thank Kelsey for that address. But she'd left the office under a small cloud after discovering in herself an unexpected sensitivity to questions of guilt and innocence. Moving to Austin and the Assets Forfeiture Division of the attorney general's office, dealing only with property, had been like pleasant semiretirement for Kelsey.

Now, though, on her own, heading into what for her was uncharted geography, she remembered the satisfaction of prosecuting a tough case, the confidence of being perpetually on the high moral ground. It would be nice to uncomplicate.

She remembered the baby again. After two weeks the search for her had dwindled to background static. No one had officially announced the presumption of what had happened to a five-month-old girl missing for three weeks, but everyone could figure it out for themselves.

Still, the missing baby would be part of Kelsey's case. It was another crime, kidnapping at the very least. She would be the one who would have to speak the presumption of murder in a courtroom. She wondered if she was still as hardened as she'd been in her prosecution days, when she could hold small bloody clothes dry-eyed in front of a jury.

At least there'd be no surviving, grieving parents to handle.

A green sign told her when she'd entered Defiance County. The sign was almost lost in the green background of tall pines.

Kelsey felt a little lost herself. She had only been driving an hour and a half from Houston, but she'd never been in this part of Texas before, and she felt hidden in the back of beyond. The town of Galilee lay somewhere just ahead of her, but a bigger city than that could have been hidden in these piney woods. It was strange country. Kelsey had lived in Texas all her life, in several parts of the state. She was used to wide vistas, flat, dry land, or woodsy acres with hills in the distance. East Texas was different. The soaring pines came up close to the highway. As she tried to peer more deeply into the woods, the pines seemed to cluster closer, blocking her view. Shorter greenery obscured the ground so that the pines seemed to rise out of a dense, bristling fog. In the near distance the shrubs and the trees became darkness, even in midmorning.

Kelsey tried to imagine living here. How isolated people must feel. How lonely. The feeling of being alone in the woods must scare some people. Others it would imbue with a sense of power.

A family of three had been staying here, in a house in the country close to town. Someone had come into the house, creeping out of these woods, and murdered the parents and taken the baby. Kelsey passed a house in a small clearing and slowed to look at it. It was a small cabin with a narrow front porch of unpainted boards and a cedar-shake roof that looked too heavy for the old wooden frame of the house to support. She imagined the crime happening inside there, three grown people trapped in its narrow confines, screaming, enraged, terrified, one firing a gun; and the baby in her crib screaming, too, with no idea what was happening.

Kelsey focused on the imagined face of the baby as the crime began to grow real for her. The killer might have had real grievances against the husband and wife. But there was no excuse for the baby. Kelsey continued to drive slowly until she realized she wasn't seeing the road any more. Her hands were gripping the steering wheel so tightly they hurt. She took a long breath and forced herself to relax, but the feeling didn't go away; the feeling that she was responsible. No one else here could be trusted, so she'd been given the responsibility. Maybe for the wrong reasons, but nevertheless she was here. Had that couple in the woods ever wondered to whom they could turn for protection if they needed it? The answer had turned out to be no one, but in a way Kelsey was their protector after the fact. She remembered as a prosecutor developing this posthumous protectiveness toward victims. She could no longer save their lives, but here she was riding into town like a hired gun, sent to exact official vengeance for their deaths.

The woods began to draw back from the road. The landscape opened up. She was on a little two-lane state highway, having left the interstate fifteen miles back. The road began to widen, preparing to turn into the main street of Galilee. Before she left the woods, Kelsey rolled down the window and felt thin streams of cool air seep into the car. It was October, summer wasn't long over where she came from, but in east Texas winter seemed to lurk in those perpetually green woods. Something else intruded into the car: the pungent smell of decay, pine needles and the detritus of the woods packing down into humus that would become soil for later growth. Kelsey continued to drive slowly, looking around. She passed a house, then another, then the houses began to cluster together. There was a two-pump gas station with a little store; next to it a much more modern Dairy Queen with a bright red plastic roof. Kelsey pulled off into the gas station and got out, mainly to take a break from driving. She didn't even know where the courthouse was. No one stirred inside the store. She leaned on her folded arms on the roof of her car and looked toward town. The town was somehow reassuring after the road that had seemed like a tunnel through the pines, but as she stood on the concrete slab, Kelsey's eyes were drawn back to the woods, rising on a gentle upslope visible above the town. A vertical line caught her eye, a smudge against the sky.

Smoke was rising out of the woods. Not the smoke of a forest fire, just the thin, wavering line of a man-made fire, someone burning leaves or trash. As Kelsey watched, the narrow finger of smoke grew paler and dissipated to nothing.

The town was bigger than she'd imagined. Galilee could not have been lost in the woods after all. Kelsey drove without stopping to ask for directions, turning off into residential sections, trying to get a sense of the town. She found a neighborhood of weathered houses little more than shacks, where driveways were only ruts in the mud, but she also drove through neighborhoods of well-kept brick houses, most middle-class, some distinctly more expensive than that. The town impressed her. She passed a large modern grocery store with a trash-free parking lot and freshly changed signs advertising specials. Several banks sat staunchly in their lots behind landscaped hedges and flower beds. There were empty stores and buildings for rent, but not as many as she usually saw when passing through small Texas towns. The high school looked as large as the one Kelsey had attended in Waco.

Eventually she came across the courthouse, which occupied its own block in the middle of downtown. The courthouse was made of native Texas stone, the building wider than it was high, with tall windows. It looked to be of 1920s or 1930s vintage. At some time the courthouse doors had been replaced. The aluminum-framed, plate-glass, whoosh-opening doors looked out of place in their stone doorways, like cat's-eye glasses on a matronly woman's stern face. Kelsey walked around the building before entering, unsure of what kind of reception to expect. She was here as a prosecutor, so should naturally be a colleague of the local district attorney, but if the DA could have handled this case himself, she wouldn't have been in Galilee. The man charged with the double homicide was the district attorney's brother. So Kelsey was prepared for hostility, overt or subtle, from the local prosecutor. She pulled open one of those anomalous grocery-store doors and went into the Defiance County Courthouse to find him.

"You don't exactly come to us trailing clouds of glory from your last prosecution, do you?" Morgan Fletcher said. Kelsey was so taken aback her face couldn't find an appropriate expression. In the next sentence Morgan's tone changed measurably. He was earnest, serious, a colleague. "A big-city DA's office isn't really the place for an ethically independent person, is it? Bastards." Again he changed abruptly, not only before Kelsey could reply, before she could even settle on the right tone. He drew back, becoming distant and a little stern, while still looking at her with deep concern. "But I hope you've put all that behind you. Because the case you're here on is the most important case in the world."

Morgan Fletcher stood from where he'd been leaning back on a corner of his desk. Kelsey noticed the breadth of his shoulders. Fletcher was a little under six feet tall, athletically built, somewhere in his forties, when a man's decline in physical power begins to be replaced, if he's lucky, with moral authority. Morgan Fletcher dripped moral authority. He stepped close to her. The district attorney had one of those heads that could make a man a movie star or a good trial lawyer: slightly oversized, with expressive features. His eyes were deep and sorrowful. "I know you hear that about every criminal case. No one knows that better than I do, right? But in this case it's true. In our little corner of the world this is the most important case there is. I know you have your own life and problems, this"—he picked carefully through her feelings—"may seem like small potatoes, but I hope I can make you see—"

"There is nothing small about this case as far as I'm concerned," Kelsey said. "I don't know what your experience is of special prosecutors, Mr. Fletcher, but believe me, I'm not distracted. This case is the only thing in my life right now."

Still studying her, he smiled slightly. "Thank you.

"Now," he said more briskly. "Let's get you started. You're going to have to guide me through this. I've never worked with a special prosecutor before, let alone been replaced by one. I realize our contacts should be minimal, but any resource we have is yours. We've cleared a room for you here in the courthouse to use for an office if you want. You can make use of any of our secretarial staff, word processing, of course any office supplies. Our records are all open to you. But I imagine the attorney general's office takes care of all that for you, don't they?"

Maybe they did. Kelsey wouldn't know, never having been a special prosecutor before. But she wasn't going to tell Morgan Fletcher that, partly because she didn't want to expose herself to any doubts about her abilities. The other part was a reason she'd just developed in the last two minutes: Morgan Fletcher, in spite of his deep voice and confident manner, seemed to need reassurance.

His office was large, bright and sunny with all the shades

raised to the October day. Good solid old wooden moldings adorned the tops of all the high walls and surrounded the windows. The furniture matched the molding in its wooden sturdiness. The walls were whitewashed plaster. Kelsey felt taken back in time. Morgan Fletcher fit the office well, in his dark, three-piece suit. She felt his eyes on her, studying her—as was only natural of a man meeting the woman who would not only take his place but would be trying to send his brother to prison—but she sensed no hostility.

"You'll have an investigator?" he asked as Kelsey stood and he guided her subtly toward the door.

"Yes, a Texas Ranger's supposed to be meeting me here."

"Good. I'm sure, though—don't let me walk over you, I'm just trying to imagine what I'd want in your position—you'll probably want someone local as well, just for background if nothing else. You wouldn't want one of our investigators since I've recused the whole office, but I'm sure Sheriff Early will assign someone to you. You can make as much or as little use of him as you want."

They went out into the outer office, where Morgan Fletcher's secretary glanced up from her computer. Kelsey smiled. She and the secretary had already been introduced. The fiftyish woman moved her head ever so slightly, more a tremor than a nod, but watched Kelsey steadily through her glasses.

"Down this way."

The hall was dim and slightly musty. Kelsey felt Morgan Fletcher close beside her. She glanced up at him and immediately felt she'd intruded on his privacy. He wasn't looking at her, just staring down the hall with a troubled expression.

"How was the arrest made?" Kelsey asked. It was an impulsive question, shoptalk.

"Someone did send you all the police reports?"

"Oh, yes. But there was no report of the arrest."

"Maybe you should get your facts from someone other than me," the district attorney said, not harshly; if anything, he sounded apologetic.

"I will. But you're the only person I know here so far."

He smiled slightly, politely, then became serious again. "Billy—my brother—was in North Carolina by the time we had what we considered enough evidence for an arrest. I called him, he flew back and came on in to the sheriff's office voluntarily." Fletcher shrugged.

"You drew up the arrest warrant?"

He stopped, not to answer the question but to open the door to a small office. They both glanced in. "Yes," Fletcher said. "We always do the warrants for the police agencies, so I did it this time, too. I figured it would be my last official involvement in the case. And since Billy didn't give any statement as a result of the arrest, it doesn't matter how valid the warrant was."

"I wasn't implying—"

Fletcher entered the office and turned on the light. There was an old metal desk, a short bookcase, and not much room for anything else. Fletcher stopped her protestation. "You have no idea of my competence. And certainly no reason to trust any of my actions in this case. That's why you're here."

"Mr. Fletcher, I didn't mean to—"

"I know, I know." He waved his hands for a time-out. "What I mean is, I'm not sensitive. Don't worry about my feelings. That's so low on your list of priorities right now that . . ."

He trailed off and smiled slightly. Kelsey responded, wondering if her smile was as sad as Morgan Fletcher's.

"Well, why don't we go meet the judge?" he said abruptly. "Have you sworn in, get you official." They returned to the hallway, where Fletcher turned to her with another of his hesitations. "And by the way, I think it would be all right if you called me Morgan, wouldn't it?"

Kelsey had caught the district attorney's hesitations. "Well, I—"

"Since the other Mr. Fletcher you'll meet is the defendant, it would be less confusing, wouldn't it?"

And Morgan Fletcher surprised her by laughing.

2

Kelsey suffered a moment of loss that morning while meeting with the judge. Morgan Fletcher took her downstairs from his courthouse office, through the empty courtroom, and Kelsey was surprised by the name above the door: THE HONORABLE LINDA SAUNDERS. Kelsey had expected some old back-country judge, a man who'd held the bench for decades. She kept a formal face as Morgan introduced her to Judge Saunders, but the judge's expression had a tiny sheen of amusement as if she still saw the surprise in Kelsey's face. But her voice was dignified as she said, "I'm pleased to meet you, Ms. Thatch."

Judge Saunders wore a well-tailored business suit and looked like an up-and-coming executive. In her youth, not so many years ago, she must have been a beauty. Her hair was assisted blond, and still bouncy. The judge had a mouth made for smiling: an aging Breck girl, heading very unwillingly toward fifty. But aging well: her skin was taut and moist in those slides under the eyes that could turn into trenches if a girl didn't take care of herself.

"Are you ready?" the judge asked abruptly, and Kelsey didn't know ready for what: trial? the town? The judge raised her right hand and said, "Do you swear to faithfully execute the duties of district attorney of Defiance County, to uphold the laws and constitution of the state of Texas, and to seek justice . . ."

Kelsey hastily raised her hand and swore that she did.

"Then that's that," the judge said informally.

"And the end of me," Morgan Fletcher added from behind Kelsey's shoulder. When she turned, he offered his hand again and said, "Ms. Thatch, again, whatever I can do to assist. But I'm sure Judge Saunders can answer any of your questions for now. Your Honor."

He walked out of the office rather quickly, as if Kelsey and the judge had already begun a conversation on which he didn't wish to intrude. When the door closed behind him, both women were still looking in that direction.

"He, uh," Kelsey said, and changed what she was going to say. "He's been very helpful."

"I knew he would be. Morgan's glad you're here, you know. Oh, sure, he's worried about his brother. But Morgan's been absolutely walking on eggshells, trying to do everything just right, waiting for you to come and take over for him."

The judge's office was even larger than the district attorney's, with a high ceiling. The courthouse had been built in the days before air-conditioning, when the top half of a room had to be storage for hot air. Two walls were interrupted by three windows apiece. The two interior walls held tall bookshelves filled with law books. There was a credenza behind the desk, under the windows, and a long wooden table across the room. The table was strewn with books and papers, and at one end a personal computer. There were posters on the walls, green plants on the desk and credenza and on a stand in front of a window. The furnishings were old-fashioned, but the decoration showed that someone of a generation much younger than the builders had made the room her own.

Judge Saunders went on, "You know the victims were Morgan Fletcher's sister-in-law and her husband and baby. The missing baby is Morgan's niece."

"God," Kelsey breathed. "No, I hadn't worked that out from the police reports."

"So Morgan was torn every way he could be." The judge's voice had a businesslike tone, but in the very flatness of her voice was an underlying compassion. Kelsey now recognized the same toneless quality in Morgan Fletcher's remembered voice as he'd described his brother's arrest. "The first couple of days after the killings Morgan walked around like he didn't know where he was. He was the one who discovered the bodies, you know."

"Yes. But I didn't know—who they were to him."

11

"And the worst part is it may never be over, with the baby still missing." Judge Saunders was looking toward the window, with a long gaze as if she could see the whole area of the search, but with a lost expression as if that long vision revealed nothing. "You almost hope—," she said, then recovered herself and continued briskly.

"When it became clear that Billy was the prime suspect, you would have thought that was the straw that would have snapped Morgan, but instead it seemed to make him pull himself together. He was on the phone to the AG's office before they even swore out the arrest warrant. He's been so careful about not touching anything, staying as far back from it as possible while still doing the things they needed a district attorney to do. I think obsessing on doing the right thing is what's pulled him through."

Kelsey was struck both by the sentiment and by the judge's choice of words. *Obsessing* was such a guest-on-Phil-Donahue kind of word. One more indication that the judge lived at least as much in the modern world as Kelsey did.

"So we're all very glad you're here," Judge Saunders concluded. "What's going to be your first step?"

That was when Kelsey experienced the sense of loss, and of burden. She had come to relieve Morgan Fletcher of his weight of responsibility, and he had passed it on to her. As for the judge's question, Kelsey didn't have an answer. Not only had it been two years since she had prosecuted a criminal case, but when she had done it regularly, in Houston, she had been surrounded by an army of support. By the time she got a case it had already been presented to a grand jury and an indictment obtained. Witnesses would be listed in her file. If she didn't think she had enough evidence, she could turn the file over to an investigator. Then she could make an offer to the defense lawyer and more often than not have the offer accepted.

This case, she knew, would not end like that. So her first step ... The judge was watching her, with a pleasant, waiting expression.

"Interview the witnesses," Kelsey said decisively. "Put together a case to present to a grand jury as soon as I can. Is one in session?"

Judge Saunders shook her head. "We'll convene one for you as soon as you're ready."

Kelsey nodded. The women surveyed each other for a long moment. Kelsey was about to take her leave when the judge decided to speak. "I don't know what kind of relationship you're used to having with the trial judge—"

"All kinds."

"I'll expect to offer you a little more help than I'd have to give Morgan, just to bring you up to speed on local procedures, even local personalities when necessary. But of course any more discussion about the facts of the case—"

"Of course."

"—between us will only take place with the defendant's lawyer present. I know you know these things, but I want to say them explicitly. I'm not going to have any ethical problems resulting from this trial."

"No." To change the subject, which had produced some tension, Kelsey asked, "Who is the defendant's attorney?"

"Clyde Wolverton," the judge said, in such a neutral tone, with such absolute absence of expression, that Kelsey was immediately alerted.

"Clyde Wolverton. Is he local?"

"Oh, yes," said Judge Saunders.

When Kelsey emerged from the judge's chambers, Morgan Fletcher reappeared to introduce her to people she needed to know. The most memorable of the meetings was with Sheriff Winfield Early. The sheriff's face was recognizable to Kelsey from his television appearances of the last few weeks. In person his color was better and a knowing look was in his eye that the cameras hadn't picked up. Sheriff Early was about sixty; he had the creases of genuineness in his face. When he saw Morgan, the sheriff clapped him on the back, almost hugging him, and asked about his family. When he turned to Kelsey, the warmth dropped away. Only professional courtesy was left.

"Miss Thatch, pleased. We'll give you everything we've got, of course."

"Thank you." Morgan Fletcher drifted away, saying hello to others in the sheriff's offices, giving Kelsey a private moment with the sheriff. She took advantage of it to ask confidentially, "How's the search going?"

The sheriff also glanced around to make sure Morgan wasn't within hearing distance. Then he looked at Kelsey appraisingly for a long moment, deciding whether to give her the official version or the lowdown. "I wouldn't count on it," he said quietly.

They were in a small glass-walled office beside the large squad room. The big room was not a hotbed of activity. Two uniformed deputies occupied desks, one on the phone, the other typing. Across the room, at a desk set a little apart, a middle-aged woman in civilian clothes was also listening on the phone. She was sitting forward, concentrating, but after a moment she settled back in her chair and stopped making notes.

"Noreen is taking the calls now," Sheriff Early said, seeing the direction of Kelsey's gaze. "They're still coming in, but they're getting more and more far-fetched."

"What about the physical search?"

"Not a trail, not a trace. It's not just us, civilians have helped out. There's a lot of woods in this county, but we've covered most of them. If we haven't found her by now ..."

He didn't have to finish. A five-month-old baby: abandoning her would be the same as murder.

Kelsey looked into the older man's face. "Sheriff, you know everyone involved. Why would the murderer have taken that baby?"

The sheriff shook his head. It was obviously a question he'd pondered. "Normally a case like this you'd suspect one of the parents, but of course they're out. Every other possible suspect is somebody you'd think would want to protect the girl. Somebody fleeing a murder scene, stopping to take a baby along, that would only incriminate him—it doesn't make any kind of sense. All that leaves is insanity, Miss Thatch. I can't fathom a crazy person's mind."

But even the insane have their reasons. "Could the baby somehow have been a witness?"

Sheriff Early looked very tired. From the way he looked at her it was clear he thought Kelsey's suggestion ranked low on the rationality scale, even for a crazy suspect. But it was one the sheriff had considered.

"Then why wouldn't he have just killed her?" he said. "He certainly wasn't reluctant to shoot people."

Kelsey remembered the picture she'd seen of the baby girl and she felt cold, the cold of the vast piney woods seeping under her skin.

When Kelsey walked out into the main room she saw the woman named Noreen, her head turned away from everyone else in the office. The slump of the woman's shoulders was eloquent.

In parting, the sheriff said something to Morgan that Kelsey found strange. "Tell Billy to hang in there," the sheriff said, and Morgan nodded.

Her motel was an old-fashioned motor court on one of the two main roads of Galilee, less than a mile from the courthouse. Just stepping into her room was unsettling, the beginning of an unwanted new life. Someone had committed murder, but it was Kelsey who had ended up in a cell. A double bed, mattress permanently indented in the center, took up most of the floor space. In the front corner of the room, close to the only window, was a round pasteboard table, accompanied by two of the worst chairs ever manufactured: those low-slung chairs with long, padded seats and long, flat arms, with backs, also thinly padded, that sloped outward from the seats. To have any back support in one of those chairs, a sitter had to lean way back, almost to the point of looking up at the ceiling. Kelsey was familiar with the chairs from other motel rooms; they must have been designed by a chiropractor to insure steady customers for his profession.

Otherwise the room featured a pasteboard dresser bolted to the wall, a mirror above it, a closet with sliding, squeaking doors, and a framed print of a hunter passing under autumn trees with his dog. What was really sad about the room was that it reminded Kelsey of her first apartment in college and in fact was not that much less homey than her current apartment in Austin.

But Austin was home, and here she was a complete outsider. Kelsey had spent the afternoon being introduced to people she was assured would help her, but it had quickly become clear that any help would be grudging. In the courthouse and the sheriff's office she had felt constant sidelong looks, confronted flat stares whenever she turned, and found smiles rare and brief. Confirming her impression had been the sheriff's message of cheer to the defendant he'd helped arrest. It was a strange town that felt more warmth toward a presumed murderer than toward the woman assigned to prosecute him.

The contradictory impulses reflected in the place names still prevailed. The county must have been named about the time of the Texas Revolution, when defiance was the order of the day. But the town had been settled and named by devout, kindhearted pilgrims. Kelsey had seen the stony face of defiance peeking out from behind the good country manners.

Well, she hadn't come looking for approval. Kelsey squeaked open the closet door, hung her skirt neatly on a wooden hanger, hung her jacket on the same hanger, and was just sliding her half-slip down her legs when there was a knock at her door.

"Well, hell," she said. She hesitated a moment, then hastily pulled the skirt off the hanger, kicked the half-slip into the closet, and called, "Coming," as she stepped back into the skirt and got it adjusted and zipped as she hurried to the door.

There was no other knock. In fact, her visitor had already turned away by the time she opened the door. She saw a slim young man dressed all in brown. When the man turned toward her, Kelsey saw that it was a uniform he wore, and that he wasn't quite as young as she'd first supposed. He wore a badge over his left breast pocket.

"Miss Thatch?"

"Is something wrong?" Kelsey asked, causing the officer to look back over his shoulder again.

"Why?"

"Well, be— Nothing. Yes, I'm Kelsey Thatch. What can I do for you?"

"Peter Stiller. Sheriff Early asked me to drop by and introduce myself. I went by the office they gave you at the courthouse, but it didn't look like you'd been there. The district attorney's secretary told me you were staying here."

"Uh-huh?" Kelsey remained in the doorway.

With slight exasperation, Peter Stiller said, "The sheriff assigned me to assist you with the case. To give you whatever investigative help you need."

"Oh, oh." She remembered Morgan Fletcher had said that

would happen. She shook her head. "That's nice of the sheriff, but I'm having a Texas Ranger assigned to me."

Peter Stiller was about her age, she thought, early thirties. He had the look of a kind of man rural Texas produces frequently—thin but strong-looking, whittled by wind and sun. He had thick brown hair but pale eyes that remained fixed on Kelsey, appraising her as intently as anyone she'd met today, although the deputy's manner was more polite. At Kelsey's mention of the Texas Ranger he looked both slightly offended and more than slightly relieved.

"Oh. Okay. Good. Well, here's my card, and another one you can give to the Ranger. If either of you wants to give me a call . . ."

"Maybe you could help. Do you jog?"

"What?"

"I was feeling kind of restless, thought I'd go for a run. If you wanted to come along, we could talk while we run."

The deputy gave a small sigh. "No, I don't jog. I'll drive along beside you in the squad car if you want, though."

They looked at each other with the same mix of irritation and amusement, and Kelsey said, "Why don't you come in for a minute?"

After the door closed, the motel room seemed dim after the outside daylight. Deputy Stiller, carefully not looking around her room, laid his two cards on the dresser and stood waiting.

"Maybe, until my investigator does arrive, you could just give me a little background." Kelsey sat on a corner of the bed and gestured at one of the motel chairs. Deputy Stiller looked the chair over and decided to remain standing. But, "Sure," he volunteered, relaxing slightly.

"It's been a little chilly here," Kelsey said lightly.

"Really? More than Austin?"

"I mean the people. Except for the district attorney, who's the one with the most reason to resent me, nobody here has exactly welcomed me with open arms."

Peter Stiller looked at her with mild surprise. "Do they usually?"

"I have friends all over this state," Kelsey said defensively.

"I mean when you're special prosecuting," the deputy explained gently. "It seems like most people wouldn't be very happy to see you. Not you personally, you understand, but you're sort of like the undertaker, you don't show up unless something bad's happened."

He was undoubtedly right. "Or like a cop," Kelsey said.

The deputy nodded agreement. They looked at each other a moment, waiting for a tone to emerge from their meeting. Kelsey didn't feel the sense of resentment from Peter Stiller she'd sensed from so many other townspeople, though he certainly seemed watchful. He didn't initiate conversation, he waited for her.

Beneath his alertness, he looked tired, making Kelsey think that the search for the baby was not winding down into undeclared failure as she'd assumed, that it was still occupying law officers' hours and after hours.

"But there's something special about this case," she continued. "I know, I know, that's why I'm here. But what is it about Billy Fletcher? He has friends that have nothing to do with being the DA's brother. Right? Or people owe him. Is he some sort of political power?"

"Never heard of Billy being interested in politics. But power, I guess you could say that. A lot of people here owe him their livings. We've got a factory here, did you see it driving in?" Kelsey shook her head. Stiller shrugged. "Well, we've got one, and it's far and away the biggest employer in town. Hardly a family that doesn't have somebody working there. And Billy Fletcher's the general manager."

Ah. The explanation gave perfect background to the looks she'd received, the way people studied her openly or in sidelong glances, the grudging offers of cooperation.

"Something to keep in mind when you pick a jury," the deputy said. "If you get that far. Lot of people'd like to see you dismiss the case."

"People want to see crimes like this go unpunished?"

"People don't want to believe somebody they know could have done them," the deputy said flatly.

"Hmm."

"Hmm," Peter Stiller replied, gently mocking. He stood and watched her think, with a small ironic expression. After a while Kelsey returned it.

*　　*　　*

They met at a crossroads. After Deputy Stiller's departure Kelsey changed into sweats and went for her run after all. She kept running farther than she'd planned because she never reached a point where turning back toward her motel room seemed inviting. At first she was running through little neighborhoods, then through a commercial strip, then the buildings thinned out into ones requiring larger parking lots—a grocery store, a building-supplies store, Wal-Mart—into territory that was barely tended by humans, where the strip of mowed grass beside the road seemed to hunch down against the advance of its big brothers from the woods beyond. There might have been more houses set back in that wooded area, but they were the houses of people jealous of their privacy. Kelsey kept running. Cars passed. Sometimes it seemed to her they slowed. Eyes in the rearview mirrors. In the era of the cellular phone, her progress could have been reported to a wide network of locals. She dismissed the idea as paranoia, though paranoia seemed a rational response to her situation, and to the shadows spilling slowly across the road from the tall, old pines on either side. She had jogged too far, late-October dusk would soon die, and Kelsey would have provided herself with a long run home across unfamiliar ground in the dark. Still she didn't want to turn back. She wondered, as she sometimes did when running, how far it was to the next town.

Then the main road she was running beside intersected a street that ran left and right into those pines, reinforcing Kelsey's idea that secret neighborhoods were back in the trees, and Morgan Fletcher was there, standing in profile to her, looking down that road to the right.

Kelsey didn't want to run any farther, and she didn't want Morgan Fletcher to think she would turn and run away at the sight of him, so she bent and put her hands on her knees and waited for the district attorney to notice her.

Morgan was wearing a sweatsuit, too, but he wasn't sweating or breathing hard, and his hair was neat. He looked a little incongruous, as if he would doff the sweatsuit to reveal a suit and tie. He turned slowly and just looked toward her for half a minute, as if Kelsey's change in appearance made her hard to recognize. Or as if he were looking through her.

Then he crossed the street, and they offered the greetings of people unexpectedly finding each other outside their accustomed circumstances. "You run, too?" Kelsey asked.

"Sometimes. But I'm just out for a walk tonight. I live back down that way, my mother-in-law lives a little ways up this road. I thought I might check on her. Would you like to see?" he asked, his voice changing, so that Kelsey was slow to answer. Morgan lowered his eyes and added, "My mother-in-law's house is—where I found them. The murder scene."

"Oh." *No,* was Kelsey's immediate reaction, though she felt curiosity crawling up her spine, spreading through her shoulders. "I wouldn't want to bother her now. It doesn't—"

Morgan regained his composure. "You can just see it," he said, taking her arm, "so you'll know where it is."

As they walked down the road to the right, night happened. There was no subtle transition from dusk to dark; when the sun dropped below the trees, its light was extinguished abruptly. Morgan saw Kelsey looking toward a street sign across the road, but it was already too dark for her to read it.

"Morningside Drive," he told her.

Yes, this was the east side of town, the morning side, though she would have bet those woods were as grudging with dawn as they were with dusk. Out here where the town ended, morning wouldn't arrive until the sun was above the trees.

"You just passed the city limits about a block back," Morgan told her. "When Mama Beaumont and her husband built out here, they were all alone, and the town grew the other direction, back toward the interstate highway. Some people say that's how the Beaumonts wanted it."

Kelsey walked beside the district attorney in near silence, with little murmurs and head nods to show she was listening. It felt odd to be in his presence, being guided and hosted by the man she was here to replace. She wanted to ask him official questions, she wanted to say something consoling about his family tragedy, and as neither seemed appropriate, she remained silent.

"There it is," he said suddenly. They were across the street from a tall, old wood-frame house, Victorian in style, with gabled windows on the second floor and an attic above that. On the ground a wraparound porch extended out from the front and left sides of the house. On the right a driveway led back to a detached garage. Only one light was burning, in a downstairs window, as if the house were deserted, or darkness had taken its inhabitants unawares, too.

"There's one bedroom downstairs," Morgan Fletcher said. His tone was absolutely professional, but Kelsey turned to see his eyes traveling around the outside of the house, as if he could see more than he was describing. "And they'd turned the dining room into a little sitting room for the baby. That's where I found them. That front right corner there."

"Your mother-in-law was out?"

"No, she was upstairs. But in bed. She had a terrible case of flu. That's why Lorrie and Ronald had come to visit. They lived in Dallas." He had no trouble with the past tense, Kelsey noticed. "They came for visits regularly. When Lorrie heard how sick her mother was, she wanted to come help out."

Kelsey nodded. She didn't ask anything. The house might have looked inviting in daylight, with that beckoning porch, but by night, almost unlit, it repelled her, even while she felt a sneaking desire to creep up and peer through that right front window, as if there might still be bodies lying on the dining-room floor, or bloodstains on the rug.

"I can show you around inside another time," Morgan said. "Or you can look around by yourself. At any rate, you won't need a warrant. Just give me a call and I'll get my mother-in-law out for as long as you need."

"She must be devastated. I hate to intrude on her." Nothing Morgan could have said would have induced Kelsey to go in and meet the old woman at that moment. She couldn't imagine the grief filling that house. They wouldn't be waiting twenty-four hours a day for word of the search, but sleep must be rare and precious. By now the family had to be in transition from the frenzy of trying to find the baby to resigning themselves to her loss, along with the loss of the old woman's daughter and son-in-law. It was too much to bear.

"She'll want to help," Morgan said. After a moment of silence, of giving her a chance to ask questions, Morgan drew himself together and said, "I'll just run in and borrow her car keys and I can give you a ride back to your motel."

"Oh, no, don't bother. I can—"

He shook his head, accepting no argument. "Run back in the dark, beside the traffic? You're not wearing anything reflective, are you?" He craned his neck to run his eyes down her back. "Even if you were ... And I know how easy it is to turn an ankle. I'll be right back."

Kelsey didn't protest any further. Growing chilled in the October night, she wanted a hot shower as quickly as possible. Morgan Fletcher jogged across the road and up the porch steps and opened the front door of the house after a quick knock. He disappeared through the door and more lights came on inside. Kelsey watched, curious about the inside of the house. She realized she was holding her breath, watching for the sight of silhouettes hurtling past the curtains, listening for the sound of hoarse cries and a gunshot. The house remained still. It was as quiet as if no one were home.

As she waited, Kelsey remembered one thing Morgan had said, the one sentence he hadn't completed. "Even if you were" wearing reflective clothes, he'd said, and stopped. Did he mean to imply the special prosecutor from out of town might make a tempting target for a hit-and-run driver as she ran beside the road? Or was Kelsey being overly sensitive again? Galilee aroused that trait in her.

As she lay in the uncomfortable, unfamiliar bed that night, the shadows seeming to breathe the sound of wind through pine needles, it wasn't Morgan Fletcher she thought about, it was the young deputy, Peter Stiller. In retrospect, maybe only because of this damned newfound sensitivity, something he'd said had a different character. "It's been a little chilly here," Kelsey had said, and Stiller had replied, "Really? More than Austin?" Thinking he'd thought she was talking about the air temperature, Kelsey had said, "I mean the people."

Now she thought she remembered a tiny smile crossing the deputy's face, as if she'd misunderstood him rather than the other way around. Maybe Peter Stiller had been talking about the people in Austin, too, where in fact things had been a little chilly around Kelsey's office until they'd spewed her out halfway across the state. Maybe that's what the deputy had meant. After all, Morgan Fletcher had done his homework on her. Clearly he knew why Kelsey had left the Harris County DA's office, two years ago. Maybe everyone in Defiance County was equally well-informed.

Did everyone here know all her business, while they were complete enigmas to her?

3

"I'm sorry to be the one to make the case against Billy," Andrew Sims said. "Billy's a good guy. But I saw what I saw and I won't say any different." Seeing Kelsey nod, Sims added, "I won't embellish the story to help you out, either."

"I wouldn't ask you to," Kelsey said. It was Sims's turn to nod, satisfied they'd gotten their relationship straight.

Andrew Sims was a black man of imposing size and distinguished appearance. Gray flecked his hair, but aging seemed not to have made much headway below his chin. His arms strained the short sleeves of his light brown uniform shirt. Sims had been a game warden for fifteen years. His paycheck, like Kelsey's, came from Austin and wouldn't be affected by local politics or economics. He didn't seem like a man who'd worry about pressure, anyway.

They were meeting early morning in the parking lot of a coffee shop on the northern edge of town. It wasn't that Sims didn't want to be seen talking to the special prosecutor—he'd already nodded at or helloed three people during their introductions—but he was headed out and it would be easier, he'd said, for Kelsey to meet him before she went into town. He folded his arms and leaned against the door of his car. That is, his legs leaned; his back stayed perfectly straight.

"How was it you came to be a witness?"

"I didn't know that's what I was coming to do," Sims replied with a small laugh that died as he began his narrative. "I was driving by Miz Beaumont's house that morning when I saw Billy and Ronald Blystone on the front porch, and I stopped."

"Why'd you stop?"

"Because I saw two men I knew screaming at each other and I wanted to make sure it was nothing serious. Around here it's not considered polite to drive on by somebody you know without at least a honk and a wave, and I did that and they didn't even notice. So I stopped."

"Now Ronald Blystone," Kelsey said slowly, because these were still just names to her, "was Billy Fletcher's . . . brother-in-law?"

"No, he was Billy's brother's brother-in-law. Morgan Fletcher's married to Katherine, and years later Ronald Blystone married Katherine's sister, Lorrie. The two daughters of Miz Beaumont."

"Who is Billy Fletcher's employer," Kelsey concluded in minor triumph. Andrew Sims nodded, willing to take things at Kelsey's pace.

"Okay, go ahead." A passing car, demonstrating the truth of Sims's earlier observation, honked as it passed, and Sims waved. Kelsey circled him, not only to see the car, but to get the sun out of her eyes. The sun had just risen above the pines, abruptly driving long shadows out of every standing object. The morning breeze died. Kelsey's light jacket suddenly seemed excessive.

"What were they shouting at each other?" Kelsey was hearing her first report of Ronald Blystone alive and Billy Fletcher enraged and expected the case to start taking shape for her.

"That part wasn't any of my business. I think anybody in town could tell you what the argument was about, though."

"You're somebody in town."

"I just heard this much. I opened my door and stepped out and Billy was saying, 'It's not your company. It's not even hers.' Pointing inside to where I guess Lorrie was. 'You've got no right—' Something like that. That's when I gave another tap on the horn and waved, just to give them a little time-out, because they were nose to nose and fists clenched. They heard me that time and Billy waved, but I don't think it helped. And I drove on."

"Do you know about what time it was?"

"I know exactly what time it was. Ten o'clock in the morning."

"Why'd you happen to look at the time?" Kelsey asked casually.

"Because I did. It was a weekday morning and I wondered why Billy wasn't at the factory. Later I heard he'd had a plane to catch."

Kelsey knew about the plane trip, to North Carolina for a business meeting.

"Did you go back by the house later?"

Sims shook his head. "Plenty of people did, though, from all the news around town. Place must have been crawling with anybody who could pretend a good reason to be there. That's all you heard for the next week or two, about the inside of that dining room."

Which meant Kelsey could draw information from a lot of sources, but it also meant the town had its own widely held theory of what had happened.

"Do you have any relatives who work at the factory?" she asked impulsively.

"Now that's the right question," Andrew Sims said approvingly. "In my case the answer is no. My brother and I both worked there a year or so—different years—but he's in Houston now and I'm a bureaucrat for the state." At that he gave her a comradely smile.

The first time Kelsey paused before a question, Sims broke off the interview. "Gotta go," he said, and in a few long strides he was around his car and standing in the open door. But then Andrew Sims stopped, staring past Kelsey into the pine trees. "Maybe if I'd gone inside the house . . . ," he said softly.

Before Kelsey could say it wasn't that easy to avert tragedy, Sims was gone, his black-and-white car roaring toward the woods. Kelsey could suddenly picture him there among the trees, head cocked, listening intently.

"Can I use your phone?" the man asked with such barely restrained urgency that Kelsey stepped aside and gestured at the phone on her desk even though she'd never seen the man before in her life.

The man held the receiver in his hand, shaking it like an orchestra conductor's baton urging a faster pace. He punched a string of digits, more than for a local call, and as he waited, the jitters moved from his hand to his leg. He stood tapping his foot, still staring at Kelsey. They were in her small office in the Defiance County Courthouse, a place where she expected no visitors, so she assumed the man had burst through her door at random, but as he waited, he pulled aside his jacket to show the badge on his shirt pocket. Walking closer, Kelsey read the words, "Texas Department of Public Safety." The lack of uniform on her visitor told the rest of the story. Here was her Texas Ranger investigator. She went back and shut her office door.

The Ranger was a man not much taller than Kelsey, with friendly cheeks and a worried forehead. "Miss Thatch? Glad to meet you. Efran Price. Be right with you. Honey?"

He sat abruptly. "How are you doing?" he said sweetly and less urgently into the phone, then his eyes widened. "When?" he asked loudly. His eyes shot around the walls of the office, then landed on the watch on his wrist. "Bad?" Price asked. "A hard one? Well, call the doctor anyway. Call her. I'll be there as soon as I can, but it'll take me an hour. I'll call you on the radio. I'll get . . . Okay, okay. Bye. Oh, the hell with that. I love you. Lay down. No, no, walk around. Okay, what? . . . I'll be there."

Kelsey made no pretense of not listening. She looked at the Ranger expectantly after he hung up. "Something wrong?"

The two words further energized him. He leaped from behind the desk, jammed onto his head the gray cowboy hat he'd been carrying, and moved for the door. Only the fact that Kelsey was in his path returned her to his attention. He gripped Kelsey's arm and almost bumped into her.

"Oh. Hi. Efran Price. I'm your investigator. Did they tell you? Listen, my wife's in labor. Early, but I want to be there. I live in Landers, about an hour north of here, so if something happened . . ." He still had Kelsey's arm and was walking toward the door, as if he would take her with him. "Listen, I'll be back. Maybe you can call me at the Ranger office, tell me what you need, and then as soon as—"

"No, no, don't worry about me. Go do what you need. Take as long as you like. Call me when—whenever."

Price smiled for the first time. "Thanks. I'll owe you one."

And he was gone. As the sound of his heels diminished rapidly down the courthouse hallway, Kelsey looked at the paper she'd picked up while listening to the Ranger's phone call, the neatly typed list of things for her investigator to do. She gave a wry smile for nobody, as she realized that the list was now hers.

But as Kelsey ran her eyes down it, she decided something else had to be done first, something not on the list.

She was going to get her hair done.

After Kelsey was seated in the swivel styling chair, the Busy Bee Beauty Boutique grew as quiet as church; that is, there was a hushed aura that could have passed for silence, but with whispers fraying its edges. Kelsey sat as if hard of hearing, appearing to contemplate herself in the wide mirror while actually using it to survey her surroundings. Two or three free-standing, head-high "walls," of the kind that divide large office space into cubicles, provided random privacy inside the Busy Bee, but the ubiquitous mirrors helped circumvent that. From where she sat, Kelsey could see three customers and four or five employees. Every eye she could see was obliquely on her. She had a feeling her identity would be known here even if she hadn't made an appointment in her own name. A couple of the stares were overtly hostile; others showed open curiosity.

The interior of the Busy Bee was not what she'd expected. Its black-and-white linoleum floor was clean beneath the hair clippings, not cracked anywhere, nor were the mirrors frosted with age. There were a few attempts at glamour, such as the brass and tinkling-crystal light fixtures and gilt trim around the mirrors, that didn't quite come off in Kelsey's opinion, but nothing could actually be called tacky. For all Kelsey knew, this was the height of up-to-date fashion in styling salons. In fact, she couldn't remember the last time she'd had her hair "done." She had it cut, and that only when it started bothering her or someone made a remark.

"Supercuts, right?" Florence said. Florence was standing behind her studying Kelsey in the mirror, lifting Kelsey's hair out in wings to the sides.

"When I'm feeling upscale. Usually I just take a pair of hedge clippers to it myself."

Florence smiled faintly in appreciation of the joke, if that's what it was, but allowing the possibility that Kelsey was telling the simple truth. Florence was not what Kelsey had expected—fearing as Kelsey had that the name of the establishment implied that Galilee was the last stronghold of the beehive. But though Kelsey had seen at least one modified hive on the head of an older customer, Florence, the stylist Kelsey had drawn, inspired confidence with the simpleness of her own 'do. Her blondish hair was feathered in layers that Kelsey knew from long-ago experience took a long effort to produce but looked casual. Florence was in her late thirties, with strong, thin arms and makeup disguising tired eyes, but she projected reserves of energy.

Kelsey had been greeted politely, but as she'd walked almost the length of the shop to take her place, no one else had spoken. She was prepared for that. She was prepared to sit here for an hour or more, have her hair manipulated and even wrecked if necessary, and ask not one question. Not this visit. Just let them look her over.

"Just give me a little hint."

"I like the way yours looks," Kelsey said earnestly.

The compliment appeared to surprise the stylist, who said, "Honey, let's not hope for too much this first time. Today is just reclamation work."

Kelsey gave Florence her head, just asking her not to cut it too short. Kelsey's medium brown hair usually fell the length of her neck, and she liked feeling it there. As the stylist went to work, Kelsey sighed and closed her eyes.

"In town for long?" Florence asked, her indifference unconvincing. Kelsey laughed resignedly. "You never can tell," she said, and felt Florence nodding.

The appointment proceeded at the slow, unmeasured pace of beauty salons. After a while Florence turned Kelsey over to a shampoo lady, who urged her to lean back in the guillotine sink, then almost put her to sleep with the warmth of the water and the suds. Kelsey thought she felt stares on her face when her eyes closed.

Back in the styling chair, Kelsey continued her idle chat with Florence, a conversation that produced no exchange of significant information: the weather, the size of Galilee, where Kelsey was from. Kelsey hadn't expected a whispered tip on Billy Fletcher's prosecution. She was there just to begin making herself known in the town.

She did catch a break as Florence was finishing up. The atmosphere, which had thawed since Kelsey's arrival so that she heard conversations all around her, suddenly grew still again at the arrival of another customer. Kelsey was slower to catch on than everyone else in the shop, not noticing the new arrival until she heard the ever-cheerful receptionist say, "Right on time, Mrs. Fletcher."

Billy Fletcher's wife? Kelsey steeled herself for an unpleasant scene, but she somehow knew as soon as the newest customer entered the styling area that her first impression had been mistaken. The tall, stylish woman making her leisurely way down the aisle behind the chairs was married to Morgan Fletcher. As Mrs. Fletcher drew nearer, Kelsey remembered she had seen her picture in the district attorney's office.

A stylist nearer the door asked, "How's your mother, Mrs. Fletcher?" The lady murmured a reply without stopping or turning her head. Kelsey suddenly put out her foot and pushed off the counter, swiveling her chair so that she was facing out into the aisle just as Mrs. Fletcher came abreast of her. The move drew a quiet gasp from Florence and a halt in Mrs. Fletcher's progress.

"Hello, Mrs. Fletcher," Kelsey said.

The lady just looked at her in slight puzzlement. She was not as tall as Kelsey had first thought: she was wearing high heels, a black dress with an almost indiscernible flowered pattern, and she was thin. Her hair was as black as the dress, so dark its highlights were brown. But it wasn't dark from dye; undisguised strands of gray threaded back from her temples. Her hair rose slightly from her forehead, then dropped around, framing her face. It was a thin face that gave an odd impression that nature had not intended it for thinness. Her forehead was wide, there was room for expansion in her cheeks, and her lips were full. The thinness did most harm to her chin, which was a little pointy, lifted as it was. Mrs. Fletcher was not pretty, but she had style. In her early forties, she had probably never looked better than she did now.

Kelsey said her own name, realizing by the relative loudness of her voice that the beauty shop had grown absolutely silent.

3 0

Mrs. Fletcher nodded, but her face didn't become animated with curiosity or welcome. "How do you do, Miss Thatch," she said perfunctorily, then smiled slightly and said, "You must be a good investigator, you've already found the Bee."

And she walked on, Kelsey frankly watching. Mrs. Fletcher's little pleasantry had been delivered with a certain flatness, as if she could do such things by rote while her mind was occupied with more important matters. She had spoken as if being introduced to the new maid; Kelsey's duties would be explained later, by another member of the staff.

Florence delivered her first bit of gossip after Mrs. Fletcher had passed out of earshot. "She used to get her hair done in Houston, but her husband put a stop to that the last time he was up for reelection."

Kelsey was listening to the friendly greetings that accompanied Mrs. Fletcher's progress, watching the smiles that bloomed, and noting the one stark exception. At the end of the row one stylist watched the new customer with a black stare, darker than any Kelsey had received in Galilee. She didn't speak as the district attorney's wife passed. Mrs. Fletcher didn't appear to notice, but Kelsey did. When Kelsey went back to tip the shampoo lady, she made sure to note the name on the angry stylist's displayed license: Janie.

"Interview Morgan Fletcher" was the third item on Kelsey's list, but when she returned to her office, she decided to move it up. Before setting out, she put her jacket on and squared her shoulders. There was no mirror in her office and she didn't need one, but she took a moment to regain a sense of herself. Kelsey was thin, but she was no frail waif; she had never aspired to that wispy look. She was five and a half feet tall, and she insisted on a degree of strength. That was why she ran. She couldn't be as strong as an average man, but she had stamina. She could outlast anyone when she put her mind to it.

She had good cheekbones, and when she thinned her mouth, she could look stern. She knew the effect she had on witnesses when she sat silently and stared at them.

She didn't try that with Morgan Fletcher's secretary, though, she went for breezy friendliness first. "Hi. Busy?" she said as she walked briskly into the outer office. The woman only shrugged. "Thanks for that tip on where to get my hair done," Kelsey added, tossing her head slightly.

"Uh-huh. You oughta make an appointment soon. They get busy on the weekend."

There wasn't a trace of humor in the woman's voice, and Kelsey didn't know her well enough to know if deadpan was her style or her life. "May I see Mr. Fletcher?"

"I imagine so." The secretary let Kelsey get almost to the inner door, already raising her fist to knock, before turning back to her computer screen and saying casually over her shoulder, "He's down in the court."

Kelsey spun smartly and exited, and if she appeared a comic figure in retreat, she was content to let the secretary have as many little triumphs as it took to appease her hostile nature.

She slipped quietly into the courtroom downstairs. Judge Saunders, the only person facing Kelsey's direction, gave her a neutral glance and returned her attention to the two lawyers arguing to her. There was an inattentive bailiff, a couple of civilians watching their lawyers alertly, two or three spectators, but no Morgan Fletcher. Kelsey eased out the door again and walked around the corridor to the court offices, where she repeated her question to the clerk of the court.

This woman—a girl, really, who looked only a few years out of high school—was much less adversarial than Morgan Fletcher's secretary. "Oh, he's around," she said, swiveling away from her work. "He was just here, I expect he went back up to his office. Or down the hall to the sheriff's office."

The clerk's smile eased Kelsey's suspicion that she was being given the classic runaround. "How long have you worked here?"

A nameplate on the desk identified the clerk as Louisa Portillo. She was quite fair, with a sprinkling of pale freckles on her wide cheeks. "Two years," Louisa said, then leaned forward confidingly. "She's a great judge."

"I'm glad to hear that." Kelsey adopted the same confidential tone. "Are she and the district attorney—"

But the atmosphere had abruptly changed. Louisa Portillo was leaning back in her chair with an uninterested expression as if her work were being interrupted. Kelsey knew that the judge was standing behind her.

It wasn't the judge, though, it was Morgan Fletcher. Kelsey turned almost into his shoulder. He didn't step back to accommodate her. Morgan's face completely lacked animation. To the clerk he said, "Is Judge Saunders busy?"

"She's in a hearing, Mr. Fletcher."

"Would you please tell her I'll be back at lunchtime?" The district attorney turned away, giving Kelsey a smiling nod as if he'd just noticed her.

She trailed in his wake. "Do you have a few minutes for me? I'd like that tour of your mother-in-law's dining room whenever you feel would be a good time."

He was slow to answer. Kelsey felt sorry for Morgan Fletcher. Every aspect of the case—how to greet her, how much to involve himself in the investigation—seemed to raise for him a moral dilemma that had to be solved painstakingly before he could move. She had to remember that she was asking Morgan to help her put together a murder case against his brother.

Kelsey held a tiny little secret on the district attorney now: she had met his wife. She looked at his troubled face, tried to picture them side by side, and couldn't. She couldn't imagine the woman she'd met offering any form of support. Having seen his wife, she felt even greater sympathy for Morgan Fletcher.

The DA thawed suddenly, his face falling into a pleasant smile. "Now would be as good a time as any. I'll take you there myself if you don't mind stopping off for another little errand with me on the way."

"Oh, that's not necessary."

He kept the same little smile playing on her like a penlight flashlight beam. "It is if you want to get into the house. I don't want to spring you on Mama Beaumont."

Morgan Fletcher's car, parked in a labeled space for the district attorney close to the courthouse's front door, was a maroon Lincoln Continental, an imposing car that reminded her that Morgan had family money. The deeply cushioned leather seat made her feel she was out of her element, but Morgan hopped behind the wheel and swung the car casually around as if he were driving a pickup truck. The car enveloped Kelsey with a man's smells of leather and cologne and elements of whiskey and smoke. She felt more completely in Morgan Fletcher's world than she had in his courthouse office.

On the carpeted floor between them, sitting on the hump, was a plastic organizer for holding change and odds and ends. It had two holders for glasses. In one was an almost empty styrofoam coffee cup. In the other, casually resting at an angle, was a bank deposit slip. Kelsey couldn't read the digits, but she could see how many of them there were, and her eyes widened—enough, apparently, that Morgan Fletcher saw them. He glanced at the deposit slip and said, "That's the errand I've got to run. I just transferred some money at the bank and now I've got to drop this off with the bookkeeper at the factory." That veil of conscientiousness dropped over his voice again as he added, "Maybe I shouldn't involve myself at all, but Billy's on leave, and I said I'd help out. It's a family favor."

"Lot of money."

"That's the payroll account. Two hundred and seventy-eight employees, and they get paid every other Friday, come sunshine or disaster."

Kelsey heard a note of pride in his voice. "I didn't realize it was such a big operation." She was looking out the side window, feeling detached, in the heavy, well-insulated car, from the scenes they were passing: a book and music store, a stationery store, giant hardware emporium. In the climate-controlled car, seeing flourishing evergreens outside, she couldn't have said what season it was.

"It's the one thing that sets Galilee apart from the other little towns around here," Morgan said of the factory, the pride in his voice becoming more obvious. "It's the reason they're dying and our population is growing. Back during the oil boom we all had money, all the towns were fat and sassy and bought their high school football teams new uniforms and maybe built them stadiums, and that oil money flowed all over town. And then that tide ebbed and you drive through those towns now and they can't afford paint for the stadium any more and half the storefronts are empty."

"But not Galilee."

"No. And that is strictly due to Mrs. Beaumont. Her husband made the money, but she had the brains. She insisted they build something that would keep producing money no matter what happened to the oil high times. And that's why other towns are broke and dismal and Galilee is doing just fine, thank you, because we're the home of Smoothskins."

"Smoothskins?" Kelsey said in surprise. Everyone so far had anonymously referred to "the factory." This was the first time she'd heard what the factory produced. "Why, I'm wearing some of your"—she cleared her throat; *panties right now* was the truthful way to finish the sentence—"clothes all the time."

Morgan Fletcher gave her a pleasant smile, as if he had already seen through her outer clothes. "Thank you."

"Well, it's no favor. I mean, I sampled Smoothskins because of the Texas connection, you know, but I wouldn't have kept buying the—the clothes if I wasn't happy with them. You turn out a good product."

"Thanks. Actually I have very little to do with production myself."

They laughed, easing various tensions. The rest of the drive they chatted inconsequentially, Morgan pointing out town landmarks. When he pulled through the gates of the Smoothskins factory, they fell silent. Morgan parked near a side door in a parking slot reserved for a truck, said, "Be right back," and slid out quickly.

After he had disappeared, Kelsey got out of the car. The factory was a building the size of an aircraft hangar, built of brick, with clean windows open to the autumn air. There was a scattering of smaller outbuildings, trucks both parked and pulling up to loading docks, and people with clipboards crossing the vast cement apron from one building to another, giving the place an air of bustle and prosperity.

Kelsey crossed the cement and slipped through the door Morgan had entered. She was in a small room with no furnishings but a time clock and rows of time cards. The room was unoccupied. When she walked through it and the next doorway, the noise level increased abruptly. She was in a giant room holding dozens of people, but she saw the machinery and the assembly lines first. This was not a small local operation, it was regional, national. Several men were doing nothing but carrying out cartons as they were quickly filled.

Kelsey walked slowly forward, and as slowly became aware that in spite of all the noise and industry, she was the center of attention. The factory workers were arranged in rows along assembly lines, and all those lines were pointed at Kelsey. One woman at the front had stopped what she was doing and was staring at Kelsey. The man beside her glanced up and his stare held as well. The workers' awareness of the intruder spread in a semicircle, until Kelsey might as well have been onstage, in a sea of stares. It was obvious they knew who she was. The expressions ranged from blank to hostile, and that was the full gamut. No one smiled, no one even nodded.

Kelsey was unwilling to retreat. She looked around for Morgan, but he had disappeared. She crossed slowly toward the far wall, keeping her eyes on the faces watching her. To each she nodded or held eye contact, but she got nothing in return. Either the face was openly hostile or there was no one home, no one to return her offer of human contact. There was curiosity in many of the expressions, but no acknowledgment of Kelsey as a person. They watched her as they would watch an approaching hail-carrying thunderhead.

There was the harsh blat of an electric buzzer, and high overhead a red light began flashing. Most of the heads lowered to their work again. A woman five feet from Kelsey continued to stare, though.

"What the hell's going on? Millie! You hurt? Where's the holdup?"

It was Billy Fletcher. Kelsey knew it not because the man bustling up along the line bore any resemblance to Morgan, but because he was clearly the manager. He wore a white shirt with the sleeves rolled up, and a dark tie pulled askew. Billy Fletcher was shorter than his brother, and wider, with muscled forearms and a rolling gait. His sandy hair, wavy but cut close to his head, topped a broad, ruddy face with a wide mouth and small blue eyes. He was sweating in the heat and the noise of the factory. As he passed, employees resumed their work, but only as if Billy Fletcher had reminded them of it, not as if they were afraid of him. His words were snappish, but he didn't glare at anyone.

He walked straight up to the anxious-eyed woman, ignoring Kelsey, and laid a hand on her shoulder.

"Anything wrong, Millie?"

Billy Fletcher's voice was loud enough to be heard over the noise of production, but the woman's murmur wasn't. She looked down at the assembly line and began sorting the packages that had piled up in front of her. Then Billy looked up at Kelsey, and she felt the shock of her intrusion. Billy's eyebrows lowered as his stare showed recognition.

"I'm sorry," Kelsey said, turning and walking back the way she had come. She heard hurrying footsteps behind her and turned around when she judged that his hand was just about to fall on her. She was right. He was right behind her, so close she could see the tiny drops of sweat on his forehead.

"Miss? You're—her, aren't you? I don't know your name."

"I'm sorry. I shouldn't have come. Kelsey Thatch. I didn't think you'd be here."

Billy Fletcher shrugged. "Where would I go?" He looked hapless and bemused, but something was hardening in the manager's eyes. "Listen, why don't we go to my office? If I can just show you—"

Kelsey stepped back. She brought up her flat expression, the one that usually made people back off, but she kept her voice as kind as she could. "Please, don't say anything to me. I don't mean to be rude, but you don't have your attorney with you and I shouldn't be talking to you. That's the rules. I shouldn't have come, but believe me, I didn't come to talk to you."

"Look at me." Kelsey had been avoiding his eyes. It was a shock to look at his face fully, to put that face into the context she'd been imagining. His expression was pleading, but that hardness was still in his flat blue eyes. Kelsey kept looking at him, with the unnerving feeling that here was the man, close in front of her, for whom she'd had no face as she imagined the crime she was here to prosecute. Was this the kind of man who could murder two people? Often even a prosecutor loses the reality of the crime as the case proceeds, the connection between the crime and the defendant grows tenuous, even as the prosecutor tries to spin that connection. But Kelsey couldn't forget these crimes. She looked at Billy Fletcher's face, then his hands. His hands were strong, red and white, with freckles beneath the pale hairs. Quick, capable, impulsive hands.

He saw where her gaze went. "I didn't do it."

Kelsey turned away again. He caught her arm. "Why can't you listen to me for two minutes? Isn't a person's life more important than the damn rules? I can prove—"

"She's right, Billy."

Morgan Fletcher was suddenly there. He gently detached his brother's hand and stepped between them.

"What are you doing here, Billy?" Morgan asked quietly, with worn patience. "You're supposed to be on leave."

Billy looked slightly abashed, but his lower lip pushed out stubbornly. "I just came to make sure this one order gets out."

"And then the order after that."

"That's right." Billy Fletcher looked his brother in the eye.

Morgan looked very much the older brother, used to dealing calmly with temper tantrums. "I thought Miz Beaumont made it pretty clear she didn't want you here."

"To hell with her." Billy Fletcher turned his attention back to Kelsey, with such an expression that she was sure he was going to say, "And with you, too." Instead he made an obvious effort to change gears. "Listen, miss. It wouldn't take four minutes of your time just to listen to what I have to say. I can clear this up—"

Morgan's voice was a little harsher when he interrupted. "The young lady told you exactly right, she can't talk to you. It won't help to bother her, Billy. She's just doing her job."

His brother's interference brought out more blatant antagonism in Billy Fletcher. He looked past Morgan, straight at Kelsey, and said, "It's a hell of an ugly job."

Morgan just turned away, arm out to guide Kelsey, but she stood her ground. She should have kept quiet, there was no point in saying anything, but she didn't like being protected and she didn't like being cast as the stubborn villain. She looked levelly into Billy Fletcher's angry eyes and said, "If it were you and your child who'd been murdered, wouldn't you want someone looking into it? Someone who wouldn't let it drop?"

Billy Fletcher's stare faltered, but instead of giving her satisfaction, Billy's abashment only made Kelsey feel stupid. She turned and stalked out of the factory, ahead of Morgan, on her own.

They drove in silence until, just before they reached his mother-in-law's house, Morgan said quietly, looking straight ahead out the windshield, "We don't say out loud around here that the baby's dead, too. Not yet."

Kelsey gasped. *You and your child who'd been murdered*, she'd snapped at Billy Fletcher, forgetting her audience. "I'm sorry," she said, automatically reaching for Morgan. "I don't know anything, you know that, I just blurted it out—"

"It's all right, you didn't know Taylor. But for us ..." He looked away from Kelsey as he turned into the driveway. She caught a glimpse of his wet eyes. Morgan cleared his throat as he stepped out of the car. "Why don't we reenact it?"

"I'm sorry," Kelsey repeated. Morgan didn't answer. He put out his hand to slow Kelsey down. They walked slowly, side by side, up the steps to the porch.

"I came up this way. It was about eleven-thirty in the morning, I was just coming to check on everybody before I went home for lunch. Mama Beaumont had been sick for a week by then, she was a little better. And Lorrie was here." He couldn't stop himself from pausing at his dead sister-in-law's name, but then he hurried on. "But Katherine and I kept dropping by to see how Mama Beaumont was coming along."

"You always park in the driveway?" Kelsey interrupted. The way Morgan had wheeled casually up beside the house had seemed proprietary, as if he were a co-owner of the house.

"Yes." Morgan gestured to the front edge of the yard, where there was no curb. The lawn grew right up to the edge of the road. There was no place to park except the driveway. "She can get around me," he said of the double-wide driveway. "Besides, Katherine's driving her today."

As they walked on to the front door, Morgan took a key ring from his pocket and casually, hardly looking, selected a key. As he brought it toward the lock, Kelsey asked, "Did you have to unlock the door that day?"

He looked at her as if no one had asked him that before. His eyes searched the air beside her face for a second before he said, "No. No, it was open."

Too bad, Kelsey thought. The opposite answer would have been good for his brother's case.

"I didn't call out," Morgan continued as they went through the front door, which opened onto a large entryway room. To Kelsey's left, through a wide doorless doorway, was a living room. Fifteen feet in front of her a broad staircase of polished hardwood went straight up to a landing, then curved around to the right and over her head. Ahead on the right was a narrow hallway that led back, probably to the kitchen. To Kelsey's right was another double-width doorway into the dining room.

From the outside the house had looked like a pleasant, grandmother's sort of house. Inside it was much more grand. A chandelier over her head hung heavily with at least a thousand dollars' worth of glass and gold. The floors shone in a muted fashion that spoke of constant care. The moldings were carved.

Morgan moved easily through the entryway, slowing as he approached the dining room. As he turned back toward Kelsey, a woman's voice said, "My goodness, what—oh, it's you, Morgan."

The maid had crept up on both of them in her rubber-soled, sensible shoes. That's who Kelsey assumed the woman was, the maid. It didn't cross her mind that the lady in the housedress and apron might be the lady of the house. Not only did she not fit the grand appearance of the house, there was something unproprietary about the unobtrusive way she moved. Kelsey would have guessed the woman was in her midsixties, but her thirty or forty extra pounds, her wrapped-around gray hair, and her round glasses made her look so grandmotherly her age was hard to determine. Her complexion was ruddy and her hands blotchy, as if she'd been baking.

"Hello, Aunt Goldie," Morgan Fletcher said, unstartled. "This is Mrs. Beaumont's sister, Goldie Hatteras. She came from Houston to help out while Mrs. Beaumont was sick, and now she's staying on. Miss Thatch."

"Kelsey," Kelsey said. Aunt Goldie nodded vigorously and held out a hand to spare Kelsey any further need to explain, or to concern herself with the older woman at all.

"I'll just let you two go about your business. Would you like some tea or anything?"

Kelsey shook her head. Morgan said, "No thank you, Aunt Goldie. It was quiet when I came in."

Kelsey realized that he had resumed his narrative without transition. She glanced to see its effect on Aunt Goldie, but the old woman was gone, as silently as she'd appeared. Kelsey interrupted Morgan to ask, "Was Aunt Goldie here when you discovered the bodies?"

He was slow to answer. Clearly the visiting relative's presence or absence didn't alter a scene significantly. "No. She was out. I didn't call out when I came in. I didn't know if Mama Beaumont might be asleep or how restfully she was sleeping. So I just came in, expecting to see Lorrie or Ronald."

Instead he had encountered silence, like the silence of the house now in between Morgan's recounting. Kelsey realized she was tiptoeing, like an intruder. Everywhere she looked she saw signs of long-established life: pictures on that hallway wall, the stains left by hands trailing along the wall up the stairs. Kelsey was listening for the sound of a radio left on, the faint buzz of lights, the soft captured echo of a scream. There was nothing.

"Did you hear anything?"

He shook his head. Morgan walked slowly toward the dining room, keys still in his outheld left hand like a weapon. His face showed a trace of apprehension.

"I saw Ronald right away. Have you ever been in a room where a gun's been fired? You can smell it for a long time afterward. Sharp smell, bitter. When I saw him lying there, I knew right away. I didn't think he'd tripped and hit his head. That smell . . ."

He stood over the spot, just inside the dining room doors, looking down. The room had been well cleaned, to Kelsey's faint disappointment. This room was more elegant than the entryway. A mahogany dining table was impressively large, though the room easily accommodated it. Another gold chandelier aimed itself at the center of the table. There was no stain on the floor, nor any trace of the evil smell that obviously still lingered in Morgan Fletcher's nostrils.

"I bent down to feel his pulse, but that's when I saw Lorrie, too."

It was a big room, about fifteen feet by thirteen, the side walls slightly longer than the front wall with its window onto the porch, through which sunlight lit the room brightly. A sideboard was on the wall opposite the double doors, decanters and a silver tea set glittering on its top beneath a wide, old-fashioned painting showing ladies in white on a summer lawn. The wallpaper, flowers caught in vines, looked old-fashioned, too, but not faded. Fresh flowers were in a bowl in the center of the table. It was hard to picture the room serving any purpose other than its designed one.

"Lorrie was lying next to the crib." Everywhere Morgan looked it was obvious he was seeing something Kelsey couldn't. "This table had been moved up against that front wall. They'd wanted to keep the baby as far from Miz Alice as they could while she was recovering, so they'd set up her crib down here, against that wall." He indicated the most interior wall, an empty spot next to a swinging door that must have led to the kitchen. "That's where Lorrie was lying, close to the crib. Face down, and not stretched out completely. She had one leg crumpled under her, like she'd been crawling when she collapsed."

He was staring. Kelsey had abandoned her hope of trying to recreate the crime in this elegant room. She was watching Morgan Fletcher, who seemed unaware of her. It was in his face she saw the impact of the murder scene. Morgan encompassed the room. He seemed to have grown taller. One hand was extended out from his body, but frozen.

Then his eye moved, startled. Kelsey heard it, too, the sound of someone entering the house through the kitchen door. Morgan murmured something else, pointing, explaining, but they were both just waiting as the sound of voices and footsteps came closer.

No, the sound of one voice, which remained raised as the door from the kitchen swung inward. "—in here, of course," the woman's voice said as she entered, immediately fixing Kelsey with an appraisal that wasn't hostile, that didn't even request an explanation for the stranger in her house, but nonetheless offered no welcome, either.

Mrs. Beaumont—Kelsey knew at once this was the owner of the house—was not the frail elderly lady Kelsey had been expecting. She was in her sixties, undoubtedly, but she stood straight, her stride was strong, and her hair was dark. She was well fed, not fat but healthy enough that her skin was taut, relatively unwrinkled. Dark-rimmed glasses emphasized the length of her nose. Her lips were thinned in contemplation, but when she opened them, her mouth was good-sized. She was an imposing woman, even what people used to call handsome, but a confident dominance to her completely overrode the question of looks.

"Hello, Mama," Morgan Fletcher said quietly. "Excuse the intrusion, we—"

Mrs. Beaumont never transferred her gaze to him. "You're Miss Thatch." Kelsey nodded. "I'd expected you sooner." Kelsey was taken aback, but before she could respond, Mrs. Beaumont answered for her. "I suppose you've talked to other witnesses already."

"Yes, ma'am."

Mrs. Beaumont nodded approval. "She's gotten everything she needs, I hope." The statement was directed as a question at her son-in-law.

When Mrs. Beaumont's stare released her, Kelsey noticed for the first time that someone else had followed Mrs. Beaumont into the dining room. With a shock Kelsey realized that the other visitor was Katherine Fletcher, but she seemed so much younger than the woman Kelsey had met in the beauty shop. She waited behind her mother, patiently holding packages, her face concerned that she might be doing something wrong or that something rude was about to happen.

Mrs. Beaumont was speaking, raising her voice to draw Kelsey's attention back to her. "But it's important you understand from the beginning what happened here. This was a hate crime, directed at me."

"Oh, Mama," Katherine said softly.

"What would you call it?" Mrs. Beaumont was still talking to Kelsey, not to her daughter. "Someone not only kidnapped my only grandchild but murdered my only child still young enough to bear children. Someone wants to wipe my blood off this planet."

She stopped, head raised. Kelsey had no answer for her. This matriarch exuded an atmosphere Kelsey hadn't penetrated; there was no human contact between them. Kelsey suddenly pictured the old lady as the last of an ancient race of women. If the murderer had meant to injure Mrs. Beaumont, he had made a mistake. Her dignity remained implacable. Kelsey could see only anger in her face, not grief.

"Unintentionally, I'm sure," Morgan interjected. "I'd say it was a crime of passion, not a deliberate—"

"To kill Ronald, maybe. I can understand that. But not to take that baby from me. What kind of passion can you have against a five-month-old baby?"

Here was the grief. Mrs. Beaumont's eyes were suddenly wet, her skin like thin parchment held in a nervous hand. She turned her head, toward the spot where Morgan had said the crib had stood against the wall. Her eyes were downcast.

"Mama, don't." Shifting her packages to one hand, Katherine came forward and put the other hand on her mother's shoulder. Even before it landed, Mrs. Beaumont said, "I'm all right." Her voice was still so strong that Katherine's offered comfort seemed unneeded. Her half-embrace of her mother was awkward and unacknowledged.

"Go ahead with what you were doing," Mrs. Beaumont said. "Tell her whatever she needs to know."

Mrs. Beaumont stood stiffly, prepared to subject herself to hearing the ugly details again. Kelsey looked at Morgan, who had obviously lost the thread of his reconstruction. "I think . . ."

"We'd finished," Kelsey said, helping him out.

"Well." Mrs. Beaumont's shoulders slumped a little as she realized she was going to be spared the recitation.

Katherine came around her. "Should I put these things in the upstairs medicine cabinet?"

"Yes, I suppose. On the—oh, let me show you. I'll see you soon, Miss Thatch. Come back whenever you need to."

"Thank you, ma'am."

"No thanks about it. You do your job."

Mrs. Beaumont walked out, Katherine hovering attendance on

her, staying close but not wanting to offer unwanted assistance. The change from the imperious woman Kelsey had seen in the Busy Bee was remarkable. What also struck Kelsey as the two women left the room was that Katherine had never spoken to her husband or, as far as Kelsey had noticed, looked at him.

Kelsey turned to him. She did have another question, one she'd wanted to spare Mrs. Beaumont. Morgan looked abstracted again, his eyes moving slowly around the room that was very different from the one in which Kelsey stood.

"Was there much blood?" Kelsey made her tone as kind as possible, but the words still came out brutal.

"Oh, yes," Morgan said softly. His eyes dropped to the floor and moved as if measuring the blood he'd seen. His relatives' blood, spilled on his relative's floor. "Oh my God, yes."

4

Yes, much blood. Kelsey studied an eight-by-ten color photo of the crime scene when it had still been the crime scene. The picture was taken from about where Morgan Fletcher had been standing as he described being the first witness on the scene, just inside the dining room doors. In the picture the baby's crib stood against the interior wall. On the floor below it, stretched as if she'd been coming from the side wall when she'd been shot, lay Lorrie Blystone's body, face down as Morgan had described it. She lay in a great pool of blood, soaking the floor around the crib. Kelsey reflected on the unintentional cruelty of the photographer and the police investigators, who had had to overcome the human urge to rush to cover the body or offer it useless comfort. There were men's legs in the picture, in the striped trousers of police officers. They had stood around the body, looking it over, probably talking to each other, while the photographer captured his grisly record.

For Kelsey's benefit, she had her answer to what she had wondered about herself: no, she wasn't as hardened as she'd been in her prosecutor days in Houston. Perhaps because she had first seen the scene through Morgan Fletcher's eyes, the pictures had an emotional impact on her.

"That's her own blood," Dr. Broom said dispassionately. They were sitting in the doctor's office, his desk between them, as Kelsey looked at the pictures for the first time. Dr. Roger Broom was what passed for the medical examiner of Defiance County, a general practitioner who examined the occasional body for the county as needed and assessed causes of death.

Dr. Broom's face looked very dark above the white of his coat. The doctor was extremely tanned and ruddy, his black hair receding as if in flight from all that angry color roaring up his forehead. Kelsey wondered how patients could have confidence in a doctor who looked more than anyone else she'd ever seen like an imminent heart attack or stroke. He didn't have the fretful mannerisms of an overly stressed man, though. Dr. Broom sat patiently while Kelsey absorbed the pictures. They were on opposite sides of his desk, the doctor turning his head to see which photo she was viewing. He seemed in no hurry, though he had patients waiting in examining rooms. Kelsey hated that about doctors and hated being the cause of it.

"Ronald died of a head wound, single shot," the doctor said helpfully. "He would have died almost instantly, so didn't bleed much. Lorrie Blystone, though, was shot in the chest, over against this side wall—another picture shows some of the splatters on the wall—and even though the shot was just as certainly fatal, it wasn't immediate. She was pumping a lot of blood, but she had the time and the strength to crawl several feet."

"From the wall toward the crib."

"Yes."

As unnerving as she found it, Kelsey continued to stare at the photograph. Lorrie Blystone's posture of slumped crawling spoke of such determination that it put an idea into Kelsey's head.

"We've been assuming someone shot the parents and then took the baby. Is it possible it was the other way around, Lorrie interrupted someone taking the baby, that's when she was shot, and she kept trying to crawl toward the kidnapper?"

"Possible. But no, wait. No. Because of the blood in the crib."

"The baby bled?"

"No. It was Lorrie's blood in the crib. From which I take it that the baby was on the floor when the mother was shot. The baby got some blood on her, on her hands or her clothes, and then someone picked the baby up and put her in the crib."

"Or someone with Lorrie's blood on his hands reached into the crib and left bloodstains when he picked up the baby."

"Also possible."

"If she wasn't crawling toward her baby, she was trying to reach her murderer. Why would a woman do that?"

Dr. Broom had an expression of wanting to help, but he could only shrug. "I'm not the detective."

"Where was the blood in the crib?"

"All over. The top sheet, the bottom sheet, the pillowcase."

"But none of it was the baby's."

"Or anyone else's. All Lorrie's."

"Be nice if the killer'd cut himself while he was there," Kelsey said, thinking of DNA testing. "You still have the sheets and pillowcase?"

"No, the police would have that, with the other physical evidence. They have more pictures, too. I just kept the few that illustrated details of my report."

"Oh." Kelsey had come to the back of the file, to a photograph of a very young baby. A happy little face, toothless, nose almost invisible. Wispy strands of neutral-colored hair formed an aura around her face.

"That's Taylor, the baby. Mrs. Beaumont gave me that for the file. Of course, I don't have a file on the baby." The sentence ended raggedly, as if Dr. Broom stopped himself from saying, "—yet."

The baby's face seemed to change as Kelsey held the photo, as if the tiny girl heard something, a sound completely outside her small experience, coming toward her. Kelsey put the file down on the edge of the desk. She found that a professional aura had settled over her without any intention of hers. She knew that her face looked firm and officious. "Did you establish a time of death?"

Dr. Broom leaned back in his chair. He sounded relaxed. "Oh, say about ten-thirty that morning. That's as precise as I can get, medically."

"So it could have been as early as ten, or five after?" Kelsey asked routinely. Billy Fletcher had been culminating his argument with Ronald Blystone at ten o'clock.

"No." Dr. Broom shook his head. "Not when you consider that Ronald Blystone answered his telephone at ten-fifteen."

Kelsey looked surprised. The doctor pointed again at his file. "I don't do the time-of-death analysis in the dark. The police give me what information they have. There's a copy of the report in there."

There was, a brief supplemental report by an officer D. P. Thompson. A woman whose name meant nothing to Kelsey had called to ask about Mrs. Beaumont's health at ten-fifteen the morning of the deaths. Ronald had answered and said they'd have to call back later. The caller had heard Lorrie's voice in the background. Maybe the argument with Billy had still been going on.

"Both died at about the same time?"

Dr. Broom nodded. "Roughly. I'd say the sequence was Lorrie first, then Ronald. But very close, close enough that I could be wrong."

Kelsey didn't pause to ponder the doctor's answers. She was increasingly aware of those patients awaiting Dr. Broom's attention. "You did paraffin tests?" she asked routinely.

The doctor nodded. "On Lorrie's hands, nothing. Ronald's hand showed some stippling, which could mean he'd fired the gun or could mean his hand was close to it when it was fired. Struggling over the gun, that kind of thing."

"Did you do a test on Billy Fletcher?"

"No point. He'd been two days gone by the time he was arrested. Presumably washing his hands any number of times."

Kelsey nodded. Nothing was making her happy so far. "So Ronald could have fired the gun," she said slowly, "and it was his wife who was killed. Leaving the baby out of it, imagining her kidnapping was unrelated, did you consider the possibility of murder-suicide? Pretty common."

"I did. And I rejected it for two reasons, aside, as you say, from the baby. One, it makes us feel foolish to say a man killed himself when he was seen having a screaming fight with another man half an hour earlier. Then there's the fingerprint. Billy Fletcher's, on the barrel of the gun. Ronald's prints were on it, too, but that was natural, it was his gun. And of course nothing but smudges on the trigger. Too narrow to take a good print."

Well, the fingerprint was something, Kelsey thought. That and the argument with Ronald were all she had so far to pin the murders on Billy Fletcher. Not nearly enough, but it was something.

*　　*　　*

She stood on the sidewalk in front of the doctor's office, not yet thinking about what to do next, still mulling over what she'd just learned. The doctor's office was in a house on a residential side street; there was no traffic to distract her. Her gaze rested vacantly on the small woodframe house across the street. Its lines drew her eyes upward. Suddenly her gaze snapped into focus. Another finger of smoke was trailing up into the sky. This time Kelsey watched it intently. The smoke paled from the bottom up, becoming a ghost of itself. It was rising from back in the piney woods, where the town gave up and the forest deepened; on the clear day it was impossible for Kelsey to guess how far away it was, but it couldn't have been far, for her to see such thin smoke at all. Just as she thought about driving toward its source, the smoke faded to nothing.

She drove slowly back to the courthouse, stopping on the way at the stationery store she'd seen, where she bought a large square of stiff white poster paper. No one was around to see her when she carried it into the courthouse. Once inside her little office, she felt alone in the building.

She thumbtacked the poster to the side wall where it would be plainly visible from the desk and found a felt-tip pen in the desk drawer. Kelsey took off her jacket, pushed her hands through her hair, then stood for a long moment in front of the posterboard. The felt-tip pen squeaked as she wrote "October 21st" at the top—the date of the murders. Below, at the left edge of the poster, she wrote "10 A.M.: Billy Fletcher, Ronald Blystone arguing (Andrew Sims)."

She knew a little more about that argument by now. When she and Morgan Fletcher had left his mother-in-law's house, they had lingered on the front porch. Morgan seemed to be decompressing. He stared across the road into the pines, which Kelsey had already discovered were ideal for contemplation. In the quiet, comradely mood, Kelsey decided to take a chance on asking him more. She'd have to give discount credit to his answer, but it couldn't hurt to start getting a fix on things.

"What was the argument about?" she had asked quietly.

From the corner of her eye she saw Morgan start slightly. He shrugged away his first reaction.

"It would be nice to say it's nobody's business. But it's not just a family matter anymore. It's everybody's business.

"Actually a lot of people in town had a stake in that argument to begin with," he added, rising to his full height from where he'd been leaning on the porch railing. "It was about the factory, of course."

"Smoothskins?" Kelsey said, surprised. She'd expected something juicier than business.

Morgan nodded. "The business was still doing fine, getting better, in fact. It'd reached the point that we needed to expand or maybe get gobbled up. That's why Billy was going to North Carolina, to meet with some people from Sara Lee. They own Hanes and L'eggs, you know. We'd gotten some feelers from them, and Billy wanted to talk to them. What he really wanted to do was fend them off. He'd been talking to Miz Alice about it for months. What he thought we needed to do was expand into other product lines, diversify, make ourselves into a bigger fish. That would take more investment, of course. Miz Alice had the money, but at her age she was reluctant to part with a big chunk of it.

"What she was more interested in was starting to settle things. She didn't want a lot of squabbling, she wanted to have a family council where we could all agree on what was the right thing to do."

"But you couldn't." Kelsey noticed the way Morgan included himself right in the middle. Married to Alice Beaumont's daughter, he would have been part of the family council. Kelsey knew she'd have to seek out other viewpoints to this story. She couldn't help trusting what she was hearing. Morgan Fletcher's quiet voice and deep-eyed, calm countenance inspired credence.

"No. We couldn't agree. Lorrie and Ronnie had the baby, you could tell they were counting on an inheritance someday. They didn't want to see that money disappear into a factory that might go down the tubes itself one of these years."

"Might it?"

Morgan shrugged. "Who knows? Things seemed to be going fine, but it's foolish to bet on business. Sometimes trying to expand is exactly what puts a company under.

"Billy tried to convince Ronald and Lorrie that the best thing for them and the baby was having that steady source of income. But talk isn't Billy's long suit, and Ronald could always tie him up in reasoning. He drove—" Morgan checked that thought. "The sad thing about it all was that Billy didn't have a vote, and he was the one in a way with the most at stake. That was hard on him."

You're telling me motive, Kelsey thought. Then she reflected that the reason Morgan Fletcher was being so forthright was probably because she could get this story anywhere. Half the people in town must have known about the family dispute. This way she heard it first from him, with his own spin on it.

"Billy really wanted what was best for everybody," Morgan said.

In her courthouse office she moved to the right on her posterboard and wrote, "11:30: Morgan Fletcher to murder scene." She stepped back. A long blank space was between the two entries, and an ocean of white engulfed them both. Thoughtfully, she stepped back to the first entry and wrote the names of the others she knew had been in the house: Alice Beaumont, Lorrie Blystone, Taylor Blystone. It was the first time she had written the baby's name. Standing in the quiet of her office, she remembered the face in the photo in Dr. Broom's office. Who could have taken Taylor?

Kelsey wondered suddenly if ransom negotiations were going on, kept secret from her and most other people in town. But remembering Mrs. Beaumont's suddenly crumpled face when she'd spoken of her granddaughter, Kelsey dismissed that idea. But no one would give the baby up without being sure. She remembered the slump of the search coordinator's shoulders, Andrew Sims heading into the woods.

Whatever else she accomplished here, Kelsey had to find out the truth about what had happened to the baby.

Her motel room, while Kelsey changed into running clothes, suddenly looked exceedingly fake to her. Galilee seemed real enough, but Kelsey's presence there made no sense. On the other hand, where should she be? Her path to this town was hard to imagine.

Maybe this mood was a signal that it was time to move on again, from the attorney general's office. But to where? What exactly did she want? It was a question Kelsey had never confronted in a large way. She was the youngest of three children, so paths had been blazed for her all her life. It was a given that after high school she was going on to college, because that was what the children of Grace and Ben Thatch did. Her father was a middle-school principal, her mother a bookkeeper who had never acquired the credentials to become a full-fledged accountant; they believed in education. Kelsey had gone to the University of Texas, an easy choice a few miles down the road from her hometown of Waco. In her first two years she took a mishmash of courses, subjects she liked—history, political science, sociology— until called upon to come up with a major, at which point UT had come to her rescue with a degree plan called Plan II, which was a prestigious liberal arts program that allowed her to get a degree in mishmash.

But after graduation there were no jobs in mishmash to be had, so Kelsey had gone back to school, where she always felt comfortable. She chose law school, at Southern Methodist University in Dallas, the best law school in Texas as far as she was concerned. But Plan II in college had spoiled her, she'd gotten used to taking courses that interested her, and the traditional big courses in law school—property, contracts, trusts and estates— didn't interest her. It seemed to her that civil law was about only one thing, money—you ruined my reputation, give me money; you broke my leg, give me money; mom liked you best, give me some of the money she left you—and Kelsey suffered from an odd, troubling affliction for a law student: she didn't care about money. Criminal law offered better stories and a wider range of emotions, and it seemed to her what law was all about. When Kelsey had begun to concentrate on criminal law, it had been a disappointment to one or two of her professors who had been impressed by her abilities, because the brightest students went into civil, not criminal, law, but Kelsey had never regretted it.

She wanted to be one of the good guys and she wanted to get trial experience fast, so at the end of law school she'd interviewed with several district attorneys' offices. The one in Harris County seemed the most serious and the most aggressive, and they had wanted Kelsey, so after graduation she'd moved from Dallas to Houston.

She also left behind her law school boyfriend, as she'd left a college boyfriend when she'd moved to Dallas, and as in the first case a few traveling weekends confirmed for her that she'd done the right thing.

In the years since, she'd nearly always had a man in her life, usually an office romance, but never felt her feelings advance in seriousness enough to take the next step. Part of the problem was that the only men she knew were lawyers, and while she enjoyed practicing law and found her fellow lawyers comfortable enough for working or sleeping with, still, would you want your daughter to marry one? So her romantic pattern was that she and her significant other would have a spat they'd realize wasn't worth patching up, or he would develop longings he'd discover Kelsey didn't share, at which point he'd drop her and go find a woman to marry. At thirty she was still happy with this pattern, or maybe not all that happy, since it had been a while since her last romance and she hadn't gotten interested enough in anyone to make a move or let herself be moved on.

She ran. The question that had popped into her mind completely occupied her thoughts, pulsing like the beat of her feet on the pavement. *What is it you want?* Finding another job probably wouldn't be a problem. Kelsey was a good lawyer; many people would testify to her hard work and quick thinking. Now was the time to go looking, before she got involved in this messy case that had loser written all over it and would be publicized enough to taint her job prospects.

It was dusk and she had run too far again. In Galilee there was only one direction when Kelsey set out randomly: eastward, toward that dining room, that isolated house. She found herself bending and blowing across the road from the murder scene, moving her legs to keep them from stiffening, all the while staring at Alice Beaumont's house. Tonight there was a car she hadn't seen before parked in the driveway, and a light in that curtained dining room. Kelsey stood in the dark, a ghost watching for other ghosts. Her hands inside her jacket pockets were cold.

Blowing off this case was the smart thing to do. Defiance

County could find itself another special prosecutor. Kelsey had other things to do and bigger decisions to make.

There was just one problem.

The long run killed her appetite but didn't exhaust her. It was full dark by the time she arrived back at her motel, but Kelsey didn't shower and drive out on her nightly restaurant hunt. Once in a while a run energized her instead of wearing her out, and tonight was one of those occasions. Inside her room, her cooling-down stretches turned into a continuing workout. She stretched, fingers reaching. She stomach-crunched. She danced aerobically. Her mind was churning as hard as her legs, no longer on the unmixed question of her future, but also on the case she had here. The twin preoccupations kept butting into each other.

When the knock came at her door, Kelsey grimaced. She looked at herself in the mirrored door of the closet and saw a woman completely unfit to receive company. She was bathed in sweat— the room felt warm and must have smelled like a gymnasium— she was breathing heavily, and she was wearing only a short T-shirt and panties.

But damn it, this was her home, as long as she lived in Galilee. People here had to learn that she had a life of her own, they couldn't expect to drop in on her unannounced any hour of the day or night and find her conducting business. She was tempted to answer the door dressed just as she was.

She almost did. She only pulled on a pair of running shorts, draped a towel around her neck, and got to the door by the second knock. Only as she was swinging it open did she realize that with all the people in this town with reason to hate her, and with a double murderer walking around free, it wasn't smart to open her door to anyone who knocked.

But her visitor was a man carrying file folders. To put a lawyer off guard, come carrying file folders. As soon as she saw them, Kelsey felt safe, because the file folders meant work, not danger. A murderer would come carrying a gun or a knife, not manila folders stuffed with documents.

It was Peter Stiller, the deputy. Her deputy, as a matter of fact. He got a look at Kelsey before he could even say hello, and he gave her a quick scan down and up, not in a leering way, just surprised. Kelsey immediately felt embarrassed. She could feel hair sticking to her temples, and she dabbed at a line of sweat with the towel, but she stood her ground. "Is this urgent?"

"Not for me. I've got the files you wanted, the supplemental reports and pictures. I went by your office at the courthouse this afternoon but you weren't in, and I didn't think you'd want me to leave them on your desk." His voice was calm and nonjudgmental, but not prepared to take any flak, either. It was a lot like the voice Kelsey had used on him. "I guess you didn't get my message to call me."

Kelsey's attempt to embarrass him had backfired. They both knew that if she had put in a full day's work in her office, Peter Stiller wouldn't have had to invade the privacy of her "home." She was also suddenly embarrassed about the minimal way she was dressed. She squared her shoulders to fight the feeling. She crossed her arms.

"Come on in. Cold out there."

As he crossed the threshold and closed the door, Peter said, "It's not much warmer in here."

"Isn't it?" So it was only her body heat radiating through the room. She was surprised he couldn't feel it.

"Sorry to come by this late. I'm just getting off my shift."

"That's all right. On something like this my schedule's always completely out of whack."

She turned her back on him and walked to the dresser, where she had an ice bucket and a couple of bottles, but she watched Peter Stiller in the dresser's mirror. He wasn't staring at her, he just stood where he had stopped, a few feet inside the door, his collection of file folders held crooked high under his right armpit, the way a schoolboy jock carries textbooks. For some reason Kelsey didn't believe in his mild appearance. He struck her as being so unobtrusive that he must have worked at it, aware of the excesses he could impose on people if he didn't control himself.

"Like a drink? Since you're off duty?" She unwrapped a motel glass, dropped a couple of ice cubes into it, and poured Scotch over them. Peter took long enough to answer to make the question seem significant.

"Sure. Thank you."

She lifted her glass and her eyebrows and he nodded, so she

unwrapped the other glass and made one more of the same. She smiled as she carried it toward him, because she could suddenly picture herself from outside: the scantily clad woman in the motel room, advancing on the uniformed man with two drinks in her hands. She hoped Peter Stiller didn't take the image for reality, because the truth was quite the opposite. There was nothing she wanted from him. So far from trying to pry information out of him, she regarded with suspicion the files he had willingly brought her.

Kelsey thought it no coincidence that the Texas Ranger investigator she'd been assigned was so consumed by a personal crisis that he was essentially unavailable to her. Some local power, Morgan Fletcher or someone else with little reason to see her do her job thoroughly, would have chosen her local investigator just as carefully. Kelsey would learn what she could from her Defiance County deputy, but she didn't trust him an inch.

She handed him a glass, raised hers slightly, and slid into the seat behind the table. "What have we got here?"

He pushed the files in front of her and took the other chair. "You got copies of the first couple of police reports, but there were some supplemental ones I didn't think you'd seen. Plus the physical evidence."

"You've got that?"

"In the property room."

Kelsey opened the first file and saw a report from a police officer. The next report was from a sheriff's deputy.

"Why was there such a mix of cops involved in this? The house is outside the Galilee city limits, isn't it? Shouldn't this have been strictly a sheriff's office investigation?"

"Nobody gave a damn about jurisdiction at first, not with the baby missing. Everybody jumped in. And since the murders and the kidnapping were obviously connected, there was just a swarm of everybody over that house. Sheriff Early and the chief of police aren't too fussy about jurisdiction, anyway."

Kelsey glanced at the opening sentences of the next report, enough to tell her it seemed to have nothing to do with the murders. "What's this?"

He leaned across. "Oh. A neighbor down the road, after the murders, called in to report that she shooed some tramp away from her back door the evening before. After she heard about the murders she thought it might be important."

Golly swell. An alternative suspect, a stranger much better suited to play the role of mass murderer than a beloved hometown boy. And Peter Stiller or whoever had put together this package for him had wanted the report included along with all the others, right near the top. Kelsey tossed it aside lightly.

She didn't open any of the others. She leaned back and sipped her drink, an image of casualness. It was a pose. Kelsey had a secret. The one problem that kept her from driving away from Galilee and leaving these people to their own devices was that the case had become real for her. The murders were no longer abstractions on paper. They were echoes of cries in her mind and a scent that made her nostrils flare. The weight of responsibility she'd felt settle on her as she'd driven into Defiance County had grown heavier. It was what kept her from driving away.

But the one advantage she had at this point was in keeping the intensity of her feeling to herself. She thought it was a secret from Deputy Stiller, but she wasn't sure. He was watching her with the same unobtrusive but constant scrutiny as at their first meeting.

"Well, thank you, Deputy Stiller, I'll get around to these—"

"Peter. Since we're going to be working together."

She looked at him with a moment of odd recognition. She was most likely completely off target, but suddenly she felt she knew who he was. Playfully, but watching him, she said, "So you're one of these real rigid people who always went by your full name, never a nickname; even when you were four nobody called you Petey."

He didn't smile but he didn't seem offended. "What did they call you: Kelly?"

"No," she said quickly and too intensely, because she'd had to put up with too much shit over the years from people who thought her name was weird or couldn't seem to pronounce it the perfectly straightforward way it was spelled, or wanted to act as if they were her friend right away by getting chummy with her name. Truth to tell, though it sounded too petty to admit to anyone, she'd stopped dating at least one guy because of his damned insistence on calling her Kels. Well, he'd had other flaws, too.

Peter was smiling at her. He sounded like her spokesman when he said, "I have a name, it's a good name, why should I trade it in for something less—"

"Yes," Kelsey said, regaining the offensive. "Biblical. Peter. 'On this rock will I build my church.' " But the biblical Peter had also been the one who had betrayed his friend three times before the rooster had crowed twice.

Peter said, "So you had a church upbringing. That'll stand you in good stead around here. Be sure to throw some of that into your jury argument."

Kelsey didn't respond. It had been years since she'd needed help with closing argument. Peter Stiller dropped his smile and said, "What do you want me to do next?"

Kelsey wondered how she could use him in spite of her certainty that she couldn't trust him. A lot of work had to be done. Unfortunately, it was all hers. "I don't know. I guess there are other witnesses to interview, but I'll need to do that. I'll talk to you after I digest this."

He nodded and rose immediately. He had his hand on the doorknob before Kelsey could wonder if she'd have trouble getting rid of him. "You could tell me one thing," she said. "How goes the search for the baby? Honestly. Have you had leads that petered out, tips that looked good for a while?"

Peter shook his head slowly. "Not a trace. Don't quote me. But you'd better plan on leaving the baby out of your case."

"I can wait. You don't think she'll turn up at all?"

He drew a breath and held it, making his face into rigid planes. Kelsey noticed again the tiredness around his eyes. "This is a little bitty town, surrounded by a lot of woods and a few lakes. Even somebody in a hurry could have disposed of her in a way we'd never find her."

But something about the deputy's appearance belied his hopeless statement. His boots—round-toed work boots, not cowboy— were dirty. He had wiped his feet before coming into her room, but the sides of the boots displayed dried red dirt.

"Where're you going now? Home?"

Peter looked at her almost with dislike. It was a dislike of admitting the hopeless way he was wasting his time. "If she's still alive, it's because somebody's got her. Which means she can still be found if we just don't give up. That's the thought I can't stand."

Determination swept his face, wiping out the look of sadness that had flickered there. Peter opened the door but lingered to look at her a moment longer. Kelsey adjusted the towel around her neck. Then he was gone, silent until the slam of his car door. Kelsey looked after him for a minute, then suddenly rubbed her arms and went to turn on the heat in the bathroom.

5

Kelsey was an odd presence in the Defiance County Courthouse. It had been a week now, there were people who had seen her trotting up the steps every morning, but no one said hello. She worked in a building inhabited daily by a full crew, but she was alone. It was startling to hear herself greeted; it made her feel like a ghost that had suddenly shimmered not only into visibility but familiarity.

"Hi, Miss Thatch."

"Oh, hi, Louisa, how are you?"

The judge's clerk displayed her empty coffee cup and went on down the hall. Kelsey continued toward Judge Saunders's chamber, but the sound of voices made her slow and soften her step. Through Louisa's empty office Kelsey saw the open door of the judge's chamber. Morgan Fletcher stood inside, half-turned away from Kelsey. She could see enough of his face to read the seriousness of his expression. She wasn't close enough to hear what was being said; her angle of vision didn't even let her see the district attorney's conversational partner, but she assumed it was the judge.

She was right. As Morgan Fletcher lowered his head, a woman's hand came into the picture. The hand laid itself comfortingly on Morgan's arm. There was familiarity in the gesture, perhaps intimacy. All sorts of things might be read into it. Kelsey desperately wanted to crane her neck just far enough to see the judge's face, but then she would almost certainly have been seen herself. Instead she turned and walked quickly away.

Another connection, she thought. Another person she couldn't trust.

She had gone to see Judge Saunders to ask her about Billy Fletcher's defense lawyer, Clyde Wolverton. Kelsey wanted to know if Clyde Wolverton had a reputation for trustworthiness or for devious dealings. She'd just have to decide for herself. She had an appointment with him and his client at nine o'clock.

They were early. When Kelsey approached her office door, she saw it standing open. Inside, Billy Fletcher was sitting worriedly in the visitor's chair. When he saw Kelsey, he rose hastily and lunged to shake her hand. Billy Fletcher was used to putting his best foot forward in meetings, used to being liked, and he had realized he'd made a mistake at his first meeting with Kelsey.

"Hello, Ms. Thatch. Sorry to rush you. If you'd like to get a cup of coffee or something first, we'd be glad to wait." Billy Fletcher's hand was firm but fleshy, engulfing Kelsey's. His face had an unformed quality, too, as if he hadn't yet suffered the crises that would force his change from boy to man. Perhaps this was the tragedy that would do it.

"No, that's all right." She retrieved her hand from his and went to set her briefcase down behind the desk, but when she turned, Billy was right there, pressing her, eager as a dog. He saw he had startled her and stepped back. He kept his voice low and his head slightly lowered, too, so he was looking at her like a supplicant.

"I've been thinking about what you said, about wanting some-body on this case that wouldn't give up. You were right. Lorrie and Ronald and Taylor deserve that. I want you to know that I want to help. I was right there, I should have noticed something. Saw somebody as I was leaving, something. I've been wracking my brain . . ."

Kelsey made such a poor job of keeping skepticism out of her expression that Billy stopped. His head came up and his voice grew louder. "I know, you think I did it. I guess you heard about the argument and you know what the trouble was between Ronald and me. Anybody'll tell you Ronald and Lorrie being dead takes a lot of pressure off me. But it makes other problems. I don't just mean being arrested, and you, I mean Miz Beaumont blaming me for what happened, maybe her deciding herself to be shut of everything and sell, or at least fire me, which she practically has already."

"That's how it is with murder," Kelsey said coolly.

"Then there's the baby. I couldn't touch a child in anger. I've got four of my own, and I'm the biggest pushover in town. Ask anybody, ask—"

Kelsey took that in stride, too. She had met a lot of murderers, and out of a small crowd she would have picked only two or three as likely violent offenders. It was impossible to decide under normal circumstances what a person was capable of doing in the frenzy of annihilation.

"I've been out there looking as hard as anybody. Every time there's a search party . . ."

Well, the murderer would, wouldn't he, join in the searches? Kelsey hoped someone was paying attention to where Billy Fletcher *didn't* lead search parties.

Billy saw her looking at his hands again. Raw, red hands, like a field-worker's. Either of his hands was bigger than the baby's face. Billy rubbed those thick hands together. "I didn't do it," he said in a heartfelt voice.

"There, Billy, calm yourself." His lawyer finally spoke. Billy Fletcher had none of the traditional reserve that is the refuge of defendants. Clyde Wolverton apparently had more than a lawyer's share of reserve. He'd hung back, letting his client make the appeal, before finally stepping forward. He guided Billy back to the visitor's chair, then presented himself before Kelsey, standing at attention with his hands folded like a boy on his first day of school, smiling. His appearance surprised Kelsey, because he was a man of about sixty, with white hair drawn back from a lined forehead. He had a long nose, a thin-lipped but wide mouth, and cheeks with no extra flesh in them.

It was his age that was surprising. If a man had been practicing criminal law as long as this man's age implied and was good at it, he would have a statewide reputation at least among other criminal lawyers. But Kelsey had never heard of Clyde Wolverton.

He had a confident air, though. "Ms. Thatch. Clyde Wolverton. I'm pleased to meet you. That's not just an expression, either.

I'm glad to finally meet you, so we can start resolving this matter. It won't be time-consuming, let me tell you. May I show you my proof?"

"Please," Kelsey said in slight wonderment. Wolverton had such an air of pleased anticipation, and the exaggerated quality of a person who spends professional time with children, that she wouldn't have been surprised to see him set up a puppet theater and stage a reenactment of the murders.

He placed his soft leather briefcase on her desk and after a search through it long enough to put a crease between his eyebrows, produced two things. The first, the stub of a plane ticket, he placed in Kelsey's hand.

"This is the receipt for an airplane flight Mr. Fletcher was on that left Houston Intercontinental Airport at eleven-ten on the morning of October twenty-first for a flight to Raleigh-Durham Airport. You can see the ticket was stamped at the boarding gate, showing that he boarded the flight."

Kelsey held the stub, unimpressed. "This proves that someone had a ticket stamped at a gate at the Houston airport. Prove to me that your client was actually on that flight, and we'll have something to discuss."

Wolverton smiled thinly and handed her the other document from his briefcase, a single sheet of paper. "This is a sworn affidavit from Mr. Howard, the executive vice president of Sara Lee with whom Billy had his meeting later that day."

So it was. Kelsey skimmed the statement quickly—easy to do as the two paragraphs were not profligate with details. But it did verify Billy Fletcher's arrival on time for his meeting in North Carolina.

"A meeting he could only have made by catching that flight I showed you," his lawyer was saying with satisfaction. Billy was seated again, looking up at her expectantly. His lawyer had folded his hands in benediction.

"This is better. May I keep a copy of this? Of course I'll have to do some investigation of my own, timing the drive to the airport and so forth—"

"Please do," Clyde Wolverton said.

"—but what would just about wrap it up is my talking to

someone who saw him on the plane." Silence answered her. "Have you found such a witness?" she had to ask.

Clyde Wolverton sounded just as confident, but he no longer had the easy smile. "Not so far. The passengers are scattered. I've talked to some of the airline staff, but so far they're not helpful. Billy didn't get drunk, he didn't make a pass at the woman next to him, he didn't have a long conversation. He sat and worked and dozed like most airplane passengers, so there was no reason for him to stand out in the flight attendant's mind. Just one of a million passengers."

But one with bloodstained hands, Kelsey thought. She needed to track down the airplane witnesses herself. "Well, I'll look into it."

"And we'll continue to do so, of course." Clyde Wolverton looked worried now. His expressions were no harder to read than those of his client, who was looking at Wolverton nervously. "But I think once you talk to Mr. Howard, you'll see—"

"Yes, I will." It was rare for a suspect to have even this good an alibi, one not involving relatives, who could be presumed willing to lie for him, but Kelsey didn't trust it. She wished the defense lawyer had given her more, or less. She wished they were discussing a guilty plea.

"This is a very simple case of mistaken arrest," Wolverton tried one last time. "We'd like to get it resolved right away. You can imagine the strain on Mr. Fletcher and his family. His record is spotless, you can check."

"Yes. We'll talk again," Kelsey said dismissively. "In the meantime, though, I'm going to pursue my investigation, and when I feel ready to obtain indictments, I'll go to the grand jury. I don't want to surprise you about that."

She had. Clyde Wolverton was looking at her as if he were accustomed to dealing with more reasonable people. Billy Fletcher's look had grown harder and less pleading, too. But Kelsey could play that game with anybody. She just looked at them, pleasantly and silent, until they pulled themselves together and shuffled out the door. Kelsey picked up the affidavit from Mr. Howard in North Carolina, carried it to her posterboard chart, and began to write.

* * *

The defense lawyer was right, though. The case against Billy Fletcher had started out not very strong, and it was getting weaker by the day. If Wolverton brought Kelsey just a little more, he was going to get his dismissal.

She didn't look forward to dealing with the defense lawyer again. Lawyers have all kinds of acts, but Kelsey had a strong urge to tell Clyde Wolverton to drop his folksy rube pose. Billy Fletcher, with his brother advising him, would not have hired a fool for a lawyer. She would have to watch out for Clyde Wolverton.

She assumed the police station would be close to the courthouse, so was surprised to learn from Louisa Portillo's directions that she had to drive halfway across town to get there. As she left the courthouse, she saw Morgan Fletcher coming her way, half a block away on the sidewalk. He waved, Kelsey waved back, but she didn't stop to talk to him.

The police station was a low, modern building, all chrome and glass and plastic-looking aqua panels. The nonuniformed clerk at the front desk took Kelsey's self-identification at face value and directed her through a door deeper into the building. In his office she found Simon Perez, whose title was deputy commander. In his forties, his jawline was going a little fleshy but his eyes were piercing. Brown hair, eyes, and a thick mustache. Perez wore a white shirt, black tie, and maroon sports coat. He swiveled and stood to meet her and already knew Kelsey's name. Their interview didn't seem private, as Perez left his office door open and the office walls were half-windowed so he could look out into the squad room, which he did several times while talking to Kelsey. She resisted an urge to look over her shoulder.

"I've read your report."

Perez smiled tersely. "Didn't keep you up late, did it?"

"No. Just the first day at the crime scene and that was it."

Perez shrugged. "I wouldn't have written a report at all, except I was the first officer to talk to the witness—to Morgan Fletcher. But I was just a drop-by. After that first day I wasn't part of the investigation."

"Then why did you go? You were the first or second officer on the scene, from what I could tell."

"Just coincidence. I was out, on my way to lunch, when I heard the call on the radio, and I was close to the Beaumont house so I swung by. I got there before the ambulance, just ahead of the uniforms."

Perez answered her questions fully enough, but Kelsey had the impression he wouldn't volunteer anything. He had an air of enclosed confidence about him, that of a man who has already decided exactly how much he's going to give up.

"Where was Morgan Fletcher?"

"Well, he came to the door when I knocked. Then he led me to the dining room and we stayed there in the doorway. I didn't want to go in and mess up the evidence. I could see enough from where we were to see what we were dealing with."

"What did Morgan say?"

"Nothing at first. We just stood there. Morgan"—for the first time Perez's voice took on color, as if he were remembering instead of reciting—"he looked stunned. He had that can't-think look about him, you know, like he had to stop and figure out how to do it before he could take a breath. They were his family members, you know."

"Yes."

"I asked him a few questions, he told me how he'd come across them, then the place started filling up and I left. I wanted to make sure somebody was taking care of Mrs. Beaumont, but after Mrs. Fletcher got there that seemed taken care of, so I went on."

"Mrs. Fletcher. Morgan Fletcher's wife?"

"Yes. Katherine. She got there right after I did."

Kelsey found herself unexpectedly curious. Her next question was for herself. "Did you see her come in?"

"Yeah. We kept her away from the dining room, of course, but she could see what was going on."

"She went to her husband, I guess."

"No. They looked at each other, she saw he was okay, and she went straight on up to her mother."

"I don't have a statement from either of them."

Perez shrugged again. "Katherine hadn't been in a position to see anything, she'd been playing bridge at her house all morning. And her mother—well, somebody asked her questions later, but I guess she didn't say anything worth recording. The lady was recovering from a really killer bout of flu, she was under medication, she'd been asleep upstairs the whole time." He looked at Kelsey levelly. *Around here we treat old people decently, even ones who've had the bad luck to have their relatives killed underneath them.*

Kelsey nodded as if she approved, not that Simon Perez cared about her approval. Their interview ended with a string of negative answers.

"Did anyone take plaster casts of tire tracks?"

"No."

Kelsey had seen photographs of the outside of the house, surrounded by cars as police and others came and went. Any evidence outside had been obliterated by now.

"Fingerprints?"

"We took some. They didn't tell us anything. Found a couple of unknown prints, like you would in anybody's house, but we never had anybody to try to match them against."

"Take a blood sample from Billy Fletcher to see if his matched any blood at the scene?"

"No. Maybe the sheriff did, check with them."

"Someone checked inside Billy Fletcher's car for traces of blood?"

"I'm sure somebody did."

Perez didn't offer any excuses. He and Kelsey looked at each other flatly. Neither of them bothered to hide their expressions. Kelsey didn't think much of Perez's police work and he didn't care what she thought.

She drove back to the courthouse, which also housed the sheriff's office, carefully not thinking about why she'd derived satisfaction from having her insight about the condition of Morgan Fletcher's marriage verified. A stranger had noticed how affected Morgan had been by what he'd seen, but his wife hadn't taken two seconds for the two of them to cling to and comfort each other. The image probably gave Kelsey an unfair image of Katherine Fletcher. After all, she'd had her sick mother to worry about. But it didn't sound like the warmest of marriages.

She went to the sheriff's office to get the rest of the photos and to make sure the physical evidence was properly stored. The sheriff's office was satisfyingly old-fashioned inside, with wooden desks and linoleum floors. No one there denied Kelsey anything, but they seemed willfully slow. She glanced into the squad room, saw that the woman Noreen wasn't at her desk, and noted no other sign that this was the command center of an intensive search campaign.

In the property room she found the package that contained the baby's bedclothes, but didn't open it. She laid her hand on the manila envelope holding the bloodstained sheets, but it was just an envelope, it had no special feeling. Kelsey's face was solemn when she emerged from the property room. Peter Stiller was standing there. She almost walked into him. He had a similar envelope in his hand.

"I was just coming to leave something," he explained.

"What a coincidence."

It was past noon. After they talked for a minute Peter asked her if she wanted to have lunch, and the idea of eating a meal with another human at the table struck Kelsey as such an attractive novelty that she said yes, though she didn't feel very warm about this particular human's company. They went through the line at a nearby cafeteria and emerged holding their trays into a large room furnished with bright metal and plastic kitchen tables and chairs. Nearly every table was taken. Kelsey and Peter sat in a booth to one side, and after they arrayed their food around them, she found herself talking freely to the deputy. She had no one else to talk to and she didn't have to worry about giving anything away, since she had precious little, and nothing that wasn't common knowledge.

"After I talked to Andrew Sims I figured the case was off to a good start, but it's not going much further. I can reconstruct it to make Billy Fletcher the murderer, but I can also put it together so that he's not involved at all."

Peter nodded. "And if Billy *was* on that plane leaving Houston at eleven o'clock, he would have had to jump in his car and scoot right after Andy Sims saw him arguing with Ronald. He would have had to set some speed records at that."

Kelsey silently agreed. "What about the baby? Any luck, any leads?"

The deputy's eyes were down on his food. He didn't raise

them, or his voice, as he said, "I think you'd better just leave the baby out of your case. We may never figure out that part."

His voice was so bitterly sad that Kelsey went silent, struck with the feeling she'd habitually had since coming to Galilee, of wanting to offer comfort but feeling it wasn't her place. She almost reached for Peter Stiller, to free him from the bitter reverie that obviously gripped him.

The clatter of plates and silverware at nearby tables disturbed their silence in a good way. She heard Peter take a breath, changing the subject in his mind, which also returned Kelsey to the professional problem at hand.

"I have had better cases."

"Some people'd be glad to hear that," the deputy said neutrally. That was the kind of remark that fueled Kelsey's suspicion of him.

"You're not really a criminal prosecutor, are you?" Peter asked suddenly, watching her. "This case is a little outside your field of expertise, isn't it?"

Kelsey heard herself saying something that surprised her. "I've tried a whole lot of criminal cases, Deputy. Like to hear about my last one?"

Peter shrugged. "If you want. But it's none of my business."

Kelsey studied him. His face belied his words. Not that he appeared eaten up with curiosity, but he looked like a man who considered almost everything his business. He had the most watchful gray eyes Kelsey had ever seen, and determination in his jawline. Peter was young, barely over thirty, but he had a mature air of slow decisiveness.

Kelsey's decision was quick. She started talking. "I was your typical Harris County hotshot. After I'd been there a year I'd try anything. The closer the case the better. Defense lawyers hated me, because I didn't want to plea-bargain away anything. You know the saying prosecutors have? Anybody can convict a guilty man; it takes a real prosecutor to convict the innocent. That was me."

"I doubt you saw too many innocents in the felony courts in Houston."

"No," Kelsey said, glad he understood. "That's why I went so hard at every case. I figured anybody who'd gotten himself arrested for one crime had gotten away with ten others.

"So finally they gave me my first capital murder. Typical convenience-store murder, we had dozens like it. I was the second chair on the case so I didn't have all that much to do. My main job was to question the one eyewitness."

"You had a surviving eyewitness?"

"Yeah. A boy named Bobby." Kelsey pictured the boy, thinking how old he was now, whether he had a stepfather, how he was doing in school. "Seven years old. He was really too young to be a witness, but we needed him, the judge knew that, and she ruled him competent.

" 'Don't ask him too many questions,' the first chair told me. 'Just the important one. And ask him about seeing his father dead.' " Kelsey heard Peter sigh. "Yeah. Well, you've got to do that. The jury has to see some emotion. Poor little Bobby." Kelsey could still picture the crime vividly, though she had never seen it. "He just went to the store with his daddy, at the wrong time. I think all he *did* remember was his father lying dead practically on top of him." She stopped again.

"You don't have to—"

She hurried on. She wanted to say it. "But he'd identified the shooter from a picture spread. I think the cops may've helped him out, but if they did, they'd done a good job, because by the time I had him, Bobby could pick that picture out of a crowd. I was confident of his testimony. But the funniest thing happened. We were in the little witness prep room just before he was going to go on the stand and I said, 'Are you ready, Bobby?' and Bobby just looked at me. Just looked, he didn't say anything, but I knew. He wasn't sure. He looked scared to death, and not just of testifying.

"I knelt down beside him and I said, 'Bobby, you don't have to say what they told you to say. Just tell the truth.' "

Kelsey suddenly realized she couldn't see the room very well; it shimmered. She sniffed hard and got a grip on herself. "This was a boy who didn't have a daddy any more, who just had a mother who cried all the time, and I'd gotten to be his friend because that was my job, and I'd made it clear to him that his job was to point at the bad man in the courtroom and say, 'He did it.' But I looked at him in that moment before trial and I knew he wasn't sure.

"But just then the first chair came in and said to hurry up, and then we were on. I asked Bobby the questions and he came through like a champ. The defendant's lawyer couldn't shake him at all. It took the jury about twenty minutes to vote for death.

"And the next day I gave the defense lawyer an affidavit to attach to his motion for new trial, saying what I just told you, that I didn't think my witness had been sure of his identification."

"Whoo." Peter took in her rigid posture. "That must have made you beloved around the office."

"The district attorney was very gracious. He said I had to do what I thought was right. I said it wasn't for that scum that'd gotten convicted, he probably had it coming. It was for Bobby. I couldn't let him live with that for the rest of his life, thinking maybe he'd lied an innocent man onto death row. The DA said he understood. He stood there on the high moral ground with me."

"He made you uneasy as hell," Peter guessed correctly.

"He made me feel like I was still part of the team. And the next thing that happened was that the felony chief asked if we could go over my testimony for the hearing on the motion for a new trial, and I said of course, I didn't want to be hardheaded."

Kelsey went silent long enough that Peter prompted, "And at the hearing . . . ?" Kelsey glanced at him sharply, expecting ridicule, but saw only a tight-lipped sympathy, as if he knew the people who'd done this to her.

"They ripped me apart." She laughed. "I helped them do it. The poor defense lawyer was so smug, I said on the stand just what I'd told him, that I'd been sure Bobby wasn't sure of his identification, but then on cross-examination the prosecutor made me look silly. 'Bobby didn't actually *tell* you he was unsure, did he?' 'In fact he'd always told you he *was* sure, didn't he?' 'So you're just substituting your judgment for the jury's, aren't you?' I answered just the way I was supposed to. Somebody'd done the same number on Bobby, too, he said he was sure as shooting. The motion was denied, the death sentence stood."

"And you were back in good graces in the office."

"I got transferred to the bond-forfeiture section. And soon after that this job offer from the attorney general's office came along, like a life raft floating by, and I jumped on it." By then Kelsey had wanted out of Houston and away from criminal law, which was too mean, too tough on all sides, where questions literally of life and death lay waiting as part of every day's work.

Peter's food was cold. His arms were folded, he was watching. Kelsey looked for judgment and didn't see it.

"Morgan Fletcher knows this story," she said. "He made some reference to it the day he met me."

Peter shrugged. "It's not a bad story. It just says you tried to do the right thing."

"Yeah. Up to a point."

Peter's eyes were still watchful, but Kelsey wasn't sure what he was looking for. His hand moved as if he would reach for hers, but he merely picked up a fork.

They ate in silence. When Kelsey glanced at Peter again, he was looking past her, watching people come and go. She didn't turn her head, since the faces probably wouldn't mean anything to her. Instead she surreptitiously watched Peter Stiller's face. Once he nodded as he lifted his eyes, another time he lifted his hand in the slightest of waves, but he didn't call hello and no one came over to chat with him. He had that same watchful expression he'd trained on Kelsey—friendly perhaps, even sympathetic, but watchful nonetheless. His eyes met Kelsey's and it took him a moment to smile. It wasn't something that came naturally to him.

"You said people would be happy if I dismissed the case. Did everyone hate this Ronald and Lorrie Blystone so much they don't mind that somebody killed them?"

"Not Lorrie," Peter said quickly, then realized what he'd said and sighed at the thought of longer explanation. Kelsey thought how perfectly sincere he looked as he began to speak. If they'd thrown at her an investigator whose job was to gain her confidence, they'd had a good sense of casting.

"Not Ronald, either. I mean nobody wanted him dead, nobody'd threatened him as far as I know. But a lot of people'd have taken it as good news if they'd heard Lorrie was divorcing him. That was the great hope around here, especially before the baby came. Lorrie was a hometown girl, people liked her, but she'd been gone for years, and when she came back with this guy, nobody took to him. He was so full of himself, he had ideas . . ."

"We're talking about the factory."

"Of course." The Smoothskins factory, the town's economic heart, was the background to every conversation about the murders. "Katherine Fletcher and Lorrie were Mrs. Beaumont's only children, so someday, we assumed, they'd inherit. Which scared some people because nobody knew what Lorrie thought anymore, and this husband of hers thought he was some kind of financial wizard. He kept talking about taking the company public, or better yet selling it and investing in something that would produce a better income. That's what he kept trying to talk Mrs. Beaumont into."

"And that word *sell* made people awful nervous."

"Well, sure."

Kelsey was still trying to get the players straight. In a way it was harder now that she'd met all the surviving ones. She had to fit her present impressions into what she was learning of the past. "What about Katherine, what did people think of her?"

"Oh, Katherine, nobody worried about her. Katherine is her mother's arm, she's just like the old lady."

Kelsey had her own opinion about that. She'd seen Katherine Fletcher twice and had seen two different people. One, indeed, had the imperiousness of her mother; the other seemed intent on nothing more than pleasing that mother.

"Besides, Katherine was with Morgan, and no one questioned his loyalties."

"And of course Morgan's brother was the one with the most to lose if the factory did go south," Kelsey said. It was odd to sit there over baked fish and overcooked green beans musing on these matters as if they were possible moves in a board game, when to living people close at hand they were literally questions of life and death. Kelsey turned and saw that the cafeteria was almost empty. A busboy moved among the tables with his cart.

Thinking of the Fletcher brothers and the Beaumont family, Kelsey said, "There sure are a lot of connections between people here, aren't there?"

"Remember your high school class? Imagine you'd spent the

rest of your life with those people—that's who you married, that's who you worked with, that's whose children your children went to school with. This is a small town, that's what life is like. If you only find two connections between some of us, you're still only on the surface."

Peter gave her a friendly smile that made him look handsome and boyish but that did nothing to decrease Kelsey's suspicion— of Peter Stiller and of his whole town.

"Can you tell me why you haven't gotten an indictment yet?"

Kelsey was in her office in the courthouse. She had been staring at her chart, thinking of what she could add to it, thinking, too, of how the blankness of the chart mirrored the nondescript quality of the office she'd been given. The small room looked exactly like a place being temporarily used by someone who didn't live there. A five-foot-tall bookcase was by the door, inhabited by someone else's books. A tall, old metal cabinet stood against another wall. It held only generic office supplies: this office had until Kelsey's arrival been a storeroom. The only frame on the walls enclosed an amateurish drawing of a bear standing up and growling, with two buckskin-clad hunters pointing rifles at the bear. Obviously it was here because no one had wanted it in his own office. Other than the bear print, only the sole window broke the blankness of the enclosure.

The surface of Kelsey's old metal desk was almost empty, too, making her feel that she had accomplished nothing so far. So she was not in a perfect mood to receive a visitor who quickly implied that Kelsey wasn't doing her job.

It was Alice Beaumont, who had appeared in the doorway, taken the only visitor's chair as if she'd had an appointment, and with only the barest of preliminaries began questioning Kelsey like a supervisor ready to receive a report that hadn't been tendered quickly enough.

"Have you learned anything that makes you think Billy is not the best suspect?" Mrs. Beaumont continued.

Kelsey choked back her first response. "No, ma'am, I haven't."

Mrs. Beaumont sat with her hands in her lap, her shoulders squared, her gaze direct. Though erect as a flagpole, she looked comfortable as well, as if stiffness were her natural posture.

"Then do you think someone screaming threats at a man who is found dead shortly after, with the screamer's fingerprints on the murder weapon, is not sufficient evidence to obtain an indictment?"

This time Kelsey didn't suppress her response. "Mrs. Beaumont, I'm evaluating the case. I don't need to report my conclusions to someone not involved in the investigation."

"You mean you're not used to keeping the victim informed of a case's progress?"

Kelsey faltered. It was hard to think of Alice Beaumont as a victim, but it was true she had suffered the worst losses from the crimes. What was remarkable about Mrs. Beaumont was the way she could make her demands in an even tone, with an almost pleasant expression. It was a trick Kelsey had expected to learn as adulthood overtook her, but hadn't.

"Yes, ma'am, I'm used to keeping survivors informed. In this case, though, you obviously know as much as I do, because you just summarized everything I've learned that implicates Billy Fletcher."

"Well, there must be more. He's not careful enough to have covered up for himself."

"He wasn't careful at all, if he was the one who killed the Blystones. Unfortunately, it's those unplanned crimes of passion that are sometimes hardest to prove. What about you, Mrs. Hatteras, were you in Galilee that morning?"

Aunt Goldie Hatteras seemed surprised that Kelsey had noticed she was in the room. Mrs. Hatteras had slipped into the office behind her sister and had done nothing to call attention to herself. She seemed intent on blending into the wallpaper. This afternoon she had traded her apron for a black bulky sweater. She carried only a small beaded purse, which she clutched in both hands. Her lips were clasped as tightly shut as her purse. Addressed directly, she actually blushed.

"No, I wasn't, at least not—not when it happened. Alice was doing better, and she had plenty of help, so I'd gone back to my house in Houston that morning. Had to cook and freeze a few more meals for Edgar, you know." She laughed embarrassedly. Edgar, Kelsey assumed, was her husband, though he could have been a cat. "I came back that afternoon when I heard what had happened."

So another potential witness was of no use. Kelsey turned back to Alice Beaumont with a slight lift of her eyebrows that said, *You see?* "Do you know something more, Mrs. Beaumont? Why are you so convinced of Billy Fletcher's guilt?"

As if she'd been waiting to be asked, Alice Beaumont said immediately and articulately, "Because this was a very stupid thing to do. And of all the people involved, Billy Fletcher has the poorest brain."

"Why do you say the killings were stupid?"

Mrs. Beaumont lifted her hand, palm upward, and her eyebrows, as if the answer were obvious. "Don't you realize that by destroying Lorrie's entire family somebody thought he was insuring that Smoothskins would stay in Galilee, in the branch of the family that's here? Wasn't that the obvious motive? But if someone thought like that, he's an idiot. Did he think I'd let a scheme like that succeed? I'd chain those gates tomorrow morning, I'd do it myself if I thought that damned factory had cost me my babies." Her face closed in on itself, lost for a moment, but then Mrs. Beaumont's face unfolded into its stern contours. "That's why I know it was Billy. Like Morgan said, it wasn't a well-thought-out thing. It was a crime of passion. Billy was the passionate one. You should have heard him try to argue, it was pitiful. One time he staged a confrontation with Ronald for my benefit. It was at a family picnic, and it was so obvious the way Billy worked the conversation around to the future of the company, with Ronald sitting there and me within earshot. Billy sounded like he was reading from a cheat sheet. But Ronald, lying there on a quilt half-dozing from being full of potato salad, wouldn't let Billy get up a two-sentence head of steam before he'd interrupt and say, 'Why do you assume that?' or 'The experience of sixty-two percent of regional companies that try to go nationwide is not only that they don't expand their markets but that they lose share in their own regional base.' " Mrs. Beaumont's face grew more elastic and her voice deepened as she tried to impersonate her late son-in-law. Aunt Goldie smiled appreciatively. Mrs. Beaumont laughed in a way that said she understood how obnoxious Ronald's quoted words sounded, but she had enjoyed his performance anyway.

"Billy got red-faced and started yelling. Morgan had to bail him out, as usual. Morgan and Ronald matching wits, now there was a fair contest."

"And Lorrie?" Kelsey asked quietly.

"Lorrie?" In her momentary confusion, Mrs. Beaumont's face looked much more vulnerable. Her blue eyes softened; age advanced on her. "I don't remember Lorrie expressing an opinion at the picnic. She agreed with her husband. She wanted what was best for Taylor."

Kelsey wasn't ready to talk about the baby. "Mrs. Beaumont, I'm confused. If you thought so little of Billy Fletcher, why did you put him in charge of your company?"

"Billy wasn't in charge. I am." Alice Beaumont's face regained its assurance. "Billy just ran the factory. I'll tell you exactly why. Billy was the fourth manager in four years when he started. The first three were young, smart MBAs I'd stolen from bigger companies. They knew all the latest techniques, they were full of ideas. They could look over a schematic drawing of the assembly line and tell you right where the bottlenecks were. They talked about niche marketing and test marketing and marginal expansion. They would take your breath away in a job interview, let me tell you. So I hired them and turned them loose on our poor old line workers and nothing happened. Every time. They'd make me spend my money on their ideas and nothing came back. So I'd fire one and start over."

From the relish with which Mrs. Beaumont spoke of firing, Kelsey wondered if there'd been some other force at work in the failures of the bright young managers.

"Billy would hold things together while I looked for a new boy wonder. Finally after the last one I was tired of looking and I just left him as manager for a while. Morgan kept trying to get me to give Billy a chance, and I finally gave in.

"And something strange happened. Productivity went up. Not big, you understand, but it'd been flat as a tree stump before. And when Billy would go on a sales trip, he'd come back with orders. He couldn't tell you why, he couldn't train other salesmen to do the same thing, but—"

"People liked him," Kelsey said.

Mrs. Beaumont frowned, gaze abstracted, thinking there must be a better answer.

"So there he stayed," she said quietly, surprised herself at this past turn of events. "Things seemed fine, but still—Billy's no long-range thinker. Ronald made a lot of sense, some ways."

The office grew quiet. Kelsey glanced at Aunt Goldie, who had been staring at Kelsey but averted her gaze when Kelsey looked at her. Kelsey kept her eyes on the aged relative as she said, "Thank you. That's helpful."

Billy was the champion of the status quo, the inarticulate proponent for holding on to all those jobs that fueled the economy of Galilee. Times are always fearful for farmers and factory workers. How they must have relied on Billy Fletcher. They all must have known about the debates with Ronald Blystone, in which the out-of-towner argued blithely and abstractly for doing away with their jobs. The people of the town would have known how those debates went, and there must have been many whose first reaction to the news of Ronald's death hadn't been sadness.

Those people who worked harder for Billy than they had for the bright young MBAs would not be willing to convict him in court. And in a town with a jury pool as small as Galilee's, those 278 employees would inevitably have representatives in the courtroom.

With a tiny smile Mrs. Beaumont changed subjects. "And how do you like the attorney general's office, my dear?"

"It's fine," Kelsey said, suspicious of this sudden personal inquiry.

"That's good, I'm glad. You wouldn't have lasted much longer in Houston."

Houston. It was becoming a word of omen for Kelsey. She stiffened. "Mrs. Beaumont, you may think you know—"

"I do." Alice Beaumont's smile had sunk into her face, leaving her with a knowing expression. From her purse she pulled a newspaper clipping. It was a headline from the *Houston Chronicle,* letters big enough to read from across the hall. Kelsey recognized it without reading: "Prosecutor Accuses Own Witness of Lying."

"I collect interesting stories," Mrs. Beaumont said. "And when something catches my eye, I make inquiries."

Seeing the clipping in the woman's hand recalled for Kelsey
the horror of seeing the headline the first time. "No!" she wanted
to shout, then and now. *It wasn't like that.* It must have been a
slow news day two years ago in Houston: the story had made
the top of the first page of the Metro section. Kelsey had seen it
that morning on every desk in the DA's offices, imagined it blinking in every hand in the courthouse.

Kelsey glanced up at Aunt Goldie. The older woman's expression, before she quickly lowered her eyes, was sympathetic.
Kelsey frowned. She didn't want anyone's sympathy and she
certainly didn't want this old tyrant in front of her looking at
her so possessively.

Alice Beaumont continued, with relentless beneficence. "Wanting to follow your conscience isn't such an ugly fault in a public
servant. And you did help your office smooth things over very
nicely. But I knew as soon as the publicity died down, you'd be
quietly let go."

"I never—"

"Don't be naive, Ms. Thatch. I know how these things work.
Do you?" Kelsey didn't have an answer. "So I made a suggestion
to my friend the attorney general. He's inclined to listen to me."

Kelsey did know enough about the way things work that Mrs.
Beaumont didn't have to say the phrase *campaign contributions.*
The matriarch remained sitting, and her voice stayed mild, but
her eyes were fastened on Kelsey.

"I don't believe this."

"You don't know me well enough to call me a liar," Alice
Beaumont replied, her voice gaining only a slight edge. "You're
not the only one like you, you know. I've made other suggestions
to other friends in office. You were just the only one in the attorney general's office at the moment."

Clearly she meant that she had requested Kelsey's services and
been accorded that favor. What was so terrible about this implica-
tion of Alice Beaumont's was that it made sense. It explained
why Kelsey was in Galilee, which she hadn't been able to figure
out before.

Kelsey had to put a stop to this at once. Alice Beaumont
thought she had some hold over her, but, "Mrs. Beaumont, if
what you say is true, I thank you for your recommendation. But

unlike everyone else in this town, I am not on your payroll. I work for the state."

"Yes," Alice Beaumont said, her small smile returning. *For the moment*, that smile said clearly.

"I'll tell you what I'm going to do, Mrs. Beaumont. You're right on one point, I probably do have enough evidence to ask a grand jury for indictments—in the murder cases. That's what I'll do, very soon. But that's all for now. The kidnapping—"

"But that's the most important thing," Mrs. Beaumont cried, rising suddenly to her feet.

"That's the most difficult thing. There's no evidence of what happened." Kelsey tried as delicately as possible not to mention the possibilities. The probability. "As you said, I can give Billy a convincing motive for the murders. But taking the baby, that was crazy. It's best if I just leave that part out of it, unless something more—"

"No." The old lady shook her head emphatically. She was leaning forward against the desk, reaching for Kelsey, who found herself leaning forward, too. Mrs. Beaumont's eyes glittered with the effort to make Kelsey understand. "The baby's what matters most. You have to indict him for taking her, too. That's the only way to make him bring her back to me. That's the only way to get Taylor back."

Kelsey's mouth opened, but futilely. She had no idea what to say.

It was the middle of November of Kelsey's first east-Texas autumn. From midafternoon on, the light was tinged by dark green that was like a harbinger of both night and spring. Evergreens predominated, so the landscape didn't change much as winter approached. The air itself seemed to change. Those pines exhaled their cold breath on the town, like Norse giants in a grim mythology. Kelsey would look up from her desk at four o'clock in the afternoon and think she'd stayed late. Like the town, the courthouse grew dark early. Kelsey found herself sitting alone, trying to think and failing. Abruptly she picked up the phone.

"This is Kelsey. I want to talk to Len." The attorney general, in jolly first meetings with his new assistants, urged them to call him by his first name. It was a privilege Kelsey had avoided using until now.

"He's a little busy right now, Kelsey," the secretary said. "Can I—"

"Tell him I know," Kelsey snapped. The secretary didn't ask anything else—maybe she heard this kind of declaration every day—and in a minute the attorney general came on the line. "Know what, Kels?" he asked with studied good nature.

"I just met the boss here in Galilee, Len. Who came to explain the nature of my duties."

"That woman is not your boss," the AG said quickly. Then he cleared his throat. "It just so happens that what she wants from you is the same thing I want, a good, tough prosecution. Any conflict there?"

From the moment he'd cleared his throat, Kelsey had had no more questions. She put the phone down gently, trying to remember what her office in the attorney general's building had looked like.

Everyone knew about Houston, about the story Kelsey had told Peter Stiller. Peter had said the moral of the story was that Kelsey tried to do the right thing. But it could also be evidence that Kelsey would do as she was told: "smoothed things over nicely," as Mrs. Beaumont had put it. And from Mrs. Beaumont's own account of the way she ran her business, she was used to having her orders obeyed.

This new aspect of the case made Kelsey want to strike out in a way none of her bosses or would-be bosses would expect. That was a tendency she should resist—to strike back at any pressure, even if that pressure was toward doing the right thing.

So dismissing the prosecution against Billy Fletcher was no longer an option, not if she wanted to keep her job. But she hadn't wanted to dismiss anyway. She just wanted a stronger case. Mrs. Beaumont's account helped a little, it demonstrated Billy's long-simmering antagonism toward Ronald Blystone. Was that motive strong enough? The trouble with that question was that it was asked by rational people, which took it out of the realm in which murder is committed. Kelsey had prosecuted people who had killed over a dog, over what TV show to watch.

Murder is a moment of madness, the culmination, usually, of years of resentment. The "motive" the moment before the trigger is pulled is a flimsy thing, not understandable by people untouched by the madness.

Judge Saunders, hanging up her robe in her chambers, looked up a little surprised as Kelsey walked in and closed the door. Quickly Kelsey said, "I think the court should know that there is someone in town who expects to influence my decisions in this prosecution."

The judge's fine-featured face slipped into a smile. "And how does Alice expect to accomplish that?"

Kelsey told her. Judge Saunders stood with her arms folded, appreciating the story. "So she pulled one out of the file folder." At Kelsey's questioning stare the judge explained, "She does collect stories—and people—she thinks she can use. What else does she have to do all day? She's the J. Edgar Hoover of east Texas."

Kelsey hadn't come for personal advice, but the judge's calm acceptance prompted her to ask, "Why would she do this?"

"Because she can. It's a small favor to ask, to give a job to a competent person. Why should an elected official to whom she's given tens of thousands of dollars turn her down? And when he does the small favor, then Mrs. B. has someone in place in a state agency who owes her a favor without even knowing it. And someday . . ."

Linda Saunders sympathetically left the sentence unfinished. "There are always contributors like Alice Beaumont who ask for something in return. It's a 'Do you love me?' thing. Every elected official has to deal with contributors like that."

Kelsey looked at the judge more searchingly. "So she contributed to your campaign?"

"Of course," Judge Saunders said lightly. "And all she got out of it was a good judge."

She didn't ask Kelsey anything in return. Kelsey said slowly, "I guess I should inform the defense of this."

"I guess you should. But don't expect to surprise them."

6

Kelsey ran a few steps, then winced and started walking again, hands on her hips, blowing hard. She was sweating even though the temperature was around forty-five. She was walking on the left side of the road, facing the traffic, so when she heard a car roll to a stop behind her, she jumped aside, then winced again as she landed on her sore right leg.

The crunch of tires advanced. Kelsey turned and saw the squad car. The driver's window came down and Peter Stiller stuck his head out. He wore dark glasses. "You need a ride?"

"No, thanks," Kelsey said, and started walking again.

He rolled slowly abreast of her. He was driving the wrong way, but on this small side street a few blocks from the court-house there was little traffic. Small shops forlornly faced the street. Peter rolled along beside Kelsey. "D'you fall down?"

Kelsey whirled on him, instantly ready for a fight. She was mad at the world and Peter was the only piece of the world handy. The pain in her leg made her mad. She'd been trying not to limp and had obviously failed. "No, I didn't fall!" she snapped, wincing at the next step. "Somebody hit me with a rock."

The squad car lurched as Peter slammed it abruptly into park and the next minute he had his arm around her. Kelsey resisted her urge to slump against him—for a second or two. But when he opened the passenger door, she stiffened again. "I can walk."

"Get in, let's go find them."

That was a clincher to the short argument. Kelsey settled into the squad car with another wince; Peter whirled the car in a tight circle and sped back down the street. "What did they look like?"

"I don't know, it had tinted windows."

"What kind of car?" Peter watched the street grimly.

"A pickup truck. Dark color."

Peter slowed the car. "You're not helping me a whole lot," he said quietly. In the block they were passing through, five pickup trucks were parked at the curbs. "Pickup is kind of the vehicle of choice around here."

"Sorry. If I see it again, whoever's driving it is going to be in a world of hurt, I can tell you that much."

That was one reason Kelsey had wanted to keep jogging. She wanted to announce loudly to the town, *I'm still here.*

"Maybe I should run you by a doctor's. At least he could give you something for pain."

Kelsey closed her eyes wearily. "It was just a kid with a rock. No big deal."

Peter kept driving, making random turns. Kelsey glanced at him and saw his eyes moving steadily. He looked very coplike, his gun strapped on, other equipment jingling on his belt, a black tie with his brown uniform, but somehow he didn't quite fit the image. He didn't look like the first thing that sprang to her mind—a boy playing cops and robbers—but like a new recruit, taking the job much more seriously than the veteran usually assigned to it would.

"Let me ask you a question," Kelsey said. "Out of that batch of reports you gave me, how come there was no report from you?"

"I didn't write one."

"But you were there. That was you I saw in one of the pictures." She'd only seen a pair of legs and a back and the side of a head, but she'd been sure it was Peter Stiller, standing straighter than everyone else in the picture.

"Yes."

"So aren't you supposed to write a report after you make a crime scene?"

"Only if you're assigned to it. I wasn't, I wasn't even supposed to be there. I just went when I heard on the radio where it was and what they'd found. So did some others."

He spoke simply and without hesitation, but Kelsey kept looking at him. "I don't suppose you saw some sign of Billy Fletcher lurking about?"

Peter shook his head. "He was already on that plane leaving Houston by the time I was there. I'm surprised he even made it, as little time as he had."

Acknowledging this reminder of Billy Fletcher's probable innocence, Kelsey said wearily, "Which probably puts Billy in the clear, assuming your so-called medical examiner is right about the times of death being around ten-thirty."

Peter said softly, "I was there at eleven forty-five, after Morgan called it in about eleven-thirty. They'd been dead a while, I can tell you that without being any kind of expert. The blood had started to congeal. It had that skin on it, you know."

He stopped abruptly. Either Peter Stiller hadn't made many murder scenes, or this one had been special to him. Kelsey couldn't be professionally contemptuous. By the time she became involved in a case, the bodies were long cooled and decently put away. She had only seen murder scenes in photographs, the immediacy of standing near dead bodies leeched out of the experience.

Peter's face was strained. They were stopped at a stop sign, but he sat as if driving very carefully, both hands on the steering wheel. Kelsey wanted to reach out and put her hand over his. As if he heard her intention, Peter suddenly looked across at her. Their eyes held on each other's in a stare that had nothing to do with the Defiance County murder cases at all. It was a stare in which they simply recognized each other.

Peter suddenly yawned, a yawn that consumed his whole face. While one moment he seemed alert, eyes unnaturally wide, in the next he would blink rapidly and appear to forget himself. Kelsey had seen this kind of behavior both in suspects and in herself. In suspects, it indicated drug use. But when it had been her, it had meant:

"You were up all night, weren't you?" she said, looking at his boots.

He was slow to answer, then smiled and said, "No, I dozed a little."

"What, while driving?"

"Oh, you know that trick, do you?" Peter grinned again.

"Yeah. I know how it comes out, too. One of those little three-second catnaps goes on too long and you end up wrapped around a tree—or running into the back of a gasoline truck."

The deputy didn't lose his smile. "No, a truck'll move over for a squad car coming up behind it."

"Will a tree?"

"Haven't tried that one yet."

Kelsey kept studying him. Neither his smile nor his sleepiness masked his intentness. She asked quietly, "Where is there left to look for her, Peter?"

He changed the subject. "What about what happened to you?"

Peter drove on slowly toward the motel. Kelsey said, "Oh, somebody just drove by me and yelled something. I ignored them and the next thing I knew there was this—" She sucked in breath as she shifted in the seat and reached to hold the underside of her thigh.

Peter pulled into the motel parking lot and turned off the car. "Do you mind if I see?"

Kelsey's immediate negative reaction rose to her skin like a blush. But she remembered the night Peter had come to her motel room, when she'd been barely dressed, and she had watched him without his knowing it in the mirror over the dresser. Peter had had a perfect chance that night to check her out but instead had kept his neutral stare on a far corner of her room.

"Come inside," she said.

The motel room was cool and dim. Kelsey sat on the edge of the bed and pushed her sweat pants down her legs. Underneath she wore running shorts, navy blue with white trim. Her legs looked pale; their only color was the blue of blood under the skin. Goose bumps rose.

She stood, tossed the pants into a corner, and turned around. Peter's leather gunbelt creaked as he squatted behind her. In the mirrored closet door she could only see the top of his head. She winced in anticipation, but when he touched the back of her thigh, it was so gently she could barely feel it. She felt his fingertips circle the injured area, gently stretching the skin around the bruise. Her leg was tight already, from her run, from the cold. Kelsey stood stiffly, feeling the warmth of his skin, thinking of his training those so-watchful gray eyes on her leg.

He sucked in his breath quietly. "What?" Kelsey said. "What is it?"

"It's a damned deep bruise," Peter said, rising. The sleepiness was gone from his eyes. He looked at her with concern. "I think a doctor—"

Kelsey sat on the bed. "Believe me, I've had bruises before. They go away on their own."

Peter turned away abruptly and went out the door. Maybe she'd offended him. Kelsey stretched out on the bed, face down. She could still feel his fingertips and his breath.

Just as she was getting drowsy, the motel-room door opened again. Peter stood there, outside light making him a silhouette. He held up both hands. In one was an ice pack, clattering with its contents, in the other a heating pad.

"I don't know which—"

"Heat," Kelsey said.

She remained full length on the bed. Peter found a plug for the heating pad and wrapped it around the back of her leg. As the warmth began, he adjusted it again. Kelsey felt like a patient, or a child. "Thanks."

"If you see that truck again, you let me know."

"Yes, sir."

She smiled drowsily, feeling his eyes on her.

No one knew where the baby was. That was what added genuine mystery to the case, lifted it out of the ordinary. The missing baby hung like a pall of smoke over the town. When the subject of the baby came up, Kelsey saw people's faces turn grim or sad or even some variety of guilty: *I would have saved her if I could.* Kelsey felt the loss herself, nagging at her to hurry, to do something. But the baby was largely abstract to her. These were people who had seen her, who had spent long weary days and nights searching for her, finding no trace. Some of them had even heard little Taylor's cries or giggles when she'd been as safe as any other infant. A few of them had held her.

"What time did you leave here that morning, Mrs. Hatteras?"

The gentle-faced lady raised her hands and moved them in circles of erasure. "Why don't you just call me Aunt Goldie, miss? Everyone here does."

"I'm not from here," Kelsey said, smiling to take the sting out of it. "You did leave before the—crimes occurred that morning, you said?"

"Yes, I went back to Houston," Aunt Goldie said sadly, acknowledging her dereliction of self-imposed duty. "It was after breakfast. About nine o'clock, I guess." She shook her head at the coincidence of it.

There'd been no timemarks to place anything for Goldie Hatteras. She hadn't had to be anywhere in particular, she'd gone home to an empty house, her husband, Edgar, at work, and she'd left again to come back to Galilee without seeing anyone in Houston. Time wasn't a concern for her. "I'm sorry," she said.

They stood on the front porch of the Beaumont house. Aunt Goldie had answered the doorbell, and since she was the one Kelsey wanted to question, preferably alone, Kelsey had resisted her invitation and instead drawn Goldie outside. It was a cool but bright morning, a breeze carrying the scent of pine needles from across the road. Kelsey felt invigorated, but Aunt Goldie hugged herself and blinked, as if her natural habitat were indoors.

"That's all right," Kelsey said. "I just wanted to ask what you remember from before you left. Was the baby awake?"

"Oh, yes, she was always awake before seven." Mrs. Hatteras smiled as if to say what an endearing quality this had been.

"So Ronald and Lorrie were up, of course."

"Yes, of course. We had breakfast together."

"Was the baby fussy?"

"Taylor? Oh, no. She played on the floor. I carried her a little before I left, to give her parents time to shower and dress." Her hands unconsciously shaped a baby. Suddenly Aunt Goldie was crying, keeping very quiet, trying to hold it in. Kelsey stepped close to her and put her arm around the older woman's shoulders, but Mrs. Hatteras shook her head. She didn't want her grief acknowledged. Kelsey quietly went back to questioning her.

"Do you remember what they were talking about?" There was no way to edge subtly into the subject of Ronald and Lorrie's marriage. Kelsey was inclined to consider Aunt Goldie a trustworthy observer, as a comparative outsider in the house.

Aunt Goldie sniffed, wiping the underside of one eye. "Nothing in particular. Alice's health, of course. They talked about when they might go back to Dallas, how much work Ronald was missing."

"Was he upset about that?"

"He just mentioned it."

"Did they argue?"

"No, no, nothing like that."

"Had you heard them argue before?" Aunt Goldie shrugged, frowning. Her tears had stopped. "It's not gossip, now that they're dead."

Quietly, Mrs. Hatteras said, "They had their bad days, like any young couple. Sometimes it seems . . ."

"What?"

Aunt Goldie was blushing at her own boldness. "Sometimes I think young couples today don't try as hard as we used to. They always think they have other . . ."

"Options?"

"Yes. Isn't that what all the magazines and TV shows say? 'What are your options?' When I was young we didn't think we had so many choices."

Kelsey regarded her with more interest. "Were things that bad between Ronald and Lorrie, that they talked about their choices?"

"Oh, no, I don't mean that. I'm just running on, just talking about things in general."

"Were they arguing that morning?"

Aunt Goldie shrugged, a more truthful answer than the one she said: "No, I don't think so."

"When you left—"

The front door opened. "Aunt Goldie? Oh. There you are."

Kelsey wasn't surprised to see Katherine Fletcher. Her dark green Buick was parked in the driveway, behind Aunt Goldie's older-model Chevrolet, leaving a clear lane in the double-wide driveway so that Mrs. Beaumont could back her car out of the garage if she chose.

"Hello, Mrs. Fletcher," Kelsey said, to which Morgan's wife only replied, "Hello," as if she couldn't remember Kelsey's name. Katherine Fletcher looked cool and smooth this morning, her eyes dark, her skin pale. She was dressed in gray, pleated slacks and wore a black cable-knit sweater over a simple white blouse. It was nine o'clock in the morning and she looked as if she'd been up for hours.

"I have a statement from you in my records," Kelsey said to her, "but it didn't say much. I'm sorry, I'm sure you were in shock when you were questioned." Katherine didn't answer. "Have you remembered anything more?"

"There's nothing I could remember. I wasn't here all that morning, until Morgan called me and I came, close to noon. It was all over by then. Long over, they tell me."

"Yes. And you had company at your house that morning, didn't you?"

"My bridge group. They started arriving by nine-thirty and were there—well, until I left. I think I gave the officer some of their names, didn't I?"

Katherine's voice didn't reveal concern or nervousness. She sounded deadened, as if she'd been over this too many times already. At Katherine's appearance Aunt Goldie had gone completely silent, looking down at the porch floor.

"You didn't come over here before then?" Kelsey asked. "Or call?"

Katherine shook her head. "I didn't need to come, since Lorrie and Ronald and Aunt Goldie were here." There was an edge to her voice that even her aunt seemed to hear. Aunt Goldie's head jerked slightly. Kelsey resumed questioning the older woman.

"So the baby was still here, and fine, when you left, Mrs. Hatteras?"

"Yes." Mrs. Hatteras looked puzzled by the question.

"And you didn't see Billy Fletcher?"

"No, miss. He must have come well after I left."

Kelsey returned to the district attorney's wife, and to another subject. "Maybe you could tell me, Mrs. Fletcher. Did you hear Lorrie and Ronald argue frequently?"

For the first time Katherine looked at Kelsey, staring at the prosecutor as if she were being unforgivably rude. "They lived two hundred miles away, Miss Thatch. I didn't see them often and I didn't try to intrude on their privacy when I did."

"You and your sister didn't talk on the phone? She didn't talk to you about her marriage?"

Katherine made a harsh exhalation of breath like a laugh. "No."

"Well, but when you did see them, did they seem happy?"

"Happy?" Katherine said, as if it were a bizarre question. "I never saw Lorrie run across a room and throw herself into his arms. Did you, Aunt Goldie?"

The question only flustered the older woman, who made no attempt to answer.

"But they didn't snap at each other constantly either," Katherine continued. "I suppose they were happy. What did they have to be unhappy about?"

Return to the Busy Bee, Kelsey thought. This time she was armed with a dangerous thing. She thought she was beginning to understand the Beaumont/Fletcher family. She had a few questions and felt entitled to ask them. This was her fourth visit to the Bee, and she hadn't asked a question yet. On the first two visits she'd just gone in and slumped in her chair, like a working woman being beaten down by a hard day, and chatted minimally with Florence while the stylist did what she wished with Kelsey's hair. During the first visit, when she'd met Katherine Fletcher, Kelsey had sensed icy quiet all around her. Defenses were up. By her most recent visit, she'd sensed puzzlement, even irritation. They were all prepared to brush off her questions—wasn't she going to ask any?

By this, her fourth visit, Kelsey hoped she had shown herself not a hostile outsider but just a woman with a hard job, and fast-growing hair. This time she was greeted by name by the receptionist, and two other employees said hello as Kelsey took her seat on a vinyl-covered couch in the styling room, early for her appointment. Florence, her regular stylist, looked over the mound of hair she was coloring, noted Kelsey with surprise, and said, "I didn't see you on my card today, honey. Shopping around? I promise you, we're getting there. If you'd blow-dry it like I told you, instead of just toweling . . ."

"I'm very happy with your work, Florence. But you didn't have any openings this morning, and I just needed a quick trim before the weekend."

The sixtyish lady whose hair was being manipulated said to Kelsey, "You look tired, dear."

Kelsey smiled valiantly. "I'm used to having some staff help, not being completely on my own like this. And, well, maybe I don't get the cooperation a man doing my job would."

She noted two or three feminine heads around the room bob understandingly, and she ventured a joke. "Is there some code phrase I need to use to show I'm a good old boy at heart? Something about hunting, or beer?"

"Something about hunting beer," Florence said, to chuckles in which Kelsey joined.

"She's working hard, I'll swear to that," said the lady under Florence's hands, smiling on Kelsey benignly. "She interviewed me, didn't you?"

"Yes, Mrs. Olsen." Mrs. Olsen, the wife of the man who owned the local independent drugstore, had been one of the bridge players in Katherine Fletcher's home the morning of the murders.

"Oh, are you a suspect, Mrs. O.?" Florence asked, winking at someone across the way.

"Gracious," said Mrs. Olsen, and Kelsey answered for her. "No, and thanks to Mrs. Olsen and the rest of the bridge group, neither is Katherine Fletcher."

"You mean she was?" asked a voice from the corner.

Kelsey shook her head. "I just need to check everyone out. I know if my sister ever gets shot, somebody'd better find out where I was at the time."

She heard the clucking of a remonstrative tongue, but also an agreeable chuckle or two. In fact, the district attorney's wife had been an attractive candidate for murderess from the moment Kelsey had seen her walking coldly down the aisle in front of this couch, but she turned out to be one of the few potential suspects with a rock-solid alibi. Kelsey had interviewed all five of the other bridge players (they hadn't had enough for two tables, they'd taken turns playing) and found to her slight disappointment that Katherine Fletcher had been in her own house while her sister was being murdered down the road. Katherine had been at home until the call came from her husband, the discoverer of the bodies. As always with witnesses, there was wide discrepancy in their accounts of when this call came in; the earliest said about ten forty-five, the latest close to noon. Kelsey knew from the police officer she'd interviewed that Katherine Fletcher had arrived at the scene shortly after her husband's eleven-thirty call. So she'd gotten the call well after the murders must have been committed. She was in the clear.

A voice from over the partition said, "The case sure seems to be moving slow. Billy Fletcher's being put through the wringer—for nothing, some people say."

"I'm sorry about that," Kelsey apologized to the air. This was strangely like being interrogated by space aliens—voices invisibly from the air, the mirrors giving her random glances of questioners and listeners. The few faces or parts of faces Kelsey could see were thoughtful, curious, listening intently. "I probably have enough evidence to go to a grand jury," Kelsey went on, "but first there are these other nagging possibilities I have to resolve, just in my own mind."

"Like what?" Florence asked. She had stopped cutting, she was just standing looking at Kelsey.

"Oh, Lorrie and Ronald, mainly. What kind of marriage they had. Because you know, the facts of this case, a wife and husband found dead like this, normally the conclusion would be murder-suicide. If not for the missing baby . . ."

All the expressions turned solemn. A woman around the corner dabbed at her eye with her protective sheet. There were murmurs of sorrow, but one strong voice cut through them. It was the voice from the back corner of the room again.

"I'll tell you who took that baby. God took that baby."

There was an audible gasp or two, the sound of chairs swiveling toward the voice, and one stylist saying in outrage the voice's name. "Janie."

The woman in the corner was heavy in a way that made her look sturdy, not fat. Her face had one deep crease across the forehead and few other lines. She had steely eyes that could have been pretty in a less cold face. She stood wearing a white smock, swept the sheet over her styling chair like a matador, and motioned to Kelsey. As Kelsey stood, Janie continued talking. She had everyone's attention.

"Anyone who cared about that baby would have taken her after her parents were dead. If she was yours, would you have wanted her left there to grow up in that house? Miz Beaumont would've turned her into the worst spoiled brat on this earth, and Katherine—Katherine couldn't bring herself to touch that baby. Did you ever see her hold her? Or even stay in the same room where Taylor was?"

"Hush, Janie," said a quiet voice, but no one contradicted Janie, and as Kelsey crossed the hard black-and-white floor toward the stylist, she saw one woman nodding and more than one turning away somberly, as if from the harshness of truth. As Kelsey settled into the chair, she said, "But Ronald and Lorrie, did they get along?"

Janie offered no opinion about that. She began rearranging Kelsey's hair. Silence was the only immediate reply, and Kelsey let it continue until a woman on the other side of the partition said, "They got along just fine, just like Harold and Hattie Lovera. Everything's hunky-dory as long as they're of the same opinion on everything—and it's Hattie's opinion."

Apparently the Loveras were a well-known local couple frequently used as an example of delicate marital relations, because several women chuckled. But Florence added, "Only it was the other way around with Lorrie and Ronald, it had to be his opinion."

This pronouncement met with no dissent, and one woman murmured, "Bully."

"You'd think a poor boy who married into a rich family would keep his mouth shut once in a while," said someone else.

A tall, thin stylist with an unlikely shade of red hair, whom Kelsey had noticed on her earlier visits but who had never distinguished herself by commentary, said suddenly, "Oh, Lorrie got her licks in, too, once in a while, I suspect."

Murmurs rose to a few audible words. "Did she tell you that, Bev?" "You used to do her hair, didn't you?" "Remember that time—?"

Abruptly Janie swiveled Kelsey out of the conversation. Kelsey found herself facing the mirror, looking into the small blue eyes of her stylist, one Kelsey had deliberately asked for because she remembered this expression, the hostile glare the woman had turned on Katherine Fletcher when Mrs. Fletcher had appeared in the Busy Bee.

"What are we doing today?" Janie asked. Turned toward the mirror and the corner, their conversation became private.

"Just a trim. I take it you had to decline your usual invitation to the bridge party at Katherine's that morning."

Janie just stared at her in the mirror for a moment, then grimaced. "I guess they would've had me in to serve canapés if I'd asked for the job."

"The first time I saw her," Kelsey said carefully, "I thought, 'There's a woman who could commit murder and not lose sleep over it.'"

Janie's long, thin scissors clipped near Kelsey's ear. Her voice came hard. "Why don't you tell her that? She'd love people to think that about her. The way she prances around and looks down her nose at people. But you just look back at her and see how long she can look you in the eye."

As if demonstrating her own capability, Janie stared at her customer in the mirror. She knew she was being used, she knew Kelsey was trying to tap her for information, but it just happened that Janie wanted to be tapped. Kelsey had read the stylist's expression correctly on that first visit. Here was someone with a long-smoldering resentment of the Beaumont clan and of its elder daughter in particular, ready to burst with the desire to share her anger. How easy it was, Kelsey thought, if you chose your target wisely.

"Some of us find that act of hers pretty funny," Janie said quietly, "because we remember what a mousy little thing she was. She shouldn't try to pull that off around people with memories as long as ours."

"Is it an act? I've seen her act completely differently around her mother. Almost like a little girl. Which is the act?"

"The little-girl part is real. Kathy'd do whatever her mother asked her. Anything. Just hoping the old lady'll drop her some crumb."

Kelsey waited. Janie continued to fluff and arrange her hair in a distracted way, clipping off tiny ends of hair. Finally Kelsey said, "You have an example." Not a question.

Janie looked at her in the mirror. Odd nickname for a woman nearing fifty, as if she were stuck thirty years in the past, or everyone thought she was. Again her expression told Kelsey she knew she was being probed, but that Janie had a purpose of her own. Kelsey looked back just as flatly, not trying to cajole the woman. *Yes, we want to use each other. Let's get started.*

"You know about the abortion."

Kelsey raised her eyes, shook her head.

"Somebody'd tell you, sooner or later. If anybody even remembers." Conversation in the rest of the shop had become general. In their corner, Kelsey and Janie were alone. "Kathy did try rebelling, years ago, but she couldn't pull it off. When she was a teenager, her daddy had already started making money in the oil binness, and Miz Beaumont was intent that her daughters was the most proper things in town. Kathy fought her sometimes, she'd sneak out and run with who she wanted to. Then in her senior year she turned up pregnant. She said she was going to go home and tell her parents she was getting married and having the baby, but that's not the way it happened once she got home."

"You were one of the ones she'd sneak out and run with?"

Janie shrugged. "I heard about her. But nobody heard what happened inside that house when Kathy went home. Except that she caved in. Her mother must've laid down the law to her that she wasn't going to have Kathy marrying some trash and being a teenage mother. Not and have people snicker and whisper behind Miz Beaumont's back. No, ma'am.

"They took her to Houston, both her parents, and they found some doctor who did it, and when Kathy came back, she didn't sneak out her window anymore. She wouldn't even hardly talk to the boy again."

"How is it you know about this? I'd think it was something the Beaumonts would try to keep quiet."

"You can't keep something like that quiet. Not with as many people as knew. Mr. and Mrs. Beaumont, Katherine . . ."

"And the boy."

Janie's hands held Kelsey's head, turning it, changing the angles in the mirror. The stylist's grip was firm but gentle. "Happens he was a friend of mine. No, not like that. Just a friend, a good friend. We used to talk. Poor stupid boy, he'd made plans. He really thought this was his life starting. And then he didn't just lose the baby, he lost Kathy, too. It was after that that she started dogging her mother's footsteps like she does, waiting for

JAY BRANDON

those crumbs to fall. You could see it in her face: she'd done exactly what her mama wanted, wasn't Mama supposed to love her now? But that's not the way Miz Beaumont is. Old Miz Beaumont ain't one to coo over people and pat them and give out hugs and kisses."

"What happened to the boy?"

Janie's voice didn't soften. "Vietnam happened to him. If he'd had a wife and a baby, he never would've been sent. I hope that's something Miss Katherine Beaumont Fletcher thinks about when she lies awake nights."

The hair cutting continued in silence after that, until Janie was doing the last brushing-out, when Kelsey asked casually, "And ever since then Katherine has been her mother's shadow?"

"Not quite," Janie said in a voice without undertones. She was brisk, wrapping up business. "That fall Katherine went off to college in Houston. When she didn't come back after graduation, some of us thought maybe she wouldn't. When she did, it was because she was Mrs. Morgan Fletcher. I don't know how that happened. I know what she's been like for the twenty years she's been back, though, and it makes a person want to laugh."

Janie was speaking in the abstract, though, because her face was not one about to be overcome by laughter. Kelsey thanked her, tipped her carefully, and thought for a moment the stylist was going to throw the money in her face. Then Janie shrugged and pocketed the bills.

Before she turned away, Kelsey asked, "So did Morgan and Katherine start going out in high school? After—what you told me about?"

"Not hardly." Janie almost snorted. "Morgan, he was the golden boy. Everybody always expected great things of him. Morgan could've had any girl he wanted, and he sampled around." Janie looked grimly amused. "No, you've met Morgan's best girl from the old days." Kelsey lifted her eyebrows, puzzled. "Years later, he helped her get elected judge."

As Janie had obviously expected, she left Kelsey blinking.

The harsh smells of the beauty shop clung to her when she was outside again. Kelsey felt fumes threatening her eyes, odors trapped in her clothes. She felt dirty. She was accustomed to having law officers do her investigating for her. Did investigators sometimes have this dirty feeling? Where was the line between investigation and snooping? Kelsey felt sure she had crossed it in the beauty shop. Katherine Fletcher's relationship with her mother didn't have anything to do with the murders. Katherine wasn't a suspect. Kelsey had just been curious about her, and she'd used her official position to satisfy her curiosity.

She continued to question people the rest of the day—at the diner where she had lunch, the fountain of the drugstore where she took a Coke break, the grocery store—but she avoided the subject of the district attorney's wife. Some of the people she questioned closed up on her, but some Galileans were willing to talk. They had a lot to say about the Beaumonts, about Lorrie and Ronald Blystone. Mrs. Beaumont didn't seem to be the beloved matriarch of the town Kelsey had thought her. Yes, her careful planning had supplied Galilee with its economic heart, the Smoothskins factory, but Mrs. Beaumont wasn't one to let people neglect their gratitude. Resentment of her was palpable. Kelsey understood it. She had felt the exact same hostile-employee attitude toward Mrs. Beaumont herself.

People were willing to talk about Mrs. Beaumont's younger daughter, Lorrie, too, and her husband, Ronald, though they weren't as well-informed on that subject, since the couple had lived in Dallas for several years. But a drugstore clerk had heard them arguing on an earlier visit to town, and a waitress was willing to swear she'd seen a scratch on Ronald's cheek, of a kind a man didn't give himself shaving.

And everywhere, no one had anything but good to say about Billy Fletcher. One or two were slow to answer when Kelsey asked about his temper, and all would concede he wasn't the brightest member of the clan, but no one thought him capable of murder; at least, no one would say so to the out-of-town prosecutor.

When Kelsey dragged back to the courthouse late in the afternoon, she found herself thinking about Katherine Fletcher again. Janie's story had had the reverse effect of what Kelsey knew the stylist had intended: Kelsey now felt some sympathy toward Katherine.

And she was almost willing to ask herself why, aside from the woman's cold manner, she'd resented Katherine Fletcher from the moment she'd seen her.

Peter Stiller was waiting in her office, sitting near her still-mostly-blank chart. When Kelsey limped in, he looked at her leg, and she made an effort to walk more evenly. Peter was in civvies today, faded blue shirt, jeans, and hiking boots. The boots were dusty, the knees of his jeans crumpled and stained, but Peter himself looked fresher than Kelsey did. He'd obviously gotten a good night's sleep since the day before. "Arrested anybody yet?" she asked him.

"No. You?"

She sat on the edge of her desk, close to him. "Mine's not as cut-and-dried as I thought. I knew it wasn't a very strong case against Billy Fletcher, but it gets worse the more I learn. It seems any number of people might've been willing to kill Ronald Blystone, including just about anybody in his own family."

From the way Peter looked calmly back at her, it was clear this news did not come as a revelation. "Including Lorrie?"

Kelsey nodded.

"Or Katherine?"

The name almost made Kelsey jump, it had been so much on her mind that day. Why did Peter focus on her, too? "No," Kelsey said slowly, "Mrs. Fletcher's the only one in the family no one saw have any quarrel with her brother-in-law. Probably because no one ever heard Katherine express an opinion about the factory, either. She didn't seem to care. As a matter of fact, Katherine was probably glad Ronald Blystone came along, because he took her sister away, out of their mother's sight, so Lorrie wasn't there to soak up what little bit of maternal affection Mrs. Beaumont dispenses.

"But no one else in the family had any reason to like Ronald."

"Can I do anything to help?"

Kelsey fixed him with a harsher look. "Maybe you could tell me why I'm missing a report. The one showing the result of someone checking the interior of Billy Fletcher's car for blood traces." The cop, Perez, had assumed that had been done. Kelsey didn't believe in inadvertently sloppy investigation, not in this case. She should have such a report, but she didn't.

Peter looked puzzled. "I haven't seen one. I'll see—"

"Maybe I'll just do my own search of Billy's car," Kelsey interrupted.

"Hello."

With the greeting came the sound of a light knock on the frame of the open door. Morgan Fletcher was already inside, smiling questioningly. "Oh, I'm sorry," he said at once. "I thought you were alone." When he turned to go, Kelsey hurried toward him.

"No, no, that's all right, it's just—"

But when she glanced back at Peter, she thought for a moment that it *wasn't* all right. The young deputy looked very stiff as he rose to his feet. His civilian clothes didn't disguise his status at all.

"Oh, yes," Morgan said, recognizing him. "Hello, Deputy."

"Hello, sir."

"You and your investigator are discussing the case," Morgan said to Kelsey. "I'll come back."

"That's all right," Kelsey insisted. "We're not saying anything important. Do you have some news for me?"

"No, an invitation. I thought you might like to come to a party. Well, *party*'s too festive a word for it, but it's the regular Friday-night gathering at the club. I thought you might like to get out, maybe meet some people you'd want to talk to. Unless you already have plans?" He held out a questioning hand toward Kelsey and Peter.

Kelsey smiled at the idea of having plans. Peter Stiller, only slightly less stiff than before, said, "I'm on duty tonight."

"Well, then," Morgan said in a hostly, all-settled voice. But Kelsey asked, "Is—your brother likely to be there?"

Morgan smiled a frowning sort of smile. "Billy's not a member. Is that fine, then? I'll pick you up. Seven-thirty or so. There'll be a buffet supper. Good-bye, Deputy."

Morgan walked briskly out, and Kelsey turned to her other visitor. "The club?" she asked.

"The country club."

"Hm, nice. I didn't know there was one. What's it like?"

"I'm not a member either," Peter said, and walked out.

7

If Kelsey had had more time, she might actually have bought a dress. But Morgan Fletcher's short invitation hadn't left her time for that, and her wardrobe didn't occasion much dithering over what to wear. Of the two dresses Kelsey had brought to Galilee, neither was appropriate for an evening out. Well, she wouldn't be the only person at the country club wearing a businesslike suit. Except all the others would be men.

When Morgan had said he'd pick her up, Kelsey expected to ride with both the Fletchers, but when Morgan appeared at her motel-room door he was alone. He wore a freshly pressed dark gray suit and somehow seemed both to fit the suit perfectly and to strain it. Morgan exuded health and competence. His face was tan and crinkled just the right amount around the eyes. And he smelled good. Kelsey had never smelled a men's cologne she liked, and she wasn't sure this was a cologne; it could have been the natural scent of Morgan Fletcher, a man who seemed both pampered and hardworking.

Morgan put his hand on her arm and her waist, ever so lightly, as he opened his car door for her. Kelsey settled into its comfortable enclosure, smiling at herself. Their drive was into darkness, westward out of town, but on a different road from the one that had brought Kelsey into town. The Smoothskins factory lay along this road, but she and Morgan were so well into conversation by the time they passed it that the dark looming of the factory didn't even rise between them.

Morgan had quickly explained his wife's absence: "Katherine's riding with her mother. That way we have an extra car there, so if anyone gets bored she can leave. Katherine's never reconciled herself to being a politician's wife," he added with a smile.

"Is that how you think of yourself?"

"You know, I don't, but the sad truth is to keep doing the job I love I have to get reelected every four years. I just think of myself as a prosecutor. That's my only love."

There were a number of ways to interpret that sentence. Kelsey went silent. Morgan had to start up the conversation again. "Going more slowly than you'd expected," he said unobtrusively.

"Yes. I'm not used to being the investigator as well as the lawyer."

"Yes, the Harris County DA's office will spoil you in that regard, won't it?" He spoke reminiscently. "That's where I learned my trade, too."

"Really? Houston?"

"Mm-huh. Went to law school there, U of H, then into the DA's office. Before your time, of course, but I'm sure we know some people in common. Ever try a case against Floyd Palmer?"

Just hearing the name, of a well-known incompetent Houston defense lawyer with an inexplicably large load of clients, made Kelsey laugh. Common experience made their conversation easy and pleasant after that. Morgan barely watched the dark road as he drove, casually with one wrist on the top of the steering wheel. His right hand was down near the seat, patting, gesturing, always close to Kelsey's leg. She kept waiting for that hand to fall on her thigh, or at least brush it. She didn't know what her response would be.

"And Houston's where you really met your wife."

"That's right," Morgan said easily. "Of course I knew her from home, but barely. When we met again in Houston, two little fish, it seemed like we had a lot in common. I was ready to come home by then, so was Katherine, and it seemed . . ."

He shrugged. It had seemed like a natural alliance, Kelsey finished for him: the rich girl and the up-and-coming golden boy. He must have come to regret that alliance in the long years since. Kelsey could see it in his face.

The woods parted for them and they drove down a lane

formed by tame oaks, with a golf course stretching around them, up to a building that would have been huge for a house but was modest by country-club standards. It featured an expansive veranda, where two or three couples stood looking out at the night. Behind them, the interior of the building burst with light.

"Hello, Henry," Morgan said to the white-jacketed, gray-haired black man who held the club door open for them. "This is Miss Thatch, my guest for the evening." Henry nodded deeply in acquiescence.

Inside was a small, dark-paneled anteroom and cloakroom. Through the interior door they stepped into a light-filled ballroom, with a gleaming floor, scattered tables, and across the room a buffet set up. A man in a tall paper chef's hat stood ready to carve roast beef. A few couples, dressed as if for an evening at the theater, wandered the room. The average age of the few men Kelsey saw was about sixty; the women about the same, though most of them were at some pains to disguise their age. More than one lady who shouldn't have displayed bare shoulders.

Kelsey was, as she'd feared, underdressed. She saw this fact in the glances a couple of the women directed at her as she crossed the room, but Morgan Fletcher carried her, hand under her elbow, as if she were the guest of honor. "Ed, have you met Ms. Thatch?" he asked a man with thick, curly gray hair and flushed nose and cheeks.

"No, but we saw each other across a crowded room," the man said jovially, and Kelsey realized she had seen him that afternoon, wearing a white apron and chatting with customers behind the meat cooler of the grocery store.

"Ah," Morgan said to Kelsey, "you've either been grocery shopping or sleuthing. Ed was probably sweeping up when you saw him, but don't let him fool you, he owns the place."

"Pleased to meet you, Mr. Thorpe," Kelsey said, assuming his name was the same as the store's.

"Oh, you are a detective," the grocer said. "Maybe you can tell me what my employees say about me behind my back."

"Aren't you more interested in what the customers say?"

Not even glancing at the new participant in the conversation, Ed Thorpe said, "Miss Thatch, have you met my wife? Now, if it's dirt about somebody you want to know ..."

"Isn't someone going to bring us a drink?" Mrs. Thorpe said pointedly. A tall lady, she was thin enough that her collarbones and the tendons in her neck were overly prominent. Her gaze was very direct.

While Mr. Thorpe made his genial way toward the bar, Morgan started to accompany him, then veered off. Looking past him, Kelsey saw that Alice Beaumont had entered with her daughter Katherine. They stopped only a few feet inside the doorway and looked around the room, but didn't acknowledge anyone. They were dressed elegantly in full-length dark dresses and jewelry Kelsey could see from across the room. Morgan joined them, and it was his mother-in-law who put up her cheek for him to kiss.

"The call of duty," Mrs. Thorpe muttered. Kelsey realized that not only were they both watching the entrance, so was everyone else in the room.

"Morgan, you mean?" Kelsey asked.

"Among others," Mrs. Thorpe said with quiet irony. Kelsey saw the people in the ballroom slowly converging, some in spiraling curves like asteroids plunging into the sun, toward the Beaumont contingent. Alice Beaumont didn't move, waiting to receive them.

Kelsey slipped away when the Thorpes went to take their turn greeting Mrs. Beaumont. Kelsey watched the patterns, all centered around Mrs. Beaumont, with interest. Everyone went to greet her, but only some stayed near, while others slipped out of earshot, beginning to talk to each other and glance back at Alice Beaumont and her daughter.

"Are these small-town rituals intriguing, Ms. Thatch?"

"Oh, hello, Judge," Kelsey said, startled at Judge Saunders's appearance. Kelsey had been right, the judge was a beauty when she tried, and she had tried tonight. Her off-white dress showed a good portion of her chest, the paleness of the dress making her skin look tanned and flawless. Her blond hair was both flowing and confined, and her face showed no lines. Her cheeks lifted winningly when she smiled, as she did easily. The judge, too, held a flute of champagne.

"I think we can make it Linda when we're not in the courthouse, can't we?" she said in a friendly way.

"I'm not sure, maybe—Linda."

Both of them listened to the sound of that, wearing matching small frowns. "No, I was wrong, let's stick with Judge."

"Thank you," Kelsey said.

But Judge Saunders remained friendly and casual, prompting Kelsey to ask, "Is she really this important? Why hadn't I heard of Mrs. Beaumont before now?"

"You would have, if you moved in the right circles and paid attention. Your boss certainly knows her. She pays for favors, and some people say she buys secrets."

"Seriously?"

Linda Saunders smiled at Kelsey indulgently. "It's just gossip, honey. But it's gossip about money, and that's the most serious kind."

Kelsey wondered if that was Judge Saunders's first glass of champagne. Encouraged, she asked in the judge's casual tone of voice, "Don't people gossip about sex any more?"

The judge's eyes roamed the room, but her answer disappointed as well as intrigued: "Who knows? Maybe I don't hear it."

On her wedding finger the judge carried a diamond half as big as the Ritz. Kelsey wondered at Judge Saunders's original social status, before being elected judge.

Realizing as she asked it that her question was an unsubtle transition from the judge's last remark, Kelsey asked anyway, "Is your husband here, Judge? You are married?"

"Not during hunting season," the judge said unresentfully. "You might meet Hank one of these days, but not during a weekend in the fall." She was still watching other people in the room. Her eyes changed as one broke away and came toward them. Kelsey followed the judge's gaze to see Morgan approaching.

"I seem to have a couple of extras," he said, handing them each a new glass of champagne.

Judge Saunders raised her new glass in a toast to the man who had brought it to her. "The chevalier of unescorted ladies. Is there enough of you to go around, Morgan?"

"I'm thinking of being cloned," he answered, and the judge laughed.

A few minutes later they were joined by someone else. Judge Saunders had just handed Morgan her empty champagne flute when Katherine Fletcher walked up and did the same. She glanced at the other glass but not at the woman who had handed it to her husband. Before the moment could become awkward, a waiter appeared with a tray on which Morgan deposited the empty glasses and then passed out full ones easily, like a host.

They were all still watching the core group, a small circle around Mrs. Beaumont, apparently chatting easily but falling silent when Alice Beaumont opened her mouth.

Judge Saunders didn't seem tipsy, she still seemed like the same woman Kelsey had met in chambers, but her personality had expanded in this larger room. "What did you and Mama talk about on the way over, Kath? Who she has to suck up to to get elected president of the Garden Club?"

Katherine Fletcher actually smiled faintly. Of all the people present, Kelsey most wanted to get Katherine alone. Katherine knew she wasn't a suspect in the murders, and everyone said she'd never taken a position on what should become of the Smoothskins factory, so maybe she'd be willing to talk freely, if Kelsey could just approach her the right way—and out of her mother's shadow.

"No, it was the usual," Katherine said. " 'This will be fun, don't you think?' No answer. 'Well, let's just go eat at Luby's instead.' No answer. 'Or I could drive us both into a tree.' "

Her voice had started out light and mimicky, but had changed. Linda Saunders put a hand on Katherine's arm, watching her intently. She made her voice light. "Well, Kathy, if you'd just answer your mama's questions, you'd have much more fascinating conversations, I'm sure."

Katherine laughed a slightly forced laugh. Kelsey boldly spoke up. "Maybe you should find her a man."

The trio turned to stare at her. "Mrs. Beaumont, I mean," Kelsey stammered.

"Well, I hoped you didn't mean one of us," Judge Saunders said.

"Maybe it would help," Kelsey went on. "Maybe—"

"Oh, honey," Katherine said. "At that age you're not interested in sex any more."

"I will be," Morgan said quietly. The group turned to watch Mrs. Beaumont speculatively. A rather distinguished-looking man, the president of the bank, was leaning close to her ear, and Alice was leaning close as well, whispering toward him. "Hmm," someone said, but,

"I may be interested, too," Judge Saunders said authoritatively, "but when I get to be Miz Beaumont's age, I'll be damned if I'll let anybody see me naked."

"Well, you can't have it both ways," Katherine said.

"Oh, but you can, Kath. They have the most ingenious underwear now. I'll loan you my catalog."

Katherine whooped into her champagne, softening it as much as she could, but her laugh was still, for a moment, the loudest sound in the room. She turned toward Saunders and slapped the judge's arm, saying, "You are bad," and for a moment Kelsey saw Katherine young and unguarded. The two women leaned their heads together and giggled.

But Kelsey looked past them and saw that Katherine Fletcher's laughter had drawn the attention of the most important person in the room, and either Mrs. Beaumont didn't like her daughter laughing or didn't like the person Mrs. Beaumont was looking at: Kelsey. Alice Beaumont marched out of her own conversation, leaving it in staring remnants, across the room toward Kelsey.

The lady walked straight up to her, staring hard. Kelsey felt the group around her part and draw aside, though not out of earshot, not remotely.

"Well, Kelsey," Mrs. Beaumont said without preamble. Kelsey found she didn't like the sound of her own name in the woman's mouth. "I'm glad you're finding time to socialize. Obviously the job you're here to do isn't taking up all your time. If it were, we might have had some results by now."

There was a shocked silence. Kelsey was part of the silence for a moment, but did not feel chastened. "I have been doing my job, Mrs. Beaumont, with the limited resources I have. It's turned out to be a more complicated case than I'd been warned."

"Only if you make it so by prying into things that aren't part of it," the older woman snapped. "Like trashy gossip. I hear you've been asking questions about my daughter."

Katherine Fletcher's eyes lifted, startled, to Kelsey, but in her next sentence her mother made it clear it was not her older daughter, the living one, in her thoughts. "Just because she had the bad luck to get herself murdered, now her whole life is exposed to public ridicule?"

"The condition of Lorrie and Ronald's marriage is very much relevant," Kelsey said. "I don't indulge in frivolous gossip, but I have to find out everything I can about the circumstances."

"The circumstances are that Billy Fletcher came into my home and murdered my daughter and stole my grandbaby. Even from the few things I know about the case, I know a halfway competent prosecutor could at least have gotten him indicted by now. Maybe then he'd be in jail instead of—"

"The few things you know," Kelsey repeated, losing her temper. "Don't you realize that I know even less? You should be my best witness, you were right there! I wasn't, I'd never heard of Galilee then. But you were right in the middle of it. What did you hear, what can you tell me? Nothing, like everyone else!"

Mrs. Beaumont faltered for the first time. Her expression turned inward, an uncharacteristic look for her. "I should," she said to herself. "I should at least have— But I—" She looked up at Kelsey, straining to be helpful. "All I remember is hearing the baby cry."

Her daughter, perhaps emboldened by her mother's unaccustomed loss of confidence, said from behind her, "You couldn't have heard anything, Mama. You were so sick and medicated. You just remember the baby crying from another time. God knows we heard it enough."

"That's not true, Katherine. She was a good baby."

Katherine Fletcher rolled her eyes, but Kelsey could only spare a glance at the daughter. Kelsey was still, like everyone else in the vicinity, staring at the transformation of Alice Beaumont. The matriarch looked suddenly old. Her face had wrinkled as it drew in on itself. She stood unmoving, head cocked as if she still heard the cry of her missing granddaughter. As if she could follow the sound.

"Nothing else?" Kelsey asked. "Not gunshots?"

"I must have, mustn't I?" Mrs. Beaumont acknowledged. "But like Katherine says, Goldie had given me my medicines early in the morning, and with the fever . . . I dozed and I woke and I can't remember now what was dreams and what wasn't. I just remember Taylor crying, for a long time. I kept thinking I needed to get up and go see her."

Some of the other guests had joined the circle around Alice Beaumont, staring at her in sympathy or surprise. One of the newcomers was her whispering partner, the banker, who stepped forward and put his arm around her. "Come on, girl," he said quietly. "Let's go think about it together."

As the two walked away, murmurs nibbled at the silence, but no one broke it completely until Judge Saunders said to Kelsey, "Don't let her tell you you haven't done anything. You've handed me a new sight. That's the first time I've seen anyone get the better of Miz Beaumont."

Kelsey felt no satisfaction. How tough was it to triumph over a woman by plunging her back into the worst tragedy of her life?

But Alice Beaumont's recitation had done something else. It had made Kelsey realize something that was missing from everything she'd heard so far.

Before she had a chance to inquire, though, she saw that Katherine Fletcher was alone, isolated by the crowd's breaking up. Kelsey hurried to join her. "Mrs. Fletcher? I take it you wouldn't put much stock in your mother's memory?"

Even after their earlier companionableness, Katherine didn't invite Kelsey to use her first name. Kelsey was beginning to admire Katherine's aloofness. She understood it.

"That baby should not have been in the house," Katherine said without heat. "She cried all the time, she disturbed Mama's rest. Lorrie was supposed to be there to help, but she just made more work for everyone. I started avoiding the house when I could."

"And the baby."

Katherine stopped walking. She gave a slight sigh. "I'm sure people have told you I didn't like Taylor, but that's not true. I just don't dote on babies. I'm a freak, I'm a failed woman. If I liked children, I would have had children."

Kelsey could have questioned that statement with the information she had, but there was no reason to tell Katherine Fletcher that she already knew the ugly secret of her teenage years. Instead she said, "And you say Lorrie caused trouble in the household?"

Katherine began to show anger. "Look, what are you trying to make me out? That I hated my sister? I'm sure spiteful people say that, too. Is gossip part of your case? You know I was nowhere near that house when she died. And I'm very sorry about Lorrie, if I could bring her back—"

"Mrs. Fletcher, I have a sister." Kelsey stopped as if that explained all.

Katherine said wearily, "And are you good friends?"

"We get along just fine. Especially since she moved to Chicago with her husband and her two brats and I see her about once every two years."

Katherine Fletcher smiled slightly. She looked Kelsey in the eyes for the first time. Kelsey shrugged. "Actually, that's a slight exaggeration, to say we get along fine. Those occasions once every two years, well, after the second or third hour I have to go for a drive or something."

Katherine laughed quietly in agreement. She looked down again, into the past. "Lorrie was like Mama, strong. Strong. Sometimes I felt squeezed between them. That's when I had to get out. But then when I'd come back, they'd be laughing and leaning on each other and sharing some new private joke and I'd think . . ."

When it was clear she wasn't going to finish her sentence, Kelsey did. "That Lorrie'd gotten what she wanted. Squeezed you out on purpose."

Katherine didn't admit the accuracy of Kelsey's speculation, except indirectly. "Everybody thinks Ronnie was the boss of that family, but he was no match for Lorrie. Nobody was."

Kelsey could suddenly see the dead family members. No one had done that for her before. She saw mental images of Lorrie and Ronald Blystone, moving, speaking, eyes flashing.

She asked, "So you think Lorrie would have jumped into the argument between her husband and Billy Fletcher? She could have made Billy just as mad as Ronald did?"

"If that's what the argument was about," Katherine Fletcher said, and resumed her course toward the bar.

Before Kelsey could hurry after her to ask what she'd meant, Morgan Fletcher appeared in front of her. He seemed to feel responsible for Kelsey. Taking her arm again, he introduced her to more prominent citizens. The pattern of their occupations made clear why Alice Beaumont was the center of attention at the country club. The grocer, the banker, the owner of a trucking company: none of them would have lasted a week in business without the Smoothskins factory and the paychecks its almost three hundred workers took home every week. Later Judge Saunders, who was beginning to show her champagne by then, put it bluntly. "She's not all that rich, you know. Not by Texas standards. She probably doesn't rank in the top three hundred in the state. It's not that she's got all the money in the world. Just all the money in town."

Kelsey got a ride home from Morgan and Katherine. Morgan had to pull himself away from half a dozen people who wanted his ear for one last chat. His wife walked out unimpeded, looking tired. Morgan put his arm around her as he opened her car door. Katherine didn't respond.

"Do you think the judge will get home safely?" Kelsey asked. She waited for Judge Saunders to emerge on the tide that was carrying the last of the celebrants out the door, but didn't see her.

"She's had practice," Katherine said, a snide remark that made Kelsey warm to her. It was a sign of emotion.

The atmosphere in the car was rather heavy. The night was black, the road unlighted except for their headlights, which reflected back a faint glow into the interior of the car. Kelsey could just see her hosts in outline. She asked the question that had occurred to her hours ago.

"The morning of the murders, where was the maid?"

For of course there must be a maid. Aunt Goldie was here to help at the moment, but in ordinary times Alice Beamont wouldn't go to the grocery store herself. She wouldn't make her own bed.

If Kelsey had hoped to startle an admission from Katherine or Morgan, she was disappointed. "Where was Helena?" Morgan asked his wife musingly. Katherine only shrugged.

"Helena?"

"Helena Parker. What became of her, Katherine?"

Katherine Fletcher's voice came low and unconcerned. "I told you, she quit. Went back to Louisiana, I think. I keep after Mama to let me hire someone else, but she's not satisfied with anybody I suggest."

"Surely someone questioned her?" Kelsey asked Morgan.

"Oh, yes. She wasn't in the house at the time, I remember that. Doing the shopping or something. Didn't you get a report mentioning her? Ask your investigator about it. How are things working out with you and your deputy? Is he any use to you?"

"Some."

"Let me know if you want Sheriff Early to assign someone else. Young Peter, he's thorough, but his people skills . . . Has he told you about the time he ran for sheriff?"

"Peter Stiller? Ran for sheriff?" Kelsey couldn't picture it: Peter shaking hands, smiling broadly, asking people to do him favors and put up his signs in their yards.

"In an abortive fashion," Morgan chuckled. "Peter didn't seem to have a flare for politics."

The district attorney laughed.

The next day was Saturday. It was a gray November day, temperature in the fifties, but the air carrying a wet chill. Saturday meant nothing to Kelsey. It had been years since weekends had mattered, but the years when they had had been Kelsey's formative years, and some part of her still thought of Saturday as date night, and of herself as a failure if the weekend found her alone. But she wasn't here for romance. She had responsibilities. She had an adult life. It was hard to convince herself of that, living in one room, fast-food boxes filling the trash can, seeing her few clothes hanging in the mostly empty closet. Kelsey put on jeans and tennis shoes and went for a walk.

The high school football team was playing in the stadium that afternoon; the town was nearly deserted. She kept half-expecting Peter to come gliding to a stop next to her. Occasionally she felt watched, but there was nothing over her shoulder when she turned. She walked on, down the town streets, cutting through the grocery-store parking lot. Autumn aroused a sense of nostalgia, but for what she didn't know. She felt tugged by sights that should have meant little to her: the grocery-store windows advertising specials, a lady fitting a little boy into the shopping-cart seat, a man working on a car parked in his driveway, a cottonwood tree losing its big leaves, revealing limbs that would let a child climb almost to its top. Kelsey recognized her feeling as just a mood, not an actual longing. Nostalgia was a fake commodity for her. There'd been no portion of her life in which she'd wanted to linger. She hadn't liked the helplessness of childhood, she'd been impatient in school—and college, and law school. If she chose, she could work up a sentimental twinge over Tom, her law school romance, even imagine the life they might be having now, but she stubbornly knew that she'd been the one to end it, without real regrets. But something was supposed to come and take the place of the things she'd shrugged off. Jobs had been her life, a life that satisfied her, but Saturday, damned Saturday kept coming along to make her think she'd forgotten something.

She heard a roar from the direction of the stadium. It wasn't sustained, it was a quick shout from hundreds of throats, the kind that came when something quick and good happened: a pass batted down, a hole suddenly opening in the line. Kelsey smiled. Rah.

Lorrie had been strong like her mother, she remembered someone saying. Strong women in a small town. What did you do with that strength? Kelsey looked around at the little houses, the pine trees in the near distance, the way nature mocked everything here. Her fake nostalgia suddenly fastened on the town. She tried to imagine settling here, putting down roots, learning everyone's secrets and living with the knowledge that her neighbors knew some of hers. The background hum of lives too intertwined to be unraveled.

She laughed at herself.

"I'm going to run a search warrant. Want to help?"

Peter nodded, setting down his coffee cup. "What are we searching? Billy Fletcher's house? We never did because when he left the scene, he headed straight for the airport. We didn't figure he'd bring anything incriminating home."

"We're not searching anything. We're seizing."

It was Monday morning. Kelsey was eager to get started. A search warrant might lead to nothing, but it was movement. Questioning witnesses required delicacy, and Kelsey was weary of deciding who was telling her the truth and who wasn't. The thought of seizing physical evidence was exhilarating.

She had called the sheriff's office that morning and been told Peter Stiller wasn't on duty, but as she'd been deciding to get some police officer picked at random to accompany her, Peter had called back, from home, and he'd met her at the diner for breakfast. Kelsey didn't know his schedule, he could have come off duty an hour ago. It was one of his tired-looking days, she was a little sorry to have dragged him out into the daylight, but she was also glad to see him. In her present circumstances, Peter Stiller looked like an old friend.

Peter wore old jeans, a khaki shirt, and a dark brown jacket. She would have preferred him in uniform, but in Galilee everyone would know his official status. He laid a bill on the check sitting on their table and said, "If it's his car you're thinking of, we already went all through it. Billy let us. Didn't you see the report?"

"No," Kelsey said pointedly. "Who censored the reports before you gave them to me? That one's missing. So is the one from whoever interviewed Helena Parker, Mrs. Beaumont's maid."

"Maybe it never got written. I remember somebody talked to her. But she was at the grocery store that morning and didn't know anything."

That was another oddity that had struck Kelsey. Katherine Fletcher stayed away from the house that morning, and the other occupants, Aunt Goldie and the maid, had taken off first thing, as if they had all cleared the way, knowing a killer was on his way. Only sick Alice Beaumont had been left behind with the eventual victims.

"Didn't anybody think it significant," Kelsey asked, "that this maid quit her job and fled town right after the murders?"

"Uh-huh. In the good old days we would've dragged her in and beat a confession out of her, but you damn lawyers have come up with all sorts of bleeding-heart reasons why we can't do that any more. Now we've got to have evidence to arrest somebody, and skipping town isn't enough. Some people just don't fancy working someplace where people've been murdered. They think it's bad luck."

Kelsey decided not to debate. "Let's go. I've got to go type my affidavit and dig up the judge."

"I'll drive you," Peter said, standing with her.

"No. You find Billy Fletcher and keep him and his car in sight. I have a funny feeling about people making phone calls while I'm on my way there with the warrant."

Peter raised his eyebrows, but he didn't contradict her.

"What are you hoping to find?" Judge Saunders asked.

They stood in the open doorway of the judge's chambers. Kelsey closed the door, trying not to be pointed about it.

"Blood."

The judge looked up at her sharply. "The baby's blood?"

Kelsey stood trying to look sure of herself. "No. Lorrie Blystone's. It's all there in the affidavit."

Judge Saunders held the warrant application and its accompanying sworn statement from Kelsey. Quickly she finished reading, and when she looked up again, her expression was more careful. "I'm not sure you've got enough here."

"I do," Kelsey said flatly. "I've had search warrants using virtually identical language upheld on appeal more than once. Both state and federal."

Kelsey stared levelly at the judge, not asking for any favors. The country-club camaraderie between them was gone as if it had never been. A prosecutor or police officer asking a judge to sign a search warrant is asking the judge to risk making a mistake. Good judges don't think of themselves as partners in the search process, they should assume the impartial criticalness that is supposed to be the judge's function. Kelsey didn't know whether Judge Saunders's hesitation was because she was a good judge.

But suddenly the judge took the pen Kelsey had clipped to the warrant and rapidly signed the second page. Briskly she handed it back to the prosecutor.

"Thank you, Judge."

"Uh-huh," the judge said impartially.

Seizing the car was as awkward as it could have been, because the car was parked in the parking lot of the Smoothskins factory.

Peter had already secured the vehicle when Kelsey arrived—he was sitting on the hood of the car. He had also managed to locate Billy Fletcher inside the building. Billy was standing in his shirtsleeves, chatting to the deputy, but his eyes locked on Kelsey as soon as she stepped from her car.

"You just want to humiliate me if you can't convict me?" he said gruffly.

He meant the eyes Kelsey could feel on them from all over the huge lot and every window of the building.

"I'm sorry, Mr. Fletcher, I truly am. I would rather you had been at home, but this was rather urgent."

"How urgent can it be, a month after the fact and after I've already let the car be searched once?"

He had a good point, but Kelsey didn't have the report of that first search, and no guarantee she'd ever find it.

"I have a warrant to impound this car," she said formally, handing Billy a copy. He barely looked at it, just turned to the page that carried the judge's signature. Peter Stiller held out his hand and said, "Please."

Billy Fletcher pulled his car keys from his pocket but held on to them. "How'm I supposed to pick my kids up from school?" he said harshly.

"Take mine," Peter said kindly. Billy shrugged, and the men exchanged keys. For a moment it looked like some faintly silly lodge club ritual. Then Billy turned and stalked away. A crew stood on the loading dock, frankly staring. One of them clapped Billy on the back as he passed. All glared at Kelsey and Peter. The deputy didn't seem to notice.

"I'll take this one," Kelsey said of Billy's car. "You follow in mine, because we'll have to leave this one there."

Peter accepted his assignment without objection. "Where are we going?"

"Houston."

The drive took more than an hour. The highway wasn't crowded, it was a bright, clear morning. It felt strange to be driving Billy Fletcher's car, taking the route he had taken leaving the murder. Kelsey found herself topping the speed limit, racing to see just how fast someone could drive this car from Galilee to the Houston airport. Peter stayed right behind her in her car.

Kelsey kept glancing at the empty passenger seat beside her. Billy's car wasn't nearly as grand as his brother's: it was a Chevrolet with fabric seats. She was happy to note the latter, thinking fabric would retain stains better than leather. She didn't play the radio. In the crackle of the passing miles she had the illusion she could hear a baby's cries, and a man muttering to himself as he drove. She noted the number of rivers and creeks she crossed, and the miles of woods. It was no wonder the search for the baby had failed.

She passed the exit for Houston Intercontinental Airport in an hour and five minutes. In Houston she made sure Peter Stiller was still behind her as she led him through a maze of freeways and downtown streets to the medical examiner's office. In her Houston DA days this had been a regular stop for her, and Kelsey still had at least one friend here. She had brought the car where she was sure she could trust someone.

"Hello, Lydia. You didn't have to do this personally."

"Someone says 'blood,' I appear."

Lydia Cadena, the assistant medical examiner, wore a white lab coat. Even in the bulky cover-up she looked tall and thin. With the white coat covering her from collar to knees she looked like a secular angel. Lydia's face always made Kelsey wish she herself had a less boring genetic heritage. The assistant ME's flat cheeks, long nose, full lips, and piercing brown eyes evoked images of Indians, Mexicans, and Africans. She wore her tightly curled hair short, an aura around her head. What Kelsey remembered about working with her was Lydia's serenity. Even peering into gore that made Kelsey's eyes seek a neutral corner, Lydia Cadena seemed to be operating on a different plane.

She had a stern, fiercely competent look on the witness stand. When she smiled, as she did now in greeting, her face changed completely. Neither she nor Kelsey was a hugger, but the assistant ME gave Kelsey a little pat on the shoulder. Their friendship had formed over late nights preparing testimony and had endured after Kelsey had left for Austin.

Kelsey had pulled Billy Fletcher's car into one of the vehicle bays of the medical examiner's office. Peter parked Kelsey's car some distance away and joined them. "This is Deputy Peter Stiller of Defiance County. He helped me run the warrant."

"Hello, Deputy," Lydia said with light irony. Peter smiled at her. Oddly, Lydia gave him one of her little welcoming pats on the shoulder, too. Kelsey got down to business.

"I want you to go over the whole interior, of course, even the trunk, but I figure either the passenger seat in the front, maybe the backseat, possibly the floorboard, who knows? This guy wasn't behaving rationally."

Lydia Cadena opened the front passenger door and peered into the interior of the car. She nodded approvingly at the fabric upholstery. "Let's see what we've got." Producing a pump-spray bottle from a pocket of her lab coat, she stooped and sprayed a small area of the car's front seat.

"What's this?" Kelsey asked.

"You've been out of it awhile, haven't you, Kelsey?" Lydia teased. "This is the latest thing, child. It's called luminol. It reacts to blood. We don't have to do all that scraping and squinting any more. Just spray."

"And then what?" Kelsey asked. She looked at Peter, who was following the procedure curiously.

"Then we turn off the lights." Lydia pressed a button and a garage door rumbled down behind Kelsey, enclosing the three of them with the car in a much smaller space. When Lydia turned off the overhead lights, claustrophobia breathed on Kelsey's neck.

"Look," came Dr. Cadena's disembodied voice.

There was only one source of illumination, a greenish glow, so faint Kelsey could barely see where it was.

"Bingo," Lydia said.

When the lights came on again Kelsey found she was looking at the passenger seat of Billy Fletcher's car. "That's it?"

"That's what you wanted, Kelsey dear. There's blood on that seat." Lydia shifted uncomfortably and unbuttoned her lab coat. *"Now* I have to do the tedious recovery part—that is, if you want it tested."

"Definitely."

Lydia knelt and peered into the car. Delicately, with a pencil, she pushed down the padded seat, peering underneath the back.

"Mm-huh. You can see the stain." She breathed through her nose. "That's blood, all right. I'll bet you a dollar."

But Kelsey wasn't looking at the car seat. She was looking at her old friend's abdomen. Lydia's lab coat had fallen open, and her hand unconsciously covered and rubbed the slight mound of her stomach.

"Dr. Cadena, you're pregnant."

"Oh, my God, really?" Lydia said, smiling. Her old serenity was enhanced, it kept making her smile. They did hug then and talked about due dates and Lydia's husband, while Peter Stiller smiled awkwardly. Kelsey was reluctant to return to the subject at hand. It was Lydia who did.

"But you don't think this is the baby's blood?" the assistant ME asked, staring at the car seat with a solemn study unlike the serene detachment Kelsey remembered of Lydia Cadena's working attitude.

"Lydia, wouldn't you like someone else to work on this?"

"No. Tell me the scenario."

"The mother—bled. A lot. She was crawling toward the crib. Toward her baby, I think. The bedsheets in the crib were blood-stained, the mother's blood. My picture is the baby was on the floor and she got her hands in the blood. Then somebody picked her up and put her in the crib."

"Then somebody took her," Lydia said flatly.

"That's right. No sign that he washed her up or changed her clothes. I think the baby would still have had bloodstained hands—Lydia?"

"Go on."

"The baby still had her mother's blood on her when he put her in his car. She would have left smears or something. That's what I was hoping."

Lydia Cadena shook her bottle of spray. "Looks like you hoped right. And you can get me a sample of the mother's blood for comparison?"

"Uh—"

"Yes," Peter Stiller said, his first contribution to the conversation. His voice in pronouncing the one syllable carried a grimness that made Kelsey glance at him, but Lydia only nodded with satisfaction.

"You're sure about this test, Lydia? You're sure what you've got there is blood?"

Lydia cocked her head, giving her friend an ironic eye. "By tomorrow I'll be sure, Kelsey. You can quote me."

Exactly what Kelsey planned to do.

Kelsey and Peter were quiet when they left the medical examiner's office. Kelsey drove aimlessly, not heading out of town right away, and found that she made her way naturally to the Harris County Criminal Courthouse, her old haunt. She stopped the car across the street and stared at the imposing but rather nondescript eight-story building where she had learned her trade. In her first three years in the DA's office she'd been moved from section to section by a design that stood her in good stead now because she knew how to prepare a warrant, how evidence was collected, how to present a case to a grand jury. Her education here might have been designed to prepare her for what she was now doing: solo-practitioner prosecution. But it wasn't a career path. There was no such thing as a freelance prosecutor. Kelsey was struck by the fleeting regret that she had left her job as an assistant district attorney too soon. She'd always been a quick study. Maybe she'd been too quick.

The streets and buildings had a comforting familiarity. Kelsey felt no urgency to drive back to Galilee.

"I wish I could talk to that maid," she said, thinking aloud.

"Why?" Peter's voice was a little startling. She'd almost forgotten he was there, he'd been so quiet.

"Because she saw something or heard something or knows something that scared her. That's why she ran. Not just the murders. She's still scared of someone. That's what I'd hope, anyway."

"She was already questioned."

"Only about where she was at the time of the murders. Not about what she might have seen before she left, or something she already knew about the people involved. Right? People nearly always cover up something the first time they're questioned. You've got to go back. Sometimes witnesses know something they don't even know is important." She hesitated, still thinking. "Maybe she even knows something that would tell us who took the baby."

Peter exhaled, tapping his fingers on his armrest, coming to a decision. Then he stared straight ahead. "Let's go ask her."

Kelsey stared at him. Finally, "I don't have time for a trip to Louisiana today," she said.

"Who said anything about Louisiana? Take a left here."

Kelsey glanced at the deputy as often as she could in the Houston traffic as he directed her into the Fifth Ward, a neighborhood where white Houstonians normally found no reason to go. Peter Stiller appeared magical to her: she asked for something and he produced it. But that meant he had been keeping it hidden until she'd asked.

"How did you find her?"

"She's got a sister in Galilee. I kept following her until she finally led me to Helena."

"Here in Houston. Have you questioned her?"

"No," Peter said quickly. "She doesn't know I know she's here. I've been watching her, hoping she'd lead me to the baby. Hoping, like you said, that she knew something."

"But she hasn't led you anywhere, that's why you're willing to give her up now."

Peter looked at her. "I'm giving her up because you said you need her."

They were driving down a block of shotgun shacks, narrow clapboard houses that Kelsey knew from experience of interviewing witnesses harbored three rooms apiece. From the front door of one of these houses one walked straight through a living room, into the kitchen, and through that to the only bedroom. Kelsey had known of families of eight living in such houses. It was a dispirited neighborhood, houses where people lived in the last extremity before homelessness, littered streets that anyone with any resources or any hope would get out of fast. A young man who wanted out might decide to get money the fastest way possible, and what was the threat of prison to a boy who lived in this neighborhood?

"Besides," Peter continued, "maybe you're right, maybe you can get something out of Helena we didn't. She certainly doesn't look like she's going to lead me anywhere."

"How can you have kept her under surveillance all this time?"

"I've got some buddies on the police force here who've been helping me out. And I've been standing a watch myself every third night or so."

That accounted for his occasional sleepy look, and his perpetual grimness. This wasn't an assignment for Peter, there was something personal in it, a purposefulness that wouldn't let him give up when everyone else had. Kelsey started to ask him a question, but said nothing.

"Here. Stop." Kelsey applied the brake a little too sharply, jouncing them forward. Peter pointed. "All right, her car's there. You walk on up and I'll drive past, up to the next corner. When you finish, walk down that way to the end of the street. I'd just as soon she not see me."

A little amused in spite of herself at Peter's stealthy precautions, Kelsey said, "So when I appear at her door, I'll look like I just beamed down from outer space."

Peter looked at her, then his eyes moved past her, to the rows of grim cottages. "Uh-huh."

Kelsey felt conspicuous walking to the house. Then her car drove on up the block, and she felt alone. She walked up onto the narrow porch and knocked loudly on the screen door, rattling the flimsy door in its frame.

She felt sure someone was home, from the car in the gravel driveway and from the fact the heavier inner door of the house was standing open, but after a minute it seemed that no one was going to respond. Just as she was about to call out, she realized someone *was* standing there a few feet in front of her, the woman's body hidden by the door and her face blending into the gloom inside the house. Kelsey's intake of breath turned into a slight gasp.

She recovered quickly and slipped into her assistant AG voice, the one that sounded as if its owner expected answers and had never for a moment considered being afraid of anyone. Kelsey knew the phoniness of the voice, but it was amazing how she could use it for minutes at a time without remembering that. It was a sincere phoniness.

"Helena Parker?" she said firmly.

The young woman didn't answer. Kelsey removed her identification from her jacket pocket and flipped it open. "My name is Kelsey Thatch, I'm an assistant attorney general, on special assignment to the District Attorney's Office in Defiance County. I need to ask you some questions."

"You here to arrest me?" The young woman's voice came softly through the screen door, carrying no suggestion of how she felt about the idea of being arrested.

"If I'd come to arrest you, I would have brought a cop with me."

They stood there regarding each other, until the silence was broken by a baby's cry. Kelsey's eyes widened. Helena Parker's hand moved quickly toward the screen door, but Kelsey was quicker, pulling the door open. Without the door between them, the women locked eyes for a moment, then Kelsey pushed past her. Kelsey felt the woman close at her back as she stepped into the threadbare living room. The baby's cry came again, from farther back. Kelsey crossed the living room and went through a swinging door into the kitchen, tiny but neat. Kelsey noticed a pan of water on the stove, heating a glass baby bottle. Kelsey almost ran through the room, holding her breath, listening to the baby cry, wondering if she would recognize Taylor Blystone when she saw her, from the one photograph she'd seen.

She flung open another door into the house's only bedroom. Across the room a small lamp on a table beside the double bed provided the only illumination. In its feeble light she saw the crib. She rushed to the baby, who was standing, stopping her cry to look curiously at Kelsey as she came toward her. Kelsey reached, almost touched the baby's arm, then came to an abrupt halt.

The baby reaching a pudgy hand toward Kelsey, tilting her head to look at the intruder from a new angle, was black. Stringy black curls adorned a plump brown face with large, staring black eyes.

At Kelsey's hesitation the baby began to cloud up again, but then Helena Parker was there, lowering the crib rail and picking the baby up. Briefly she rubbed noses with the baby, smiling, until the baby was laughing. Then Parker settled the baby on her hip and cocked an eye at Kelsey.

"Yours?" Kelsey asked, then they were interrupted by another voice.

" 'Lena?" A toddler came through the bedroom door, pushing it open with effort. The newcomer was probably a boy, less than two years old, wearing blue overalls and slippers. This child was dusky, too, though of less immediately identifiable heritage than the baby. Helena Parker took the little boy's hand and stood posed for a minute as if for a family portrait. Kelsey couldn't see the resemblance, but then she never could in babies.

"No, neither," Parker said. "I'm just keepin' 'em."

Kelsey followed her slowly back through the kitchen, where Parker picked up the baby's bottle from the stove, tested its temperature on her wrist, and stuck it in the baby's mouth, then back into the living room, which now that her eyes had adjusted to the inside Kelsey found wasn't so gloomy after all. She stopped behind a green, scratchy-fabricked couch of a color and style one couldn't imagine anyone's having bought originally, which seemed destined to have been the hand-me-down it now obviously was, and saw in a corner of the room a playpen, and toys scattered on the floor rug.

"It's just temporary," Helena Parker said. She laid the baby in the playpen, where the baby put her feet up in the air and continued gurgling down the bottle, one bright eye fixed on Kelsey. "Their mothers work, they need somebody."

Kelsey nodded blankly. The sudden expectation of the triumphant rescue of the kidnapped Taylor and the quickly following disappointment had left her feeling dislocated. "You used to work for Mrs. Alice Beaumont?"

"She send you?"

"No," Kelsey said, more irritably than the question deserved. She saw the former maid smile slightly and felt a momentary kinship with her. "No, I found you to ask you some questions."

"Then you wasted a trip. Didn't they already tell you I didn't know nothin'?"

Parker knelt on the floor to hand a squeeze toy in the shape of a clown to the boy. Kelsey knelt, too. "Yes, they did. But I don't take you for that stupid. I don't think you could've spent as much time as you did in that house without knowing something."

Parker shot a glance at Kelsey. She could have been a pretty young woman in other circumstances, in something other than the shapeless blue housedress she wore, if her knuckles hadn't been enlarged and raw from work. She had great cheekbones, and a makeup artist wouldn't have needed to work long to make those eyes wide and gorgeous. But Parker's expression slipped naturally into sullenness when she had no other. It was a face of lost possibilities.

"I was at the grocery store when those people got killed. Lots of people saw me."

"I don't suspect you, Ms. Parker. I want to know what life was like inside that house."

Parker looked away, as if weighing obligations. Kelsey prompted her, "You and Aunt Goldie sure cleared out fast that morning, like you were expecting trouble."

Parker smiled slightly, as if being reminded of a figure from her long-ago past, and repeated, "Aunt Goldie," in a tone between derision and affection, but then her face sobered. "We could tell it was gonna be one of their days."

"Whose days? Ronald and Lorrie's?"

With great deliberation, as if afraid anything she said were being recorded, Helena Parker nodded.

"Why? What happened?"

Parker gave Kelsey a penetrating look, wondering why she should tell her story to this woman. But it was a story she'd obviously been hoarding, that she wanted to share. Kelsey had seen this effect dozens of times. It was the tale-bearing urge that led to confessions, and good gossip.

"Somethin' had already happened before breakfast," Parker said. "I don't know what. But you coulda got electrocuted walkin' between Lorrie and Ronald that morning when she gave him a look. He musta been the one handin' out the shit before they come to the table, 'cause at breakfast he was already tryin' to make up, tryin' to get her to laugh. He said somethin' to her like, 'Just one of my quirks you have to learn to live with.' He was always usin' words like that, like he was English or somethin'.

"And Lorrie just looks straight at him and she says, 'No, I don't. They've got a great little invention for fixin' this kind of problem now. It's called divorce.'"

Parker glanced at Kelsey to see if she was following, then hurried on, "That's when I started puttin' away the breakfast things and decided there were groceries I needed."

"You'd heard them argue before, hadn't you? It wasn't uncommon, from what other people have told me."

"No, but that was the first time I heard her use the D word. It put a chill on breakfast, I tell you that."

"What else did you hear?"

The onetime maid hesitated so long that the momentum of her story was gone. She looked nervous, not exhilarated by the telling. "They'd moved into the other room. As I was going out the back door, I heard Lorrie say, 'Maybe you could take lessons from Morgan.'"

"Morgan? Lessons in what?"

"In being the perfect son-in-law, I guess. I'm not sure, I didn't hear the first part. I was movin' fast, by that point."

"So Ronald and Lorrie were already fighting before Billy ever arrived," Kelsey mused. "The argument must have been Lorrie and Billy against Ronald, once he got there."

Helena Parker shook her head. "That was the thing about Lorrie, you couldn't predict her. She could be cutting Ronald into little pieces with her tongue, then if somebody else come in and looked at him cross-eyed, she'd jump on *them* for not treatin' her husband right. That's why it was best to leave the vicinity. I checked on Miz Beaumont one more time and I got my purse and told Lorrie I was goin' to the store. I offered to take the baby with me"—Parker suddenly stopped, stared into an alternative world for a moment, and sniffed—"but she said no. And that's the last I saw of any of 'em."

Kelsey mulled it over, wondering what else she should ask. But the former maid's story had had the sound of completeness. Kelsey could hear the kitchen door slamming as Parker had gone out it, escaping the house. The imagined sound made her think her last question superfluous.

"Why did you quit?"

But Helena Parker's answer surprised Kelsey. Her eyes going liquid again suddenly, she said, "I couldn't work in that house and hear that baby crying all day long." She gave Kelsey a desperately puzzled look. "How can *she* live there?"

When Kelsey came out of the house, the narrow street was empty of cars. Hers wasn't in sight. Kelsey walked toward the end of the block where Peter had told her he'd meet her. It was a sunny late-November day in Houston, where it had, of course, rained recently, so the air carried more than a trace of summer's mugginess, and the yards were spongy. Kelsey walked in the unevenly paved street, having to watch her footing to avoid turning an ankle. Most of the houses Kelsey passed had open windows, some screened, some with curtains blowing out. Kelsey felt observed. From one front porch an old man in an undershirt watched her quite frankly, nothing moving but his eyes.

The air shivered, and Kelsey looked up warily before she recognized the sound as music. Loud rap, coming closer. She hurried toward the corner.

And stopped. She looked carefully in all four directions and didn't see her car. From the right the rap sound grew louder. A red Pontiac was coming slowly toward her, shaking from poor tuning or from the angry talk blasting out of its radio.

Kelsey turned away from the car, left, hoping that was the way Peter would have gone, hoping the occupants of the Pontiac would ignore her. She shouldn't have given them her back, she realized. She waited for the car to pass her, but it didn't, its music just grew so loud it seemed to be screaming at her.

The short side block took her quickly to another corner. Her car was still nowhere in sight. She stepped into the street, then stopped abruptly as the red Pontiac swung in front of her, close enough to scrape her if she'd kept walking. The driver's window rolled down. A leering face behind black sunglasses said, "Need a ride, lady?"

Four of them were in the car, four black teenagers wearing backward caps, shirts with the sleeves torn off, and more paraphernalia than clothes. They looked like a parody of white panic, but their stares were real as asphalt, and Kelsey felt a wave of coldness sweep through her as the one closest to her stepped out in front of her.

Then he stopped, and Kelsey knew without looking that Peter was behind her. She remembered that Peter wasn't in uniform and wondered what it was about him that made the teenager stare. She also wondered if Peter was armed.

In a voice that came out surprisingly strong and jaunty, she said, "You guys done your homework yet? Tomorrow's a school day."

Give them something to jeer and catcall about, something other than the view of her ass as she turned and walked away from them, toward, sure enough, Peter Stiller standing at the open driver's door of her car. His arms were folded, he didn't look particularly menacing. He pushed the door wider open and Kelsey brushed past him into the driver's seat. After Peter walked around the car and slid in beside her, she took off and said in a voice made irritable by the passing anxiety, "I didn't need a rescuer, I just needed you to be where you'd said you'd be."

She realized as she said it that she'd counted on his reliability. Peter spoke comfortably. "I went to find a phone to get somebody over here to watch if Helena takes off. And on my way back I chased those same jerks away from some girl they were hassling."

"Maybe you were just interfering with young love."

"If you'd seen her hunch her shoulders like what they were saying to her was cold rain falling on her, you wouldn't have thought so."

Kelsey felt abashed, and she couldn't allow that for long. The more she drove the steadier she felt, as the Fifth Ward receded in her wake. Once she got to the freeway, the ugly neighborhood would barely exist any more. "Where'd you get this vigilante complex?" she asked idly.

"A vigilante," Peter said professorily, "is a civilian taking the law into his hands. I'm a professional."

"Yeah, but you don't mind putting in unpaid overtime at it. Why are you such a crusader?"

He said stonily, "Maybe because of my best friend being kidnapped and murdered when we were twelve."

"Oh, my God." Kelsey turned toward him, stricken. Peter was staring out the window. "Really?" she asked gently.

After a long pause, he said, "No, not really. But lots of people do have stories like that, and I'd think you'd want to make sure I wasn't one of them before you went smarting off."

"God," Kelsey gasped. The relief she felt was thin, diluted by outrage, annoyance, and uncertainty as to whether he was telling her the truth now. "Sorry," she said sharply. "A sensitive sheriff's deputy is outside my experience, I didn't mean to intrude."

From the corner of her eye she saw him shrug, which she took as his acknowledgment that he'd overreacted. She glided up an entrance ramp onto the freeway, avoided being swerved into by veering cars, managed to edge into the lane she needed, and drove in silence for a couple of miles, until Peter muttered, "Sorry. I'm not usually like this. Well, yeah, I am, pretty much, but not this much. This case ... So what did Helena tell you?"

Kelsey recounted the little she'd learned, then abruptly said, "Before we plunge back into the boonies, how about a real metropolitan lunch?"

She realized what had been most sorely lacking from her life while she'd been exiled in Galilee: Mexican food. She found her way to the Merida restaurant, on Fulton, which she discovered had moved a couple of blocks into a larger, brighter location Kelsey didn't like as much because it didn't have a place in her memory. But the food was the same, traditional Tex-Mex dishes plus what Kelsey had come for, specialties from the Yucatán. Since those were unfamiliar to Peter, she told him to order the special, a sampler of everything, most of them featuring *cochinita pibil*, the savory shredded pork that probably went straight to her arteries, but hey, why else did she jog all the damned time? Peter didn't look like someone who cared much about food, but he dug in appreciatively. Kelsey watched him surreptitiously. When he first tasted something unfamiliar, he looked like a suspicious child, then he smiled slightly and looked remarkably handsome and didn't revert to his habitual sternness. She was catching him at ease for the first time and was about to ruin the experience. She'd had an insight. Peter had muttered about "this case," implying its unusual effect on him. Everyone had been affected by the missing baby, but no one had worked at finding her like Peter Stiller had. He couldn't have cared about Ronald Blystone, but Peter had been almost a contemporary of Lorrie's, they would have grown up together, and as he'd told Kelsey, there are always extra connections among people in a small town.

"You were in love with Lorrie," Kelsey said suddenly.

Peter stopped chewing. He didn't look at Kelsey and it didn't seem he was going to answer until he said with equal abruptness, "No." That obviously wasn't the whole answer, from the pain that crossed his face, but it seemed to be all he was going to say. Then he looked into Kelsey's face, she raised her eyebrows, and Peter said, "But I could have been."

What a strange answer. Kelsey just said, "Oh?" but Peter understood she was asking for more. He chewed and swallowed, drank tea, and continued, eyes glazed as he stared into the past. "I liked her a lot. There was a time when she liked me, too, when we were just kids, really, and thought liking was all there was to it. But then we realized—she wanted out of Galilee, I didn't, I didn't want to look like I was courting her family's money, she wanted to not care what people thought . . ." He shrugged, and his eyes focused on Kelsey again. "But we could have overcome all that. We could be married now, she'd never have met that damned Ronald Blystone, none of this would've happened. We could have been in love."

It was the second time he'd used the expression. "Could have been?"

"Yeah," he said, not understanding her puzzlement.

"What makes you think you 'could have' fallen in love with her? If it didn't happen then, what makes you think—"

"Don't you know that's how love works? You spend time with somebody, you find things you like about them, you let them know things about you, you get closer than either of you is to anybody else, and then . . . What did you think, love is something that sweeps over you the first time you look into some stranger's eyes? That ever happened to you?"

"As a matter of fact it has. Three times."

He looked at her with concern—not for her but concern that he was having lunch with a space alien. "Really?"

"No, not really, but I could be one of those people, and I'd think you'd want to find that out about me before you go smarting off about love."

He laughed. Kelsey maintained her look of mock indignation for two more seconds before joining him. Other diners looked at them and smiled. The waitress brought them more iced tea, smiling.

"Thanks for clearing that up for me," Kelsey confided to Peter. "Now I know what I've been doing wrong. I can stop staring into strangers' eyes and just concentrate on hanging around one guy all the time until we realize how fascinating we are."

"Sure, sure, my method'll work with anybody. Probably during trial you'll be spending so much time with Billy Fletcher, close behind him at the lawyer tables, you know—"

"One late evening I'll look up and say, 'Why, Billy, I'd never noticed before how the light glints off the little hairs growing on your ears, in a strange, lovely . . .'"

Peter was laughing again. "Find someone for me."

"Well, there's Florence at the Bee, I sense a lot of stored-up passion there that a man could—"

"Actually Florence and I dated for years. We used to be engaged."

"Really?" Kelsey said, and the word set them laughing again, as Peter shook his head.

"I don't think Billy . . . ," she began.

"No, not Billy for you, but there's other choices. Clyde Wolverton now, you might try to look beyond the seersucker suits. . . . Or there's Morgan."

Kelsey kept smiling, but neither of them laughed. Peter was looking at her, smiling, too, but his eyes seemed knowing. They let the game die after that.

Back in her car, on the road, there was a comfortable ease between them. "What'll you do now?" Peter asked. They were into the east Texas greenbelt, the highway miles unscrolling before them. Peter was leaning back in his seat, one leg propped up, looking more comfortable as he scanned the pines around them. Houston had been green enough, but now they were plunging back into territory where the air itself seemed verdant. The pines came toward them with a feeling both confining and liberating.

"Get Billy indicted," Kelsey answered, "if anyone in Galilee will give me an indictment. The blood in his car seat puts the case over the top for me."

Peter nodded, but said, "You won't know whose blood it is for a while."

"Right, he just happens to have traces of blood on his front seat. Doesn't everybody?"

"Works for me."

Did the gentleman protest too little? In Peter's daylong company Kelsey had forgotten her initial certainty that he had been assigned to her to keep track of her and to prevent her from making a strong case against Billy Fletcher. Peter had never done anything to justify that suspicion, and she was beginning to take him at face value. What harm could it do to have a little faith in Peter Stiller?

She said musingly, "I still have a little trouble with motive. Murdering a whole family over a job . . ."

"More than a job. I thought you got that by now. You come into Galilee and see everything static, like it's always been the way it is. But you take it back a few years, Billy Fletcher's just a factory worker with a lot of kids to support. Part-time farmer, like nearly everybody around here. Work like slaves." Peter sounded as if he spoke from experience. His voice was soft but vibrant. "Forty hours a week on the line, probably another forty in the field, sitting on a tractor if you're lucky, weeding with a hoe on bad days. And a farm wife's schedule makes that one sound like a holiday in the Bahamas. That was Billy's family, that was his lot in life. If he hadn't had Morgan Fletcher for a brother."

"Everybody says Billy's a good manager."

"He was, he is. But he didn't have the ambition to get the job on his own. If his brother hadn't been married to a Beaumont, Billy never would have gotten a shot at the job. And look at Morgan." Now Peter's voice became tinged with resentment, or was that Kelsey's imagination? "You see him now he looks like an imposing figure. He is. I can't think of anybody better respected in the county. But if he weren't married to the heiress, people would've had no reason to notice him. If Mrs. Beaumont's money hadn't helped get him elected DA the first time—which she did just to have another powerful person in the family, beholden to her; it was just coincidence he turned out to be good at the job.

"And Katherine gets more notice than she would just from being Mrs. Beaumont's daughter because she's also the district attorney's wife. And she doesn't work, but with her share of the income from the factory, they live better than they could on his salary. That car he drives represents a good chunk of Morgan's annual salary. You know what DAs in small counties make. Not enough for Morgan and Katherine to live the way they do."

"Hasn't she ever worked?"

"It would be beneath her. Or beneath her mother's idea of the family. She fills up her time, she does volunteer work, mostly in Houston. You know, literacy, time at a nursing home, a family-planning clinic . . ."

Kelsey remembered with a shock the story she'd heard in the Busy Bee, Janie's narrative of Katherine's forced abortion as a teenager. She imagined Katherine in a clinic, facing girls in a similar situation, maybe talking to parents as she'd never been able to face up to her own.

"About once a year they go to Houston for her to get a plaque from somebody," Peter continued. "Gets Morgan's picture in the paper, too. He's always got to be looking to the next election." He returned to his theme. "If Morgan had gotten divorced, if Billy'd lost his connection to the family . . . That job meant Billy's life. Take it away and he'd be worse off than he'd ever been. Back in the fields, maybe bagging groceries on the side. Poorer and older, and still with kids growing up . . ."

Kelsey realized how real the alternative life Peter was describing was to him; he must know people who lived it. "I don't have to tell you," he concluded. "You've prosecuted people who killed for a lot less."

Kelsey was feeling more confidence in Peter. "Speaking of elections, somebody told me about your political aspirations."

Peter laughed, not happily, more a snort. "Yeah, that was a heady week."

"That's all your campaign lasted?"

"Not much more than. I never— You want to hear this?"

She did. "You couldn't stomach kissing the babies?"

"You know how you get a job you've always wanted, and you feel lucky to have it, and then it's not long before you start looking the boss over and thinking, 'I could do that better than he does'?"

Kelsey nodded. Peter didn't continue his narrative. "Do you?" he asked.

Oh, yes. She remembered very well thinking that if someone handed her the job of district attorney of Harris County, or later on of attorney general of Texas, how well she could perform it, aggressively, boldly, with no consideration for power or politics. She remembered the fantasies; they were with her still. "Oh, yes."

Peter appeared satisfied. He gave her a slight, comradely smile. "Well, I got that bug. So much so I actually started telling people I was going to run for sheriff next election. Without insulting anybody I suggested that it was a new era in law enforcement. And that—well, you know. People took me seriously, I think."

"And what happened?"

"And I got sent out on a domestic-dispute call one night. I knew the house. It was my best friend who opened the door. Known him since we were eight. He said hi and offered me a beer, and I said, hi, Jesse, how's life, what's the trouble, and he said no trouble, everything had settled down, and I said let me see Anne. And she came out of the bedroom and she had a black eye."

Peter winced as if he could still see the bruise; feel it. "What we're supposed to do in those family cases is talk to the people. You know, try to back out gracefully, let the folks take care of the problem themselves, only intervene if the situation looks really dangerous. Sheriff Early even had us all take a counseling course."

"So you . . . ," Kelsey pursued, suspecting the answer.

"So I arrested the son of a bitch. I'm no counselor. But I

know a man who hits a woman's going to do it again, probably worse the next time. I hauled him out of there. Jesse screaming and tugging at my one arm, Anne crying and pulling at the other, begging me not to take him. I didn't make any friends. Even the sheriff let him go again without ever putting him in a cell."

Kelsey sympathized. She remembered this well, taking a more stubborn position than her supervisor would allow. "And the upshot of this story is . . . ?"

"Is that people saw there wasn't much use in being a friend of mine. That's what people expect, you know, you don't vote somebody into office unless you think somewhere down the line he might be inclined to cut you some slack. Not for criminals, of course, but for good, fine upstanding citizens who just have a misunderstanding with the little woman or have a couple of drinks too many some night before they drive home, a man ought to be understanding about things like that. And if you're the kind of tightass who'd put your best friend in jail, when even the high sheriff thinks jail is too extreme, well . . . That's what people decided about me, and what I decided was if they expected me to be anything different, to hell with politics."

Peter was breathing more heavily when he finished. Kelsey's response was automatically cynical. *Good story,* she thought. *But then it is one he told about himself.* But it was Kelsey who'd asked him for the story, having heard a hint of it first from Morgan Fletcher.

Then she wondered if most people would have her reaction to the story. It made Peter Stiller more trustworthy in her eyes, but it had had the opposite effect on many of the voters of Defiance County. It wasn't the first time Kelsey had suspected she might be different from most people. This time the realization had more impact, because she was sitting next to another outcast with a badge. She recognized Peter's passion now, the smoldering subsurface life that kept him so watchful. She recognized it because Kelsey suffered from the same passion, one that had to be kept secret from almost everyone. When she spoke lightly, she was making fun of herself as well as him:

"Just hate to see anybody get away with anything, don't you?"

"With hurting somebody, yeah. If I'd caught him taking a deer out of season, that would have been a tougher call. This was easy."

Peter looked at her directly, a glint in his eye similar to hers. He wasn't fooled by her sarcastic tone. He recognized her, too.

Shrugging acknowledgment, Kelsey nevertheless said her next cynical thought aloud. "So in other words you're telling me Sheriff Early assigned me an investigator nobody likes much."

Peter laughed ruefully. And didn't deny the truth of her observation.

The green miles unwound. Peter became more relaxed. His stare grew longer, his days of too-little sleep began to overtake him. Kelsey stopped talking to him, she just watched him out of the corner of her eye. Finally Peter closed his eyes and didn't open them again. Kelsey could look him over freely, with that common illusion that a sleeping face can't hide its character. Peter retained a certain relentless quality. The bridge of his nose creased suddenly in a frown, even in his sleep. He was having a dream confrontation. Finding the baby's abductor, maybe. Peter seemed the only person in Galilee who wouldn't give up on baby Taylor. But she'd had to drag his concern out of him. She understood that. Why had she turned to criminal law, after all, except that cruelty pained her personally? She'd wanted to make a difference in victims' lives. But you couldn't say that to people.

Peter's face smoothed out; he looked like a baby himself, a big, ungainly baby, taking up more than half the space in the front of the car, one leg bent toward her. His body looked so trusting in her car. His long legs were awkwardly imprisoned in the confines of the front seat. Kelsey wanted to touch him.

A car whooshed by and he stirred but didn't wake. Kelsey reached out as if to comfort him, toward that uncomfortable crease in the bridge of his nose. Her hand lingered over his face, then fell, ever so softly.

"What? Something wrong?"

"I was afraid your leg was about to hit the gearshift."

"Oh. Sorry."

"It's okay."

Peter sat up a little straighter, but still relaxed, still at ease with Kelsey. They let the car stay quiet, their hands close on the seat between them.

* * *

138

It was Thanksgiving week. No prospective jurors had been called, the courthouse was quiet. In Judge Saunders's courtroom a few lawyers halfheartedly argued motions that wouldn't take long to dispose of. When Kelsey's turn came, the court's business was done, at ten forty-five in the morning, but a couple of the lawyers lingered. Kelsey could feel their eyes on her back.

Judge Saunders sat back in her tall chair. The zipper of her black robe was pulled down several inches below her neck, displaying the cream-colored, scalloped collar of her blouse. The judge raised one eyebrow at Kelsey. "Should I have Clyde Wolverton come over for this?"

"It isn't an adversarial proceeding, Your Honor. But I'm ready to make it one. I'd like you to convene the grand jury you told me I could have when I was ready."

In the pause that followed, Judge Saunders seemed to be studying Kelsey rather than what the prosecutor had said. Kelsey watched the judge as well. Linda Saunders and Morgan Fletcher had dated when they were young. That past could cover wide ground: forgotten minor incidents, lifelong lingering love, anything in between. Kelsey had seen that some affection remained between Morgan and the judge.

"Actually there's a grand jury finishing up its term today," Judge Saunders said. "But maybe you'd like to wait to convene a new one, even a special—"

"No, thank you, Your Honor. I wouldn't want to put the court to any special trouble." *Of handpicking a grand jury for me to try to sell on indicting Billy Fletcher.* Better to try her luck with leftovers. As it was, it probably wasn't possible to convene a grand jury in Galilee that wouldn't include friends of Billy's.

"I was going to dismiss them this afternoon. I could give them to you instead. Tomorrow morning."

"I'm ready now, Your Honor." Time was not Kelsey's friend. She knew in a matter of moments word of what she was about to do would start spreading, and the grand jurors would start getting phone calls.

"After lunch, then. Two o'clock. Does anyone else have business with the court? . . . We're adjourned, then."

When Kelsey returned from a solitary, distracted lunch, the story had quickly spread. A glaring Clyde Wolverton, accompanied by his client, met her on the first floor of the courthouse. "I understand you think you have something worth taking to a grand jury." He sounded restrained, but his face was red.

"Yes," Kelsey said shortly, and started past him, but Wolverton grabbed the prosecutor's arm to stop her. "Doesn't it offend you to prostitute yourself like this? Everybody in Galilee knows who is behind the prosecution! Before I'm done, everyone in the state will know you are just the puppet of a vindictive woman. The attorney general will have no choice but to fire you in disgrace. Such blatant disregard for truth—"

Kelsey had resolved to let him talk himself out, but as he did, she got mad, until she leaned forward and blasted him back. "If she's vindictive, it's because Billy Fletcher murdered her child! I don't have any personal stake in this case. The truth is all I care about. Personal motives don't matter as long as I have the evidence. And I do, Mr. Wolverton. You ask your client whose blood is in his car!"

Billy started to shout something, but his attorney, finally controlled, put a hand on Billy's chest and quieted him. Wolverton looked stonily at Kelsey. "I hope some other profession interests you, Ms. Thatch. After this proceeding you will be such damaged goods that no one will hire you to practice law anywhere in this state."

Well pleased with this exit line, the defense lawyer turned smartly and took his client in tow. Billy Fletcher was furious, but expostulations so crowded his throat he couldn't say anything until he was almost out of sight down the corridor, when he screamed, "Don't you have a conscience?"

Kelsey didn't reply. As she stood watching Billy and his lawyer disappear out the doors of the courthouse, she realized someone was standing just behind her. She felt his presence as a blocky warmth and knew who it was even before Morgan Fletcher put his hands on her shoulders. "Of course you do," he said of Kelsey's conscience. "Don't mind—"

"I don't." There was something frighteningly alluring about Morgan standing close behind her, so that she was immobilized. She knew she should step away from him, but she wanted more to put her hand over his. Obviously sensing her feeling, Morgan kept his hands on her shoulders, holding her for a long minute in the empty hallway.

There was another surprise visitor to the courthouse, sitting on a hard bench outside the grand jury room.

"Mrs. Beaumont," Kelsey said. "Can I help you?"

"No, thank you. Move aside, please, dear."

Kelsey did so, puzzled, and saw that Mrs. Beaumont was craning her neck to watch the grand jurors approach. They did so in straggling order, in no hurry, men in suits, women in dresses nice enough for church. Some of them were chatting as they came down the courthouse hallway. Each stopped or glanced nervously upon sight of Alice Beaumont.

"Ed." "Gordon." "Hello, Mrs. Davies." Mrs. Beaumont spoke to some of the grand jurors. Each she fixed with a steely eye. The reason for her presence was clear. She was watching them: they had better do what was expected of them.

But Kelsey walked away a few steps and saw what Alice Beaumont couldn't see. As they saw her, each man or woman on the grand jury acknowledged the matriarch. But as they passed out of her sight, their faces changed. It was those faces they presented to Kelsey when she followed them into the narrow grand jury room and shut the door behind her: skeptical faces. A few, particularly among the seven men, actively frowned at her. Mrs Beaumont had had the opposite effect from what she'd wanted. She had stiffened the grand jurors' resolve not to be sheep. Not to do as they were implicitly ordered by the woman who controlled the fate of their town.

These were Billy Fletcher's people. Not Alice Beaumont's, and certainly not Kelsey's.

"You are the grand jury. I'm coming in late, I didn't hear your instructions. Did they tell you about how historically you're the body of citizens who stand between someone accused of a crime and the power of the State?"

One woman nodded. The grand jurors were casually arrayed around the room, only about half of them sitting at the long conference table. Two of the women and one of the men looked familiar to Kelsey; she hadn't met them but she had seen them, in the town or during her evening at the country club. Solid citizens, they all looked like. The average age was about fifty, and she couldn't tell from their hands or their faces which worked in offices and which had spent years in the farm fields. They all looked like hard workers. They looked like Billy Fletcher's peers.

"Well, I'm the power of the State." Kelsey hoped to draw a chuckle, at least a few wry smiles. Make the grand jurors acknowledge that in this case the array of power was behind the suspect, not the prosecutor.

But no one acknowledged her little joke. They stared at her grimly. The best she got was a look of quiet neutrality, from a lady wearing a cotton print dress and a small hat. Her green sweater was draped over her shoulders, as if she were cold or as if she didn't expect Kelsey's presentation to detain her long.

"My job as the prosecutor is to present to you the evidence I've been given in this case, to convince you that enough evidence exists to put my suspect to trial. *Not* to convince you of his guilt. Guilt isn't an issue here. Your job is only to say whether I have probable cause—just enough evidence that you think I should have to go to trial and let a jury decide whether the defendant is guilty or not guilty. You're not calling him a criminal just by issuing the indictment. You're just saying the case should go to trial."

Kelsey spoke firmly and professionally. She wasn't going to rely on emotion.

"The cases I'm presenting to you are the murders of Ronald Blystone and Lorrie Blystone, and the kidnapping of their daughter, Taylor. I'm going to ask you to indict Billy Fletcher for those crimes."

There was only a gentle stir. They all knew why they were there. Kelsey outlined the facts of the cases, facts with which the grand jurors must be as familiar as she was. Kelsey passed around pictures of the crime scene, of the bodies, the pool of blood. Some grand jurors studied the pictures briefly, others only glanced at them, wincing. The lady in the green sweater didn't do that much, just took each photo in turn and passed it on, without looking at any.

"Shortly before the murders, Andrew Sims witnessed a very angry argument between Billy Fletcher and Ronald Blystone,"

Kelsey continued, but was interrupted by a standing man who spoke to the room at large, not bothering to whisper.

"Not safe to have an argument with anybody any more. You'd better not say what you think in this town. Next thing you know somebody'll be dead and you'll be blamed for it."

"Would you rather I not tell you the evidence I have?" Kelsey asked, walking around the table toward the man, who stiffened and glared at her.

"Hush, Norman," one of the women at the table said softly. "Let her talk."

The admonition did not reassure Kelsey. It sounded to her as if the woman meant they should let the special prosecutor finish as quickly as possible so they could all do what they'd come to do.

Kelsey told them about Billy Fletcher's fingerprint on the murder weapon. In a grand jury proceeding she didn't have to present live witnesses, she could simply describe the evidence she had. Kelsey was the only witness the grand jury would hear. She tried to keep her voice level and detached, as if she had already made the judgment for them. But some of the things she chose to tell them were brutal.

"The baby crawled in her mother's blood. Then someone put the baby back in her crib. We know that from the bloodstains on the baby's sheets. Then someone took the baby. I expect her little hands and gown were still bloody."

The room was dead still. The air was very close. The heat was on that morning in the courthouse, and in the little grand jury room the heat breathed in through the vent and had nowhere to escape.

Some of the grand jurors frowned down at the table. A few frowned at Kelsey. She knew they didn't like to hear about the baby. Hadn't someone warned her that the kidnapping of the baby actually weakened her case against Billy Fletcher? Because while people might be convinced that he had killed Ronald and even Lorrie Blystone in the heat of passion, taking the baby was the act of a madman, and no one in Galilee could believe good old bluff Billy Fletcher capable of such an act. Kelsey might have been well advised to lay off the baby. But today that was her trump card.

"Yesterday morning I seized Billy Fletcher's car and had it searched. An assistant medical examiner in Houston examined the car and confirmed that what she found in the front passenger seat was traces of dried blood."

Now she did get gasps. Some of them looked shocked. All stared at Kelsey.

"The baby's blood?" one woman asked quietly.

Kelsey shook her head. "I assume it's Lorrie Blystone's blood that the baby had on her hands and clothes." A couple of people nodded, having followed her reasoning. "I don't know yet, it will take a while for tests to determine whose blood it is. What I'm telling you this morning is that the man who argued with Ronald Blystone, whose job was threatened by Ronald and his wife, whose fingerprint is on the gun that killed both of them, who was the only one we know of in a position to take the baby—that that man has traces of blood in his car. Traces such as the baby would have left when he took her with him when he drove away."

Kelsey saw her words take effect. The man who had interrupted her looked down at the table, lips moving as he mumbled something inaudible. He had the look of a man trying to explain a puzzle. Others wore the same expression. A few simply looked horrified. "That's my evidence." Kelsey closed her file and picked it up, ready to walk out. The law required her to leave while the grand jury voted. They could do what they wanted behind her back.

Kelsey was proud of herself for the professional way she'd presented the case. She hadn't raised her voice and she hadn't argued. She hoped her quiet authority had convinced them.

But she didn't think so.

It was a relief, though, to be finished. As she turned to go, Kelsey had the ugly thought that it would be okay if it did end here, if the grand jury did refuse to indict and she could go home, to tell people it had just been too tough a case, too much of a hometown boy for a suspect.

Then she turned back to the grand jurors.

"You may think you'll be doing Billy Fletcher a favor if you refuse to indict him," she said harshly. "But you took an oath not to do any favors for anybody. And I'm not sure you'd be doing Mr. Fletcher any good by not indicting him. Everyone's going to know what I've discovered. And even if you no-bill Billy Fletcher, after his friends congratulate him and he goes back about his normal business, everyone will remember for the rest of his life. Everyone will wonder. Won't they? Imagine him in church someday ten years from now, passing around the collection plate, and someone nudges a new member and whispers. Someday somebody will even say it to his face: murderer. And the only thing Billy will be able to say in return is, I never got indicted. But everybody will know that had nothing to do with whether he did it or not."

"You'd better watch your—," the gruff standing man began, but Kelsey looked at him and he subsided. She swept her gaze around the table. Anybody else?

"If you want to give Billy Fletcher his only chance to clear his name, if you want this thing thoroughly thrashed out to a conclusion that will satisfy everyone, issue the indictment."

Only a couple of them looked as if they found that convincing. Kelsey said the last thing she had to say.

"If you give a damn about the truth, if you want to know about that blood, if you want to know where the baby is, issue the indictment."

She stood and looked at them all, but no more than five or six of the grand jurors met her eyes.

Alice Beaumont was waiting for her when Kelsey came out of the grand jury room. "What did they decide?" she asked quickly.

"They're deciding now." Kelsey felt tired. She needed to run again.

"They'd better do the right thing."

Mrs. Beaumont was wearing a green dress, dark but with white highlights at the collar and wrists that saved the dress, and her, from drabness. She carried a black shawl, a mourning cloak she could put on or off. Mrs. Beaumont stood so erect that in her heels she was taller than Kelsey.

Kelsey had the drained feeling that her time in Galilee was over. But there was still much she wanted to do here, and even more she wanted to understand, starting with Alice Beaumont. She was a woman who insisted on being in charge. Her life had

been devoted to gaining dominance over her whole world. If
people got hurt along the way, if bystanders like Kelsey had their
lives changed, that hadn't mattered to Alice Beaumont. Why?
What had she been after?

Kelsey felt free enough, almost on the highway out of town,
to ask her. "Mrs. Beaumont, did you ever have a plan?"

The old lady looked at her, startled.

"Everybody says what a great thing you did for the town,
getting your husband to build the Smoothskins factory. And the
way you've used the factory ever since to keep everybody in
line—what did you want from it all? Was there some goal, or
was it just beating down resistance just for exercise? What did
you want?"

Alice Beaumont peered at her as if trying to discern what
Kelsey was asking. The woman's eyes didn't look as piercing as
Kelsey remembered: they were the faded shade of bluebonnets
in May, but Mrs. Beaumont squinted them as if trying to make
her eyes see as sharply as ever. Then her voice came out angrily.

"I wanted what anybody wants. Everybody. I just worked
harder for it than most people are willing to. I wanted my children around me. I wanted family, babies crawling under the
table. Playing in the yard, not having to worry. I wanted to sit
on my porch and watch them . . ."

Her voice softened and her lower lip began to tremble. "One
baby, that's all I had," she sobbed. "One baby to watch grow
up. To remember me. And he—"

Kelsey put her arms out and Mrs. Beaumont lowered her head
to Kelsey's shoulder, but as soon as they touched, the older
woman stiffened again. She drew back and her eyes went fierce.
"What do I want?" She clenched her fist. "I want the respect I've
earned. But they wouldn't let me have any of that." She glared
at Kelsey. "Now I want what the law owes me: revenge. Or I'll
kill this town."

It was a death threat cold with sincerity and stony with the
power to carry out the threat. If Alice Beaumont's target had been
a person instead of an entire town, she could have been arrested.

Kelsey stared at her, somehow looking for a resemblance to
herself. In a way Mrs. Beaumont was an admirable woman, a
role model. Young during an age when a woman could never

seize her full potential, Alice Beaumont had learned through romance and ingenuity and finally brute force to control her life and every life around her. But in the end her power hadn't even protected her family. And she was counting on Kelsey to right that wrong.

They heard the sound of rising voices from the grand jury room, but not what they were saying. The vote on Billy Fletcher's indictment was not going smoothly. "At least I got to some of them," Kelsey said.

"I did," Alice Beaumont corrected her.

But Kelsey knew she herself had won over some of the grand jurors. She'd seen it in the anguish in their faces during her final short speech about the baby. She wanted to burst back into the room and say more.

There was silence. It went on, the silence of justice fled. Kelsey was suddenly angry. She was walking toward the grand jury room door when it opened. The woman in the green sweater said, "Ms. Thatch, we're ready for you."

And Kelsey was ready for them. *You've disgraced this town,* she was going to say. She wasn't going to let any of them off. She had changed her mind. She wouldn't let it die here. She would ask for another grand jury. She would find more evidence. She—

"There," said the tall man she'd clashed with before. He threw her papers down on the table, scowling. "There's your damned indictment," he said angrily.

"All right," Kelsey snapped. "If you won't do your job—" But then she looked at the document before her and saw that it was signed. She also saw that the angry man throwing down the indictment was the foreman of the grand jury. He was the one who had signed the indictment: Norman Gray.

"Thank you, Mr. Gray," she said levelly. She looked around at all the faces. None of them looked happy. The lady in the green sweater, though, who had taken her seat at the table, had a certain look of satisfaction, and she gave Kelsey a nod of approval.

"I'd like one more thing. I'd like you all to sign. Everyone who voted to issue this indictment. I'd like you all to put your names to it."

They didn't like that suggestion, but none of them balked. It turned out to have been unanimous. Maybe some of them had voted out of fear of Alice Beaumont, rather than Kelsey's persuasiveness, but it didn't matter. She had her indictment. Billy Fletcher was going to trial.

Coming out of the courthouse, Kelsey turned in a slow half-circle. It was a habit she'd developed in Defiance County, perhaps the habit of a woman who had no one to watch her back. Today, though, she felt a proprietary interest in the town she saw arrayed before her. She was going to be here a while longer.

She lifted her eyes to the horizon, the pine trees as always drawing her gaze. She hadn't thought she was looking for anything in particular, until she saw it:

Smoke rising.

It had been days since she'd seen one of the thin columns of smoke. This one was just starting: a crinkle in the sky, a shimmering of the air, then the smoke. Thicker this time than she'd seen it before.

Kelsey ran toward her car.

9

The smoke had paled to invisibility by the time Kelsey reached the woods, but she thought she could still find its source. She left her car on the side of the road and plunged into the trees on foot. Almost immediately, she was lost. These woods were so thick, the pine trees so tall, that even in broad daylight sunlight only pierced the shadows in streaks, in sudden rays that would blind Kelsey as she stepped into one, then disappear when she took another step. Gloom rose like mist. She tried to hurry, looking for a clearing where she could get her bearings. Pine needles were a skidding carpet underfoot. There were fallen branches, too, that threatened to trip her.

She stopped suddenly. The forest did not fall instantly silent. Twittering of birds continued, distant enough that the sound was eerily hard to identify. But what Kelsey listened for, and thought she heard, was a thud on the forest floor, like the amplified echo of her own step. She didn't hear the sound repeated. But she began moving more quietly.

Kelsey couldn't see a trace of smoke any more. But her nose told her she was close. The general smell of the forest was ancient, the smell of decay and undisturbed must, faintly tinged by the clean smell of new growth. But a more acrid odor cut through the general smell. Kelsey walked softly from tree to tree, wondering not just who but what kind of person would be setting fires in the woods. Arson indicated deep anger, she remembered that. Kelsey realized she'd have trouble finding her way back to her car. She tried to become invisible, drawing herself up behind a tree trunk, peering around it, before moving on.

But she heard nothing else and the smell of smoke grew stronger. Ahead she saw light. The woods were aflame. Through the trees thirty yards in front of her, she saw a wall of light, and flinched from it.

But what she saw was sunlight. Ahead, sunshine poured down so strongly compared to the surrounding dimness that the clearing there looked like a lighted stage.

Kelsey stopped behind a last tree and looked. No other human was in sight. She stepped out. After a quick glance around—the woods looked even more impenetrable from the vantage of this cleared space—she concentrated on the fire. It had been built like a large campfire, rocks creating a circle three feet in diameter. The fire was still fighting to breathe, smothered by the bulk of cloth that had been dumped atop it. Kelsey went closer. No one was tending it now, but the fire had been built by someone who knew how, with twigs and old dead branches underneath, larger pieces of wood on top. It would have been a good fire that could have burned all night if fed gradually, but it wasn't strong enough to consume the clothes, the purpose for which the fire had apparently been built. The clothes were singed and had smoldered to a black silhouette in places, but were still identifiable.

Kelsey turned away from the fire, looking for a long stick with which to rescue the evidence. Away from the soft crackle of the fire, she heard the sound of someone coming through the woods. She jumped, but the sound was too close, she could never reach the shelter of the trees in time. She whirled toward the sound of the footsteps and saw Peter Stiller emerge from the woods.

"What are you doing here?"

"Following the smoke." Peter walked quickly toward the campfire. "What is it?"

He squatted to look closer, while Kelsey found a stick and poked something out of the fire. Peter patted it lightly with a flat rock to put out the last of the fire. He and Kelsey stared. Kelsey said it aloud. "Baby clothes."

The burned outfit was a one-piece pink coverall. Whatever ornamentation of bows or ribbons it had had were burned away.

The surviving patch of unsinged fabric looked soft, like velour. "What size is it?" Kelsey whispered.

With a twig Peter fished out the size tag, which was darkened. He leaned close to read it. "Twelve months, I think it says."

"Too big."

"You have to buy baby clothes bigger than the baby's age," Peter said with quiet authority. He took off the leather jacket he was wearing and laid it atop the fire. A few seconds later, before the jacket could burn, he lifted it away. There were no more visible flames. Peter took the stick from Kelsey and lifted out another garment, laying it carefully on the needle-strewn dirt. He covered the fire again, laying his jacket on it as gently as covering a sleeping child with a blanket. This time he left the jacket in place for a full minute.

Kelsey looked at the newly saved outfit. It was a little dress, about the right size for a five-month-old baby. The skirt had been made of some frilly material that had burned away quickly, leaving only traces, but the top remained. It had been a cherry-colored dress with long sleeves and white trim. Kelsey unconsciously reached to smooth it out. Peter's hand grabbed her wrist. He shook his head. Kelsey nodded.

When Peter lifted his jacket off the makeshift campfire, a ball of black smoke rose. Beneath it, the fire was out completely. They saved everything they could, spreading out the clothes in the sunlight, creating a scene like a weird laundry. Primitive peoples might have laid their clothes out like this to dry. They were all baby girl's clothes, four outfits in all. There was no doubt whose clothes they were.

"I remember this one," Peter said, kneeling over a tiny green sweater dress. "Taylor was wearing this one in one of the pictures we used for identification, to show people."

"Why?" Kelsey asked quietly, and Peter knew what she was asking. He stood beside her, surveying the clothes. "Maybe Billy grabbed up a bunch of her clothes when he took the baby, and now he's getting rid of the evidence?"

Kelsey had already considered that. "But he—," she began, then screamed.

"What? What?" Peter shouted, trying to shield her, but Kelsey pushed him back, still screaming, "Owwwwwww!" She was jumping in place, slapping at her legs. Peter looked down, suddenly said, "Oh, hell," and picked her up and carried her several feet away.

"Ant bed," he said, but Kelsey was still saying ouch, ouch, ouch. Peter looked more concerned. "Fire ants?"

Kelsey was in no condition to answer. She was clawing at her jeans-clad legs. The fiery pains climbed higher. Kelsey unsnapped and unzipped her pants. Peter started untying her tennis shoes. Kelsey struggled awkwardly with her pants. Peter suddenly sat down, sat her in his lap, and pulled off her shoes and socks and jeans. Kelsey rubbed her legs feverishly. Peter helped her slap off the last few red, stinging ants. But that didn't stop the pain.

"Come on," Peter said. Abruptly he picked her up and carried her. Kelsey put her hands around his neck. The bouncing as Peter half-ran through the woods intensified the pain in her legs for a moment. He almost ran them into a few trees, but managed to dodge through them. Luckily, Peter had known better than Kelsey how to come through the woods. He'd parked on a side road, barely a dirt track, that had left him only a short plunge through the woods to the campfire. In only a couple of minutes he came out of the woods and set Kelsey down beside his squad car. "You have first aid?" Kelsey asked, still feeling such pain from her bites that she wasn't yet noticing the strangeness of the situation.

"Better than that." Peter stuck his head into the car and quickly emerged holding a pump-spray tube with a green cap. "Bactine."

Almost as soon as he began spraying her legs, the relief was wonderful. Peter stopped to rub in the medicine, his hands soothing her calves, his fingers almost liquid around her ankles. "Better?"

"Oh, yes."

As the pain ebbed, Kelsey came to her senses enough to realize where she was, standing in her Smoothskins panties beside a country lane, with a man kneeling at her feet spraying her legs and then rubbing in the comfort. Peter apparently came to a realization of the moment at about the same time, as his hands rubbed and soothed her left leg, rising above her knee. He looked up at Kelsey, his hands stopped, and after a moment he handed her the spray. "Maybe you'd better take it from here."

Kelsey looked down at him and quite deliberately said, "No, you go ahead." Slowly, he continued, spraying her thighs and circling them with his hands, smoothing and massaging. He was looking into Kelsey's face as he soothed her legs. She gave him a little smile and saw it reflected in Peter's expression.

He stood up. "God," Kelsey breathed, meaning to say how much better she felt, how grateful she was, something like that. Peter nodded, and Kelsey put one hand on the back of his neck and pulled him down. As they kissed, Kelsey put her arms around his neck. Peter put his hands on her hips, then brought them around her back, slowly, stopping to feel her skin. She felt her muscles relax where he touched.

When they broke apart for breath, Peter said, "Let's get you out of here."

He opened the front passenger door of the squad car and Kelsey got in, sitting demurely with her legs together. Peter leaned in to kiss her again, then abruptly pulled away and ran back into the woods. Kelsey sat there feeling like an arrested suspect, wondering what she was doing, but she knew she had already decided that, days ago. Peter returned quickly carrying her jeans and shoes. He dropped them into the floorboard in front of her and kissed her again.

When he slid in beside her and started the car, Kelsey said, "I don't want to go to the motel."

"Okay," Peter said shortly as he pulled out onto the little country road.

"And don't run the siren."

Peter grinned, then stepped on the brake in order to pull her close and kiss her again.

Kelsey began to feel embarrassed as he drove. She knew how awkward pulling her pants on would be in the confines of the car, but she was about to try it anyway when Peter said, "They might still have ants in them."

"Oh, sure. You just want me—" She couldn't bring herself to finish the sentence.

"Yes, I do."

Peter never got back on the main road. No one saw them. In only a few minutes he turned onto what Kelsey at first took for another narrow country lane, but then realized was a driveway.

She got a quick look at a small rock house with an attractive front porch, then Peter followed the gravel drive around and behind the house, another hundred yards into the woods. He parked in front of what was little more than a log cabin; but a pretty log cabin, with a stone chimney and clean windows. "What is this?"

"My house." He pulled open her car door and offered his hand. Kelsey stepped out daintily, barefoot on the pine needles, which were oddly soft and comforting underfoot. She followed Peter onto the narrow front porch. Before accepting his gestured invitation to enter, Kelsey stopped in front of Peter and asked, "Are you on duty right now?"

He smiled. "No, ma'am."

"All right then." She began unbuttoning his shirt.

Later—it seemed both a short, feverish time and a long, lingering idyll—Kelsey stuck her right leg straight up into the air, her pointed toes reaching toward the ceiling of the only bedroom in Peter's little cabin. Lying on her back in Peter's bed, she examined her leg in the soft light that filtered in through the trees and the windows. She could see half a dozen little welts, white bumps surrounded by small red mounds that looked painful, but she couldn't feel them any more. Kelsey started laughing.

Peter's arm was across her chest. He turned his face toward her, his hair falling down his forehead. "I hope it wasn't something I said," he said huskily. "Or did."

"God, I wish I could tell someone about this," Kelsey said, still laughing. "This must be a first. Seduced by Bactine."

"Kind of a dirty trick. I hate to use it, but I will when I have to."

It wasn't long after that that his arms tightened around her and he kissed her again, almost with the urgency of that first passion. Kelsey felt a flinch of alarm because she knew the kiss for good-bye.

"I got to run," he said, confirming her fear.

Kelsey leaned up on her elbow. "Why?"

"Because we've got evidence laying out in the woods waiting to get stolen or rained on."

"Oh, hell." Kelsey jumped out of bed and was dressed before he was. They jostled each other in the doorway of the cabin like the Three Stooges, but more enjoyably. Kelsey oddly enough had little trouble changing gears, maybe because the sexual interlude hadn't taken her completely by surprise. But things were unquestionably changed. Peter held her hand as he drove, and once he lifted her fingertips to his lips. Kelsey leaned against him. She drew back and they looked at each other questioningly, surprised to find they looked more or less the same as they had two hours earlier. But they didn't talk about themselves. When Kelsey spoke, when they were almost back to the part of the woods where they'd left the baby clothes, what she said was, "How are we going to account for the missing time?"

"What missing time?"

"Gee, thanks. It was memorable for me, too."

Peter still didn't get her. "Who the hell do we have to tell?"

"Well, the cops. The evidence technicians, when we call them in to collect this stuff."

Peter pulled the squad car to a stop, about where he'd been parked before. He got out of the car and opened the trunk. Lifting out a case the size of an overnight bag, he said, "I'm the evidence tech."

He took a big roll of butcher paper out of the trunk as well, and they went back into the woods, conscious of disturbing the trail. Birdsong had returned to the pine forest. The serenity of the woods felt old again. Kelsey's shoulder bumped against Peter's arm. For the first time in a long while Kelsey felt as if she had a partner.

As they neared the clearing, she had a sudden premonition that when they stepped into it everything would be gone—the clothes, the fire—not as if the scene had been covered up, but as if it had never been. Then would she report the finding of the burned baby clothes to someone anyway? Someone who would ask, "Why did you leave the scene?"

But the clothes were still there. A breeze stirred the pine needles and pulled Kelsey's hair across her cheek, but the clothes lay inert. The way they were scattered and singed made the scene look like the aftermath of a plane crash. A tear stung Kelsey's eye.

Peter put out a hand and stopped her, then he went ahead, bending to peer at the ground. A few feet in front of the campfire he squatted in front of a patch of bare ground and studied an impression.

"Find something?" Kelsey called softly.

"Yeah. It looks like I'm getting a hole in the sole of my boot." Peter looked at what she assumed was another footprint, then looked back at Kelsey, at her tennis shoes. He walked on.

They didn't find any usable prints or tire tracks. The fire builder could have entered the woods from any of dozens of points. The ground was hard and the pine needles made a natural carpet so that shoes didn't touch the bare ground. After a while Peter carefully stacked up the four baby garments, separating them with sheets of the butcher paper. "I'll send them to Houston," Kelsey said.

Peter didn't object. "Send the rocks, too, though I doubt they've got usable fingerprints."

The next morning Kelsey was sitting at her desk, staring at the chart on her wall. The chart was filling up with names and places from the time of the murders—Aunt Goldie on the highway to Houston, Helena Parker at the grocery store—but it wasn't divulging a pattern. The little office felt strange to Kelsey. Her skin seemed to sense people moving in the courthouse around and below her. By now the whole town knew about the indictment she'd obtained.

She was waiting. When Peter Stiller appeared in her doorway, she knew that's what she had been waiting for. He was crisp in uniform this morning. He was just the same as the first time she'd seen him—tall, watchful, slow to speak—but now Kelsey looked for and found landmarks on his face: the creases beside his eyes, the few pale freckles that appeared only across his nose. And she saw what might have been there all along, the way his mouth was ready to ease into a smile. In fact, he was smiling, most of the time, but only in his eyes, so she might have been the first person who'd ever noticed his capacity for joy.

"Who was burning those baby clothes?" Kelsey asked him. "I've sent them off to Houston, but they're not going to tell us anything. The baby's gone, the clothes aren't evidence of anything."

That wasn't what she'd planned to say when she'd first seen him in the doorway, when her heart had lightened and she'd felt for the first time that morning like smiling. Paradoxically, for the last hour she hadn't been able to think about the case for thinking about Peter, but as soon as he appeared, when she had him there close, her thoughts could return to what had brought her to Defiance County.

Peter came and sat on the edge of the desk close beside her. He took her hand and drew her up. He put one hand on her cheek and one on her hip but didn't pull her any closer, just stared into her face. He touched a spot near her temple, stroked the line of her chin with his finger. Kelsey watched his gray eyes as they shifted around her face. She had thought his face rather stony, but now knew that wasn't true. There were subtle shifts to his expressions. His eyes didn't just stare, they questioned, responded, longed.

She leaned forward, or he did, and they kissed for a long moment, balanced lightly, bodies barely touching. When they broke apart, Peter touched her cheek again, then stood and went back around the desk.

"I can't think of any reason." He was talking about the burned clothes.

"Let me tell you a rule of investigation," he went on. "When you can't answer a question, ask one you can answer. Who's burning the clothes? Who has access to them?"

"If the kidnapper took a bunch of clothes when he took the baby, I guess he'd still have them and want to get rid of them," Kelsey said slowly.

"Not like this." Peter said aloud what she'd already thought. "He would have dumped them all long ago."

"You probably would have gotten a report about the missing clothes, too, if it had happened when the baby was taken."

Peter shrugged. "We scattered right away, looking for Taylor. People didn't spend much time searching the house. And her parents were dead, they couldn't tell us anything was missing. Just the baby. Everything took second place to her."

Kelsey saw him go into a reverie and knew Peter was wondering what he could have done differently, better, in those first frantic minutes so that the search would have ended with his reaching out and taking the missing baby into his arms. She had talked to people who'd joined in those searches. They had been uncoordinated at first, people running off in all directions. The searchers remembered now where they had looked, they remembered the relief and the disappointment of pushing aside bushes and finding nothing, but in most cases they didn't remember who had been with them. Sometimes people had started off together but then separated. It was impossible now to reconstruct who had had an alibi and who had been alone long enough to hide Taylor.

And Billy Fletcher had had a long head start on all the searchers.

"If someone still has her—," Kelsey began, then her brief hope died. "But getting rid of her clothes wouldn't help. The baby herself is what's most identifiable. Why keep . . . ?"

"They change so fast at that age," Peter said, echoing what Kelsey had heard all her friends who had children say. "In another few months she won't even look the same; her grandmother could glance at her and never even think it was Taylor."

On the other hand, Mrs. Beaumont might think that every baby she saw for the rest of her life was her missing granddaughter. Kelsey shook her head. "Wasn't your question who? Who's burning the clothes? It wasn't Mrs. Beaumont, I can tell you that. I had just left her in the courthouse when I saw the smoke and raced out to the woods."

"Unless she ordered someone to do it."

"Who could—" Kelsey stopped, realizing Mrs. Beaumont could order damned near anyone in Galilee to do anything and expect to be obeyed.

"I assume the baby clothes they brought for the trip are still in the house," Kelsey said. "Aunt Goldie's there all the time, I guess Katherine can come and go there whenever she likes . . ."

"Morgan."

"Destroying potential evidence against his brother? But that brings us back to the question you told me to stop asking. What are the clothes evidence of?"

*　　*　　*

Whatever it was, the lab in Houston couldn't tell her. They were baby clothes, burned. No traces of blood or other unusual stains. And as Peter predicted, the rocks around the fire hadn't retained any fingerprints.

Thanksgiving came, making occasion for a sweet farewell to Peter, dinner in his cabin, a long quiet evening in front of the fire, talking softly about their lives, gradually falling against each other. Kelsey was sorry to leave him, but not as sorry as she'd expected. She liked getting away to think about this new development, but found on the long drive to Waco that thoughts didn't form, only memories. She remembered Peter as if he'd been at places where she had never seen him, waiting in the background of her life for Kelsey to notice him.

In Waco, the holiday seemed odd. Perhaps it always had been, the longest holiday weekend of the year, long enough that people weren't just counting the hours until it was time to go back to work again, when Kelsey could let the fantasy overtake her that she still lived in her parents' house where she had grown up, with a life of such stupefying leisure that she could sit for hours on a couch drinking coffee and letting parades and football games flow over her.

She could leave any time, make the short drive down the highway to her apartment in Austin, but why? One of these days she would see her boss the attorney general again, and though he hadn't done anything wrong in sending Kelsey to Defiance County, his motive hadn't been admirable, either.

But who said you had to admire your boss?

"Your Honor, this is outrageous!"

"Counsel?" Judge Saunders said to Kelsey, in the bored tone with which a judge conveys that she is totally disinterested, don't bother wasting a passionate plea on her. Save it for the jury, as lawyers say. But Judge Saunders was looking at Kelsey keenly from beneath her slowly blinking eyelids—almost with amusement, as if Kelsey were committing some fundamental blunder unknown outside the Defiance County Courthouse. "You have some rationale for this request?"

It was the following week; they were arraigning Billy Fletcher on the indictment, to which he had entered a plea of not guilty.

Billy sat glowering and sweltering in spite of the cool air, looking like a laborer who rarely has to cram himself into a suit. His lawyer, Clyde Wolverton, was displaying the first fire Kelsey had seen in him, standing so tall he looked stretched, his mouth staying open in outrage even while his opponent spoke.

"I think it's obvious, Your Honor," Kelsey said calmly. She held up the indictment, with its long three paragraphs, for emphasis. "Twelve grand jurors, Mr. Fletcher's peers, have found there is probable cause to believe that the defendant murdered two people and kidnapped a totally innocent baby. To insure the safety of the surviving citizens of Defiance County, I think a bail of five hundred thousand dollars is not excessive."

"It's ridiculous!" burst in Clyde Wolverton, with the moral fervor of a man whose client is about to be forced to pay out thousands of dollars that could much more satisfactorily be spent on attorney's fees. "There is still a presumption of innocence at work here, in spite of this indictment."

With Clyde Wolverton's red face turned toward her, Kelsey felt a great calm settling on her, because her opposing counsel looked like a man who knows he must lose unless he wrings everything he can out of the only weapon on his side: bluster.

Clyde Wolverton turned to the judge. Tightly he said, "As Your Honor well knows, Mr. Fletcher is a very responsible citizen of this county. He has a family of a wife and four children to support. He has many, many more people than that dependent on his managerial skills to guide and shepherd a business enterprise that—"

"From which he's been suspended and ordered to stay off the premises," Kelsey interjected.

Wolverton whirled on her. "Is that in evidence?" he shouted.

"Is anything you've said?"

"Address your arguments to the bench," the judge said, and what both lawyers heard her actually say was, *Children, children.* "Ms. Thatch, correct me if I'm wrong, but isn't your theory of the case that this defendant wiped out everyone who represented a threat to him? That being so, where is the continuing danger to the community if he remains free on bond?"

Kelsey's mind raced while her mouth moved silently. Judge Linda Saunders was a much more formidable arguer than Clyde

Wolverton was, and Kelsey saw against whom the judge's arguments would be directed.

"Your Honor, that argument leads to a rationalization that if a man commits a crime monstrous enough, he should walk free, because he's already completed all the evil he ever contemplated, so that—"

"Of course not," Judge Saunders said. "He should be punished, as this defendant should be if he's found guilty. But as our constitution says and our Court of Criminal Appeals has often reminded trial judges, a bail bond isn't punishment, because this man hasn't been convicted of anything. The bail bond is just to insure his appearance for trial. Do you have some evidence that makes flight a likely possibility?"

"He'll be here," Clyde Wolverton snorted, "because when that trial is over, Billy Fletcher's going to be the first person walking out those courtroom doors."

The judge ignored him, watching Kelsey with a politely waiting expression. The longer her wait, the more apparent it was that Kelsey had no answer. "I'll continue the fifty-thousand-dollar bond Mr. Fletcher has already made," Judge Saunders finally said.

"I'm thinking about going for a football theme in jury selection," Kelsey said. "Ask people if they're Oiler fans or Cowboy fans. If they like the Cowboys, that means they go for a winner. There has to be something bigger-hearted about somebody who roots for the Oilers, season after damned season. Don't you think?"

"Or psychotic," Peter Stiller said. He watched her with a lazy smile but penetrating eyes, as if egging her on, as if he could see a wilder, looser side to her personality about to emerge. Peter lay stretched out on a quilt, head propped up on his hand. Kelsey sat cross-legged in front of him. Under Peter's regard she felt herself expanding. She talked more freely. Closed chambers of her life were opening, so painlessly Kelsey didn't realize the source of this lightness, only felt it like sunlight on her face.

She'd only had one glass of wine, so it wasn't that.

"Then if somebody says he's an Oilers fan, I need to ask—subtly, of course—if he sticks with the team because he thinks the players are better than their coaches and their management. Does he feel sorry for a team that hasn't been led right? You know, so he could vote to convict Billy without thinking that was an indictment of the whole town. But would he think I was talking about Billy, or about Mrs. Beaumont? Is Billy a winner or a loser? The trouble is, I can't figure out if I'm the Cowboys or the Oilers."

They were sitting and lying on their picnic quilt in a clearing in the piney woods, in a part of the woods behind Peter's house. It was amazing how you could walk out the door of someone's house and in two minutes be so deep into the forest as to feel lost from civilization. Maybe that was part of the liberating sensation Kelsey felt. The clearing seemed both spacious and private, the pine trees standing like guards. Sunshine could find them here, but no one else. Indian summer made the air mild but invigorating. Kelsey stretched out her bare legs and laid them across Peter's jeans-clad legs.

"It doesn't matter what you say," he said. Kelsey raised her eyes. "That's just an excuse so they can hear you talk and look at you and make up their minds about you. You've got to make some rapport with them."

"I can do that."

Peter looked skeptical. "There's something unapproachable about you, Kelsey."

She stared at him, comically wide-eyed. "It is now four weeks, three days, and about seventeen hours since the first time I ever laid eyes on you."

Since they were lying on a quilt in the woods, both of them half-naked, her point was obvious. Peter acknowledged it by putting his hand on her thigh and softly stroking the length of it. "But I'm a pretty extraordinary person," he said. "You can't expect jurors to be as relentless as I am."

Had he been relentless? Had Peter Stiller pursued her? That wasn't how it seemed, it had seemed like a delightful accident, so much so that Kelsey had been afraid when she'd returned to Galilee after Thanksgiving that she and Peter would act as if nothing had happened between them before she'd left. She'd been afraid that the first meeting with him after their separation would be as awkward as a second kiss. But Peter had made it simple. She had been turning her key in her motel-room door after her rough morning in court when she'd suddenly turned to see him sitting in his squad car, wearing civilian clothes. He'd stepped out of the car just enough to show her the basket he was carrying and to say, "I'll wait while you change into something picnicky."

As if she were a man, as if she could just run inside her room, drop her suit on the floor, pull on jeans, and be ready to go. She'd needed time to think about what to wear. Fortunately, the motel-room closet had shown her her choices were limited. What she'd chosen was something she'd gone by her apartment to pick up, swinging by Austin to check in at the office on her way back to Galilee from Waco. She'd picked out something from her hippie period. Everyone who's lived in Austin has had a hippie period; Kelsey's had lasted about fifteen minutes one Saturday afternoon at an arts-and-crafts fair. That was when she'd bought the skirt that she later drew out of the closet to wear on her picnic with Peter. The skirt was basically brown, but shot through with a pattern of yellow and blue and green. It was long, ankle length, but light as a scarf. It would rise about Kelsey's hips when she spun around—at least that's what the genuinely hippie salesgirl who'd sold it to her had said. Kelsey hadn't tested the promise.

Above the skirt she'd put on a simple white top, almost sleeveless, three buttons in front, and run, then walked sedately, outside to join Peter. He had been waiting beside her motel-room door when she opened it, not looking impatient, just positioning himself so that he could kiss her as soon as she came out; not taking her by surprise, leaning in slowly, putting his hand on her neck. A soft kiss, not quick, a reestablishment rather than a greeting.

Then they'd driven to his cabin in the woods and walked deeper into the woods to this lovely clearing, talking about the holiday they'd spent apart, and Peter had spread the quilt and then stood close to her and kissed her again, more lingeringly, his hands on her bare upper arms, then moving down to her waist, which coincidentally was where the long skirt buttoned. *I'm not ready for this*, Kelsey had thought, but her fingers were unbuttoning his shirt.

Then the long scarflike skirt had whispered down her legs and Peter had knelt in front of her, first kissing her leg, then picking up the skirt so that Kelsey had stepped out of it. Then he'd done the strangest thing. Peter had lifted the skirt, smoothed it by floating it in the breeze, then walked to a tree that had a branch conveniently at eye level, from which he'd hung Kelsey's skirt, making sure it hung straight. Then he'd finished removing his own shirt and had hung it from the end of the dead branch, more carelessly. Kelsey had watched this performance without saying anything, just waiting to see what it meant. And Peter had turned to her and put out his hand for hers and said, "Come and eat."

Maybe that, too, helped account for the extraordinary ease she felt lying there on Peter's quilt in the woods, her bare legs stretched out to catch the sun, thinking that in a moment she was going to run her hand across his chest to see if she remembered exactly how it felt: that Peter hadn't rushed her at all, that even though he'd started undressing her, and himself, he didn't seem to expect anything except to have a picnic lunch with her and listen to her talk about whatever she wanted to say. Kelsey tried to remember if she'd ever before known a man who wasn't in a hurry.

"You have to make friends with at least twelve people here," Peter said. He stroked her thigh again, his hand coming close to her Smoothskins panties. Kelsey sank lower, full length on the quilt.

"I don't have to be their friend," she murmured. "Just make them trust me."

Peter shook his head. His thick, light brown hair glinted with scattered hairs the sun had turned blond. "You ask people to think about something horrible, then do something they never thought they'd do, it better come from a friend," he said.

But she wasn't thinking about trial, and he couldn't have been either. Kelsey reached down and touched his neck. "You like those thighs?" she asked playfully.

His answer was indistinct but definite.

"Then why did you offer them potato salad?" She laughed.

He rose up, laughing, too, and put his arms around her. They were mismatched, his bare abdomen and chest pressing against her blouse, Kelsey's naked legs sliding along his jeans. They needed to do something about that.

"Next time tofu and sprouts," Peter promised.

That was her last great moment in Galilee. More lovely days followed, days preparing for trial and evenings with Peter, moments tender and raucous and joyful. They had special occasions, their own little Christmas by his fire on December 27, New Year's Eve in Houston, but by then her life was overshadowed by the coming trial. Their best day was that long afternoon in the woods when everything seemed fine. When trial was still more than a month away and Kelsey couldn't foresee the crash that was coming; later she could hardly remember that golden day in the woods when she still thought she had a case and still thought she could trust Peter Stiller.

10

Trial began on a Tuesday in January. By the first day, Kelsey had received two very bad pieces of news. The first was that the case she had to take to trial wasn't as strong as the one she'd presented to the grand jury. The second piece of news hurt much worse, because the news about her evidence wasn't Kelsey's fault, it didn't make her review the past three months thinking how stupid she'd been.

The first bad news came in a call from the medical examiner's office in Houston, from her friend Lydia Cadena. "How are you doing, Lydia?" Kelsey asked cheerfully, sitting at the desk in her still-underfurnished office in the Defiance County Courthouse. "Are you taking care of yourself? Is everything . . . ?" Not finishing the sentence because you don't want to ask a pregnant woman about her pregnancy. But Lydia cut right through the personal.

"It's not the mother's blood, Kelsey."

Kelsey found herself on her feet, mouth open, her mind uselessly formulating questions that wouldn't help.

"It's not the baby's, either. We know her blood type from her birth certificate, and it doesn't match up. It's not the baby's blood."

Kelsey found her voice. "What about Ronald?"

"No, Kelsey. I'm sorry. Not his either." Lydia's voice was patient. She knew the devastating impact her news was having on her old friend. Kelsey had been waiting for this last bit of evidence to make everything fall into place. Instead it was smashing a giant hole in her case.

"The only blood we found was there on the front passenger seat. None in the trunk, the other seats, the floorboards, the brake, the gas pedal. The car was clean except for that one small area."

After a long silence Kelsey said, "Thanks, Lydia."

"I'm sorry, Kelsey. Mine's doing great," she belatedly answered her friend's question. "When he's not kicking me, he's got hiccups. My belly's just a little playground."

"That's great, Lydia. Tell him I said hello. I'll see you."

"You bring me some other blood to test against this and I'll see if it matches up," Lydia said gently. "When's your trial start?"

"Tomorrow."

Without that phone call Kelsey would have entered the courtroom next morning with an air of confidence. She had won every pretrial motion hearing, so Kelsey now had a short history of winning against the defense lawyer. Lawyers get used to these positions. She would have been confident of beating Wolverton again—if she'd had a case.

The courtroom was rather large and old-fashioned, with dark-stained wooden pews for the spectators. Large windows filled its back wall, behind the spectators, and the long side wall. The judge would sit with her back to an interior wall and so would the jury, to the judge's left. The witness stand was on the jury's side of the judge's bench. Outside at eight-thirty in the morning the temperature hadn't yet risen above freezing, but from inside the courtroom what could be seen through the windows were evergreen trees and bright sunlight, a timeless view of a side street that could have been any season of the year, and except for two parked cars, any decade of the century. The glass in the windows was old and rippled, so that as Kelsey walked up the aisle, the view elongated and distorted. In imagination the cars turned Depression-era, to match the facades of the buildings.

A scattering of spectators already in the seats. The bailiff, a tall black man in a blue uniform that stretched tight across his stomach, yawned behind his desk inside the railing. There was nothing of watchful alertness about the bailiff even though he was sitting only a few feet from the defendant charged with two murders and the kidnapping of a baby. But Billy Fletcher was on bond, free to come and go like anyone else, and the bailiff's attitude seemed typical of the town's. People might argue the theories of the case, but no one could take seriously the idea of Billy as a mass murderer.

The accused was sitting huddled with his lawyer, having some important last-minute discussion. Kelsey came up the aisle toward them feeling like an underrehearsed actor.

"Good morning," she said to her opponents as she set her briefcase on the prosecution table, the one closer to the jury box. The two men looked up at her, their urgent conference interrupted. Kelsey glanced perfunctorily at the defendant's face, then stopped. Billy Fletcher's wide, almost featureless face was already familiar to her: white, the eyebrows sketchy to the point of invisibility, his forehead blank of lines. It was an empty space waiting for emotion and thought to color in a countenance. But that morning, in the first bright, empty moment in the courtroom, Kelsey saw Billy's face utterly changed. She could picture it sliding into that of the affable country boy everyone knew so well. But she could also see his face changing in another direction, the forehead drawing down, the mouth snarling, Billy's whole face reddening into darkness.

For a long, silent moment she could see both faces reflected in his blank expression. Was Kelsey the only person in Galilee who could see that hidden face of rage? Was that because Billy had turned it on her? In his clenching heart, was he still?

As Kelsey looked out over the array of fifty potential jurors Judge Saunders had ordered, she was slightly surprised to see no familiar face. She scanned the faces quickly from row to row, occasionally nodding, making eye contact with everyone who would let her. They had the usual wary but curious faces of potential jurors. The youngest was a man who looked to be about twenty, but from there the age of the next youngest skipped up at least a decade. Young people generally left Galilee for bigger cities.

She lowered her eyes to the printed list the bailiff had handed her. From the corner of her eye she noticed that Clyde Wolverton was still nodding and smiling to the potential jurors. He didn't need the list. His client, too, saw people he knew. He presented to them the concerned, baffled face his lawyer must have told him to prepare.

More than potential jurors were in the courtroom. For jury selection the lawyers and the defendant were facing out into the spectator seats. The fifty potential jurors were seated on the left side of the courtroom. On the right side, those few spectators from eight-thirty had grown to a small crowd, including people Kelsey recognized. Alice Beaumont avidly divided her attention between the lawyers in front and the citizens across the aisle from her. Her daughter Katherine accompanied her. She nodded at Kelsey and smiled slightly. Kelsey had an odd relationship with Katherine Fletcher. Kelsey hadn't been able to put aside her suspicion of the district attorney's wife, because that suspicion hadn't been based on facts, but on Katherine's haughty manner. But knowing that Katherine couldn't have been involved in the murders, Kelsey still felt Katherine had something significant to tell her.

Standing at the back of the courtroom was Peter Stiller, who smiled at Kelsey in that slight way she wasn't sure anyone else would call a smile, but that made her feel suddenly much less alone.

"Do you understand what this indictment means, Mr. Jones?" Kelsey held up the document.

The potential juror, a thin man in a white shirt and old suit jacket, looked at her as if she couldn't really expect him to speak, but as Kelsey waited, he managed to say, "It's what brings him to trial."

"That's right." Kelsey nodded. On her feet, facing the potential jurors, she held up the indictment. It was longer than average, three dense paragraphs. "I wrote this. I wrote it to conform, I hope, to the law of what a prosecutor has to prove for a murder conviction and a kidnapping conviction. There are require-ments—the 'elements' we talked about. But what makes up those elements are events. I filled in the blanks. 'Billy Fletcher,' 'with the intent to cause death,' 'shot Lorrie Blystone with a deadly weapon, a handgun,' and so on."

"I investigated the facts of this case, and then in this indictment I wrote what I think I can prove happened."

Clyde Wolverton's suspicious expression was growing toward anger. Kelsey heard the legs of his chair scrape the floor as he prepared to stand to object. "But I'm not the one who gets to decide what Billy Fletcher is charged with," she said. The defense lawyer kept his seat. "Once I've written this document, I have to take it to a grand jury. Twelve citizens whose job is to look at this skeptically, listen to the evidence I have, and then endorse this indictment or not." Chair legs scraping. "By doing that, they have not found Billy Fletcher guilty of anything." The defense chair was silent again. "They have said only that they've heard enough evidence that they think he should stand trial on these specific charges. Do you understand that, Mr. Jones, and all of you? No one has found Billy Fletcher guilty of anything just because those twelve people, unanimously, issued this indictment. All they decided was that there's enough evidence that I should have to prove these charges to twelve other people beyond a reasonable doubt, or let Billy Fletcher walk free. Are there any questions? This is the only time you get to ask."

A woman on the fourth row, who probably hadn't had to raise her hand to ask a question in a long time, did so. She wore a flowered dress, with a heavy brown coat. Her voice squeaked a little but she raised it. "But didn't you say you don't have to prove all of it?"

"That's right." Kelsey kept her indictment raised aloft like a flag. "There are three paragraphs here. This charges the defendant with three separate crimes. The jury will have to deliberate over all of them, it's not an all-or-nothing proposition. The jury will be able to find him guilty of only one of these charges, or two, or three, or none."

Clyde Wolverton rose. "It may be that the jury won't even consider all these charges."

Kelsey looked at him politely. "That may be."

"How could that be?" the lady in the brown coat asked.

"That will be up to me," Judge Saunders said. The judge, behind her bench, looked over the standing lawyers' heads at the jury panel. "If I find that the prosecutor hasn't presented enough

evidence on one of the charges, I won't even give it to the jury
to consider."

"*You'd* be finding him not guilty?" the lady asked.

"In effect, yes." Judge Saunders smiled. Kelsey was impressed
with the judge's quiet authority. In her robe she looked no more
impressive than she had in her office in a suit, and Judge Saunders hadn't portentously donned any added dignity, but her
bearing projected confidence. She could easily handle the burden
of deciding whether to take the case from the jury. Kelsey wondered at that possibility, and at what lay behind the judge's calm,
pretty face.

"Or I might withdraw one of the charges for some reason,"
Kelsey said.

She was pleased with the way this part of the jury selection
was going. While carefully explaining that the indictment was no
proof of Billy Fletcher's guilt, she intended to convey precisely
the opposite: twelve citizens of Galilee had had the chance to
make sure this case never got this far, and they hadn't taken it.
They hadn't set their friend Billy free even though they could
have.

Kelsey even liked the judge's interjection. She hoped the jury
would remember it. Whatever charges came to them would come
with the judge's implicit stamp of approval.

Among the potential jurors, Kelsey discovered nine who either
worked at the Smoothskins factory, used to work there, or had
family members who did. Six of the nine were honest enough to
admit that their liking for Billy Fletcher was such that they
couldn't possibly find him guilty of murder; they were dismissed
with the court's thanks. Beside the other three names Kelsey pen-
ciled *S*'s on her jury list. She struck those, but when the jury
was seated, it must still have included people sympathetic to
Billy Fletcher.

"Ms. Thatch, do you wish to make an opening statement?"

Kelsey was sitting so still at the prosecution table that unknow-
ingly she had become the center of attention in the courtroom.
Her otherworldly preoccupation looked to some like deeply troubled concern. Others took it for some ritual preparation.

"Yes, Your Honor." She stood up slowly, turned blindly

toward the jury, and suddenly saw them before her. She was standing stiffly as a cardboard cutout and felt the tension in her shoulders and neck.

"Could we *all* stand up?" she said suddenly.

The jurors looked at her blankly. Kelsey looked back over her shoulder at Judge Saunders. "If I can, too," the judge said with a smile, and rose to her feet.

Hastily, the jurors stood. Kelsey shook her hands and pivoted her head on her neck. Some of the jurors followed suit, some just stood with their hands in their pockets. "We're all going to be sitting a lot of the next few days," Kelsey said. "If any of you need a break, let us know. All right, thank you."

The courtroom's silence was broken. The jurors smiled at each other nervously and shook themselves out of solemnity like worshipers rising at the end of church service. The atmosphere had changed. They looked at Kelsey expectantly.

"This is the beginning of trial, when I tell you what I expect the evidence will show. But first I want to tell you what I *won't* be able to prove."

She began to toy with a button on her blue blazer. "There are always mysteries in life." Kelsey was almost mumbling, preoccupied with the button. "They happen every day, things we can't explain. A picture falls off the wall in an empty room and we hear the crash and come running, but we can't see why it happened. Even things involving people are mysteries sometimes."

A couple of the jurors were annoyedly leaning forward. A couple were watching Kelsey's fingers instead of her face. Suddenly the button popped off her blazer and rolled away.

"Where'd it go? It doesn't matter, it's not important. Unless I got murdered later today. Then everything would be significant, including a missing button. But if I hadn't made a point of losing it in front of witnesses, no one would ever know. Some scenes we cannot ever re-create. The detectives would be baffled over what they would be sure was a missing clue.

"There are always mysteries left over." Kelsey paused before concluding more routinely, "But I expect the testimony to show you quite enough to convince you that Billy Fletcher murdered two people and kidnapped their baby. I will not be able to explain every detail of what happened. Too many people are gone for that. But I expect the evidence to show that this man had reason to commit the murders, he was at the scene at the right time, and he held the murder weapon. The evidence will be sufficient to convince you of his guilt. Please, don't let the small leftover mysteries distract you. Thank you."

Clyde Wolverton said immediately, "We would like to invoke the rule, Your Honor."

The one rule always referred to as "the" rule is that which allows either side to exclude all witnesses from the courtroom, on the theory that someone who is going to testify shouldn't be allowed to listen to other witnesses. The hope of the rule is that a witness should tell his story without adapting the story to earlier versions.

"Will everyone expecting to testify in this matter please come forward?" Judge Saunders said.

They trickled forward, coming from the spectator seats and from the back of the courtroom: Andrew Sims, Morgan Fletcher, three police officers, Alice Beaumont. Peter Stiller wasn't in the room to join them.

Morgan was the first to the gate. He held it for the others, nodding to each as if it were he who had called them forward. Mrs. Beaumont's face was sternly set. She didn't glance at her son-in-law. The small crowd assembled in front of the judge's bench. Morgan was behind the others, closest to Kelsey. He stared at the judge, his old friend, with the close attention of someone who had never seen a trial before.

"Do you have defense witnesses present, Mr. Wolverton?"

The defense lawyer casually shook his head. "Not here, Your Honor."

A crease appeared between Kelsey's eyebrows. She looked out at the filled spectator seats. So none of these people would speak for Billy Fletcher. She saw Katherine Fletcher, the place beside her where her mother had been sitting now vacant. Kelsey had had no use for Katherine as a witness. Apparently the defense didn't either. Katherine was dressed as if for a rather formal party, in a long dark skirt and a long-sleeved white blouse, elegant in its simplicity. Her hands were folded in her lap. She watched the scene at the front of the courtroom, her expression blank.

"Very well. Raise your right hands, please. Do you swear that the testimony you will give in this cause will be the truth, the whole truth, and nothing but the truth, so help you, God?"

They did. "The rule has been invoked," the judge explained. "That means you will not be allowed to listen to the testimony given by other witnesses in this trial. You must remain outside the courtroom until you are called. Don't discuss the case among yourselves until after the trial is over. Ms. Thatch, who—"

"Your Honor." It was Morgan Fletcher's voice, quiet but easily penetrating Judge Saunders's question. "As an officer of the court, may I be excused from the operation of the rule?"

Linda Saunders glanced at him, her face neutral. "I see no reason why not, Mr. Fletcher. Objection?"

"None from the defense," Clyde Wolverton said quickly.

Kelsey walked around her table, closer to Morgan, who turned to her full face and stood as if offering himself for inspection. His face was impossible to read. "This is Mr. Fletcher's courtroom," Kelsey said to the judge. "I certainly wouldn't ask that he be excluded from it."

Without an objection from the defense, Kelsey felt certain that her objecting to Morgan's sitting through the trial would be useless. So she gave in graciously. Morgan gave her an ever so slight bow, which she returned.

Their roles were set in opposition, though. Much as Kelsey had come to like Morgan Fletcher, even as helpful as he'd been to her, she had no illusions about whose side he was on. She was certain of Morgan's loyalty to his brother. In his cordial, gracious way, Morgan was determined to see Kelsey fail.

He took his seat in one of the chairs just inside the railing at the front of the courtroom, on the defense side, a few feet behind his brother.

"May I stay?" This voice was equally identifiable. Its peremptory tone made the question not a question.

"I'm afraid not, Mrs. Beaumont," Judge Saunders said to her with a smile.

"This is my family," Alice Beaumont said grimly, standing her ground. "This is about him killing my baby. Do you think I can't listen?"

She stared a threat at the elected judge. Linda Saunders didn't acknowledge it with even a moment of hesitation. "I'm sorry, Mrs. Beaumont, but the rule is the rule. It has very few exceptions."

Outrage entered Alice Beaumont's stare. But Linda Saunders wasn't dueling with her. "Call your first witness," she said to Kelsey.

Mrs. Beaumont frowned, with her first trace of uncertainty. Then she turned to Kelsey, with peremptorily raised eyebrows. That face: didn't the old lady know the effect it had on people? Kelsey felt her own back stiffening.

But for the first time she saw herself in Mrs. Beaumont's place. She saw her sternness for what it was: outraged helplessness. Kelsey reached for Mrs. Beaumont, only planning to guide her out, but instead put both arms around the matriarch and hugged her close. "I'll do everything I can," she whispered. "I'll bring her back."

Mrs. Beaumont suddenly slumped against Kelsey's shoulder. The two women stood in silence for a long minute, oblivious to the courtroom, before Mrs. Beaumont made her slow way out, looking defeated.

Clyde Wolverton looked solemnly satisfied. Kelsey realized that the defense lawyer thought she had just proclaimed herself Mrs. Beaumont's servant, and he was pleased: if the trial was a popularity contest between Wolverton's client and Kelsey's, Mrs. Beaumont would lose.

"The State calls Andrew Sims," Kelsey said.

She took her seat, pulled a smaller file from her voluminous accordion file, and drew a legal pad toward her.

It had been years since Kelsey had tried a criminal case. She had forgotten her role models. She had planned to try this case absolutely by the numbers, dot one to dot two, dot dot dot, but something had happened, the shock just before trial of losing her vital evidence had left her strangely exhilarated. Everything seemed fresh to her. She thought she could explain every facet of the crimes. She could picture the scene so well, as soon as the game warden began speaking.

"What time of day was it, Mr. Sims?"

"Ten o'clock of a weekday morning. I believe it was a Wednesday."

Sims was wearing his brown uniform, but he'd left his jacket and his hat in the hallway, and he didn't wear a gun or a badge, so he looked rather unadorned. The unshowiness of his appearance added to his competent look. Sims spoke up clearly, looking at the prosecutor in concentration.

"I was driving out Morningside Drive on my way out of town, just passing Miz Alice Beaumont's house."

"Did you know anything about Mrs. Beaumont's condition that morning?"

"I'd heard she was sick with flu, and that her daughter was visiting her with her husband and baby girl."

Kelsey felt slightly jarred, like bouncing over a small pothole in the road. What Sims had just testified to was hearsay, something he'd only heard, without knowing from his own experience, and Kelsey had expected an objection. She glanced at Clyde Wolverton, looking thin in a black suit, and saw him watching her witness intently. So the defense lawyer wasn't one who blindly enforced the rules of evidence. That opened up the trial. Kelsey felt both hopeful and nervous.

She remained aware of Morgan Fletcher at her back, staring at her and at her witness, with the knowledge of a lifetime Kelsey couldn't hope to duplicate. For any sentence of testimony, there was so much more Morgan would know both about the scene and the witness than Kelsey could possibly understand. He sat there close, where he could convey any vital discrepancies to the defense. Having him sitting behind her made Kelsey feel like a student with an instructor observing her closely.

"Did you know Mrs. Beaumont's daughter and son-in-law?"

"Yes, ma'am. Lorrie Blystone and Ronald."

"Did you see either of them as you drove by the house on October twenty-first?"

"It wasn't Ronald I noticed at first, it was Billy Fletcher."

"Did you have your car windows rolled up, Mr. Sims?"

"Yes, I did."

"But you could still hear Billy Fletcher?"

"I'm not sure I heard him or saw him, but something caught my attention. And as soon as I saw him, it was obvious what was going on."

"What was that?"

"An argument. Billy arguing with Ronald Blystone."

"Mr. Sims, it seems to me you say that in a sort of weary way. Was that something you'd seen before, an argument between Billy Fletcher and Ronald Blystone?"

"I don't think I'd ever seen it, but heard enough to—"

The defense lawyer rose briskly and said, "We'll object to anything Mr. Sims only heard, Your Honor."

"Sustained."

Kelsey asked, "What did you do when you saw this fight going on?"

"I wouldn't call it a fight. I didn't see anybody hitting, just arguing." Kelsey gave her witness a thin smile. "I slowed way down. I was driving my patrol car, and usually that makes people do a double take, thinking it's a police car. But Billy and Ronald didn't notice. So I gave a little tap on the horn. But they still didn't look. So I stopped and climbed out."

"Mr. Sims, what did you see that made you think you should stop?"

"Oh, nothing much." Kelsey waited for the right answer. "It looked like the kind of thing that could get out of hand."

"What did you do?"

Sims went on with his story, in a quiet even tone. He had gotten out of his car, honked again, then waved at both men, who had paused, red-faced, to wave back. That is, Billy had waved.

"Did you hear what they said, Mr. Sims?"

"No, ma'am. I didn't stop to chat. I figured they'd cool down and Billy'd leave. I drove on myself."

"Did either of the men have a gun when you saw them?"

"I'd never have driven away if they had."

Kelsey nodded. "Was Lorrie Blystone there, too, at the time you saw Billy Fletcher arguing with her husband?"

"I heard her voice when I first stepped out of the car, calling something from inside the house."

"Just one more question, Mr. Sims. Did you hear the baby?"

The tall man's gaze grew abstracted. He was back there at the scene, before the murders. "That's what I keep asking myself," he said softly. "Was the baby still there then? Could I have walked in and taken her out? Or just gone up and put my hand on Billy's shoulder and say why didn't he leave with me? He would've, I'm sure. Then we . . ."

Wouldn't be here now, Kelsey willed him to finish his thought, but Sims didn't, he just trailed off. Kelsey was sure she wasn't the only person who'd heard what he was thinking, though.

After Kelsey passed the witness, Clyde Wolverton sat looking at him for such a long time that Kelsey turned to stare at the defense lawyer. He looked friendly and musing, an appreciative audience. There had been nothing startling in Andrew Sims's testimony. Didn't Wolverton have any cross-examination prepared? Judge Saunders, too, was watching the defense lawyer, but she didn't prompt him to begin. Maybe this was a familiar habit of Wolverton's. Kelsey got the tingling along her forearms she always felt when something was going on that she didn't understand and didn't like.

When Wolverton finally spoke, it was anticlimactic. "Hello, Andy."

Sims nodded. "Clyde."

"Did you see anybody else outside the house?"

"No."

"But you only stayed there what, a minute? Maybe two?"

"Maybe two."

"Did you go inside the house?"

"No, sir. Not even up on the porch."

"So you don't know who all might've been inside?"

"No."

Clyde Wolverton's courtroom voice was higher pitched than Kelsey remembered it, with a twang that reverberated annoyingly in Kelsey's ear. Andrew Sims was looking at the defense lawyer almost with a glint of amusement, as if watching a familiar comic who hadn't yet said anything amusing. Once Sims's gaze slid past Wolverton to Billy Fletcher, and Sims's expression turned appraising.

Wolverton said, "Did you know Billy had to catch a plane in Houston that morning?"

"Objection to hearsay."

"Sustained," said the judge.

Wolverton had no more questions. Kelsey had a couple. The first was in response to Wolverton's speculations about other people in the house. "Did you notice any cars around the house, Mr. Sims?"

Sims frowned in memory. This wasn't something he and Kelsey had touched on while going over his testimony the day before. "Only two," he said slowly. "Both parked in the driveway, side by side."

"Did you recognize them?"

"The one on the right was Billy's, that old Chevrolet Caprice. The other one was a pretty new model foreign car, Toyota Camry, I think. I assume it was Ronald's."

"No more questions."

The defense lawyer had no more either. How many had he asked, two? Kelsey rubbed a hand down her left forearm, soothing its tingling. Wolverton hadn't even tried to back Andrew Sims down about the quality of the argument he'd seen. Either the defense lawyer's competence was questionable, or Sims's testimony hadn't hurt him, and Wolverton was smart enough to know it.

"Call your next witness."

That would be the one sitting behind her. "The State calls Morgan Fletcher," Kelsey said.

He came forward slowly but with his shoulders squared. He didn't look at his brother's table. "You've already been sworn, Mr. Fletcher," Judge Saunders said, barely glancing at him. Morgan nodded and took his seat. He looked at the jury—no, at the jurors, individually. Kelsey interrupted his concentration. "Please identify yourself."

It was the traditional first question, a requirement for the record, but asking it suddenly made Kelsey feel mortally stupid. Everyone in the building knew Morgan Fletcher, knew him better than Kelsey ever could. When Morgan Fletcher talked, it would be to a jury of more than peers, of friends. The same was true for every witness who would be called in this trial.

Kelsey resolved not to be stupid any more. She wasn't going to worry about the record for appeal and she wasn't going to play by tradition. She might be ignorant, but she wasn't going to be a rigid fool.

"Mr. Fletcher—Morgan—do you love your brother?"

Morgan was taken by surprise by the question, but responded

quickly. "Of course. But I certainly don't intend to violate the oath I took to tell the truth. Or the oath I took as a prosecutor to see that justice is done."

"I wouldn't suggest that you would. My question is, do you think you're the only person in Galilee who loves Billy Fletcher?"

She had managed to awaken uneasiness in Clyde Wolverton. The defense lawyer sat up alertly, looking uncertainly at the witness. But why would he object to giving Morgan the opportunity to say how lovable Wolverton's client was?

"I know for a fact many people in this town love Billy," Morgan said with smiling enthusiasm.

"And do you think Billy returns their love?"

"Yes. Billy's always had a great concern for people."

Clyde Wolverton was actively frowning now. He was sitting up very straight, the closest posture to standing a sitting man could achieve.

"And he actually carries responsibility for a great many people here in Galilee, doesn't he?"

The defense lawyer bolted upright—Kelsey had a strong feeling he would have no matter what question she had just asked—but then spoke slowly. "Your Honor, I have to question the relevance of this line of questioning."

"It goes to motive, Your Honor," Kelsey said calmly.

"Motive?" Wolverton asked, baffled.

"I'll move on," Kelsey offered.

"Thank you, Ms. Thatch," said Judge Saunders. The judge didn't look as puzzled as the defense lawyer. Neither did Morgan Fletcher.

"Morgan, where were you late in the morning of October twenty-first of last year?"

"I was at work in my office in this courthouse."

Kelsey nodded. "What time did you leave the courthouse?"

"It was about eleven-thirty in the morning. I decided to go check on my mother-in-law, who was down with the flu."

"Didn't you expect your wife would have looked in on Mrs. Beaumont?"

"Katherine had company at our house that morning. I didn't think she would have been able to get out."

"What time did you arrive at your mother-in-law's house?"

"It didn't take long. Maybe five minutes."

"What kind of car did your brother-in-law drive?" Kelsey was looking at a photograph taken from across the street from the Beaumont house. It had been taken by a police photographer long after the murders, after police had arrived on the scene. In Mrs. Beaumont's driveway Morgan Fletcher's Lincoln was parked behind a deep blue sedan. Katherine's Buick was parked beside the blue sedan. Police and sheriff and emergency vehicles crowded the roadside.

"Ronald and Lorrie had a Toyota Camry," Morgan said.

Kelsey carried the photograph to him on the witness stand. "This car?" She pointed to the car parked in front of Morgan's Lincoln.

Morgan gave the picture more than a glance, but didn't see anything unusual in it. "Yes."

"Do you recognize this place in the photograph?"

"It's my mother-in-law's house. Alice Beaumont's house."

"Is this how it looked when you arrived that morning about eleven thirty-five?"

"No. It was very quiet when I got there. I hadn't called the police yet, of course, because I didn't know anything was wrong."

"So if we mentally erase all these law enforcement cars and the ambulance and so forth, this picture would show us what you saw when you arrived that morning?"

Morgan frowned slightly at her question and studied the picture again. It was obvious he thought Kelsey was trying to slip something by him, but he couldn't see what. "Yes," he finally said.

"So there was no other car near the house when you arrived? Only Ronald and Lorrie Blystone's Toyota."

"Yes, that's true."

Kelsey carried the picture back to her table, looking it over. Barely visible in the photo, peeking up into view through the rear window of the Toyota, was the top of a child's car seat.

"You went inside?" she asked abruptly.

"Yes. I knocked on the front door. No one answered, but that wasn't unusual. With Mrs. Beaumont so sick the household routine had broken down somewhat. And since I hadn't seen the maid's car or Goldie Hatteras's, I assumed they were out." Morgan had gotten Kelsey's point with the photograph. There had been no other murder suspects on the premises. "So I knocked and went in."

"Did you call out when you went in the front door?"

Morgan stared at his hand on the railing in front of him, concentrating. "I don't think so. I started to, but something stopped me. It was so quiet in the house."

It was equally quiet at that moment in the courtroom. The spectators and jurors, even Judge Saunders, leaned toward Morgan, stilling their breaths. Most of them must have heard about his discovery of the bodies, but probably none of them had heard it firsthand like this, from Morgan's own lips. He spoke quietly, but his voice hung perfectly audible in the still air of the courtroom.

"And almost right away I smelled blood. That stopped me. I just stood there for a second, listening, but as soon as I took another step, I saw Ronald."

"Where was he?"

"Just inside the doorway to the dining room. He was lying on the floor. For a second I thought he was just hurt. But when I got close to him, I saw the bullet wound and I knew there was no chance he was alive."

"Where was the wound?"

"Here." Morgan touched his left temple. "There was a black ring around the hole, so I knew it was a contact wound."

"Which means what?"

"That the barrel of the gun had been touching his head, or almost touching it, when it was fired. That's my understanding."

Kelsey was trying to go slowly, to let the horror of the scene come alive for the jury. As a witness, Morgan wasn't helping. His testimony had none of the dramatic quality his voice had had when he'd reenacted the finding of the bodies for Kelsey in the dining room of his mother-in-law's house. Today in court Morgan was much more businesslike. He wasn't cold, his voice was too alive for that, but he showed no sign that the scene had affected him emotionally.

"Did you touch your brother-in-law?"

"No. I don't think so. It was obvious I couldn't do anything for him. I didn't want to disturb the scene."

"You were already thinking about that?"

Morgan fixed her with a look. "It's amazing how in a crisis your personal feelings just shrink away from what you're seeing and all that's left is this sort of—professional shell that goes about its business. If you've never experienced that, Ms. Thatch, you're a lucky person."

It wasn't a rebuke. Morgan looked abstracted. In the slow spacing of his words was the first emotion he had shown. Judge Saunders watched her old friend with a look of undisguised sympathy, an expression reflected on most of the jurors' faces.

Kelsey nodded in sympathy as well. "What did you do next?"

"I turned and saw Lorrie. I hadn't noticed her before; you know how your eye passes over a room and you see what you expect to see instead of what's really there. It was Ronald who took my attention first because he was closer to me, and Lorrie was down on the floor. She was stretched out full length, her head down so I couldn't see her face."

"Close to her husband?" Kelsey asked solemnly.

"No. There was a crib next to the side wall. Lorrie was there, almost next to it."

"Her body was parallel to the crib?"

"Just about."

"How far behind her was the far wall of the room?"

"Six feet. Something like that."

"Did you notice a stain on that wall?"

"Not then, no."

Kelsey was satisfied with that answer. "What did you do?"

"I went to her, of course. I reached for her neck, and then her wrist, and didn't feel any pulse. By that time I'd noticed the blood and I knew there was no chance."

"Where was the blood?"

"Everywhere," Morgan said simply. "Lorrie was lying in it, she had dragged herself through some of it, and there was a pool of blood around her. A great deal of blood."

"Did you stay there beside her long?"

"No." Morgan's voice quickened. "I thought of the baby. I jumped up and tried to step around the blood and I went to the crib. I realized I hadn't heard Taylor crying and I was afraid what that meant. There were covers spread in the crib, so at first I couldn't see. I was so afraid she was under there that when I pulled back the covers, I thought I saw her. But it was just a stain on the underneath sheet. Taylor was gone."

"What did you do next?"

"I called the police, from the phone in the entryway."

"And your wife."

"Yes. I called Katherine."

"Why?"

"I knew she'd hear very soon what had happened, and I wanted to be the one to tell her. And I knew she'd want to come take care of her mother."

"Had you already checked to make sure Mrs. Beaumont was all right?"

Morgan frowned. "I don't— No. I ran upstairs right after I'd called the police."

Morgan hadn't called 911, he'd called a homicide detective he knew, so there was no recording of the call. She saw no reason to delve into it. There was another call she wanted to ask about, though.

"How long was it before other people arrived?"

"Not long. Five minutes."

"Your wife arrived quickly?"

"Yes, just behind the first police officer. They came in almost together."

"What did Katherine do immediately?" Kelsey felt malicious asking this question, as if she wanted Morgan to announce the information publicly for Kelsey's satisfaction.

"She ran straight upstairs to be with her mother."

"Did she ever go into the dining room, in your memory?"

"No. By the time she came back down, they had tape across the doorway, they wouldn't have let her in where they were investigating. Katherine isn't the kind to want to stare at bodies, anyway." His eyes sought his wife's in the audience, with a tender, apologizing expression.

Kelsey had asked about Katherine because she wanted the jury to know why Katherine wasn't being called as a witness: she hadn't seen anything. Unless jurors were informed of that sort of thing, they tended to speculate what the missing witness would have said.

"What did you do during those five minutes while you waited for someone else to arrive?"

"After I checked on Mama—Mrs. Beaumont—and saw that she was all right, I went back downstairs and just waited. I sat at the bottom of the stairs, I think."

"Did you think of your brother?" Kelsey asked suddenly.

She imagined she felt a rush of air as Clyde Wolverton hit his feet.

"Objection, Your Honor. What the witness may have thought is irrelevant."

Bad move, Clyde. Tell the jury you didn't want them to hear what Morgan had thought as he sat in that house with the bodies, and the jurors knew what he had thought. Kelsey didn't mind at all when Judge Saunders said, "Sustained."

While Wolverton was still savoring his triumph, Kelsey said, "You had gotten a call from your brother that morning, hadn't you?"

In the pause that followed, Kelsey drew another file toward her and began shuffling through the papers inside. She felt Morgan's stare and imagined what he was thinking. If she had obtained the courthouse phone records with a subpoena, why hadn't someone told him? But that wasn't the source of Kelsey's information.

"Yes," Morgan said slowly.

"Where was he calling from, if you know?"

"He was calling from his car. At least that's what he said."

"What time was that?" Kelsey asked casually, drawing the answer toward her. The document she had was a copy of October's bill from the company that operated Billy Fletcher's cellular phone. Kelsey had arranged to have the record subpoenaed through a friend in the Houston district attorney's office. The cellular phone company was also in Houston. They had handed over the information without balking, and without informing their customer. Kelsey had wanted to have at least one surprise at trial that the wide network of informants in Defiance County wouldn't know about.

"It was about ten-thirty when he called me."

"Would you agree ten twenty-five?" Kelsey asked, looking at the phone record.

Morgan shrugged. "He was already on his way to the airport in Houston."

Kelsey had expected that explanation. "Could you hear anything in the background? Road noise, or a voice?" She watched Morgan intently.

He hesitated, making Kelsey's heart lift. She hadn't expected for an instant that Morgan would blurt out, "Yes, I heard a baby crying in the seat beside him." But a pause, from this witness, was almost as good. It made Morgan look for the first time as if he might be hiding something.

"It wasn't a very good connection. It kept fading in and out, like he was traveling. I could barely hear Billy's voice, let alone anything in the background. It sounded like a call from a moving car, though, passing from one cell coverage to the next, getting weaker and then stronger."

Kelsey let him get away with that without challenge. "Why did he call you? What did he say?"

"Well, to let me know he was on his way to catch his plane."

"Didn't he tell you he'd been by Mrs. Beaumont's house?"

"Yes. He said he'd gotten into an argument with Ronald there, and I said when I got a chance, I'd go by there and try to smooth things over."

"So that's why you went to your mother-in-law's house an hour later," Kelsey said neutrally.

"That and to check on her, as I said." Morgan didn't have the self-justifying tone of a man patching up an explanation. He still spoke calmly.

"Did Billy routinely call you to report every argument he had with your brother-in-law?"

"Objection," Wolverton said. "Assumes a fact not in evidence, that there were any other arguments."

"Sustained," said Judge Saunders in a slightly weary voice that reflected the common thought: everyone in the room knew there had been many such arguments. Kelsey had regained her confidence. She was on the knowing side again. Now the defense lawyer was the one who sounded naive.

"Had your brother Billy had other arguments with Ronald Blystone?"

"A few."

"Some of them in your presence?"

"Yes."

"What did they argue about?"

"Objection," Clyde Wolverton said, briskly on his feet again. "Relevance again."

This time Kelsey stood, too. "This is extremely relevant testimony, Your Honor, concerning motive. It also goes to the prior relationship between the defendant and the deceased, which is specifically admissible in a murder trial."

Judge Saunders pursed her lips. "That objection is overruled," she said slowly.

Kelsey relaxed a little as she sat down. No matter what secret allegiance the judge harbored, she also had a concern with her appearance of neutrality. She would follow the law—for the time being, at least.

"That means you can answer the question, Mr. Fletcher," Kelsey said to Morgan.

Straight-faced, he said, "Thank you for the legal explanation, Ms. Thatch," causing a ripple of amusement through the courtroom. "They argued about what should be done with the Smoothskins factory. Billy favored keeping things the way they were, the way that had worked fine for twenty years. Ronald wanted to make changes."

"Who won most of these arguments?" Kelsey asked, expecting Morgan to answer as he had on the front porch of his mother-in-law's house. But this time he was evasive.

"Hard to say. I guess you'd have to say Billy won them, since the factory stayed in business like always."

"But the arguments upset your brother, didn't they? They made him mad."

"Some people might think that. Billy's one of these people that turns red-faced real easily. It makes people think he's madder than he is. I could make him blush right now, in about three words. Billy. Emily Fay Vincent."

The defendant wouldn't look up from the defense table. He

looked abashed, very much the little brother. "Morgan," he muttered warningly. And his face reddened.

It was an effective demonstration, not just of Billy's complexional volatility, but of the relationship between the brothers—jocular, affectionate, with Morgan very much in charge. She had never seen Billy Fletcher look less threatening than he did in that moment. Kelsey felt blood rise to her own face.

"If the arguments were no big deal to Billy, then why did he call you to tell you about this one?"

Morgan blinked. The defense lawyer gave him more time to think, with an objection: "Asks him to read another person's mind." Judge Saunders agreed.

"I mean if he told you," Kelsey said doggedly. "Was this argument different, worse than the others?"

Morgan had his answer ready now. "He didn't say that. It's just that Billy was on his way out of state, he thought Ronald and Lorrie might go home to Dallas before he got back, he didn't want there to be bad feelings in the family."

"Why didn't he just call them himself to make up?"

"Oh, I was used to being the peacemaker," Morgan said easily.

"So this family needed a full-time peacemaker."

For an instant Morgan's eyes penetrated hers, in a flash Kelsey didn't think anyone else could see—a flash of anger, or even of congratulations. But when he spoke, it was quite calmly. "Hardly full-time. I'm just maybe a little more articulate than Billy. I'm in the word business, he's not."

Kelsey hesitated, so long the judge turned toward her inquisitively. Kelsey liked something about that answer. She could imagine using it in her final argument. It would probably be the strongest finish she could draw out of Morgan Fletcher.

"Pass the witness," she said.

Clyde Wolverton sat forward eagerly, with a pleasant smile. "Mr, Fletcher—Morgan—what is your professional title?"

"District attorney of Defiance County."

"Normally you would be the one prosecuting a case such as this, would you not, rather than my worthy adversary Ms. Thatch?"

"If I thought the evidence sufficient to take to trial, yes."

"At what point did you decide you had to recuse yourself from this case?"

Morgan was leaning forward, his fingers interlaced, sounding professionally detached. "When we learned about Andrew Sims's report that he'd seen Billy at the house soon before the murders— although we didn't yet know the times of death, we didn't know how far apart those incidents were. But just as a precaution Detective Childers had Billy's fingerprints tested against the ones found on the pistol in the house. When one of them matched, that's when the chief decided he had to make an arrest and that's when I called the attorney general's office to say we needed a special prosecutor appointed."

"Morgan, how many felony indictments have you obtained from grand juries in your career?"

"Hundreds."

Kelsey saw where this was going. She prepared to rise and was surprised by how stiff she felt. The first objection in a trial was always the toughest one. It seemed rude. She had known lawyers who could never gather their courage to make that first objection and so let their opponents run roughshod over them. Not unlike the average soldier who never fires a shot during combat.

"Have you obtained any murder indictments?" Wolverton asked.

"Fortunately murders have been very rare during my tenure as district attorney of Defiance County," Morgan said, and Kelsey heard a sound like extremely muted applause, or like a hundred faces simultaneously breaking into approving expressions. "But during my early days in Houston I obtained my fair share of murder indictments from grand juries. Prosecuted several, too."

"In your professional judgment, was the evidence you had against Billy Fletcher at the time you recused yourself from this case sufficient to take to a grand jury?"

"Objection." Kelsey was gratified to find her voice working fine. In fact it rang out more loudly than it had during her questioning. "The jury doesn't need a supposed expert evaluating the evidence for them. They can do that perfectly well for themselves."

The judge didn't even look up. "Overruled." Kelsey remained

on her feet a moment longer, but no one would return her look. As she sat, the defense lawyer repeated, "Was there enough evidence against Billy?"

"No," Morgan said confidently. "With only that, I wouldn't have taken the case to a grand jury. Certainly it wouldn't have been enough to convict." With a nod of professional courtesy he added, "However, I'm sure Ms. Thatch has more evidence than that by now."

He knew, of course. He knew that when Kelsey had taken her case to the grand jury, she'd had the evidence of blood in Billy's car. With that evidence, she had obtained the indictment only by the skin of her teeth. And she no longer had the blood. Kelsey wouldn't look at the jurors, but she felt some of them turning toward her questioningly.

11

It already seemed late in the day when Kelsey called her second police witness. It was a surprise to remember that this was still the first day of trial. She was already getting into the heart of her case.

Sgt. John Zuniga was the fingerprint examiner for the Galilee police and a general evidence technician. His testimony was going to be about guns—not Kelsey's field of expertise, as she had never fired one.

She had practiced holding one, though, so that she could do this: walk up to the witness, pick up the pistol from the railing in front of him, and hold it casually, not betraying the shock it was to pick the thing up, the impression it made all the way up Kelsey's arm.

"This is the gun you examined, Sergeant Zuniga?"

"Yes, it is." Zuniga was shy of forty by a year or two. He had curly black hair and a mouth made for smiling. The breadth of his shoulders and chest were rather out of keeping with the relative fineness of his features. Zuniga sat unmoving on the witness stand, watching Kelsey carefully.

"Could you describe this for the jury, please?"

He said briskly, "It's a thirty-eight-caliber semiautomatic handgun."

"Semiautomatic? You mean it can fire a lot of shots at once?"

"No, ma'am, it just means there's not a hammer you have to cock in order to fire it. You just pull the trigger. It still only fires once each time you pull the trigger."

Kelsey continued to study the gun as she asked questions about it. She wanted the jurors' attention fastened on that weapon. She was not pretending her own fascination. The gun was heavier than she had expected. No one could wave it around casually or forget that he was holding it. Its weight announced its purpose.

The gun was hungry. Kelsey could feel creeping up her arm and shoulder the desire to aim and fire it. The gun only had one purpose. Holding it, she could feel that purpose.

"How did you come into possession of this gun, Sergeant Zuniga?"

"Officer Dial brought it to me."

James Dial had already testified to finding this gun close to Ronald Blystone's hand. It was the murder weapon.

"Did you try to obtain fingerprints from it?"

"Yes, I lifted three sets of prints."

"From the grip?" Kelsey offered him the gun and felt relief and loss when Zuniga took it from her and held it easily in his large, thin-fingered hand.

"No, ma'am. You see this grip? It's plastic, with a very rough surface. This textured pattern. It's good for gripping, but terrible for retaining a usable fingerprint. I need a smooth surface to lift a print."

"Where did you find a good surface?"

"Under here." He indicated the front of the grip, which was steel, unadorned by the plastic plates on the sides of the grip. "And two here on the barrel."

"None on the trigger?"

"No, it's too thin. I need a certain amount of flat surface to retain a whole print, one large enough to compare. This trigger is just too small."

Kelsey took the gun back from her witness. It nestled into her hand. "Sergeant, did you compare the fingerprints you found on the gun against known prints?"

"Yes."

"Did they match up, so that you were able to identify the prints on the gun?"

"Yes, I identified all the fingerprints. Two of them were Ronald Blystone's."

"The owner of the gun."

"Yes."

"And the third print on the gun?"

Zuniga looked toward the defense table. His voice remained level. "That one was the defendant's."

"Billy Fletcher's."

"Yes, ma'am."

"Where did you find Mr. Fletcher's fingerprint on the gun?"

"On the barrel. About here."

"Sergeant, could you please show me what a man would be doing to leave a fingerprint on that spot on the gun."

Zuniga sounded relaxed. "He could just be picking it up. Not a very good way to pick up a gun, but people do. Or if someone else were holding the gun, like you are now, Billy could've left his fingerprint on the barrel like this."

The burly sergeant reached out and wrapped his hand around the barrel of the gun. Kelsey let it go, so it looked as if Zuniga had taken it from her.

"Then he'd just turn it around," she said, as the police sergeant did just that, holding the gun in firing position, "but not leave a fingerprint on the grip or the trigger."

"Right. No one did. Nothing I could use, anyway."

"And you didn't find any other fingerprints on the gun?"

"No."

"Did you take Lorrie Blystone's fingerprints?"

"Yes, ma'am. But I didn't find them on the gun."

Kelsey walked thoughtfully back to her table. She opened her briefcase and took out three clear plastic bags. As she did so, she glanced at the defense side. Morgan Fletcher was in his spot behind the defense table. He returned Kelsey's look, his eyes deep and sad. He seemed to know exactly what was coming, and what he was going to do in response, so that in a way they were acting in tandem. It was a comradely look he gave Kelsey, but a mournful one.

Kelsey walked slowly back to the witness stand and handed one of the bags to her witness. "Can you identify the contents of this bag, State's exhibit eighteen?"

Zuniga held the bag up, so that some of the jurors might have been able to identify what was inside as the twisted, ruined remnant of a bullet. Zuniga peered at the yellow label on the bag. "This is the bullet that was removed from Ronald Blystone during the autopsy."

"Did you receive it from Dr. Broom?"

"I was there. He gave it directly to me."

"Thank you. And this bag, State's exhibit nineteen?"

This bullet was in slightly better shape. It had only penetrated flesh, not a skull.

"This is the bullet removed from Lorrie Blystone." Zuniga set it down carefully beside the gun on the railing.

"And finally this third bag, State's exhibit twenty."

"Those are three bullets I fired from the gun myself and recovered from a tank of water."

"Then what did you do with them?"

"I compared them to the bullets removed from the victims' bodies."

"And what was your conclusion, Sergeant Zuniga?"

"That this was the murder weapon." He held up the .38 automatic again. "This is the gun that fired the bullets that killed Lorrie and Ronald Blystone."

"Thank you, Sergeant. I pass the witness."

The defense lawyer sprang up from his seat and buttoned his suit coat as he walked toward the witness. "Would you pick up the gun again, John?"

The sergeant did, looking unperturbed and barely curious as Wolverton came toward him. Zuniga held the pistol by its handgrip, its barrel aimed up toward the ceiling.

"Point it at me, please," Clyde Wolverton said, coming to a stop in front of the witness stand. "You have removed the ammunition clip, haven't you? . . . Good. Now you testified that Billy's fingerprint could have gotten on the barrel in the place you found it if he took the gun away from someone holding it. Let me ask you if it could have gotten there like this."

Wolverton reached out, moving his hand slowly, and pushed the barrel of the gun aside.

Zuniga watched him. "Yes, sir, that would work." He said it so quickly that Kelsey was certain he had answered the question before.

"Thank you, Sergeant." Looking pleased with himself, Wolverton returned to his seat.

All right, Kelsey had been expecting this defense tack. But then Wolverton opened up a new subject, one that took her completely by surprise.

"Sergeant Zuniga, you were also in charge of collecting blood samples at the scene, weren't you?"

"Yes, sir."

"Where there was a good deal to be collected, but did you also attempt to collect blood evidence anywhere other than at the scene of the homicides?"

"Yes, sir. When"—Zuniga nodded toward Billy with slight embarrassment—"your client became a suspect and we learned he had flown out of state, I went to Houston Intercontinental Airport and found his car and tested it for traces of blood."

"This is a copy of your report, is it not?" Wolverton said pleasantly. Kelsey stared as the defense lawyer handed her witness a one-page form Kelsey had never seen.

"Yes, sir, it is."

"And what was your finding, Sergeant Zuniga?"

"No trace of blood in the defendant's car."

"Did you check everywhere in the interior of the car?"

"Yes, sir. The seats, the floorboards, even inside the trunk."

"And you found no blood at all?"

"No, sir."

Wolverton turned to Kelsey with a bland smile the jury couldn't see. Her shock was apparent. "Thank you, Officer. No more questions."

Kelsey couldn't think of any either. Not to ask the witness.

Judge Saunders began speaking. When it became clear she was dismissing court for the day, Kelsey gathered her things quickly, and as soon as trial was adjourned, she went quickly out the side door and down a narrow corridor to a side exit from the courthouse she'd discovered. When she threw open the door, the cold air hit her unexpectedly and she realized she'd forgotten her coat. But she wouldn't turn back. As she started down the short flight of concrete steps, a hand fell on her arm. She immediately flung it off.

"Kelsey—"

"No!" she screamed the word, already enraged, answering the loud voices in her head.

Peter came after her, having to walk fast to keep up. When she felt him reaching for her again, she made a slashing gesture with both hands. "Listen," he said.

"No! God damn you. You let me get sandbagged. Why didn't you give me that report?"

"I never saw it, Kelsey."

"Bullshit. Where'd you get the ones you did give me?"

"From the sheriff. He told me those were all there were."

She stared at Peter, at the tension of his arms wanting to reach for her but knowing that would enrage her further. His face was desperate with longing for her to believe. But she couldn't. Nothing had been what it seemed in Galilee. Kelsey thought of his hand on her and her skin crawled.

Suddenly she had a much worse thought. "You were the only person who knew I was going to have Billy's car searched. By the time I got there and you had the car, all it had in it was some stranger's blood. Planted so I'd think—"

He shook his head. "Not by me. I swear, Kelsey."

"But if you called someone as soon as you knew . . ."

He shook his head again. Kelsey looked at him and felt herself wanting to believe him, which sickened her. "Did they tell you to romance the special prosecutor, or was that your own idea?" She had the terrible feeling her voice sounded pitiful.

Peter stepped back as if he'd been hit. "Kelsey, you can't think—"

That was exactly right. She couldn't. Apparently thinking hadn't been her strong suit all along. Suddenly she just wanted away. She didn't want to argue, she didn't want to scream at him, she just wanted to pretend he'd never existed.

"Kelsey."

"No."

He reached for her again and she turned and ran, shaking her head as if she could shake memory out of it. When she heard him following, she screamed, "No!" again and ran faster. She stumbled around the corner of the courthouse, wanting just to keep running. Almost by accident she found her car, fell into it, and slammed the door. In the narrow confines of the car she pounded both hands on the steering wheel until her arms were tired and she couldn't see for the tears.

The sun was still barely up, but it couldn't penetrate the insulation of cold air that covered the ground to a height, Kelsey imagined, as tall as the pine trees. In the late afternoon the light seemed three shades less than white. In that strange filtered light the landscape was dim, aging like an old photograph. The sun was low, threatened by the tips of the reaching trees.

Kelsey ran. In her sweatsuit, with an extra nylon jacket, she was warm enough as long as she ran fast, but the air she kept pulling into her lungs was icy. The ground beside the country road was almost as hard as the pavement. She felt it all the way up into her hips every time her foot hit that lifeless dirt, but still she ran.

When she'd reached her motel room, the phone had been ringing. Kelsey had stayed there only long enough to change, then had driven away toward the back roads near the Beaumont house. She had parked off the road near the site of one of the fires she'd investigated and begun running. At first she'd been stiff after her day in court. The first mile had been hard as slogging through wet concrete, fighting her body. Her mind had been the same way: stiff with unwillingness to give up its presumptions.

Her search of Billy's car had been both useless and anticipated. Someone—the sheriff, Peter, someone else in the loop—had deliberately kept from her the report that proved there'd been no blood in Billy's car in the days after the murder. But there had been when Kelsey had searched it a month later. That could have been accident—Billy or a passenger had cut himself between the first search and Kelsey's. Kid with a nosebleed. But Kelsey couldn't believe in accidents, not in Defiance County.

But why would someone keep from her evidence that tended to prove Billy innocent, when the whole town was rooting for him to be cleared? Obviously not everyone. More than one force was at work behind the scenes in Galilee. Someone had tried to frame Billy. Who would do that but someone with what Kelsey had called a vigilante complex? If Peter had been convinced Billy had killed Lorrie, the woman Peter "could have been" in love with, would Peter have planted the evidence that would help convict Billy?

Mrs. Beaumont would. Maybe someone had been acting on her orders, covering up the first report and planting blood in Billy's car. But that still left Peter involved, because he had been the only person to whom Kelsey'd announced her intention of searching the car.

She tried to think if she'd accomplished anything that day in court, before her case had been twisted away from her. Her examination of Morgan Fletcher had been a battle—conducted cordially and with mutual respect, but a battle nevertheless. Morgan had been determined that Kelsey would extract nothing from him that would harm his brother. Kelsey had been equally determined that Morgan play his part as a witness despite his personal involvement, and she thought she had gotten as much as she could have hoped for.

But there was something more. She remembered Morgan during her first days in town, how he had apparently given her everything he could, in supplies and space and painful memories. Even though she'd known his perspective, she hadn't been able to help feeling she could trust him. That feeling persisted, even after today's duel. She remembered Morgan's eyes on her, that one prideful flash she had interpreted as his silent congratulations to her on having asked the smart question.

Morgan was still trying to tell her something. Something that hadn't come out in court at all.

Her ankle almost twisted as her foot came down hard on a rock, and her memory picture of Morgan fractured like a dropped mirror. How could she imagine she understood anyone? She'd drawn so close to one person here she'd thought she knew him so well it made her understand herself better, and what a stupid illusion that had proved. Kelsey felt at her core a cold loneliness that the warmth generated by her pumping legs couldn't reach. A void where she felt not only the loss of love but the nibbling away of her self-image. She had reached the age of thirty thinking herself a cool career woman, then she'd come to Galilee and found herself so apparently needy that she'd lost her sense.

But she wasn't going to think about Peter Stiller. Not now, and not later when the trial was over.

In pushing him away, she felt the foreignness of Galilee reassert itself. For a brief, heady time she'd thought she knew the town well: wisecracking Florence and her pals at the Busy Bee, the hard workers of the town fearful for their jobs, the Beaumonts and Fletchers straining to turn new money to old before another generation passed, and Alice Beaumont, who insisted on owning it all like a Monopoly board. But now they had all regained their air of strangeness.

She was finally in her rhythm, where her mind worked independently of her body. As her legs moved, she was barely aware of the whisper of fabric across her thighs, lubricated by her sweat. When she reached this point, she could run for miles. But Kelsey knew how quickly night fell here. In five more minutes it would be dusk; ten minutes after that, deep night. It was time to turn back. Time to prepare for the next day of trial.

Kelsey didn't like calling Mrs. Beaumont as a witness, but she'd known she would have to. The matriarch was one of the few people to have seen most of the arguments between Billy Fletcher and Ronald Blystone. Morgan had made the arguments sound too casual. Kelsey needed better than that. She had considered calling Katherine for this purpose. Of all the family, Katherine seemed the least passionately engaged in the business fights. Katherine would be the one most likely to give an objective account of the disagreements between Billy and the dead man. But a trial lawyer doesn't want objectivity.

Even before Kelsey finished announcing her name, Alice Beaumont came through the doors at the back of the courtroom, with a long stride like a tiger released from too confining a cage. Her chin was up. She wore a black dress with a cluster of lace at her throat, and simple pearls. Kelsey had seen her that morning enter the courthouse wearing a full-length mink, but the coat now lay across Katherine's lap. It was hard to say whether Mrs. Beaumont had dressed up for her court appearance. She looked very much herself. Her face was pale except for dark red lips set in a tight line and thin black eyebrows that had been applied by God, not an eyebrow pencil.

Kelsey still felt a trace of the sympathy she'd felt for Mrs. Beaumont at the beginning of trial. But this was also the woman who had left Kelsey with no respect for her employer and little trust for institutions she had once admired. Mrs. Beaumont had done that for Kelsey entirely incidentally, in pursuit of the bigger fish of the moment. And thought she was due gratitude in return. Kelsey understood exactly how the citizens of Galilee felt about Alice Beaumont.

That was why Kelsey had been reluctant to call her as a witness. She realized the woman's great potential to alienate the jury. But Mrs. Beaumont wasn't only a witness in the case, she was the last victim left grieving. Kelsey had to use her.

Mrs. Beaumont stopped in front of Billy Fletcher and stared down at him. Billy looked up without flinching. Billy understood that his future was ruined no matter how the trial came out. He had nothing more to fear from Mrs. Beaumont. He stared at her flatly, like a man expected to confess but who instead had grievances of his own to blurt out.

Judge Saunders interrupted the staring match. "Take your seat, Mrs. Beaumont. You understand you've already been sworn in?"

"Yes," Mrs. Beaumont said shortly. She settled herself into the witness chair and gave the jurors a searching look. Mrs. Beaumont was still offended, Kelsey knew, by being excluded from the courtroom until her testimony. Kelsey wanted to wipe that aggressive look off her witness's face as quickly as possible. It would do her case no good if it looked as if all this were an exercise in achieving Alice Beaumont's vengeance against Billy Fletcher.

"Mrs. Beaumont, I want to ask you about the events of October twenty-first of last year. Where were you then?"

"I was at home in my bed. I had a very miserable case of the flu."

"Who else was in your house that day?"

"Well, my sister Goldie, and Helena. And of course my daughter Lorrie and her husband and daughter were staying with me. I'm not sure who else."

"You weren't in condition to observe much that day?"

"No, miss, I wasn't. I'd had about three kinds of medicine,

and fever, and I hadn't had anything to eat but broth for two or three days. I couldn't get up to go to the bathroom by myself."

"Did you know Billy Fletcher had been in your house that morning?"

"No."

"In fact, did you ever go downstairs that whole day of October twenty-first?"

"No. Goldie came back to sit with me, all that day and night, until Katherine could come back. I asked them to bring the baby to me, because I'd heard her crying. They didn't tell me about the baby that day. I knew something had happened to Lorrie, because she didn't come to see me, but nobody told me about the baby. I thought they were just keeping her away so she wouldn't catch my flu."

Mrs. Beaumont was holding a handkerchief. As she talked about her granddaughter, she clutched it harder. Her hand above the rail of the witness stand whitened as she talked. The round bone in her wrist grew prominent. The skin there was white and spotted, as if that were where age had gathered in her body.

Mrs. Beaumont's tone had changed in the few minutes since she'd sat down. She no longer stared at anyone. She looked down into her thoughts of the past, or her future. Kelsey gently led her back further.

"What relation is Billy Fletcher to your family, Mrs. Beaumont?"

"He's my son-in-law Morgan's brother. And he was the manager of my factory."

The past tense stood out prominently in this recital of Billy Fletcher's position in the world.

"Was he a good manager?"

Mrs. Beaumont's eyes flashed as if she would say something harsh, but what she said was, "Yes. I'd kept him longer than anyone else."

"What made him a good manager?"

"It wasn't brains, I'll tell you that. Billy wasn't nearly as bright as some of the geniuses I'd had to fire. But he knew his way around the factory better than I did, and I built the place. Billy practically grew up there."

"So Smoothskins is a sort of family business, isn't it? Are you the sole owner?"

"No. My late husband and I gave shares to each of our daughters. I kept the majority, though."

"Even the baby was a part owner, wasn't she?"

"Yes." Mrs. Beaumont had to stop to swallow, though the memory made her smile. "I gave Taylor a few shares when she was born."

Kelsey had followed that paper trail. The baby had been an heiress. If she had lived, with her shares and those inherited from her mother, baby Taylor would have owned the largest share of Smoothskins stock, except for her grandmother.

"Was your daughter Lorrie active in the management of the company?"

"No. She never seemed to care much about it one way or the other, at least until she married Ronald."

"So Ronald expressed opinions about the direction the company should take?"

"Express? Yes. Ronald wasn't shy."

"What sort of suggestions did he make?"

"Big ones," Mrs. Beaumont said with a small laugh mixing annoyance and admiration. "One week he'd say we should sell out, then the next time he'd say we should expand but we should start by moving the manufacturing plant to Mexico. Or Hong Kong." She shook her head as if she thought the idea bizarre. "Just leave that big old factory here standing empty and going to rust."

"You sound as if you didn't think much of Ronald's ideas, Mrs. Beaumont."

"Oh, he made sense sometimes. He had a degree in economics, you know. He taught college."

"So you listened to what he said."

"I don't think I could have stopped him from talking."

But Alice Beaumont said it with a chuckle hidden in her voice. With a quick glance Kelsey noticed the jurors staring at her witness. Kelsey was watching Mrs. Beaumont with the same almost horrified curiosity. She sensed that Alice Beaumont had never taken seriously her son-in-law's proposals, that she had encouraged him to talk only for her amusement—or the amusement of the effects he had on other people.

And there she still sat with a smugly contented face, a spoiled child pleased at causing an uproar. Didn't she realize even yet where her games had led? Didn't she feel any responsibility for her daughter's death?

In a hollow voice, Kelsey asked, "When Ronald talked, did you sometimes act as if he'd convinced you of the wisest course of action to take regarding the Smoothskins factory?"

"Well, as I said, he *did* make sense a lot of the time. He certainly knew more about economics than any of the rest of us."

"Was Billy Fletcher present sometimes when Ronald Blystone was making these arguments to you?"

"Oh, yes."

"Did Billy seem to take him seriously?"

"Oh, yes. Ronald would make Billy furious. They'd have almost screaming fights. Well, Billy screaming. Ronald would just sit back with this little smile, or this perplexed look like Billy spoke some brand of childishness Ronald couldn't follow. That, of course, would make Billy even madder."

"How do you know he was mad?"

"He'd yell, like I said. His face would get red as a brick, he'd clench his fist."

"Did you ever see Billy Fletcher hit anyone?"

"No, I never did. Once he did break one of my end tables, slamming his fist down on it. My fault, I guess, for letting them argue in a room with such flimsy furniture."

Kelsey hated the lightness of her witness's tone. "Mrs. Beaumont, did you stop these arguments?"

"I told them to settle down, not to make such a fuss, that it wasn't up to either of them anyway."

"Did you ever tell Billy, 'Don't worry, I'd never shut down the factory here in Galilee'?"

"No," Mrs. Beaumont said firmly, as if this suggestion had been put to her before. "I did have to think about the future. That business is almost my only source of income. And it's my family's future."

Mrs. Beaumont blinked. Kelsey sat silent, letting the realization settle on the older woman that when she said "my family" she was talking about a greatly diminished entity. The future she had planned for in fact had a foreseeable end, not far ahead in the dimness. Mrs. Beaumont put the handkerchief to her mouth.

"Did your daughter Lorrie join in these arguments?"

"Yes, some—" Mrs. Beaumont cleared her throat. Her eyes were reddening without tears appearing. "Sometimes. But she wasn't consistent like the others. You couldn't ever tell which side Lorrie would come down on."

Kelsey had heard this from others. Lorrie had been like her mother, a flirt, using ideas to tease. She wouldn't have played for her mother's favor as obviously as the others—and perversely had won that favor easily. The note of affection in Alice Beaumont's voice when she spoke of her younger daughter was obvious.

"What about the rest of the family?"

Alice mused. "Katherine, never. Even when I'd press her for what she thought, she'd say, 'Whatever you want, Mama.' Katherine—" Mrs. Beaumont stopped herself, shooting a sharp glance at Kelsey as if she were intruding.

No, Katherine wouldn't be drawn into her mother's game. As she'd told Kelsey, Katherine had long ago given up trying to get between her mother and Lorrie. Kelsey could imagine Katherine just staring back placidly in response to her mother's sly questioning. Had it been a hard lesson, had Katherine fallen into the trap early on, trying to say what would please her mother and finding that only dispute pleased Alice Beaumont?

"What about your son-in-law, Mrs. Beaumont? I imagine Morgan took his brother's side?" Kelsey was no longer following the careful story line of Billy versus Ronald. She was asking the questions she thought she'd want answered if she'd been observing this family from the outside for years but had never gotten inside. From the way the jurors' attention remained fastened on Alice Beaumont, Kelsey thought she was doing the right thing.

"Usually he did, yes," Mrs. Beaumont answered. "That was the only time Ronald got as good as he gave, when Morgan would light into him. Not yelling like Billy. Morgan was so quiet and so—insinuating. It was like watching a little trial in my living room. Ronald knew to sit up straight and keep his wits about him when Morgan spoke up."

Kelsey had heard this before. In her witness's recital of praise for the district attorney, only one word had caught Kelsey's attention. "Usually?" she repeated. "Usually Morgan would take up for Billy?" She glanced aside. Billy sat with his fist in front of his mouth, staring. His expression was no longer deadened as he watched his boss testify. Behind him, his brother sat straight but at ease. Morgan's face was interested but uninvolved, the way a good lawyer's is during trial. Kelsey hadn't seen him once lean forward to whisper to Clyde Wolverton.

"Yes, usually," Mrs. Beaumont said, frowning in memory. "Just lately, the last I don't know how long—their last two or three visits?—anyway, Morgan had stopped joining in. Like the arguments bored him. Once he even said, 'Maybe he's right,' about what Ronald was saying."

Kelsey heard the stirrings of disbelief among the spectators. Obviously the citizens of Galilee had expected their elected district attorney to take up for them not only in the courtroom but in the private confines of his family. Maybe that was part of the reason for Morgan's electoral successes. He was meant to be Galilee's emissary to the Beaumont house; like his brother.

Kelsey asked, "Did Morgan's withdrawal from the debates put a stop to the arguments between Billy and Ronald?"

"Oh, no." Mrs. Beaumont sounded surprised at the suggestion. "If anything, that made it worse. Made Billy sound more desperate."

"Was there a time limit to this ongoing discussion about what was to be done with the factory? Did a decision have to be made soon?"

"No," Mrs. Beaumont said firmly. She had that expression on her face again, the slight movement around her mouth that wanted to rise into a sly smile. She was like a child hiding a cookie behind her back. The decision on the factory's fate would never have been made, Mrs. Beaumont's face said clearly; not as long as she could keep them dancing attendance on her, paying her court with their supplications. That game could have gone on indefinitely. Soon it could have been blended into the changing-the-will game; the which-heir-loves-me-best-this-week game.

Kelsey stared at her and let the jury do the same. She decided to do it now.

"May I approach the witness, Your Honor?"

Judge Saunders nodded.

Kelsey took with her the file folder she'd prepared. She held it in her right hand and tapped it against her left palm as she slowly approached Alice Beaumont. Inevitably the woman's eyes attached to the thin file folder. Kelsey barely cracked it to draw out the first picture.

"Can you identify this?"

Mrs. Beaumont took the four-by-six photo from her. "This is Ronald."

"Your son-in-law Ronald Blystone?"

"Yes."

"Mark it, please," Kelsey said to the court reporter sitting close by at her stenography machine. As the court reporter put a small sticker on the picture identifying it as a State's exhibit, Kelsey looked at the man in the photo again. Ronald Blystone had been in his midthirties. The photo was a professional full-face study, though Ronald still looked casual in the picture. He had a wide forehead made wider by his dark hair drawing back from the temples. A straight, thin nose led the eye down to a mouth like Mrs. Beaumont's, one that held a secret. His eyes gave the same knowing, almost smiling impression. Even though Ronald held a rather formal pose, his cheeks were stubbled. He looked like a man determined not to put himself out for anyone.

"And this one?" Kelsey asked, handing her witness an eight-by-ten color photo she'd removed from a frame in Mrs. Beaumont's bedroom.

"That's Lorrie. My daughter Lorrie."

Kelsey reached for the photo, but Mrs. Beaumont held on to it. Mrs. Beaumont's voice had been strong when she identified the picture, but her mouth was squeezed small, no longer pleased with itself. The photograph had been professionally taken but was a lucky shot. Lorrie appeared to have ruined the photographer's careful preparations by moving her head just slightly. She was barely starting to smile spontaneously as if just before the picture was snapped, someone Lorrie was delighted to see had stepped into the room behind the photographer. It was obvious why her mother had kept it near her. Anyone would have wanted that delighted expression of Lorrie's turned in her direction.

Lorrie was casually beautiful in the picture. A girl with honey-colored hair, full cheeks, white teeth, and wide blue eyes, her freshness undiminished by life. Even in repose she seemed to be lunging forward, looking for what came next.

The picture began to flutter. When Kelsey pulled it gently out of Mrs. Beaumont's grasp, the witness put her hands together, but she couldn't stop their shaking. Kelsey handed the picture to the court reporter and pulled another from her folder. She handed it to Mrs. Beaumont without a word.

"This is one of their wedding pictures. Obviously," Mrs. Beaumont added, trying to strike a light note, but her voice wouldn't support her. Her eyes were glistening.

A conventional wedding photo of the couple cutting the cake, the photographer would probably again have culled it because instead of beaming carefree smiles Lorrie and Ronald were glancing askance at each other, privately ridiculing the public ceremony. Lorrie was getting a good laugh out of the occasion, but Ronald had his knowing smirk. Kelsey had chosen it out of many choices.

"And this?"

"Oh, my." A genuine laugh was surprised out of Mrs. Beaumont. "That's the three of us, one time when I went to visit them in Dallas. Who took this? It was a picnic, some company picnic for the insurance office where Lorrie worked. Ronald wanted to skip it and go some place fancy for lunch. So did I, really. How many years had it been since I'd sat on the grass? But Lorrie insisted we go, and it turned out—turned out nice."

The picture was nice, too. The three of them sat on a quilt, Ronald to the side, one knee up, a hand holding a glass of white wine resting on the knee. What Kelsey liked about the picture was the mother and daughter. Lorrie was smiling into the camera, easily, as if a smile had just happened to be the expression she was wearing when she'd turned toward the camera. Beside her, her mother was smiling, too, but not at the camera, at her daughter, leaning toward her, putting her hand on Lorrie's arm, like a child trying to get her mother's attention. Lorrie just beamed placidly for the camera.

Mrs. Beaumont seemed to be studying what the picture revealed, too, but she let Kelsey take it without clinging. Kelsey busied herself with the court reporter for a few moments, letting Mrs. Beaumont remain the unoccupied center of attention. Mrs. Beaumont didn't seem to be aware of her audience. She put her hand to her mouth, jerked it away as if she would reach for one of the pictures again, then stopped. Mrs. Beaumont looked much older than when she'd taken the witness stand; not as if she'd spent more years on earth, but as if she were closer to the end of her life. The photographs made her an old woman, just as the pictures would grow older themselves, much studied because they would never be replaced by newer ones.

Mrs. Beaumont had completely lost her self-satisfied insouciance. Kelsey had wanted to remind her with the pictures what her game-playing had accomplished. But Mrs. Beaumont didn't look guilty, she looked bereft. Her shoulders had drawn inward. She looked cold, with no one to offer her a wrap.

This was Kelsey's other purpose in having Mrs. Beaumont identify the photos of her dead relatives. The prosecution always required this in a murder case—having a surviving victim show off her grief in public. Morgan hadn't been good enough, he hadn't given any sense of the lives lost forever. Kelsey needed to show the jury the suffering caused by the murders, the suffering that would go on until at least one more death. From Mrs. Beaumont's shriveled expression, it was clear Kelsey had succeeded admirably. She felt ashamed. But the dirty work was far from over.

"I'd like you to identify this one, please, Mrs. Beaumont," Kelsey began, but Clyde Wolverton interrupted her by rising to his feet.

"This is repetitious, Your Honor," he said respectfully. "The witness has identified sufficient photos for the State's purposes."

"This is something fresh," Kelsey said.

"Overruled," Judge Saunders said quietly. Kelsey was already handing the next photo to Mrs. Beaumont. She would have no matter what the judge had ruled.

Mrs. Beaumont smiled. Then memory twisted the smile and squeezed a tear out of her eye. Mrs. Beaumont turned the picture as if she would display it to the jury proudly or as if she couldn't bear to look at it herself. "This is—" She had to stop. She looked at the picture again and couldn't help smiling again, the saddest smile anyone in the courtroom had ever seen. Tears were welling out of Alice Beaumont's eyes now. She took a deep breath, giving her voice strength. "This is Taylor. Lorrie's daughter. My grandchild."

It was just a baby picture. Kelsey had looked for a recent one, in which the baby might have displayed more personality, but instead had seized on this one taken when Taylor had been about four months old. She wore a yellow sundress that left her shoulders bare, and someone had put a silly hat on her in a vain attempt to disguise her baldness. The baby lay on her back, not focusing on the camera. Her mouth was open in a little *o*, perhaps surprise, perhaps the beginning of a yawn. She wasn't particularly pretty and her expression didn't display incipient genius. Nothing in the picture would set off a burst of ancestral pride. What the baby mostly looked was helpless.

Kelsey had Mrs. Beaumont identify two more photos, but she began to hurry. Mrs. Beaumont was crying steadily. She wasn't making a display of it, in fact the sight of her grief was more wrenching because of Mrs. Beaumont's obvious efforts to keep it in check. She had long made up for her knowing glances during her earlier testimony. She had suffered enough. Kelsey handed her the last picture.

"Oh, not this one." Mrs. Beaumont's tears stopped in surprise. "Why would you—"

"Please identify the people, Mrs. Beaumont," Kelsey said evenly.

Mrs. Beaumont put the picture down on the railing in front of her and didn't look at it again. "It's Lorrie and Ronald and Taylor."

All eyes were on that mystery picture as Kelsey handed it to the court reporter, who glanced up at her sharply and marked the picture with a sticker. That was the one they were waiting for, State's exhibit number twelve. Kelsey offered the pictures into evidence and handed them to her opponent. While the jury watched, Wolverton flipped quickly through the short stack to the last photo. He looked up at Kelsey distastefully. Billy leaned over to look at the picture, then quickly turned away.

"Objections?" Judge Saunders did a good job of keeping her voice unconcerned, but she already had her hand out, waiting for the pictures to be handed to her.

"One, Your Honor." Wolverton came quickly forward and handed the pictures to the judge. "To State's exhibit twelve. I believe the basis for my objection is obvious."

Judge Saunders was studying the picture. She didn't display the squeamishness the other people who'd viewed the picture had shown. She kept looking at the picture as she said, "Make it more obvious, Mr. Wolverton."

"Well, the picture is—it's medical in nature, Your Honor. It makes the people in it look—injured."

"Injured?" Linda Saunders looked up at him. The judge would probably have awarded this contest to the defense lawyer, but he had put her off badly with the wording of his objection. "Try again, Mr. Wolverton," she said coldly.

He pleaded quietly, "It's unnecessary, Your Honor. They are all identified in other pictures. This one—"

Kelsey interrupted his stammering. "Part of my burden of proof is to identify the victims as they're named in the indictment, Your Honor. This does that. And of course I also have to prove that the victims were human beings, the definition of which is—"

"I'm familiar with the definition, Ms. Thatch. The objection is overruled." The judge waved the lawyers away.

"May I—," Kelsey began to ask, but the judge said yes before Kelsey could finish the question. She handed the short stack of photographs to the jurors. "I pass the witness."

Clyde Wolverton wasn't dumb enough to fall for that one. He could see where the jurors' attention was riveted. The ones in back were leaning forward to look over the shoulders of the jurors who had the pictures. Clyde Wolverton just watched them, soberly.

It was interesting to watch the reactions of the jurors when they got to glimpse State's exhibit twelve. Most of the men turned away from it after a glance, although the youngest man on the jury, a married man with two children, studied the photo rather critically, then smiled. Some of the women smiled, too. Some of them just stared, as if lost in memory.

Exhibit twelve was a small family portrait, taken with an instant camera in the delivery room. The light was intense. Lorrie lay on the table, leaning forward to see her newborn baby. Ronald was holding Taylor. For once Ronald had lost his knowing expression. He looked enormously weary, much more so than his wife, who had just given birth. Ronald's expression as he looked at his baby was mostly stunned—and nervous. The baby's mouth was open and her eyes closed in a screech. Lorrie's beaming smile held nothing but joy and pride.

It was the only picture that showed the family together, as they had been that fatal morning. It fulfilled Kelsey's burden of proving that the victims were human, which by legal definition meant they had been born and were alive. Probably no one in Texas had ever proven this quite so definitively.

Kelsey had chosen this picture for yet another reason. Clyde Wolverton had wanted to keep the picture out for that same reason, though he hadn't been able to articulate his objection. The picture showed the Blystone family captured in the midst of life—at life's beginning, with what should have been long lives ahead of them.

The picture showed something more. A sheet had been pulled discreetly across Lorrie's body, but the baby was naked. The baby had been quickly cleaned before the picture was taken, but still carried evident traces of what showed on the sheet as well: her mother's blood.

12

As Kelsey turned away from the jury to take her seat, she caught a glimpse of her audience. The spectator seats of the large courtroom had filled to capacity. Citizens of Galilee were packed in shoulder to shoulder, and a dozen more stood in the back. Kelsey hadn't been aware of the crowd because they had sat so silently during Mrs. Beaumont's testimony.

It was an intimidating mob. In the silence while the jurors studied the pictures, many of the spectators turned toward Kelsey. Some expressions were hostile, but most merely intense with curiosity and a muted horror, as if they might ask, *Why are you doing this?* In reply, Kelsey could ask them, *Why are you watching?*

The only open space in the crowd was around Katherine Fletcher. People gave her space on both sides, so she stood out as if in a spotlight. Katherine was also set apart, again, by the relative formality of her appearance. She wore a pale blue blouse with a scoop collar, severe in its simplicity, and a black suit jacket. Her clothes made her look as if she'd dressed to perform some official function. Katherine didn't look at Kelsey, she was watching her mother on the witness stand. Katherine wasn't crying along with her mother. She wore a judgmental expression, but vacantly, as if that had been the last expression on her face when her mind had fled elsewhere. Katherine's eyes were empty. She was lost in time.

Kelsey looked again at her witness, whom she'd left in reduced circumstances. Mrs. Beaumont no longer looked the proud matriarch. The witness chair seemed to have grown larger around her. Her appearance made Kelsey feel guilty, but she wanted to answer, *What did you expect?* Mrs. Beaumont was the reason for Kelsey's being here. She had ordered Kelsey delivered like a household appliance. As always in her life, Mrs. Beaumont had thought herself in command. She had gotten the perfect person: one who would take her orders and who would convict Billy Fletcher of murder.

Mrs. Beaumont hadn't realized the contradictory nature of her desires. To win a murder case, one as weak as this one, a prosecutor couldn't let the survivors off the hook. You had to sway the jury emotionally. It was one of the things that had driven Kelsey out of criminal law. She could deal with the gory pictures and the excruciating testimony. It was this ceremonial offering of the survivor—the insistence that the victim be stripped bare in public—that had driven Kelsey away.

But when she had to do it again, she had. Mrs. Beaumont hadn't known when she'd sent for her special prosecutor that she'd also ordered up her own public devastation.

Clyde Wolverton cleared his throat. "Mrs. Beaumont, I'm sorry for your loss," he said with practiced sincerity.

Mrs. Beaumont didn't acknowledge that he had spoken. Her chin came up. If he was very smart, that had been Wolverton's purpose with his offering of sympathy. Mrs. Beaumont no longer looked like a victim.

"Mrs. Beaumont, I just have one question for you. Did Lorrie and Ronald have a happy marriage?"

"Yes," the witness answered without a pause for thought.

The defense lawyer had lied about having only one question. "Constantly?" he pressed.

Again Mrs. Beaumont didn't hesitate, though her answer was backtracking. "Of course they had disagreements sometimes. It would have been a very dull marriage if they'd had nothing but the same thoughts."

"Disagreements, of course. So they argued sometimes."

Mrs. Beaumont gave Wolverton a piercing look. Don't let him think he was smart enough to lead her down the garden path. But she said, "I suppose they argued. I don't remember. Lorrie generally took his side when the talk was about what to do with Smoothskins."

"But, Mrs. Beaumont, you said yourself there was no telling where Lorrie would come down in that argument on any given day."

"Well, no. But she—she didn't really argue. She would just make observations."

"It must have been annoying to her husband that he couldn't count on her support in these family discussions."

"Object to the sidebar remark," Kelsey said quickly. Clyde Wolverton rose beside her, taller than Kelsey even though he bent forward obsequiously, hands clasped together at his chest. "I meant that as a question, Your Honor. Let me rephrase it that way."

Judge Saunders didn't reply. In fact she wouldn't glance at the defense lawyer. Kelsey saw that she had been wrong about something. The judge clearly favored the defense in this case, but not the defense lawyer. Linda Saunders's loyalty was to the man sitting behind Wolverton and Billy. Kelsey remained convinced that the judge would do what she could for Morgan, and that meant helping Morgan's brother by ruling in Wolverton's favor most of the time. But it was equally clear Judge Saunders had little regard for the defense lawyer.

Odd. Clyde Wolverton must have had Morgan Fletcher's respect. But the judge, Morgan's—what? lover? friend?—didn't share that opinion. Kelsey paid close attention as the defense lawyer questioned her witness. "Didn't Ronald get angry at his wife when she failed to take his side during these family discussions?"

"I don't know," Mrs. Beaumont said firmly. "I didn't go and listen at their bedroom door."

"You didn't have to," Wolverton said, and before Kelsey could rise, he continued, "if their arguments were public. Were they?"

"Nothing that amounted to much," the witness sniffed.

"Mrs. Beaumont. Did Lorrie and Ronald ever argue in front of you?"

The matriarch hesitated for long seconds. Finally, "Yes," she said quietly.

She had fought so hard to avoid saying it that even that small syllable seemed to speak worlds. The defense lawyer sounded smug when he passed the witness.

"Did their arguments ever become physical?" Kelsey asked quickly.

"No."

Kelsey would have liked a moment to instruct her witness: *Don't give me that smug tone, as if you're still fighting with the defense. Let your answer ring out like simple truth.* Instead Mrs. Beaumont looked as if she were saying what she was damned well determined to say, without recourse to her memory at all.

"You never saw Ronald and Lorrie hit each other?"

"Certainly not."

"Break things, throw things at each other?"

"No."

"Did you ever hear either of them threaten to hurt the other physically?"

"No, never."

Unsatisfied, but hoping she'd put a stop to this defense insinuation, Kelsey passed the witness back. This time the defense lawyer really did have only one question.

"But you weren't awake during much of Lorrie and Ronald's last visit to your home, were you, Mrs. Beaumont?"

The witness looked confused. Her mouth opened quickly but stayed that way. Finally she said, as if trying to excuse herself for not having been all-seeing, "I was very sick."

"Yes, Mrs. Beaumont, thank you. No more questions."

Kelsey had no more either. Mrs. Beaumont stood quickly, her dignity restored. This time she didn't glance at Billy or at Morgan as she walked away. Kelsey heard the sound of her heels stop, and she turned to see that Mrs. Beaumont had made her way into the pew and plumped herself down beside her daughter. She glared back defiantly at Kelsey, who made no move to have her excluded again. She was done with Alice Beaumont.

Lead off with your second-best witness and close with your strongest one. That's what Kelsey had been taught in the Houston district attorney's office. But she didn't have a strongest witness. She had led off with Morgan Fletcher of necessity, to set the scene of the murders, then followed up with Mrs. Beaumont because Morgan hadn't been vivid enough. Maybe she should have saved Mrs. Beaumont for the end. The old woman's—Kelsey had turned her old on the stand—grief over her lost daughter and granddaughter was the strongest emotion Kelsey could display to this jury. Maybe she should call Katherine as a witness after all. But Katherine had never shown Kelsey any sense of loss over her sister's death. Who mourned for Lorry Blystone? Who in this town that had cared so intensely about the outcome of the Beaumont family quarrels could Kelsey put on the stand to weep over the dead woman and the missing child? Kelsey couldn't think of anyone.

She called two police officers and the police photographer to testify to the murder scene and identify the photographs. She called Sheriff Early to testify about the search for the kidnapped baby.

"How far did your search extend, Sheriff?"

"Well, nationwide. We appealed for leads to the whole country, and we got calls from all over. It was on every national newscast for days."

"But around here, Sheriff. How far did you search the area around Galilee?"

The creased old Sheriff stared at her as if she were an idiot. "Miss, there are five thousand square miles of pine forest around us. Not to mention two major rivers and I don't know how many lakes. We had fine volunteers, but we couldn't have searched every foot of this area if we'd had everybody in America helping us."

Kelsey had wanted that stated clearly in the courtroom: just because the baby hadn't been found by the intense search didn't mean she wasn't out there.

Kelsey stared at the sheriff, wanting to ask him while he was under oath if he had kept from her the report showing no traces of blood in Billy Fletcher's car, or if he knew who had. But it wouldn't do her case any good. Kelsey passed.

Clyde Wolverton asked no questions of the sheriff.

Her last police witness of the day was Joe Pointer, who had tested the hands of the victims for gunpowder residue. "Did you find any residue on Lorrie Blystone's hands?"

Officer Pointer was rather delicate-looking for a cop. He was thin, with a shiny forehead that his lank blond hair fell across, and an Adam's apple that moved prominently before he spoke. "No, ma'am."

"Meaning what, Officer Pointer?"

"To me it meant that the subject had not fired a gun since the last time she'd washed her hands."

Kelsey didn't like this talk of "subjects." She'd instructed the witness before trial not to do it, but he couldn't or wouldn't shake his jargon. Kelsey made a point by contrast of being on a first-name basis with the victims.

"What about Lorrie's husband, Ronald?"

"That subject's right hand did show evidence of stippling."

"Stippling?"

"Gunpowder residue imbedded in his skin."

The crowd reacted some, though this couldn't have been news to many of them. Kelsey sounded a little surprised herself when she asked, "Does that mean Ronald *had* fired a gun?"

"No necessarily, ma'am. All the test tells us is that his hand was close to the gun when it was fired."

As in a struggle over a gun, for example, but that wasn't the image Kelsey wanted to convey. "Did you examine the wound to Ronald's head, as well, Officer Pointer?"

"Objection," Clyde Wolverton said, only half-rising. "This witness hasn't been qualified to give medical testimony."

"I'm not going to ask him to say anything that calls for him to make medical conclusions," Kelsey said coolly. Wolverton should have known that, should have known what Kelsey was going to ask next. Judge Saunders did. She ruled on the objection by not saying anything.

"Did you examine the head wound, Officer?"

"Yes, ma'am."

"What did you find?"

"I found traces of gunpowder around the wound."

"And what does that tell you?"

"That the gunshot that made that wound was fired very close to his head, almost in contact with it."

"Could the same gunshot have left the gunpowder residue on both Ronald Blystone's hand and his head?"

"Oh, yes."

"Could you demonstrate the position he would have been in for that to happen, Officer."

In the days before trial Kelsey had had Officer Pointer demonstrate this to her over and over, until he fell into the pose naturally. He did so now for the jury, even before Kelsey finished the question. The officer twisted his head to the right and down, his long neck bending. At the same time he threw up his left hand close to the left side of his head, the palm open, the fingers curving, as if to catch a softball.

Something else happened when Pointer assumed this position. Either the man was a natural actor or something about turning away and throwing up a hand defensively naturally made a man close his eyes and grimace. The officer moved so quickly and squinted so fearfully that for a moment people expected a shot to ring out. He looked helpless with his eyes closed and his thin-fingered hand offering pitifully inadequate protection. Kelsey let him hold the pose until he tired of it. After several seconds Pointer lowered his hands to his lap and blinked as if coming out of a trance.

"One more question, Officer. Did you examine the defendant's hands?" Kelsey turned and looked at Billy Fletcher and caught him resisting the temptation to look over his hands himself. His hands lay on the table in front of him. They almost trembled with Billy's concentration on keeping them immobile. The tension acknowledged the power of those accomplished hands. They loomed larger than life on the defense table.

Billy's face was stiff. His eyes looked sad, but the rigidity of his face projected anger. He refused to look at Kelsey.

"No, ma'am," said Officer Pointer. "I didn't examine Mr. Fletcher's hands. He wasn't arrested until two days after the murders, there wouldn't have been any traces of gunpowder remaining."

"I pass the witness."

"May I approach the witness, Your Honor?" Clyde Wolverton asked respectfully. He, too, sat with his hands in his lap, his lanky body splayed out in front of him.

"Yes, sir."

The defense lawyer moved quickly once he had permission. Kelsey watched him suspiciously. Wolverton wasn't carrying anything, he had nothing to show the officer. Why did he need to approach him?

"You say the residue on Ronald's hand could have come from firing the gun?" Wolverton asked pleasantly.

"Yes, sir."

"And the presence of gunpowder around the head wound indicates closeness or even contact with the barrel of the gun when it was fired?"

"Yes, sir," the officer said patiently.

"May I see your hand, Officer?" As the witness brought his hand up, Wolverton continued, "You demonstrated how both these things might have occurred at once. May I offer another demonstration and you tell me if it's also a possibility? Imagine your hand holding a gun." The officer obligingly curled his fingers around an imaginary handle. Wolverton took Pointer's index finger and straightened it out to indicate a handgun's barrel. The officer's hand easily held the position, one all boys have used when playing cowboys or cops.

Wolverton gently moved the officer's hand until Pointer's index fingertip touched the side of his head. Satisfied with his human sculpture, Wolverton stepped away, leaving the officer demonstrating for the jury a man holding a gun against his own head.

"Bang," the defense lawyer said quietly.

As he turned back toward his table, Wolverton asked, "Wouldn't that produce the same effects you've testified about, Officer Pointer?"

Looking as if he were being coerced into giving the answer, by his own "gun" pointing at his head, Pointer stiffly said, "Yes, sir."

"Thank you, Officer. You may put your hand down."

But there was one major flaw to the theory of Ronald's having killed his wife and himself. Kelsey reminded the jury of that with her last witness of the day.

Over the last three months she had interviewed at least two dozen people who'd joined in the search for the missing baby, from Sheriff Early and the search coordinator Noreen Reynolds to teenage volunteers. She had chosen only one for her trial purposes, a middle-aged man with four children who'd taken time off from his factory job—Mrs. Beaumont had shut down the factory for a week after her granddaughter's disappearance—to spend sixteen-hour days for six days searching for the baby, then half-days for another week after that: an average amount of time, among the volunteers.

His name was Lewis Hanks. He didn't look like a factory worker, he looked like a farmer. In fact, he was both; he'd also interrupted his harvesting to join the search for Taylor. Hanks was so thin he looked like a man who lived on smoke instead of food. His knuckles were black with dirt so ground in they would never come clean. His face was deeply tanned, except a white band at the top of his forehead where he wore a cap when working. Wrinkles had scored his face the same way the farmer had scored the black soil all his life. His eyes were deep set and dark. Sometimes Kelsey would see a flash emerge from those eye sockets and realize Lewis Hanks would have scared hell out of her if she'd encountered him in the woods. But he was a slow-moving, soft-spoken man. He made her realize how thin a line there was between deep sorrow and meanness.

"First thing we did was search around the house. All around it. Moving fast. There were hundreds of us, and we must've covered ten thousand acres that first day. Not like Sherlock Holmes, you know, not scouring ever' inch of ground lookin' for clues. We were lookin' for a baby. Listenin' for her." He stopped abruptly, demonstrating how he had stopped repeatedly in the woods, his eyes moving back and forth, his breath still. "We were makin' lots of noise. We wanted her to hear us, if she could. We spread out, watchin' the ground, shufflin' our feet. I guess if there were any clues in there, we messed 'em up good. But we were lookin' for a live baby. We were thinkin' maybe somebody took her and abandoned her right away. If somebody was hidin' her, we wouldn't've found her. That's not how we were workin'. We were lookin' for a baby on the ground."

"How late did the search go on that night, Mr. Hanks?"

"I guess—I guess about eleven." His voice conveyed how it had hurt to give up. He swallowed and said, "Some people kept at it all night, but it's no use bein' in those woods at night. You got a flashlight or somethin' and you see that little thin beam goin' out into the dark, and it's like a fishin' line in th' ocean. You could walk right by somethin' the size of a baby and not even notice. But people were hopin' to hear somethin', I guess."

"What about the next day?" Kelsey asked softly.

"I was back out before sunup. My oldest boy, Will, came that day."

"Did you search the woods again?"

"Not those woods. Some people did, but Will and me joined the group goin' toward the highway. Police had been up and down the interstate to Houston all night, in cars, but we wanted to do better than that."

By the second day the character of the search had changed because police had identified Billy Fletcher as the prime suspect and knew the route he had taken out of town. The first day the search had been haphazard, with searchers spreading out in all directions, primarily right around the Beaumont house. Helena Parker's house in Galilee had been searched. Everyone in town, excepting Mrs. Beaumont and Aunt Goldie staying with her, had joined in the search that first night, before Billy returned from North Carolina. Morgan and Katherine had been among those out all night—not together, Kelsey had determined. Morgan and Katherine Fletcher didn't do anything together.

But by the second day the search coordinators were looking for a baby abandoned in haste along the highway from the Beaumont house to the Houston airport. The search changed.

"They'd take a bunch of us to one stretch of the highway and we'd spread out along the sides. Not too deep into the woods because we didn't figure he'd've gone too far." The former searcher watched Billy Fletcher as he said this. Hanks worked at the Smoothskins factory, Billy was his boss, but there was nothing deferential in Hanks's gaze. There was nothing overtly hostile, either: he didn't glare. But it was more than a look of curiosity. Hanks's black eyes were flat and hard. He stared as if he could see into Billy's soul. Billy couldn't help being riveted. His bright, broad face, which fell so easily into friendly smiles, grew pale. After a few seconds he shook his head.

Hanks continued to watch Billy, so levelly that Billy's lawyer squirmed, trying to think of an objection. But Lewis Hanks's intentions obviously had nothing to do with law. The man looked weary but implacable. He had not made peace with the failure of the search for the baby. If he ever found out what had happened to her, God help the person responsible.

"Besides, you couldn't go too far to the side of the interstate in most places, it was private property, fenced off. We'd search a little ways beyond the fences, but mostly we were tryin' to cover the whole length of the highway."

"Did you search in the same way you described before?" Kelsey asked.

"We were more careful the second day." Hanks's voice softened. "We had to look more closely and not count on hearin' her, because most of a day had passed by then. She was a baby who couldn't walk. We had to figure she'd had nothin' to drink. We didn't expect her to be conscious by then." Hanks cleared his throat. He looked up at the courtroom's ceiling. "I tried to stick close to Will because if he thought he saw somethin', I wanted to get there first."

Kelsey sat shrunken. She had to remember that she was supposed to ask a question next.

"Did you find anything?"

"No, nothin'. Not a baby blanket, not a scrap of cloth. I began to hope that we'd hear from town that the family'd gotten a call for ransom. That's what we were all hopin' for by the end of the second day. Because another night was beginnin'. And by then we knew how hopeless it was. That road goes over rivers and creeks. There were divers searchin' them, but—there'd been rains. The rivers were runnin' high and fast."

Only when the witness paused did Kelsey start him again with another question. At least two of the jurors were crying, one of them the young man with children. Lewis Hanks had led Kelsey past the point of endurance, but she couldn't stop. "What about the next day?"

"The next day more of the same, only more intense. We'd covered the whole fifty miles of highway the first day, but of course not very thoroughly. The next day they moved the different teams to different areas—new eyes—and did the same thing over again, but we'd spread farther out to the sides of the road. We'd go down the side roads, too, and into the woods there."

"Did you find anything?"

"Nothin'."

"What was the weather like, Mr. Hanks?"

"Hot durin' the day. We'd all end up strippin' off our jackets. Steamy in those woods. Like you could feel those pine needles compostin' under your feet. But it'd cool off fast when the sun went down."

"What about the next day of search? That would have been the fourth day, counting the day the baby disappeared."

Clyde Wolverton stood up. "Your Honor," was all he said, spreading his arms in appeal. Judge Saunders just looked at him. Her face was carefully expressionless, but the strain of neutrality showed. "You have an objection, Mr. Wolverton?" she said flatly.

"It's repetitious, Your Honor."

"It sounds to me as if she's asking about a different day."

"But calling for essentially the same testimony, over and over, Your Honor. She could break it down into hour by hour, or minute by minute, and it would be even more repetitious. More of this will be prejudicial without proving anything more."

The judge lifted her eyes from the defense lawyer, glanced briefly past him, and turned to Kelsey. "Could you ask for a summary now, Ms. Thatch?"

"Yes, Your Honor."

Lewis Hanks had sat unmoving through this exchange. He would tell the tale or not, it was all the same to him. Clearly, the days of the search were playing over and over in his head whether he talked about them or not. He was slumped in the witness chair, suppressed in failure and rage.

"Mr. Hanks, did you ever find the baby, Taylor Blystone?"

"No, ma'am. Not a sign of her."

"Did anyone find her?"

"No, ma'am."

"Was the search ever called off, Mr. Hanks?"

"No, ma'am, not officially. They never told us to stop comin', but after a week or so there was nothin' for us to do but the same things over again. People dropped out fast from that point on."

"Did you?"

"I kept givin' it some time every day for a week after that. I wanted to be sure. But it wasn't like those first few days, when we were all so frantic. After that, like I say, what we were mainly hopin' was that somebody had taken her, somebody was keepin' her somewhere. 'Cause after a week we knew we weren't gonna find a live baby in those woods."

Kelsey asked quietly, the question hurting her own heart, "Are there animals in those woods, Mr. Hanks?"

"No!"

The scream came from the audience. Alice Beaumont was standing in the center of the spectators. She had donned her mink coat, but it somehow made her look bedraggled, like a bag lady who'd found the coat on a trash heap. She screamed again at the witness stand.

Katherine was pulling on her hand. Mrs. Beaumont screamed equally at her. "No! She's not there! She's not out there!"

She fought her way to the aisle, people hastily moving their feet for her. The bailiff rose from his desk. Lewis Hanks sat as still as ever. He had emptied his emotional reservoir somewhere out in those days in the woods. He had none left to appreciate this drama. He just sat waiting.

Perhaps it was his stillness that turned Alice Beaumont away from him, as a target unworthy of her wrath. She stood spread-legged in the aisle, screamed, "No!" again, then turned and ran out of the courtroom.

Morgan Fletcher was looking at his wife. Katherine's head was down, but she must have felt his stare because she shook her head. Or maybe it was just a shake at the helplessness of the world in general. After a moment she rose and quietly followed her mother out of the court.

Silence prevailed for a long minute, the embarrassed silence that is the aftermath of fury and pity. Judge Saunders belatedly reached for her gavel, then just sat with her hand on it, because there was no noise to order subsided.

Kelsey had to recollect that the next words were hers. The rituals of trial felt useless. "I pass the witness."

Clyde Wolverton sat bemused for a moment as well. Then he gathered himself, smiled futilely at Lewis Hanks, and said, "Do you know whether Billy Fletcher joined in the search for the baby, Lewis?"

"I know he did," Hanks said, giving his boss that flat stare again. "I saw him a time or two."

"And he gave you and everyone else who worked at the factory all the time off you wanted to help look for the baby, didn't he?"

"I think that was Mrs. Beaumont's idea."

"Yes, but—" The defense lawyer lost his thread. He stared at the witness, his ideas breaking apart on that stony countenance, and finally said, "No more questions, Your Honor."

Kelsey just shook her head.

"We'll start up at nine o'clock in the morning," Judge Saunders said, and she fled the bench.

Kelsey was on the phone talking to Dr. Broom when the knock came on her motel-room door. It was a quick, peremptory rap, the knock someone makes just before turning the doorknob. The knock of someone who doesn't feel he needs to knock.

Kelsey hastily ended the call and hurried to open the door. She had to lower her gaze.

"How did you get to be such a monster?" Alice Beaumont said.

"Mrs. Beaumont, I tried to keep you out of the courtroom. I knew the testimony would be difficult for you to hear."

Mrs. Beaumont pushed past Kelsey, into the room. Her sister Goldie was standing behind her. She gave Kelsey a long-suffering smile and waited on the threshold for an invitation. Alice Beaumont grabbed Kelsey's arm.

"That mean-spirited, hateful talk with no purpose but to hurt me. You should—"

"Hurt you?" Kelsey asked, baffled.

"I know what you think of me! That I manipulated you and my own family and didn't care about this town, but you *know* I love that baby. For you to attack her like that—"

"Mrs. Beaumont, I don't know what you're talking about."

"Having that man say those horrible things about Taylor lying in the woods. I don't know what your purpose is, but those lies have no place—"

"Lies?" Kelsey remained lost in the older woman's rantings.

"Taylor is alive." Mrs. Beaumont's voice softened in wonderment that Kelsey really didn't seem to understand. Kelsey just gaped at her. "Of course she is. They didn't find her, did they? He has her. Don't you understand anything?"

"Who has her?"

"Billy, of course. Who did you charge with kidnapping her?"

"Billy," Kelsey acknowledged faintly.

"Yes! He has her. Why do you think he took her? Was he just crazy? No. Taylor's his job security. He knew I'd fire him and have him sent to prison after what he did to Lorrie. So he took Taylor, so I couldn't do anything to him. He's still got her somewhere. His job, that's the ransom he wants."

What a novel theory, Kelsey thought. It was the first good explanation she'd heard for why anyone would have taken the baby. But it created so many more questions. Where had Billy stashed her? With whom, while he was gone to North Carolina? His own family? Could they have kept such a terrible secret, while all their neighbors and friends were out searching the woods every day for the missing baby?

Had Helena Parker, Mrs. Beaumont's former maid, for some reason been Billy's confederate? She had never returned to the Beaumont house after that awful morning. Kelsey remembered the testimony that Helena's house in Galilee had been searched first thing, but she also remembered the house in Houston where Kelsey had found the maid, baby-sitting.

"Has he said anything to you?" Kelsey asked wonderingly. She turned and found herself looking at Aunt Goldie, whose expression bore none of her sister's crazed hopefulness. Goldie shook her head minutely at Kelsey, answering more than her one question.

"Of course not," Alice Beaumont screamed. "He won't until after the trial. Until he needs me. Don't you see?"

Yes, Kelsey saw. In Goldie Hatteras's hopeless expression she saw the truth behind Mrs. Beaumont's theory—the truth of a woman who had always had her way and been able to control events and couldn't accept that life had had the temerity to deal her such a blow.

"I see," Kelsey said to Aunt Goldie.

"Not that this is going to let you off the hook," Mrs. Beaumont went on angrily. "When this trial is over, I'm going to file a formal complaint with your boss. I'll have your job. Your conduct has been disgraceful. Showing me those pictures on the stand, trying to make me—Everyone saw through you. Using a trial to try to hurt me."

Kelsey didn't answer. Alice Beaumont's complaint was a more general one, and to a much higher authority than the attorney general of Texas. Kelsey let her rave herself out, agreeing with everything, until Mrs. Beaumont let her sister take her home.

Kelsey turned back to the phone. Her conversation with Dr. Roger Broom had been going unsatisfactorily. The doctor had complained that he had a full morning of appointments the next day, though he'd known for months that Kelsey would need his testimony. She remembered, too, during the few attempted rehearsals, how flat the doctor's explanations had been. She pictured him on the witness stand, resentful and in a hurry.

Kelsey picked up the phone and dialed a longer number. "Hello, Lydia," she said with false cheer. "How's the baby?"

"Wiggly," Dr. Cadena said. "What's up, honey?"

"Lydia, I need your help."

"Where are you staying?"

After Kelsey hung up the phone she crossed the tiny room and opened her door. She welcomed the chilly air invading her room. She scanned the narrow view, expecting to see a patrol car parked across the street, or cruising slowly through her motel parking lot. But nothing was out there except the black night of Galilee.

Kelsey thought about going for a run. She even considered driving to his house. Instead she just stood in the cold darkness. After a minute she began to feel spotlighted in the spill of light from her doorway. She walked through the courtyard, out the back side of the motel, where there was an open field. At the far side of the field stood a few tall pine trees. It was not the edge of the great piney woods, just representatives of the primeval forest left when the land was cleared for the town. The trees stood as if ready to reclaim the land. Kelsey stared into the darkness, thinking of being alone in the cold woods.

Who mourned for Lorrie and Ronald Blystone? Lorrie's mother did, but Mrs. Beaumont's worldview was so self-centered it was hard to say whether she grieved at the loss of her daughter or at what she perceived as an attack on herself. Kelsey hadn't found anyone else in town who grieved for the victims. She was prosecuting the most popular man in town for a double murder, and she wasn't sure she could make anyone care about the victims. They were not nice people, Ronald and Lorrie. Even Kelsey thought she'd learned enough about them to say that. They had not been pleasant and they would not be missed.

But the baby. Kelsey folded her arms against the night. That baby out there in that night. Had the baby spent nights in that dismal forest? Or did someone have her even now?

Kelsey slipped to her knees. She was crying, but the emotion that made her whole body clench was anger. She was suddenly furious. Furious with this town, that she couldn't force the truth out of it.

Whatever anyone had thought of Lorrie and Ronald, or of Mrs. Beaumont, the baby was perfectly helpless and innocent. The only innocent involved. "Taylor," Kelsey whispered. She remembered the picture of the baby's birth. It was hard to bring her alive from that, but Kelsey felt the baby growing. She was Kelsey's baby now. Kelsey was responsible for her. She remembered that feeling from when she'd first driven into Galilee, that she was the victims' defender. She hadn't realized how personal that feeling would become.

Slowly the tears dried on her face. She sat staring into the darkness.

13

Kelsey had a surprise greeter the next morning as she stepped out of her car behind the courthouse. Katherine Fletcher stood waiting on the sidewalk. The trial had gone on for days now, and Katherine was finally repeating an outfit. She was wearing the same dress she'd been wearing the first time Kelsey had seen her, inside the Busy Bee beauty shop. It was a black dress with muted flowers, barely visible inside a long black trench coat. Kelsey recognized the coat from one of the evidence photos. Katherine had been wearing it when she'd come into her mother's house an hour after the murders.

"Miss Thatch," she said urgently, with a muted intimacy. "I need your help. You've got to keep Mama out of the trial again this morning."

"I'm sorry, Katherine. She's already violated the rule. You can't take it back. I have no reason to exclude her."

"Make one up. You can make her."

Kelsey laughed bitterly. Katherine recognized the emotion. It made her remove her hand from Kelsey's arm. "This is killing her," Katherine said hoarsely.

Katherine's cool face, the only face she ever wore in public, was coming apart. Her eyelid trembled. Kelsey had thought Katherine's habitual passivity a result of coldness—perhaps willed coldness after a frightened, lonely adolescence. It could also, she saw now, be a sign of a strength no one suspected. And a caring.

"I've never seen her like this," Katherine said. "She threatened you, didn't she? But at home, with no one to bully, she just collapses. She feels guilty about something. I don't know what," she forestalled Kelsey's question.

"Make her give her up," Katherine said abruptly. "Make her see she has to give up the baby. Let her rest in peace, Kelsey. You are, aren't you? You're not going to try to say she's still—" Katherine's voice was hoarse but rising. Her hands reached for Kelsey again, then clawed in midair. Katherine put her arms around herself. Kelsey reached for her and her hand landed unnoticed on Katherine, the way Kelsey had seen Katherine's mother resist touches. "Make her give up," Katherine begged, staring at the courthouse. A tear streaked her cheek. "You're not going to leave her any hope, are you?"

"I'm sorry," Kelsey said, sincerely but in as hollow a voice as Katherine's. The women stared at each other with a strange sense of alliance. Kelsey felt like a little sister. "I'll tell her to stay away, if you think it would do any good."

Katherine shrugged. Still watching her closely, Kelsey guessed that Katherine Fletcher felt guilty, too—guilty that through someone else's murderous rage she'd gotten what she'd wanted: unobstructed access to her mother. For the first time in her life, Katherine was the only person available to catch whatever affection was stored in her mother's nature.

"Oh, well," she said, wiping her cheek. "I guess the worst is over. There won't be anything too terrible today, will there?"

Kelsey took her hand, but it felt false. She let it drop.

"Yes, Katherine. There will be."

Kelsey had almost no case left, as far as the defense knew. From her witness list, all that was left was the medical testimony, and there were no surprises there. Clyde Wolverton looked at Kelsey expectantly as she rose. Judge Saunders, too, waited for Kelsey's announcement, with an expression that said there must be more to the State's case.

"The State calls Dr. Lydia Cadena."

The courtroom stirred, because this was a name no one knew. At the defense table there was no concern, though. Clyde Wolverton knew what Dr. Cadena's examination of Billy Fletcher's car had uncovered. He smiled expectantly. But behind him, Morgan

Fletcher looked concerned. For the first time during the trial, he leaned forward to say something inaudible to the defense lawyer. Wolverton's smile leaked away. Billy Fletcher turned to look at his brother.

Lydia came up the aisle of the courtroom slowly, like a ship docking. She would not have appreciated the analogy. Dr. Cadena had spent thirty-some years as a thin person and had had to adjust herself to this stomach that preceded her. She was almost eight months pregnant now, and apparently carrying a big boy. She was still thin in her legs and shoulders and face, but the pregnancy interrupted her profile, a surprising parenthesis.

She settled herself in the witness chair, looked along the jurors' faces, and turned to Kelsey with composure. Lydia had testified many times, it didn't frighten her, especially when she was in the hands of a friend.

She stated her name and then listed her credentials, her medical degree, her postgraduate training, her special certifications, her current position as an assistant medical examiner in Harris County.

"How long have you been a medical examiner, Dr. Cadena?"

"Eight years."

"How many autopsies have you performed or assisted in in that time?"

"Usually more than one a day, five days a week, sometimes six or seven. Well over a thousand, certainly."

"How many times have you testified in court describing your autopsy findings?"

"Dozens of times. Maybe a hundred."

"Have you ever testified in court about the results of an autopsy you didn't perform yourself?"

"Oh, yes." Lydia sat back, started to cross her legs, then remembered that was no longer in her repertoire. "If another doctor has left the office since performing the autopsy, or for some other reason isn't available for the trial."

"Do you feel comfortable doing that?"

"Yes. The autopsy itself is usually very routine, in fact we have assistants, nondoctors, who do most of the actual work of opening the body and removing and weighing the organs. It's in interpreting the results that I have to use my medical training. That process is the same whether I was present at the autopsy or not."

"Let me hand you two documents and have you identify them for me." As Lydia took the reports, Kelsey saw that her old friend's hands were steady. Lydia was good. That's why Kelsey had called her. Until the small hours of the morning they'd had a slumber party with the theme of violent death. Lydia's face didn't betray her lack of sleep. The skin of her face was smooth and brown and her eyes were wide. Kelsey thought again that pregnancy had given her old friend a new regality.

"These are autopsy reports," Dr. Cadena testified. "The reports of autopsies performed by a Dr. Roger Broom on Lorrie Blystone and Ronald Blystone. With accompanying photographs."

"Let's go over these, Dr. Cadena, starting with State's exhibit number twenty, the autopsy report on Ronald Blystone."

"Objection, Your Honor." Clyde Wolverton finally got to say the phrase that had been on his lips ever since the smile departed them, when Morgan Fletcher had leaned forward to whisper to him. Wolverton stood tall and stiff. "This witness is not competent to testify to the results of these autopsies because she didn't perform them."

Kelsey was on her feet, too. "Defense counsel had no objection to Dr. Cadena's qualifications."

"Approach the bench."

Judge Saunders was tapping a pencil on her bench as they came up to her; tapping slowly and deliberately. "Is this witness a surprise to you, Mr. Wolverton?"

"No, Your Honor." Lydia Cadena had been on Kelsey's witness list from back when Kelsey had thought the medical examiner would have useful testimony about her examination of Billy's car. "My objection is just that she didn't perform the autopsies, so she shouldn't be allowed to testify to their results."

"But she's done that before," the judge said. "Houston courts have obviously allowed it. Any medical examiner *is* competent to analyze the results of an autopsy."

Since the judge was making her argument for her, Kelsey stood silent.

"This isn't Houston," Clyde Wolverton said petulantly. That might have been a good, sly argument to make to a judge proud of his back-country independence, but Linda Saunders was not that judge. Her pride was bound up in the idea that she was as well-versed in the law as any judge in the state. She frowned at the defense lawyer, who hastily added, "I mean, it wouldn't be error to exclude her testimony either, Your Honor."

"Can you guarantee me that, Mr. Wolverton?"

He had no answer. Judge Saunders turned her attention on Kelsey. The pencil tapped faster. "What's your purpose for this substitution, Ms. Thatch? Is Dr. Broom unavailable?"

"He was very reluctant to cancel his appointments for today, Your Honor. Of course I could force him here with a subpoena, but Dr. Cadena was available and autopsy reports are her specialty."

The judge continued to peer at Kelsey. This could be a mistake for the prosecution: using an out-of-town expert rather than the local doctor. It would remind the jury that Kelsey herself had no stake in what happened in Galilee.

"Overruled," the judge said slowly.

Kelsey quickly took her seat again. Clyde Wolverton was still walking slowly back to his when she asked, "What killed Ronald Blystone, Dr. Cadena?"

"A gunshot wound to the head. The bullet penetrated the left side of the skull and did not emerge. It would have rebounded from the inside of the skull and remained in the brain, from which Dr. Broom removed it."

"How long would it take such a wound to cause death?"

"A few seconds at most. Almost instantaneous."

"Would there have been much bleeding?"

"No, not much." Lydia's voice was placid but serious, weighing what she said. "Once the heart stopped beating, blood would not have pumped out of the wound."

Kelsey took a long moment to collect her thoughts and pull a different file toward her.

"Now to the autopsy report on Lorrie Blystone, Doctor."

The jurors returned their attention to Lydia. Ronald had been essentially a stranger to them. But Lorrie's name evoked memories. How she had died was part of her life, and they wanted to know the story.

"What killed Lorrie, Dr. Cadena?"

"A single gunshot wound to the chest. The bullet severed a major artery, punctured her left lung, and exited out her back."

"Would that wound, like her husband's, have caused death instantly?"

"No."

There was a solemn silence in the courtroom. Lydia wasn't referring to the report. She testified staring out into the courtroom, as if from memory. "Lorrie Blystone died from loss of blood. That isn't something that happens instantly. She was losing blood fast, because of the artery, but it would have taken a while, maybe as long as a minute. Maybe longer, if she staunched the flow of blood."

Staunched the flow. Held her hand over her still-beating heart and tried to preserve her life. Distracted by the image, Kelsey didn't ask her follow-up question. Lydia spoke again in her quiet, full voice that filled the courtroom, soft in every corner. "The other evidence also indicates that Lorrie lived after she was shot."

"What other evidence, Doctor?"

"The bullet, I understand, was removed from this side wall. There's also a blood spatter on that wall, indicating Lorrie Blystone was standing close to that wall when she was shot."

Clyde Wolverton had made a mistake, letting Lydia testify to that hearsay about where the bullet had been found. Kelsey glanced aside and saw that Wolverton was following the testimony for its narrative value. Beside him, Billy was leaning forward, mouth open, his chest moving as he breathed in short, shallow gasps. Kelsey wished the jurors would look at his horrified face. He looked like a man reliving a terrible experience.

"Yet her body was found in this spot." Lydia held up a photograph. "Several feet away. From the way the blood settled in her body, it's clear she died in that position, face down, one arm stretched out."

"What does that indicate, Dr. Cadena?"

"The bullet struck her. It would have been a powerful blow, probably one that would have knocked her back against the wall. Then she fell forward. The bullet killed her. She may have realized that. But she managed to lift herself up, to her hands and knees, and she crawled forward."

"How can you tell that, Doctor? That she rose to her hands and knees?"

"Because there was blood on her hands and knees. That's visible in the pre-autopsy photos. And Dr. Broom's report shows that he had that blood tested and it was the victim's own blood."

"Would the wound that Lorrie Blystone suffered be one that caused much bleeding, Dr. Cadena?"

"Oh, yes. Much blood, pumping out of her chest, because her heart was still beating. That's another way of determining that she lived for some time after being shot, because of the amount of blood in these pictures."

"So she crawled through her own blood?"

"Yes."

"Dr. Cadena, in that photograph that shows Lorrie's body lying on the floor, what object in the room is closest to her? What is her hand outstretched toward?"

Lydia didn't have to consult the photograph. Unconsciously, she was rubbing the mound of her stomach. "The crib," she said clearly.

Kelsey was looking at a copy of the same photo herself. Lorrie lying beside the empty baby crib. Kelsey had forgotten for the moment her function in the trial. She wanted to hear more of the story, like everyone else in the room. She saw Judge Saunders watching her expectantly.

"I pass the witness."

From the back of the courtroom came a minor commotion. The hallway door opened, a sound too quiet for Kelsey to have heard, except that the room was so still. She turned to look, but the door was closing again, as if someone had just glanced into the courtroom.

Clyde Wolverton seemed not yet to have collected himself. Lydia's testimony hadn't offered much room for cross-examination. She hadn't said anything controversial or overly theoretical. She had done only what Kelsey had called her to do: brought the evidence alive.

So Wolverton went to his strength. "Did you see the photographs of the interior of the crib, Dr. Cadena?"

"Yes."

"What did that appear to you to be, those stains on the sheets?"

"I would say blood."

"Correct," Wolverton said, an objectionable remark, but Kelsey let it pass. "Assuming that blood had been tested and determined to be Lorrie Blystone's, what would that tell you?"

Kelsey should object to this, too, but she didn't. She knew where the defense lawyer was headed, but he was going to help her along the way.

"I would guess that the baby had been on the floor, had gotten stained with her mother's blood, and then someone had placed the baby back in her crib, where she got her sheets stained as well."

"Correct," Wolverton said again triumphantly, not noticing the impact this simple picture had on the jury. They were distracted, lingering on the image of the baby stained with her mother's blood.

"Now, Dr. Cadena, you attempted to gather some evidence in this case, did you not?" Wolverton was almost rubbing his hands together.

"Yes."

"What did you examine?"

"I examined an automobile."

"Whose car was that, Dr. Cadena?"

"I was told—," Lydia said slowly, which dragged Kelsey to her feet to make the hearsay objection.

Silence followed, to her surprise. Finally: "Overruled." Kelsey looked at the judge wonderingly as Wolverton renewed his question.

"I was told it was the defendant's car," Lydia said.

"And what were you searching the car for, Doctor?"

"Traces of blood."

"Specifically for traces of Lorrie Blystone's blood?"

"Specifically, yes. Or the blood of anyone else connected to the case."

"And did you find any such blood inside Billy Fletcher's car, Doctor?"

"No, I didn't. The traces of blood I found in the front seat couldn't be matched to any other known blood."

"So that blood had nothing to do with this case?"

"Not as far as I could tell."

"Now, Doctor," Clyde Wolverton said, knowing but gentle, as if he didn't want to hurt anyone. "If the baby Taylor Blystone, with her bloodstained hands and gown, had been inside that car, wouldn't you expect to have found traces of that blood *some-where* in that car's interior?"

"Objection. Calls for speculation."

"No, Your Honor," Wolverton replied. "Just for interpreting the evidence, as the witness has been doing extensively for the prosecution."

That's because you were too stupid to object, Kelsey thought, but wasn't surprised when Judge Saunders overruled her objection.

"Yes, I would have expected to find blood," Lydia said, "unless the baby had been wrapped up in a clean sheet or been carried in a car seat or carrier."

Good old Lydia. If she was going to be forced to speculate, she would get in some speculations that helped Kelsey's case, too. Clyde Wolverton stopped smiling.

"Doctor," he said grimly. "Dr. Broom's autopsy reports also contain an estimate of the times of death, do they not?"

"Yes, they do," Lydia agreed, again not having to refer to the reports.

"What is that estimate?"

"Sometime between ten-fifteen and ten-thirty that morning, the morning of the twenty-first."

"Do you agree with that estimate?"

Lydia shrugged. "I see nothing in the reports to contradict it."

Wolverton had regained some of his self-satisfaction. "Pass the witness," he said loudly.

Kelsey had nothing else to ask—a terrible, empty feeling, because Lydia Cadena was her last witness. "No more questions," she finally had to say.

Lydia stepped down from the stand and crossed the front of the courtroom in her new, deliberate glide of a walk. Whispered conversations broke out among the spectators. Then Lydia was past and Judge Saunders was saying, "Call your next witness."

Kelsey shrugged. "I have no other witness, Your Honor. The State—"

"Wait!"

The next sound after the shout was the crash of the hall door of the courtroom slamming back against the wall, so that it sounded as if someone were fighting his way into the room. But Peter was moving so fast the noise of his entrance seemed unconnected to him. He was already coming down the aisle of the courtroom. His face was grim. A streak of dirt was on his cheek. He wore his brown uniform, but it was in worse condition than Kelsey had ever seen it, crumpled and dirty at the knees, some kind of ugly stain creeping up the pants cuffs. He was carrying a large padded envelope.

Peter didn't glance at Lydia Cadena as he passed her in the aisle, but he reached out and touched her arm. Lydia turned and stared wonderingly after him.

Everything else in the room seemed static: Kelsey still stood with her mouth open to rest her case. Judge Saunders posed with her gavel lifted. The jurors sat locked in various expressions like a Norman Rockwell painting of parade spectators. The defense team were all turned in their chairs watching the deputy come through the gate in the rail. Billy and his defense lawyer sat openmouthed. Only Morgan's face had moved, only he seemed to recognize Peter Stiller. His eyes were piercing.

"May we have a moment to confer, Your Honor?" Peter was the one who asked. Judge Saunders could fight off her stasis only enough to nod.

Noise resumed as Peter stood in front of Kelsey, sufficient conversational murmur from the audience to cover their whispered conversation. "Where have you been?" Kelsey was looking over his face carefully, searching for injuries. But Peter didn't even seem tired. He looked like a survivor of a cave-in, but his eyes were bright.

"I've been in the dumps," he whispered.

I've been a little down myself, Kelsey thought inanely, then realized Peter was being literal. She looked down at the envelope he carried. "What—?"

"The landfill where the trash from the highway and the trash cans at the rest stops are emptied. I've been searching it for weeks."

"How could it take so long?"

"You know how much trash gets dumped there in a day? And if a week goes by before anybody thinks to start looking there, we're talking major archaeological dig."

"But they must have—"

"No," Peter said excitedly. "Those first few days, we were looking for a live baby. Not something as small as a piece of cloth. While we were searching the woods, the garbage-collecting crews were going right on with their work. Someone probably dug through the trash cans in a hurry looking for a baby, but they never got a methodical examination."

"And that's what you've been doing? My God, Peter, what did you—?"

"Look." He turned his back on the jury and barely opened the large envelope enough for Kelsey to peer inside. She sucked in her breath sharply. She reached into the envelope and felt fabric.

Then a large hand covered hers. Morgan Fletcher was standing in front of her, straight and broad, his body hiding the envelope from the view of the audience. His face was frightening in its intensity, but he wasn't looking at Kelsey. Peter took the force of his glare.

"Deputy," Morgan said in a low voice like a quick, sharp blow to the stomach, "do you know anything about chain of custody?"

"I'm the chain, sir. I haven't passed this evidence off to anyone else. No one else has touched it since I found it." Peter gazed coolly at Morgan.

Morgan softened his voice. "Then do you understand chain of command?" Morgan took the envelope. "Your supervisor should have been the first to see this, and your next step would come from him."

"I'm on vacation, sir." Deftly, without a struggle, Peter took the envelope back from Morgan.

The rest of their conversation was unspoken, but Kelsey thought she heard it as the two men stared at each other.

"Here," Kelsey said, taking Peter's arm and turning him away. "Tell me exactly—"

"Ms. Thatch," the judge's voice interrupted. "Were you making an announcement?"

Kelsey removed her hand from Peter's arm. "The State calls Peter Stiller."

Morgan was resuming his seat. As he did, he leaned past the defense lawyer's back, and Clyde Wolverton popped to his feet. "This calls for a hearing, Your Honor," he almost shouted. "Outside the presence of the jury."

"I agree," Judge Saunders said. "Bailiff."

As the jurors were led out of the room, they all, without exception, looked at the large padded envelope Kelsey was holding in both hands. She gave them a tight-lipped smile, as if she were about to fight on their behalf.

When the jurors were gone, she motioned Peter toward the stand. The momentum of his burst into the courtroom was gone; he looked a little embarrassed at his appearance. But when he sat and looked across the room at Morgan Fletcher, his lips closed purposefully.

"The defense can't claim this witness is a surprise either, Your Honor," Kelsey said with a confidence she didn't feel. "Deputy Stiller was also on my witness list."

Taking no chances, Kelsey had listed the name of every police officer who had been in the Beaumont house the morning of the murders, not knowing which she might have to call.

"Let's just hear what he has to say," Clyde Wolverton said grimly.

Kelsey got right to it. "Deputy, what do you have in the envelope?"

At Kelsey's nod Peter reached into the envelope and pulled out its contents. There were gasps from the audience and one strangled cry. The cry told Kelsey what she needed to know: the baby gown Peter was holding had been Taylor Blystone's.

The stains on it were plainly visible.

"Can you identify that?" Kelsey asked.

"It's a baby gown," Peter said. "It's Taylor Blystone's gown."

Clyde Wolverton interrupted. "Can you really testify to that, Deputy? Have you memorized this baby's entire wardrobe? Did you ever actually see her wearing this gown?"

"Well—" Peter sounded uncertain for the first time. "It just makes sense."

"Sense!" Wolverton snorted. "I don't think that meets a legal standard."

Judge Saunders reached across her bench to take the tiny gown from Peter. He looked up at her with an open expression, eager to be questioned.

"Your Honor," Kelsey said, "I can call the baby's aunt or grandmother to identify the gown. I can say—"

"Except that both of them have been sitting through this witness's testimony, and allowing them to testify would be a violation of the rule to which the defense would strenuously object." Clyde Wolverton's voice was controlled anger.

"I could call someone else then," Kelsey said, faintly desperate. "Goldie Hatteras, who was staying in the house. Helena Parker . . ." She tried to think of someone else who might be able to tie the gown to the baby, but they were all dead or had been watching the trial.

"I doubt people who had spent only a few days in the company of the—" Wolverton began.

"It could be proved through the blood, Your Honor!"

The unexpected voice belonged to Lydia Cadena. She was still in the aisle. She came forward hurriedly. "Those stains on the gown, Your Honor. I could test them overnight, right away. I wouldn't have time for DNA results, but I could make a match for blood type. I've already typed Lorrie Blystone's blood. I could have these results for the court by tomorrow morning." Lydia stood with her hands on the railing, asking for her chance. Kelsey felt a lift of strength.

The judge held the baby gown in both hands, stroking it gently. When she looked up, the effort she was making to keep her face still was visible to everyone. She looked at Billy Fletcher and had to look away quickly. She looked past him to his brother.

Judge Saunders's voice was soft. "Let's put aside that question for the time being." She handed the gown back to Peter. "Where did you find this, Deputy?"

"In the Liston Gardens Landfill, Your Honor. It's where the trash collection company takes the garbage they collect from the highway rest stops between here and Houston."

"You were told that?" the judge asked softly, anticipating the defense objection.

"I followed the trucks there, Your Honor." Peter Stiller knew something about law himself. Judge Saunders gave him a faint smile of approval.

Kelsey asked one more question. "From where you found this gown in the landfill, Peter, could you testify when it was put there?"

"Approximately." Kelsey looked at him with a great burst of affection.

"Is that the extent of your proof?" Judge Saunders asked neutrally. "And I assume you are urging that this gown be admitted into evidence before the jury?"

"We certainly are, Your Honor."

Next to Kelsey, Morgan Fletcher was whispering urgently to the defense lawyer. With a tiny snarl of frustration, Morgan gave up on Wolverton and stood up himself. "This, of course, leaves out an essential element of admissibility, Your Honor," he said loudly. He stood very straight and looked hard at Judge Linda Saunders. "There's nothing to connect this evidence to the defendant."

"Are you speaking for the defense now, Mr. Fletcher?" the judge asked quietly, returning her old friend's gaze. There was no telling the extent of their communication.

"He'll make the same argument," Morgan said with a small, contemptuous gesture toward Clyde Wolverton. "Admitting this evidence would just be prejudicial, Your Honor. It would appeal to the jury's emotions—I believe we can all testify that the sight of it is horrifying—but it adds nothing to the proof against the defendant."

Kelsey spoke haltingly. This was all happening so fast, she didn't have time to think, only to react. "Of course it does, Your Honor. This gown is the one Taylor Blystone was wearing when she was abducted. It was found right on the route the defendant took when he left the Beaumont home—the highway to Houston."

"There's been no proof of where the defendant went," Morgan interjected.

My God, he was right. Kelsey knew Billy's alibi, but there'd been no proof of it yet. That was the defense's job. Very well, she could save the nightgown for rebuttal, after Billy testified about having to catch his plane in Houston. Just save—

"And that is a very well-traveled highway." Morgan Fletcher pronounced his final condemnation of the evidence.

Judge Saunders looked at Kelsey, who could think of no argument against that. Finally the judge spoke. "Yes, it is," she said quietly. "I believe we've heard testimony about at least two other members of the Beaumont household who left the house that morning and ended up in Houston."

Aunt Goldie and Helena Parker. But they hadn't been in a position to take the baby. Had they? Who could say they hadn't been?

"I'm sorry, Ms. Thatch," Judge Saunders ruled. "He's correct. Without evidence to tie this gown to the defendant, admitting it would be an attempt to inflame the jury. A successful attempt, I'm sure."

As Kelsey stood silent, the judge turned to Peter with a regretful expression. "You're excused, Deputy Stiller."

Peter stood slowly. He was holding the nightgown in both hands, as if the baby it had clothed had suddenly been teleported away, leaving only her empty gown. His face was stricken. Suddenly he looked as tired as he was dirty.

He looked at Morgan Fletcher, Peter's boss in a sense. Peter's chin firmed. He came down off the witness stand briskly, walking toward the district attorney as if Peter wouldn't stop when he reached him, as if he would walk through Morgan or punch him. But Kelsey interrupted him.

"Thank you," she said, wrapping her fingers around Peter's arm. Gently she took the gown from him and put it back in its envelope.

"I'm going to bring the jury back in," Judge Saunders said. "Will you have another witness to call, Ms. Thatch?"

"No, Your Honor. I'll rest my case."

The judge nodded, first to Kelsey, then to the bailiff. As the bailiff went to fetch the jurors, Kelsey turned to watch Peter walk out. Lydia Cadena was making a small, quick calling motion to her. Kelsey walked out of the gate and leaned toward her friend's mouth.

"That lack of blood in the defendant's car is killing you, isn't it?" Lydia whispered. Kelsey nodded.

"Have you considered the possibility," Lydia breathed distinctly, "that somebody gave him a ride?"

Kelsey's eyes widened.

The jurors returned.

14

The baby gown was back in its envelope by the time the jurors came filing in. When they first emerged, the jurors looked around curiously, even suspiciously, knowing everyone in the room had learned something they hadn't. But in a moment their eyes focused on the thick padded envelope Kelsey held in both hands. When the jurors were seated, Kelsey set the envelope down on the corner of her table. She didn't look at it again, but she didn't want it out of the jurors' minds. Let them go home tonight and violate their oaths, if they wanted. Let them ask around. Kelsey no longer felt above anything in this case.

"The State rests," she said formally.

"Mr. Wolverton?" Judge Saunders asked. The defense lawyer quickly stood and announced that the defense had a motion to make. The judge nodded, unsurprised.

"The lawyers and I have work to do," she instructed the jury, "so I'm going to give you a long lunch break. Remember my instructions. Be back here at two o'clock."

They were reluctant to leave. They sat for a long minute, and when they left, it was with many a backward glance, particularly at Kelsey and her mystery envelope.

The door had barely closed behind the last juror when Wolverton began making his motion for a directed verdict. "The prosecution has placed Billy Fletcher at the scene of the crimes, but not at the time the deaths occurred."

Judge Saunders sat watching him, leaning her head on her hand, her index finger stretched up beside her temple. She re-

membered the evidence as well as the defense lawyer did—
better, probably. Judge Saunders understood perfectly the weakness of the State's case.

The case was so weak, in fact, that the judge would be justified
in directing a verdict of acquittal at this point. There would be
an uproar, but not much of one. The judge might be criticized
elsewhere for not letting the case go to the jury, but here in
Galilee among the voters who had elected her, most people
would probably say she had done the right thing. She could do
the favor Morgan Fletcher expected of her and not suffer any
consequences. This, right now, was Kelsey's biggest hurdle of
the case.

"The State hasn't even proven that both deaths were murder,"
Wolverton said. "The State's own expert testified it was just as
likely that Ronald Blystone killed himself as that he was murdered. In short, Your Honor . . ."

He sat with an air of confidence when he was finished. Kelsey
presented the perfect contrast. She had been taught, as a young
prosecutor, to treat these motions offhandedly, even contemptuously, but she couldn't do that. Her voice was low and shaky as
she began.

"What the defense is asserting is that I can't prove this defendant guilty of murder because he was careful to make sure he
got rid of all the witnesses to his crime. Unsurprisingly, he didn't
commit the murders in full view of anyone except the people
he killed."

Kelsey looked up. "But the State has proven more than that
the defendant was at the scene near the time of the crimes, Your
Honor. We have proven motive and state of mind. He wasn't
just there, he was there and he was furious."

Judge Saunders remained expressionless. She watched Kelsey
steadily. She didn't glance at the defense team.

"As for Ronald Blystone's death not being a murder, we all
know what's wrong with that theory." Kelsey put her hand down
on the big envelope on the corner of her table. Its skin crinkled.
"The murderer was there to take the victims' baby.

"Let the jury decide who that was, Your Honor."

Kelsey sat down. Wolverton didn't. He looked posed for a
photograph shaking hands with his client. Billy Fletcher's hands

were on the table, ready to push himself up. He had a hopeful, open expression.

But the judge wasn't looking at him. She was looking at the envelope on Kelsey's table. Her gaze was sad, then it turned determined.

"The motion is overruled. Will you have witnesses to present, Mr. Wolverton?"

Wolverton looked stunned. He turned to his partner on the defense team, but Morgan Fletcher wouldn't look at him. Morgan's mouth was tight and angry.

"I'll have to make that decision with my client," Wolverton said slowly.

"Very well. Two o'clock," Judge Saunders said briskly. She tapped her gavel lightly and walked out of the courtroom, head down.

When Kelsey stood, she almost bumped into Morgan Fletcher. He put his hands on her arms to steady both of them. Surprisingly, she didn't find his touch repugnant. He had finally revealed himself as her adversary, but Kelsey had known that all along. What else could he do but do his best for his brother? Kelsey would do the same thing. They both knew what they both had to do. Kelsey felt comradeship in the contact with Morgan. She looked into his eyes and saw the pain she remembered. Morgan Fletcher was a torn man.

He was in a hurry, rushing after the judge. Kelsey didn't try to horn in on that meeting. Judge Saunders wouldn't change her ruling. Kelsey had a respite.

"You're not going to get away with anything, you know." Clyde Wolverton leaned toward her as he angrily snapped his briefcase closed.

"My case is over, Mr. Wolverton," she answered wearily. "It seems to me I didn't get away with much."

"You know what I mean." He came and stood in front of her. Kelsey had the choice of staring straight into the knot of his tie or straining her neck to look up at him. She chose to look down, giving him a view of the top of her head. "Hiding a witness. That's a low trick, but it won't help you."

"What are you talking about?"

"Helena Parker."

"Helena Parker? I'm the one who told you about her. That's not a very good job of hiding."

"After you knew she was safely secreted, you gave us an address that was no longer good."

Kelsey looked up, startled. "She's gone?"

"Gone good. We've had the house in Houston watched for a month now, and she hasn't come near it. Her sister says she doesn't know where she is, either."

"Well, I—," Kelsey said slowly, wondering what this meant.

"But it won't do you any good."

"What do you mean?"

He gave her a smug smile, as if the missing witness were his triumph. He turned away and took his client's arm.

The courtroom had mostly cleared out. But Kelsey's team was waiting for her. Lydia and Peter, still standing in the aisle. Waiting for her. She went to them and they each put out an arm for her.

It felt strangely right, walking out into the sunlight with Peter. They went, with Lydia, into the square across the street. It must have been cold, the square was deserted.

"Thank you," Kelsey said again, but stopped and looked hard at Peter. "Who planted that blood in Billy's car?"

"I don't know, Kelsey." His face was perfectly calm. He didn't try any theories on her.

"Who did you tell I was going to search the car?"

"Nobody."

"Well, hell. I've lost all my judgment."

Peter grinned slowly, because he knew what that meant: she believed him, in spite of herself.

"What a nasty break," Lydia Cadena said. "Don't be such a pain, Kelsey, give the man a hug."

But Kelsey was alone again at the front of the courtroom when trial resumed, waiting nervously for the defense to make its first announcement.

"Mr. Wolverton?"

Clyde Wolverton was subdued. He gave the judge a look that announced clearly he no longer considered her an ally. Judge Saunders looked as if she could handle his scorn.

"The defense calls John Howard."

Kelsey let out her breath with quiet satisfaction. Her worst fear had been that the defense would rest without calling any witnesses. That might have been a smart move. In spite of the judge's ruling, they all knew the weakness of the case Kelsey had presented. A strong, confident defense lawyer would have taken it to the jury right then, arguing that the defense didn't have to call any witnesses to prove anything, because the prosecution hadn't proven anything.

But that was a move that would have taken guts, and Clyde Wolverton apparently wasn't up to it.

This was what the prosecution wanted after presenting a weak case: for the defendant to put on his own case, giving the prosecutor a chance at the defendant and his witnesses on cross-examination. It was the chance Kelsey wanted, but it was scary, too, to sit there and have to wait, not knowing what might be coming.

John Howard was no surprise to her, though. She knew who he was, though she had never seen him before, so she studied him curiously as he took his seat. He was a solid-looking man about fifty, packed into his pinstriped suit. He had a strong jaw and an almost rectangular head, its shape accented by Howard's brush haircut. John Howard looked like a man who'd enjoyed military training.

"And where do you live, Mr. Howard?" Clyde Wolverton was asking.

"Raleigh, North Carolina."

A gentle sighing sounded in the courtroom as the spectators realized who John Howard was. He was the business executive who had met with Billy Fletcher in North Carolina the evening after the murders.

"And what time did this meeting take place, Mr. Howard?"

"It was over dinner. Started about seven o'clock." Howard glanced at Billy Fletcher, gave him a little nod of recognition, but looked at him with only slight curiosity, as if Billy's predicament were part of some bizarre hometown ritual Mr. Howard didn't care to learn any more about.

"Was this meeting hastily arranged?"

"Oh, no. We had talked to each other over the course of a few months. We were thinking of expanding our operation in the Southwest, which would have meant increased competition in Texas with Smoothskins, so Billy and I had talked about the possibility of a merger of some sort. That never worked out. But we had been talking to Mr. Fletcher right along, and he and I had made plans to meet, oh, two or three weeks before we actually did get together."

"I see." Wolverton asked his famous one last question. "And *are* you moving in to Texas?"

Kelsey thought of objecting—it wasn't relevant—but she was as curious as everyone else. Howard had no intention of revealing corporate intentions, however. "That decision hasn't been made yet," he said blandly.

Kelsey's turn. "Hello, Mr. Howard. My name is Kelsey Thatch, I represent the State here. Do you remember our speaking on the phone?"

"More than once, yes. Hello, Miss Thatch."

"How did Mr. Fletcher arrive at your dinner meeting, Mr. Howard? Did you pick him up?"

"We ate at the restaurant in his hotel. He just came down from his room."

Kelsey looked satisfied, but she hadn't gotten the answer she'd wanted—that Billy Fletcher had had a car in North Carolina.

"And what did Mr. Fletcher wear to your dinner meeting?"

John Howard answered promptly, surprisingly for a man asked a question about clothes. Kelsey had asked him this question months ago when his memory had been fresher, and she had kept him reminded of his answer. "He wore slacks, and an open-collared white shirt."

"Was that appropriate attire for the occasion?"

Howard shrugged. "It wasn't that fancy a restaurant, he didn't look out of place. I was a little surprised he wasn't wearing a suit to a business meeting, though."

Maybe that was just Billy, maybe he was a casual guy. Maybe there were knowing looks, even affectionate ones, behind Kelsey's back. She would let them know later that they had just heard something significant.

"Speaking of surprise, Mr. Howard, you said this meeting had been long planned, but were you a little surprised it was taking place at all?"

"I was."

Clyde Wolverton broke off his whispered conversation with Billy to stare at the witness. This was new ground for the defense lawyer.

"Why was that?"

Howard shrugged again. "There was really no reason for a face-to-face meeting at that point. Our talks on the merger idea had pretty much stalled out. And as for the other thing, I'd told Mr. Fletcher a week earlier that we had already hired someone else."

There was a shocked silence in the courtroom, but Kelsey waited for that silence to be torn apart by voices. They came: voices whispering and murmuring. Kelsey waited for the noise to subside, belatedly hastened by Judge Saunders's banging her gavel. The judge, too, was looking with surprise at the witness. She motioned at Kelsey to ask her next question.

"What do you mean by that, Mr. Howard? Did your company have a job opening?"

Howard spoke casually. "Well, of course, if we opened another manufacturing plant in Texas, we'd have lots of job openings. After it became clear the merger idea was off, Billy Fletcher put in a sort of informal application to be our plant manager."

Noise again from the crowd. Billy Fletcher had his head down. Clyde Wolverton was bent close, whispering frantically into his ear, but Billy didn't stir. He looked more stubborn than sorry, refusing to be repentant.

Kelsey raised her voice. "Did Billy Fletcher tell you why he was looking for another job?"

"Oh, he said the usual things, wanting a new challenge, that he'd gone as far as he could with Smoothskins and wanted to work for a larger corporation that would give him more upward mobility."

"You sound as if you didn't believe his explanation, Mr. Howard."

Howard shrugged again. "In a job negotiation, you never expect anybody to tell you the whole truth."

Kelsey stared across the room at John Howard, glad he wasn't her witness. She didn't like him much. "But you hired someone else instead?"

"Yes." Howard broke apart his blunt-fingered hands, then put them together again. "We weren't quite sure of Billy's sincerity, if you want to know the truth. We decided not to take the chance of hiring someone from a competitor."

Clyde Wolverton suddenly sat up straighter, as if he'd been poked in the back. Kelsey continued, "And you told Billy Fletcher that, before his trip to North Carolina?"

"A week before. I wanted to save him a trip. But then he said he wanted to come anyway." Shrug. "I said okay."

Kelsey made a point of turning to Billy, as if looking to him for explanation. But Billy paid her as little attention as he had his own lawyer. His head was still down, his eyes compressed. "Pass the witness."

Wolverton had on his sly face. "So did you offer any job to Billy?"

"No."

"Because you didn't want to hire a competitor, you said. Were you thinking that Billy Fletcher had applied for this job as a way of working his way into your company, learning your intentions?" Kelsey rolled her eyes. Wolverton doggedly continued, "Did you turn down Billy Fletcher because you thought he might in fact be a sort of spy for Smoothskins?"

Howard shrugged a last time. "Why take a chance?"

Neither side required John Howard to linger in Texas. Kelsey didn't even watch him depart. She was looking expectantly at Clyde Wolverton. If every defense witness did as much damage to the defense's case as their first one had, Kelsey hoped Wolverton had lots more up his sleeve. Her confidence restored, she smiled at him.

He smiled back. "The defense calls Ms. Kelsey Thatch."

Kelsey didn't move. "May I ask for what purpose?" she said distinctly.

Wolverton talked to the judge. "If the prosecutor would like to have a hearing, we'd be glad to. This concerns an unavailable witness. The only person able to relay the testimony that witness would have given if not for her disappearance is Ms. Thatch."

Kelsey sat debating for a moment, then suddenly stood and walked quickly to the witness stand.

Judge Saunders looked at her curiously, not privy to any of this. "You're not requesting a hearing?"

"No, Your Honor." No point in letting Clyde Wolverton put on a private investigator to say how he'd tried futilely to find Helena Parker, Mrs. Beaumont's former maid, then let Wolverton imply to the jury that Kelsey was hiding her. With or without a hearing, Kelsey was going to end up on that witness stand.

It might be okay, with Kelsey able to put the proper spin on what she'd heard from Helena. Like most lawyers, she'd always harbored a secret certainty that she would make a brilliant witness if she ever got the chance.

"Very well, then. Raise your right hand."

Kelsey swore with the fervent sincerity of a new citizen from an oppressed country, then sat in the witness stand as properly as her mother could have wished, legs crossed at the knees, hands atop her knee, chin raised.

Clyde Wolverton started slowly, with that sly look. Kelsey waited for just the right question to make him eat it.

"Do you know a Helena Parker?"

"I know a young woman who identified herself to me as Helena Parker."

Wolverton batted his eyes. "You have some reason to think she was lying to you?"

"No."

Out of the jumble of his papers Wolverton fished a small photograph. A young woman was standing on a wooden pier, wearing a white sailor hat and a big smile. Her day off. "This the woman you talked to?"

"Yes."

Wolverton displayed the picture to the jury. They probably all knew who Helena was. Kelsey kicked herself mentally. Pick your battles better, she thought.

"Where did this meeting take place?"

Without quibbling again, Kelsey explained to the jury how and where and when she'd found Helena Parker. She remembered the tiny house in Houston. She remembered, too, the way her heart had twisted in her chest when she'd stood on the porch of that shack and heard a baby cry inside.

"Helena told you she was in the Beaumont house the morning of the killings, didn't she, Ms. Thatch?"

"Yes, although she made it clear that she left before Billy Fletcher arrived, before any shootings."

"But she heard what went on that morning before Billy's arrival."

"Yes."

"What did Helena tell you had been happening? Between Lorrie and Ronald Blystone, I mean."

"Ms. Parker thought they'd been having an argument."

"A bad argument? One that made them both mad?"

"A pretty bad one. Although Helena didn't say they were screaming or anything like that. Nothing physical, certainly. No hitting or throwing things."

"How long had this argument been going on?"

"I don't know."

Wolverton decided to get tough. "You must have some idea. Surely Helena arrived in the house early, she had ears."

"I don't know."

"Your Honor, would you please instruct the witness to answer the question?"

Kelsey didn't look at the judge. She leaned toward the defense lawyer and said in the tight tones used to instruct an idiot, "Mr. Wolverton, I am not Helena Parker. I don't know everything she saw or heard, I only know what she told me. Maybe I should have asked that question, but I didn't. I'm sorry."

Behind the defense lawyer, Morgan Fletcher had his head bent slightly, shading his eyes with his hand. He might have been laughing at Kelsey's quiet, fierce response. Or crying quietly to himself.

"Well, let's get on with it," Wolverton said, talking to no one. "Let's get to the important question. Did Helena tell you there was something about this argument between Lorrie and Ronald that made it stand out from all the others Helena had overheard?"

Kelsey thought about objecting. The question assumed other arguments between the dead wife and husband. But everyone knew that. "Yes," she said quietly, "at one point Lorrie Blystone mentioned divorce."

"Divorce," Wolverton said with satisfaction. "So this was a very serious argument indeed."

Kelsey shrugged.

"Well, it frightened Helena Parker enough that she fled the house, didn't it?"

"Helena did say she didn't want to hear any more after that, and she left for the grocery store."

"Before she did, though, she heard something else, didn't she, Ms. Thatch?"

Kelsey frowned. She really didn't know what the defense lawyer was talking about. "Something to do with Morgan Fletcher?" Wolverton prompted, turning his reed-thin body to gesture at the district attorney. Morgan looked as if he were bearing up under a terribly sad recital. Kelsey frowned, not at her refreshed memory, but at what was troubling Morgan Fletcher.

"Yes," she said slowly, "Helena Parker said she overheard Lorrie making some unflattering comparison between her husband and Morgan Fletcher."

"Unflattering to whom?"

"To Ronald. Helena said Lorrie Blystone said Ronald could learn something from Morgan."

"Learn something about what?"

"She didn't know. That was the last thing Helena heard, she was on her way out the door."

Clyde Wolverton looked pleased. Kelsey hadn't managed to cram that look down his throat. "Pass the witness."

Meaning it was Kelsey's turn as prosecutor to rip the defense witness apart on cross-examination. She sat silent, feeling the weight of the opportunity for the perfect collusion between interrogator and witness. Judge Saunders leaned toward her. "Do you have any questions?"

To ask herself. Kelsey couldn't think of anything. Finally she said, haltingly, "Did Helena mention the baby?"

She felt tears come to her eyes. She hadn't planned this effect, she tried to fight it off. Clyde Wolverton was looking at her scornfully. That helped. "She said—" Kelsey paused to let her voice come stronger. "Helena said she offered to take the baby to the store with her, but Lorrie said no."

Wolverton continued frowning. Even he felt the effect of this last simple statement. The courtroom was very quiet.

"No more questions," Kelsey said.

A strange thing happened when the trial broke for the day. Still a little dazed, Kelsey was slow to pack up and didn't make her usual dash out the back door of the courtroom. She was so slow that she expected the courtroom to be empty when she turned, but it wasn't remotely. Most of the spectators remained, some standing, some still in their seats, all of them watching her. Slowly, Kelsey went out the gate in the railing and walked up the aisle.

Sure enough, a woman was standing almost at her shoulder, glaring at her. Kelsey walked quickly past. The spectators were converging on her. Then she felt a hand on her shoulder. The hand squeezed, softly, giving comfort. Kelsey turned, thinking Peter had found her, but it was a stranger gripping her shoulder, a man in his sixties, with a face in which all the lines showed, because he had his mouth closed tightly, as if his chin would tremble otherwise. He nodded at Kelsey and withdrew. She paused to stare after him. When she walked on, a lady reached out to pat her arm, a woman Kelsey knew she'd seen around town somewhere. The woman didn't say a word, but gave Kelsey the same sort of nod, brimming eyes conveying support.

The crowd stayed silent. Only one woman, when Kelsey was almost through the gauntlet, let her know what they all meant. The silver-haired woman wore little round glasses and a churchgoing dress. She, too, reached out toward Kelsey, but didn't quite touch her. "That poor baby," she said.

That was what they were saying. In her moments on the witness stand Kelsey had done her credibility with the townspeople of Galilee more good than in all the months before. Because they had seen she cared. She wasn't just here to take home a scalp. She cared about what had happened to Taylor Blystone. That didn't mean she was right, it didn't make Billy Fletcher guilty, but in a small, tentative way it admitted Kelsey to the town's fellowship of grief.

She left the courthouse feeling not quite so alone.

* * *

But her testimony had hurt her more than it had helped. Kelsey was the one who'd allowed the defense to begin building its case, against the victims. It was easy to see the defense argument coming: that the Blystones, left virtually alone in the house, had continued arguing, their rage escalating, until Ronald shot his wife and then, in remorse, himself. Billy Fletcher had only been an unlucky interruption. Maybe the defense even had a way to account for the missing baby.

Driving aimlessly, Kelsey tried to think of a way to refute this theory. As in her apparently random runs, she found she had arrived at her goal: the Beaumont house. The house in the dusk looked quiet and empty, in spite of the two cars in the driveway, parked side by side. Kelsey recognized them both. One was Mrs. Beaumont's white Cadillac. But that didn't mean the matriarch of the diminished family was home. Katherine had probably been driving her to the trial and back every day; they always arrived together. Mrs. Beaumont was probably at Katherine's house now. Maybe Mrs. Beaumont was reluctant to come home these days. Helena Parker had asked, "How can *she* live there?"

Kelsey parked on the side of the road where there wasn't much shoulder, then changed her mind about leaving her car sticking out into the road and pulled into the driveway behind the other car. Kelsey wouldn't be here long, and the other car's driver wouldn't be leaving until Kelsey did.

The doorknob turned in her hand and Kelsey went through the front door without knocking or calling. She wasn't sure what made her so bold. She felt she knew the Beaumont house as well as anyone now, and in a way the house had become public property. Kelsey had studied photos of this entryway and the dining room across the way until she could have re-created them perfectly—at least the way they had been.

It was a bit of a surprise then, even though she'd been here before, to see no crib in the dining room. In its place was a sideboard. Someone had rearranged the furniture. Maybe the someone standing in front of the sideboard now, reaching out to straighten the crystal vase and the pictures in their silver frames. Kelsey watched Goldie Hatteras's hand linger lovingly on one frame. Was it because the frame held a picture of Lorrie, or was it the frame itself Goldie admired, the heavy silver molded into roses and vines? From the way her hand moved from the frame to the equally strong but delicate crystal bud vase, Kelsey thought she saw envy on the older woman's face, reflected in the large mirror.

Then Mrs. Hatteras looked up into that mirror, gasped, and turned quickly. "Oh, my goodness." She put her hand over her heart. "I didn't hear you knock."

"I'm sorry, I didn't." Kelsey nodded toward the sideboard. "Your sister has some lovely things, doesn't she?"

Goldie lifted her shoulder deprecatingly. "She doesn't care about them. Except to show them off."

"Some people say that about everything in her life," Kelsey said quietly.

"She doesn't have many friends here, does she?"

Kelsey shook her head. Mrs. Hatteras turned away from her and ran her hand along the sideboard.

"I could have lived this life so much better than Alice has," she said suddenly.

Kelsey wondered if Aunt Goldie was prone to sips of apricot brandy in the late afternoon. Or maybe it was just being left alone in the big house, surrounded by her sister's possessions, that gave her voice that wistful, and defiant, tone. "How?" Kelsey asked.

"I'd be more gracious." Goldie smiled. "I'd make friends with the people in town. Alice was always—what's the word they use now?"

"Mean?"

Goldie smiled. "Mean, stubborn, hardheaded. All those. Control freak, that's what I was trying to think of. Alice always had to be in charge. And it's hard, it's impossible, to get close to people if you spend all your time trying to dominate them." She glanced at Kelsey, who tried to look sympathetic. "For a long time Alice was secretive about it. None of us knew how absolutely determined she was to get her way. Finally she has, and she's dropped her pretenses. But pretense isn't such a bad thing."

"Why haven't you been coming to the trial, ma'am?"

Aunt Goldie frowned, as if at a short, sharp bubble of gas under her heart. "I don't want to hear all that. What's going to come of your trial? Someone will be found guilty, or innocent.

What will it change? I don't want to listen to those—descriptions. It's bad enough to remember." She tried to smile brightly again. "So I take care of the house. I cook supper for them. I need to get to it."

Kelsey stopped her. "Aunt Goldie, I need your help."

Mrs. Hatteras smiled more genuinely. "Aunt Goldie. That's what everyone here calls me. Whose aunt am I now? Just Katherine's, I guess. Poor Kathy. She doesn't need an aunt, she needs ..."

When it was clear she wasn't going to finish, Kelsey said again, "I need your memory."

The old woman looked up in surprise. "What do I know?"

"What was said here that morning. You left here after Helena Parker. Maybe you heard something she didn't. Did you hear Lorrie tell Ronald that he could take lessons from Morgan?"

"They didn't mean what they were saying, they were just trying to hurt each other. I know—"

"I'm not asking you to evaluate it. I just need to know what you heard. Did you hear that?"

"Yes."

"And did you hear what Ronald answered?"

A reprise of the pained frown crossed the woman's worn face, and Kelsey felt that hopeful lift of the heart lawyers feel when a witness is stabbed by painful memory.

"Yes, I did."

Kelsey had a small urge just to walk through the next door, too, without knocking. But she had to be invited back inside the cabin in the woods. She stood on its porch for a long minute, listening. She almost turned away, but finally she tapped on the heavy door.

For such a timid little knock, it drew a big response. The door was flung open, Peter stuck his head out, then put his arm around her waist and drew her inside, as if she were pursued. Kelsey lost her breath.

He let her go and stared at her. "Hi." His voice was strange. "I went by your room but you weren't there. I thought—"

Peter probably didn't know what he'd thought. He looked bereft of thought. The only thing he was wearing was a pair of jeans. His hair was wild and his pale eyes were as Kelsey had never seen them before, tired but staring. He looked like a man who'd had a visitation from the dead. His eyes stayed locked on Kelsey's face as if it had been a long time since he'd seen her.

Kelsey opened her arms and he came into them. An expulsion of breath, a whoosh of gratitude, came from both of them. She held him tight, cheek pressed against his. "I'm sorry. I'm sorry, Peter."

"No," he murmured. "You were right. What else could you think? I don't know what to think myself. It doesn't make sense, you know. Somebody wanted to frame Billy, but so stupidly it would never hold up. They must've known the blood would be tested, that the frame wouldn't hold up. It's like some kid did it, without thinking."

Kelsey had thought the same thing. She was ready to listen again when Peter talked. One thing Peter had accomplished, with his wild-eyed burrowing through trash and his dramatic entrance into the courtroom bearing bloody remains, was to convince Kelsey that he was on her side. It could have been an elaborate ploy, a strategy to worm his way back into her confidence, knowing the baby gown wouldn't be entered in evidence against Billy anyway. But Kelsey wasn't paranoid enough to believe that. Not after watching him stand up to Morgan Fletcher. If that had been an act . . .

Well, sometimes you just had to take things on faith. Kelsey believed in Peter again. She believed in the sincerity of his arms, of the tear between their cheeks. When they finally drew back, she put a hand up to his face.

"I'm sorry," he said, sounding genuinely discouraged. "I wanted to bring you something you could use, I wanted to break the case wide open for you. But it was just useless."

"No, it wasn't. That gown was crucial, Peter. It saved the case." He rolled his eyes, the first normal-looking expression he'd worn. "It did. Because it turned the judge. I'm positive she was ready to pour me out on directed verdict. She wouldn't even have let the case go to the jury. She would have done that favor for Morgan, I think, granted the directed verdict—and my case was weak enough to justify it. But not after she saw that gown. She couldn't take her eyes off it. You saw her touch it. She wouldn't let it in to the jury and I think she was right, it would have turned them against Billy without really proving anything against him. That's what it did to Judge Saunders. She ruled in my favor on the directed verdict because of that baby gown sitting on my table in its envelope."

Kelsey was convincing. She knew that from Peter's face, the way his expression smoothed out and turned believing. For all his work to have gone for nothing, that would have been maddening for him.

"Thank you," she said.

They hugged again. Peter said her name softly. She kissed his neck and bit his earlobe gently, on her way to finding his mouth. She felt softer when they kissed. It was peculiar, this physical intensifying as she began to feel less substantial. Kelsey was enjoying the strangeness quite a lot when they broke gently apart. Peter stared at her for a long moment, then glanced from her eyes to his hands on her cheeks. Suddenly he pulled away. He looked at his fingernails, rubbed his hands together, and said in that choked voice he'd used when she'd first arrived, "I need to shower. Will you wait?"

She laughed at his uncertainty. "Go on." She pushed at his bare shoulder. He managed a smile before he went off through the bedroom door. In a minute she heard the sound of water running. She imagined him in the shower. Remembered him in the woods.

She walked around his house, feeling possessive again. The cabin was growing dark. She turned on the hanging lamp over the small dining table. The cabin was furnished in a masculine way—heavy wooden furniture, leather sofa—but with an occasional decorative touch that startled the eye, such as the blue-checked curtains around the kitchen window, over the sink.

She wandered into the bedroom, where the sound of the shower water was louder. Steam padded out of the almost closed bathroom door. Peter's jeans were laid neatly on a cane-bottomed chair. Kelsey found the bed unmade and smoothed its sheets. She wandered to the closet, the door of which was standing open, and glanced inside. What she saw saddened her expression. She glanced at the bathroom door. "Poor Peter," she said softly.

Hanging on the closet rod was a towel, still damp. Of course, he had changed out of his uniform, and he must have taken a shower then. How many showers had he taken? How hard was he finding it to wash off the imagined grime of his weeks sifting through garbage? He was afraid to touch her.

Kelsey found a hanger and began unbuttoning her blouse.

She was surprised not to surprise him when she slipped into the shower. As if Peter had been expecting her, or imagining her. Her hands on his back like the steam solidifying. He stood still when she touched him. Kelsey pressed herself full length against his back, moving her thigh along his. She was murmuring something that couldn't be heard over the sound of the water, but Peter nodded. She put her arms around him and laid her head on his shoulder. The steam crept up her legs. She felt the steam, insinuating itself up her body, more than she did the streams of water. Peter turned, the pivot against which Kelsey molded herself. Her breasts flattened against his chest. His soapy hands went down her back, slowly, slippery but not uncertain in their grip. As he turned, a spray of warm water hit her neck. Kelsey hid her face in the hollow beneath his collarbone. But his hands moving around her hips made her lift her face, smiling.

"Kelsey," he said longingly.

His lips were moist, not too wet.

"Tell me about Lorrie," she said.

They lay on Peter's bed, atop the sheets Kelsey had smoothed an hour earlier. The bedroom was dim. The only light slanted in from the lamp Kelsey had turned on in the other room, but it was sufficient for her to see the towels on the floor, her clothes hanging in the closet. Most clearly of all she could see Peter. Her head had been lying on his arm, but she raised up on her elbow when she asked the question. She could see and feel the slight flinch with which Peter heard it.

"I wasn't in love with her, or anything like that."

"I know."

"But I always expected to see her again. Not in a big way, not have an important conversation, just run across her now and again. See her on the street Christmastime, see how big her girl was getting. Maybe look at her closely enough to see how she was aging. Maybe say to somebody later, 'Have you seen Lorrie

Blystone lately? She still looks good, doesn't she?' Or, 'She's putting on a few pounds,' or something. See how we're both changing."

He stared across the room and rubbed his lips together. "I keep thinking about her. Sometimes at the end of the day I think, Lorrie'll never have another day like this. Good day, bad day, whatever." He smiled and touched Kelsey. "Never have this." She returned him the same sad smile. It was oddly intimate and affecting, hearing him talk about the dead woman. Kelsey believed Peter when he said he hadn't loved Lorrie Blystone. But it was equally obvious her death had touched him, and his emotions in turn touched Kelsey.

"I remember thinking the same thing about my dad for a long time after he died," Peter continued suddenly. "You can't just leave them in the ground, you imagine—they're here, feeling the pain of not being around any more."

Starting to feel cold, Kelsey pulled the bedspread up to her waist. "But tell me what she was like." She was still looking for a hook for her final argument—some endearing trait everyone knew about that she could use to remind everyone what a fine person Lorrie had been, what a vile act her murder was.

"She was fun if you were on her side."

"But you had to choose sides?"

"No, I don't mean that, I mean—she'd always be saying something to one person but looking at another person out of the side of her eye to see if you got it. And she would—oh, man. You know that governor you have in your head that keeps you from saying some of the things you think?" Kelsey nodded. "Lorrie didn't have one of those. She could say really hurtful things to people. Funny things, so if you knew her, you knew she had said it just because she'd thought of a funny way to put something, and she couldn't stand not to say it. It wasn't always cruel things, sometimes it was just funny things. But it didn't matter. If it was something mean, she'd expect you to forgive her, because to Lorrie it really was all just in fun. And usually people would."

Peter's voice had lifted but was now trailing off again. "Must have been hard to live with, though."

Kelsey agreed. She didn't think she'd want to remind the jury of the endearing way Lorrie had had of making snide remarks to all and sundry and expecting them to laugh it off the way she did.

But somehow the narrative made Kelsey feel even more strongly about Peter. She put her hands on his chest, rested her chin on the backs of her hands, and looked down at him, stretched out in exhaustion, to which she had contributed. Peter would be a great old friend to have.

She said it aloud. "You didn't care all that much about her, but you spend weeks in the dump digging through trash to find some evidence of what happened to her baby, or that would help solve her murder." She was smiling.

"Don't you know anything?" Peter looked at her in genuine surprise. "I didn't do that for Lorrie."

He raised up, lifting her easily, and twisted so that she fell sideways, into his arms. He held her and didn't smile as he said, "I did it for you, Kelsey."

Later, in the dead of night, Kelsey stood at a living-room window looking out. Outside, among the pine trees, a strange light, shredded moonlight, would illuminate a trunk then leave it. Fog twisted among the trees, rising then subsiding, simulating movement, so it was easy to imagine something about to come striding out of those woods. Kelsey was naked beneath the blanket she'd pulled around her shoulders. She wasn't cold, but her skin was in gooseflesh. She stood very still, staring.

He came up behind her silently, but she didn't flinch at his touch. From behind he put his arms around her. Kelsey could feel Peter's stare following hers, out into the strange moonscape among the trees. His voice came soft and hoarse.

"You can't get into her skin, Kelsey. Hers is probably rotted away by now. You still have yours."

He demonstrated with a slow run of his hands down her front, inside the blanket. It didn't seem intended to be erotic, it was just meant to remind her of her flesh, but it had both effects. Kelsey stood still for another minute. She felt what Peter had said, the immense gift of being alive, the possibilities opening up from this moment. The feeling contributed to her immobility. She felt what Lorrie had lost: the burden of unlived life.

15

The defense started off the next morning by calling an investigator who testified he had gotten into his car at ten o'clock one morning outside Alice Beaumont's house, driven as fast as he could without getting stopped for speeding, and gotten to Houston Intercontinental Airport just after eleven, barely in time to park and run to a gate for an eleven-fifteen flight. "No questions," Kelsey said.

Next Clyde Wolverton called Bill Stewart, a friend and colleague of Ronald Blystone's in Dallas, who testified to the state of the Blystone marriage.

"Were you ever witness to any of these arguments yourself?"

Stewart, a boyish-looking man in his thirties who looked more like a college student than a professor, shrugged. "Sometimes I'd catch the tail end of one, or the beginning, and I've leave. Sometimes I was around them when you could tell from the atmosphere that things weren't—very pleasant that day around the Blystone household."

"Did Ronald tell you what they argued about?"

Kelsey said, "Objection, hearsay. Also irrelevant."

"Overruled." Judge Saunders and Morgan Fletcher were carefully not looking at each other this morning, but Morgan looked more satisfied, in a stiff, grim-faced way, and Kelsey's objections were being shot down like clay pigeons.

"The usual things," Bill Stewart said. "Money, family. Lorrie thought Ronald should get a better-paying job. He thought she should be nicer to her mother. 'That's a gold mine,' he used to tell me." Stewart made a grimace of distaste that made Kelsey think he hadn't been a very good friend of Ronald's.

"Did these arguments between the Blystones ever get violent?"

"Of course I didn't see much. One time I did see Lorrie slam their front door in his face so fast it caught Ronald in the nose." From the careful way Stewart kept his face neutral, it seemed a pleasant memory for him.

"Were there times when these arguments seemed worse than other times?"

"Objection. Speculation, based on hearsay, irrelevant."

"Overruled."

Stewart nodded. "After they'd come back from a visit to Lorrie's hometown, things always seemed worse between them."

Wolverton nodded at getting the right answer. "Pass the witness."

Kelsey sat silent a moment. She had nothing against Bill Stewart, but she didn't like the way he was being used. "You taught with Ronald Blystone at the University of Texas at Dallas?"

"Yes."

"Did you ever see him teach a class, perhaps after one of these supposed arguments with his wife he told you about?" She threw in the last part just to forestall objection from Clyde Wolverton, and it worked.

Stewart spoke carefully. "I observed him teach a couple of times. I don't remember if it was after an argument."

"What was Professor Blystone's teaching method like? Did he use the Socratic method?"

Stewart smiled. "I guess we all do to one extent or another."

"So he'd try to draw answers out of students? Tell me, Mr. Stewart, how did Mr. Blystone treat students who gave answers he thought wrong?"

"Objection," Wolverton finally said, sounding puzzled. "How is this relevant?"

"Since the defense case seems to be based on arguments between the two victims, and it's the State's theory that an argument between the defendant and Ronald Blystone helped prompt the murders, then Mr. Blystone's style of argument is very much relevant."

Judge Saunders shook her head. "Sustained."

Well, Kelsey hadn't thought she'd go for it. But she persisted. "Was Ronald Blystone a popular teacher?"

"Objection."

"Sustained."

"Did students who had taken a class from him want to take more?"

"Objection."

"Sustained."

Kelsey tapped her fingers. Finally she asked, "Did Ronald talk to you about these arguments he and his wife would have here in Galilee?"

Clyde Wolverton didn't at all mind her asking this question. The witness sat for a moment, then surprised that there was no objection hastily said, "Yes. Well, some."

"Did he tell you about his arguments with other family members?"

"He'd mention it."

"Did he tell you the effect those arguments would have on Billy Fletcher?"

"Objection. Hearsay."

Kelsey stood. "Your Honor, this concerns the prior relationship between the deceased and the defendant, which is specifically admissible by statute."

"That doesn't overcome the hearsay objection, Ms. Thatch. Sustained."

Kelsey sat, trying not to show her frustration, then decided what the hell, let the jury see it. Let them see she was trying to get them evidence and being prevented.

"Did he tell you what he thought of Billy Fletcher?"

"Objection. Hearsay."

"Sustained."

"Did he tell you that he argued with Billy Fletcher just to goad him sometimes? Just for the fun of it?"

"Objection. Hearsay."

"Sustained."

Clyde Wolverton had at least learned this one successful thing to say. Kelsey turned and glared at him. Then she kept looking that way, wanting to draw the jurors' attention in that direction as well, because she saw that her answerless questions had had an unexpectedly successful result. They had plunged Billy Fletcher into his memories. The witness couldn't answer the questions about how Ronald Blystone had treated Billy, but Billy remembered. His face was flushed and furious. Billy sat there looking as stolid as he could, but his face gave him away. His eyes were murderous.

Still looking that way, Kelsey asked, "How did Ronald act when he would talk about Billy Fletcher?"

Wolverton stood confidently, said, "Objection, Your Honor, hear—," then realized something new was called for.

"Hearsay? I'm not asking the witness what he heard, I'm asking what he observed himself."

Judge Saunders looked to Wolverton. When he couldn't answer, she nodded to the witness.

"Well, Mr. Stewart?" Kelsey repeated. "How did Ronald Blystone act when he talked about Billy Fletcher?"

Stewart spread his hands and answered simply. "He'd laugh."

Billy's flush deepened.

Trial took a short break after Bill Stewart's departure, so short that though the jurors went out to their room, most of the trial participants stayed in place. Judge Saunders stood and rotated her neck, stretching her arms. It was easy to imagine the judge in an aerobics class. Kelsey remembered her the night of the country club party, how caustic and fun Saunders had been. Kelsey wished she could hear the judge's comments on the progress of the trial. It wasn't a fun job, judge, to sit stern and silent and represent the impartiality of the law.

Kelsey turned toward the spectator seats and saw Mrs. Beaumont and Katherine. Alice Beaumont was beckoning Kelsey with a peremptory hand. Kelsey decided to ignore her. She looked farther back and saw Peter. He was coming in from the hall and looked intently at Kelsey, trying to convey something. Just then Judge Saunders rapped her gavel and the jurors began returning. Kelsey shrugged at Peter.

"Is your witness here, Mr. Wolverton?" the judge asked naturally, seating herself.

"Oh, yes, Your Honor." Clyde Wolverton had gone into the

hall during the break and returned fairly rubbing his hands with glee. "The defense calls Ms. Jean Blair."

He was still standing back at the far end of the aisle, and he extended his arm like a talk show host introducing a movie star and gesturing both for entrance and applause. Then he started back up the aisle like a herald.

Peter held the door open, giving Kelsey another look, and this time he stayed in the courtroom.

Jean Blair came through the door looking straight ahead; her line of sight made a right-angled turn when she did. She strode purposefully. Young, around Kelsey's age, Blair was attractive in a stiff way, as if being pretty were a useful obligation. She wore a blue suit, her dark blond hair was neatly short, and the jurors heard the whisk of efficiency when she sat in the witness stand and crossed her legs.

Kelsey frowned because she had never heard of Jean Blair.

"State your name, please," Clyde Wolverton said happily.

"Jean Blair," she answered in a well-modulated voice.

"Where are you employed?"

"Eastex Electronics. I'm a product representative." Such a perfectly bland job title, it produced no more questioning along that line from the defense lawyer, and Kelsey could think of none either.

She thought she heard a slight stir in the courtroom, but when she turned, she couldn't see anyone whispering. Peter Stiller was no longer among the spectators.

"Where were you on October twenty-first of last year?" Wolverton continued.

"I made a business trip from Houston to Raleigh, North Carolina." Now a definite murmur arose in the courtroom as everyone realized that the case was almost over, the defense victory assured.

"Do you recognize anyone in the courtroom, Ms. Blair?" Clyde Wolverton asked in a deep, confident voice. Billy Fletcher sat up straighter at the urging of his attorney's elbow.

Jean Blair didn't need the help. She'd been watching Billy since the question began. "Yes, Mr. Fletcher, sitting beside you. He sat next to me on the flight from Houston to North Carolina."

"What time did that flight take off, ma'am?"

"I have my ticket receipt here, which says the scheduled departure time was eleven-twelve A.M., and I remember that was about what time we left. A few minutes late, of course, leaving Intercontinental."

"Was there anything particularly memorable about the flight, Ms. Blair?"

The witness thought for a moment and shrugged. "Not especially. It was pretty smooth. I remember at one point there was some kind of disturbance a few rows behind us, someone complaining about not getting the special meal they'd ordered. That's when Mr. Fletcher and I looked up from our work and introduced ourselves. I asked what business he was in, and after he told me his company, I remember being grateful that he hadn't made the old joke that he traveled in ladies' underwear. That's the main thing I remember about our conversation."

Jean Blair had a pert little nose, too cute for her otherwise patrician face, and a mouth that looked prim when she closed it, but opened substantially when she talked and could probably produce a dazzling smile. Kelsey disliked her immensely. From that dislike she had already proceeded to the assumption that Ms. Blair was lying like a thief. But how to prove that Kelsey hadn't figured out, when Clyde Wolverton turned to her pleasantly and said, "Your witness."

"How long did your flight take, Ms. Blair?"

"Two and a half, three hours, I think. Let me see, yes, my ticket says arrival time two forty-six. Of course, that was eastern time, an hour later."

"And in this two-and-a-half-hour flight you only remember the one conversation with Mr. Fletcher about what companies you both worked for?"

"There were other things, I'm sure, but nothing important."

Watching the witness intently, Kelsey continued, "After you realized you were going to the same city, did Mr. Fletcher ask where you were staying?"

"No," Jean Blair said coolly.

"You wouldn't say you made friends with him?"

"No."

"When you both left the plane, did he offer you a ride, or a local phone number?"

"No." Ms. Blair fixed Kelsey with a look. "He didn't try to chat me up, he didn't suggest we get together for a drink, and he didn't grope my leg when I had to squeeze out past him." She lifted an eyebrow, asking if she had settled all that.

"And yet you remember him."

Jean Blair wasn't flustered. "I have a good memory for names and faces. That comes in useful in business, and I've worked at it."

Kelsey could almost hear Clyde Wolverton chuckling. He'd given Kelsey free rein with his witness, and Blair had effectively put Kelsey in her place. Kelsey rubbed her forehead. She asked more questions about the flight, the times, other passengers, hearing herself growing less relevant, but still with no objection from the defense.

Kelsey turned and saw from the big clock high on the back wall that it was eleven-thirty. "Your Honor." She stood. "I have a few more questions for Ms. Blair, but I wonder if we could break for lunch now? I'd like to talk to the defense."

Without comment, as if Kelsey's request were commonplace, Judge Saunders announced, "We'll be in recess until one o'clock."

A babble of voices broke out before the judge rose to her feet. The jurors were conspicuously silent as they filed out, but they looked back at the lawyers curiously.

"You'd like to talk?" Clyde Wolverton said genially.

"I'll find you in a few minutes," Kelsey said.

First she retreated to her office on the second floor, which already had a disused quality. Since trial had begun, Kelsey had spent almost no time there. A cobweb decorated the window. Kelsey called a friend in the Houston DA's office, who did a quick computer check and found no criminal record for Jean Blair. "She did have a speeding ticket couple of years ago. Here's her date of birth. She look about thirty-two?"

"Yeah."

"That's her, then. So I can confirm she was born."

"Thanks, Alison. I would have sworn from looking at her she was created in a laboratory."

"Sorry, Kelsey. She's not a criminal."

"Thanks anyway."

Kelsey walked down the dimly lit hall, at first slowly and thoughtfully, then her pace picking up. Kelsey went straight to Morgan Fletcher's office door and opened it, interrupting a masculine chuckle. Three men turned toward her. The only one looking surprised was Billy Fletcher. Beside him, his lawyer gave Kelsey a smug look, the expression of a man waiting for an opening bid he knew he was going to refuse.

Morgan Fletcher just looked at her. He clearly had not been the one chuckling. He was the only one of the trio who seemed to commiserate with Kelsey's dilemma.

To Clyde Wolverton, Kelsey said, "Why didn't you bring this witness to me before trial? I told you a long time ago that if you could show me proof your client made that flight, I'd consider dismissal."

"It took us a while to locate Ms. Blair," the defense lawyer said, taken aback. "And you hadn't made any promises. I didn't—"

"Didn't want to give me a chance to investigate your witness," Kelsey said hotly.

"No, no. We have nothing to fear from investigation. Ms. Blair is exactly what she seems to be. I have never—"

"Why is it so hard to believe I'm innocent?" Billy Fletcher interrupted. "All the evidence—"

Kelsey stepped between them, up to her real adversary. "I would have thought you would have brought her to me if you cared about your brother's best interests."

"I thought Clyde had," Morgan Fletcher said simply, which gave Kelsey pause.

Morgan continued, "Do you mean if you'd heard her say two months ago what you just heard her say from the witness stand, you would have dismissed the case? Why don't you do it now, then—if you think that's the right thing to do."

Somehow Morgan made it sound not like a suggestion but like a question, as if he were asking Kelsey's opinion on an ethical matter.

Kelsey didn't answer.

At ten till one she was in the city square across the street from the courthouse, eating an utterly tasteless tuna sandwich strictly out of obligation, so she wouldn't feel faint later in the afternoon. On this cold, cloudy day, Kelsey had the outdoors to herself. She was mulling over Morgan Fletcher's good question. The defense testimony had been straightforward and Kelsey had no way to refute it. Was there some reason, then, she found herself so unwilling to do the reasonable thing? She had seen this happen to other prosecutors when a case was no longer about its facts; it was about a defense witness being too cool under cross-examination, about the imagined smirk on a defense lawyer's face. Kelsey tried to put all that aside and think about what Morgan Fletcher had so simply suggested: the right thing to do.

A few minutes later she turned and chucked the rest of her sandwich toward a trash can—even pigeons wouldn't want it, she was sure—and was about to cross the street when she saw Peter Stiller coming toward her. He carried a slip of paper. Without greeting he said, "I called the company she said she works for, Eastex Electronics. Talked to this man, the sales manager. That's what he said."

"Really?" Kelsey said, momentarily happy as she read the note, then growing more thoughtful, waving the paper in the breeze. "Doesn't really tell me much."

"It tells you she's a liar."

Kelsey smiled. She patted her partner's chest by way of thanks. "Can you get me something written? Can we make something bigger of this?"

"Maybe, if you give me time."

"I don't have any time."

At one o'clock Kelsey was sitting at her table in the courtroom, poring over a three-page document. She had the identifying information at the top of the page covered with a legal pad, but as Jean Blair walked past to the witness stand, she could see it was a bank statement Kelsey was reading.

The January day was growing colder. Occasionally the courtroom windows shivered with a blast of air. The weather made the courtroom seem an isolated refuge. When the jurors were back in their box and all eyes turned questioningly in her direction, Kelsey looked up for the first time.

"Did you receive a nice Christmas bonus from Eastex Electronics this year?" she asked the witness.

Jean Blair looked at her blankly, doing a mental calculation. "No," she finally said.

"Because in fact by Christmas you were no longer employed by Eastex Electronics, isn't that right? You were laid off more than a month ago."

Jean Blair's mouth was tight and small. She looked at the bank statement Kelsey was holding and made the admission. "Yes, I was—although technically, I believe, I'm still carried as an employee of the company because my benefits continue for three months. Health insurance and so on."

Kelsey let "and so on" go. She looked stern. "How much did the defense pay you for your testimony?" she asked bluntly.

Jean Blair's mouth opened, but only for the tip of her tongue to touch a spot on her upper lip, a spot that must have been dry. After the tongue's ministration she looked perfect again. "Not for my testimony. But they agreed to pay my expenses."

"Expenses," Kelsey said musingly. "That would amount to about fifteen dollars for the round-trip from Houston, if you used premium gas. Right?"

"And for my time. A reasonable amount."

"Which was?" Kelsey lifted the bank statement into greater visual prominence. She glanced at a line of it, clearly ready to compare the deposit amount with whatever figure the witness was about to say.

"Ten thousand dollars."

There were quick gasps from the audience. Their muttering continued even after Judge Saunders rapped her gavel. Kelsey distinctly heard someone say, "Miz Beaumont would've topped that offer."

"I have no more questions," Kelsey said.

Clyde Wolverton tried his best to rehabilitate his witness, asking the standard questions. The money had had nothing to do with *what* she testified, had it?

"Not at all," Jean Blair said staunchly. "I told the truth."

"Did you alter your testimony in any way because of the money you received for your expenses?"

"No, sir. Not a bit."

"Is everything you told this jury the truth?"

"It is." Ms. Blair looked straight at the jurors, in a last bid to give the defense its money's worth.

Kelsey didn't bother to question her again. Even while Wolverton did damage control, Kelsey felt eyes on her, on the document in her hand. Specifically she felt observed by Morgan Fletcher, felt him wondering how she could have gotten the documentary evidence so quickly.

Kelsey glanced at the bank statement again, which showed that Kelsey had a balance of $241 in her checking account, then she carefully folded it and put it away, back in her briefcase from which she'd drawn it to use as a prop, praying that her guess was right, that after Jean Blair lost her job she would have demanded money from what she saw as a wealthy defendant for whom she was doing a big favor.

Jean Blair left the witness stand, moving up the courtroom aisle more quickly than she'd come. Clyde Wolverton stood shakily. "Your Honor, the defense would like— May we approach the bench?"

Kelsey went with him, but she turned out not to be a participant in the conversation. "Judge, we need a continuance," the defense lawyer said softly. "There was a witness we, we didn't think we'd need, but now—" He wouldn't look at Kelsey. He leaned close to Judge Saunders. "We need a day or so to find her, Judge."

Judge Saunders did not share Wolverton's desire for closeness or privacy. Her voice was not that of a friend. "This isn't California, Clyde. We're going to have an ending to this thing this week." She paused, thinking. "I'll give you till tomorrow morning," the judge finally concluded.

"Thank you, Judge."

After the early dismissal spectators stayed in the courtroom, standing in conversational groups like people after church. Reporters at the back of the room were waiting to grab Kelsey, and cameramen in the hall. Texas hadn't forgotten the missing baby that had inspired the statewide search three months earlier. Kelsey decided to wait at her table. But her musing was interrupted by the appearance of Alice Beaumont at the railing. Mrs.

Beaumont was again dressed in black, under her fur. She reached out a hand toward Kelsey. The hand looked old, almost a claw.

"Come to my house," she said to Kelsey, but it was a plea, not a demand.

It was a strange tableau. Only a couple of feet from Mrs. Beaumont's reaching hand, her son-in-law turned away from her. Mrs. Beaumont and her onetime employee Billy didn't look at each other either. Behind Mrs. Beaumont Kelsey saw Katherine. Morgan Fletcher turned just before he left and shot a look at his wife, but Katherine was looking down, just waiting for her mother. Morgan didn't wait to get her attention. He turned quickly and exited the courtroom with the defense team.

"Please," Mrs. Beaumont renewed her plea to Kelsey.

"All right," Kelsey said, "I was going to anyway."

The Beaumont mansion was a house of women that afternoon. No one mentioned Morgan, making Kelsey wonder what his presence in the family would be like from now on. If Billy were convicted and sent to prison, wouldn't his brother become his stand-in in the family, the object of hostility? Kelsey looked at Katherine, wondering if she would stick by her husband. She never seemed to now; how would she weather her mother's anger at Morgan? There must be some secret bond in marriage Kelsey didn't understand.

In the house Katherine wasn't nearly as subdued as she'd been in the courtroom. Kelsey recognized her outfit again, classy gray slacks and a cream-colored blouse. In court, under a coat, the clothes had seemed almost mournful, but as Katherine moved with a long stride across her mother's dining room, it became a sporty outfit. "I guess we'll hear from Billy tomorrow," Katherine said casually.

"If we hear from him at all," Kelsey said. "They could've had him testify this afternoon. Makes me wonder if Wolverton'll put him on the stand at all."

"Could he not?" Mrs. Beaumont asked. She had shrugged out of her fur coat, dropped it right onto the floor in the entry hall, where it still lay. Mrs. Beaumont had emerged from the coat larger than she had seemed within its embrace.

"Billy doesn't have to testify," Kelsey said. "The defendant always has that choice. I think it would be a mistake for him not to, though. The jury will want to hear him. I don't think he can win a not-guilty verdict without getting up there and denying he did anything wrong."

"Then maybe we want him to make that mistake." Mrs. Beaumont's voice had an urgency, as if she could make happen whatever she decided was the right course for events to take.

"Don't you want to hear what he has to say, Mother? You've never let him tell you."

Katherine leaned back against the dining room table, throwing her hair back over her shoulder. Her hair was longer than Kelsey remembered. Combined with the elegant clothes, the sweep of hair gave Katherine a certain glamour. Her mother turned and gave her a hard look, but Katherine just looked back, not challenging, but not flinching, either.

Maybe there are roles in a family that have to be filled. Mrs. Beaumont had only had one challenger in her family, and she was now gone. Kelsey realized with a start that that was whom Katherine reminded her of now: Lorrie. Her posture, the nearblankness of her face, ready to turn to any emotion, reminded Kelsey of pictures she'd seen and stories she'd been told of the younger sister. Maybe Katherine had been studying Lorrie all those years, waiting for her chance no longer to be the understudy.

Kelsey turned to the other person in the room. Aunt Goldie was there, though no one noticed. Mrs. Hatteras was so self-effacing she almost didn't exist.

"I'm going to call you tomorrow," Kelsey said to her. "Are you ready?"

Aunt Goldie blushed but nodded. Her sister turned a surprised look on her. "What on earth is Goldie going to do?"

"Testify to what she heard," Kelsey said. "Which reminds me. Have you thought any more about what *you* heard, Mrs. Beaumont? Still nothing?"

Mrs. Beaumont's face fell. She turned introspective, and it didn't look good on her. Alice Beaumont needed someone to boss around, and when it was her memory she was unsuccessfully commanding, the combination of anger and abashed inability on her face made her look schizophrenic.

"I remember," she said slowly, "something woke me up. And then I heard the baby crying and that kept me awake. I kept waiting for somebody to go to Taylor. I wondered where everybody was. I heard somebody moving around downstairs. And I heard men's voices."

"Men's?" Kelsey asked.

"Yes. Only men." Mrs. Beaumont had dredged her memory for her daughter's voice and come up empty. "I drifted off again, then something else woke me. Some noise. Then everything was quiet again. Except Taylor crying. I still heard her. On and on."

Her voice had grown softer and softer. The other women watched her silently, watched Alice Beaumont diminish from matriarch to grandmother. As she lifted her face in a listening attitude, they realized she was still living that memory, listening in her empty house to a cry she couldn't answer.

Kelsey woke early the next morning, already thinking, as if dream thoughts had awakened her. She had told the jury that mysteries would remain in the case, but she didn't like them. "You haven't accounted for everyone in the house," Peter had once said to her, but Kelsey couldn't imagine Mrs. Beaumont rising from her sickbed to commit some mayhem. And if she had heard more than she'd said, she had no reason to keep it from Kelsey, did she? What about Helena Parker, why had she gone into hiding?

And, she remembered in the shower, who had burned those baby clothes in the woods, and why?

Surely this could not be the bombshell witness the defense had needed half a day to find: this little old lady coming staunchly up the aisle gripping a cane until her hand was white. She was obviously from Galilee, she nodded to people in the courtroom, and when she said her name on the witness stand, Kelsey found it vaguely familiar: Gladys Gottschalk.

"Mrs. Gottschalk," Clyde Wolverton asked gently but loudly, "do you remember an encounter you had with a stranger last fall?"

"Yes, sir, I sure do. October twentieth, it was, a Tuesday evening."

Now Kelsey remembered. She stood quickly. "Your Honor, may we have a hearing on this?"

"Approach."

Wolverton went quickly, to get in the first word at the bench. "Very simple matter, Your Honor," he said briskly. "And no surprise to the prosecution. I believe you've seen the police report," he said to Kelsey.

"I did. This is about the drifter on her porch?"

"That's right," Wolverton said, turning back to the judge. "Less than a mile from the Beaumont house, only half a day before the murders."

"Oh, please," Kelsey said. Looking at Judge Saunders's face, she saw she'd have to amplify her objection. "Do you have any evidence at all that would connect this so-called drifter with the crimes on trial here?"

"I just told you some. Why don't you listen and hear?"

Kelsey turned to the judge, lifting a reasonable hand. "Objection," she said simply.

Judge Saunders didn't seem to be paying close attention. "Overruled. I'll let the jury hear her."

Turning away, Kelsey noticed that Morgan Fletcher was absent from his habitual spot directly behind the defense table. Maybe he couldn't take it any more, after Kelsey had decided not to dismiss the prosecution.

"You said this happened on the evening of Tuesday, October twentieth, Mrs. Gottschalk?"

"Yes, sir." The old lady had a prominent chin, which became the dominant feature of her face when she closed her mouth firmly, as she did after every answer she snapped out.

"Could you describe him, please, ma'am?"

"Tall man, somewhere around forty years old. Mean look about him, even when he tried to smile and look polite."

"Where did you encounter him?"

"Right on my back porch. It was after sundown. I'd locked up and was in the front room. I heard a noise, and when I looked out, I saw this stranger rattling my back doorknob. I ran and got Mr. Gottschalk's shotgun and I opened the door and let this stranger see the gun, and he jumped back fast and tried to look polite, like I say, and asked if I had any work for him. I told him the only work I wanted to see him do was to run away from my house, and I wasn't going to pay him for it, neither."

A chuckle or two from the audience, but obviously not the big response Mrs. Gottschalk had expected. Her chin became prominent again.

"Which way did he go when he left?"

"East."

"Which direction, if you know, is Mrs. Alice Beaumont's house from yours, Mrs. Gottschalk?"

"East."

When the witness was passed to her, Kelsey said, not bothering to hide her disgust, "No questions."

Wolverton watched his witness leave, then his attention shifted. Kelsey turned, too, and saw Morgan Fletcher walking toward the front. Morgan gave the defense lawyer a grim little nod and took his seat. He didn't look at Kelsey.

"Mr. Wolverton?" the judge said.

Clyde Wolverton stood and called an unfamiliar name. She entered from the hallway and took her seat, and it became quickly clear that the defense had found their witness, a flight attendant who had served on the flight from Houston to North Carolina that had supposedly carried Billy Fletcher. The attendant, Terry Fortescue, was younger and less steely than Jean Blair had been, functionally pretty in a blue suit that approximated the look of a uniform, with a bright, fresh forehead and a mouth that fell naturally into a smile.

"Him," she said, pointing to Billy Fletcher. "I didn't know his name, but I remember seeing him on that flight."

"Do you know his name now?" Clyde Wolverton asked.

"Mr. Fletcher." Ms. Fortescue looked alert. She smiled.

"Is there some reason why you didn't come forward at once when you read that Mr. Fletcher had been arrested?"

"Because I didn't read about it. Soon after that trip I was transferred to an international route. I've been flying over the pole to Japan. I guess that's why I remember those last few domestic flights so well."

"Pass the witness," Wolverton said, trying to sound triumphant.

Kelsey spoke at once. "Ms. Fortescue, how many flights have you made as a flight attendant?"

"Goodness, I'm not sure. I've been doing it for four years."

"On a day like that October twenty-first, would the flight from Houston to Raleigh have been your only flight of the day?"

"Oh, no," the witness said brightly. "After we stopped in Raleigh, I'd work the flight to wherever the plane was going next— Nashville or Chicago or wherever—then the return trip to Houston."

"So two or three flights a day. Five days a week?"

"Five, yes." Ms. Fortescue smiled.

"For four years. Math wasn't my strong subject, but could we say that's hundreds of flights you've worked on?"

"That sounds right."

"Which would mean thousands of passengers, correct? And you remember all the passengers on all those flights?"

"Oh, no, of course not. But some of them stand out."

"Uh-huh." Kelsey stood and crossed in front of the defense table. She stopped in front of Billy Fletcher, turned her back on him, and faced the witness. "Ms. Fortescue, would you describe Billy Fletcher, please? What color hair does he have?"

"Reddish. Maybe strawberry blond. Light-colored, anyway."

"Eyes?"

"Blue," the flight attendant said confidently.

"Is he wearing a wedding ring?"

Ms. Fortescue blinked. "I think so. Yes."

"And how is he dressed?"

The witness's eyes moved, off Kelsey, trying to see past her. She could probably see a sleeve; that was enough. "A brown suit."

Kelsey gave no hints whether any of the answers were wrong or right. She moved away from Billy. "Does he look about the same as he did the day he supposedly took your flight?"

"Yes." The flight attendant was frankly studying Billy now. He smiled sadly.

"Ms. Fortescue, what is there distinctive about Mr. Fletcher's appearance that made him stick in your memory out of thousands of passengers you've seen?"

"Oh, I don't know." The flight attendant looked Billy over. "He has a nice face."

"Uh-huh." Taking her seat, Kelsey gave the jury more time to look at Billy Fletcher. His best friend would not have said that anything about Billy made him stand out in a crowd.

"Do you remember who was sitting in the row of seats with Mr. Fletcher?" Out of the corner of her eye Kelsey saw Clyde Wolverton sit up a little straighter, looking almost happy.

"Yes." Ms. Fortescue smiled. "A woman dressed for business. Blond, very pretty, about thirty?" She asked for confirmation.

Kelsey didn't give it. "What about the ma—the person directly across the aisle from Mr. Fletcher?"

"Uh . . ." The flight attendant blinked. Blinked again. "No, I don't recall him."

"Do you remember who occupied the seats on the row in front of Mr. Fletcher and the blond woman?"

"Um." Terry Fortescue gave up after a brief struggle. "No."

"White? Black? Adults, children?"

"No, I'm sorry."

"What about the people in back of Mr. Fletcher?"

"It was a couple, I think, with a child. I'm not—"

"Take your time," Kelsey said kindly. The witness shrugged.

"Ms. Fortescue, there was a little disturbance a few rows behind Mr. Fletcher and Ms. Blair at one point. Someone was causing a stir. Do you remember what the trouble was?"

The flight attendant blinked again. Her blinking became more rapid. "About—the air vent?" she finally guessed.

"Thank you, Ms. Fortescue. I have no more questions."

Terry Fortescue turned to the defense table. "Was that it?"

No one answered her.

"The defense calls Billy Fletcher." Clyde Wolverton's voice had regained its sturdiness. Other aspects of the defense case might have faltered, but the strongest part was about to begin. Billy stood in front of the judge to raise his right hand high and took the witness oath in a loud, strong voice. His posture was good in the witness stand, not the nervous, shifting stance that seat sometimes inspired. Kelsey would have bet he'd sat there before, through many a rehearsal.

"State your name, please."

"Billy Fletcher."

"And your occupation?"

"I'm not sure. Farmer, I guess. I worked for Smoothskins for almost twenty years, but not any more."

He didn't sound regretful or apologetic, just stating the facts, but Kelsey noted at least two or three jurors looking at Billy with grim sympathy, reminded that he had already been punished for incurring Mrs. Beaumont's anger, right or wrong.

"Let's get right to it, Billy," Wolverton said with admirable informality. "Why did you go to Mrs. Beaumont's house the morning of October twenty-first?"

"Because I knew Ronald and Lorrie were there. I was on my way out of town, and I wanted to talk to them one more time about the future of the factory. Everybody knows Ronald and I used to argue about that. I thought he'd be working on Miz Beaumont while I was gone, and I wanted to see if maybe we could talk reasonably while she wasn't there. I knew she was sick, and I thought maybe Ronald and Lorrie and I could reach some understanding while she wasn't listening to every word we said."

"You think Mrs. Beaumont's presence affected your arguments with Ronald?"

"Sure she did." Billy sat solidly, hands laced around one up-raised knee, which emphasized the strength in his shoulders. "Half of what Ronald said was just playing up to his mother-in-law. Maybe more than half. He wanted to show off how smart he was. And I gave him the chance, boy. He was damn sure smarter than me, everybody could see that."

Kelsey hadn't made a note yet. She just watched. Billy hadn't glanced in her direction. His attention went from his lawyer to the jury. He spoke easily, sometimes delivering what he was saying directly to the jurors, leaning toward them as if he expected them to smile or nod in response.

"Then why go argue with him again, Billy?"

"I didn't want it to be an argument," Billy said sadly. "I was hoping I could make Ronald really see that there was more to all this discussion than just the numbers he knew so much better than me."

"Is that all? Hadn't you said that to him before?"

"Yes." Then, as if the information were being forced out of him, Billy turned to the jurors and said, "Really it was Lorrie I wanted to talk to. It was hard to tell how Lorrie stood on things. Usually she'd take her husband's side, naturally enough, but— Lorrie'd grown up here. This was her town. She knew these people." The people he meant were in the audience, listening tensely. So many spectators felt involved in the argument Billy was describing. "What I really wanted was to remind Lorrie of how much her family meant to this town, and hope she'd take some pride in that, and some—compassion, I guess you'd say."

"What time did you arrive at the house that morning, Billy?"

"About nine forty-five or so. I knew I didn't have much time, if I was going to catch my flight."

"Billy, we've all heard what Andy Sims saw, so I guess it's safe to say things between you and Ronald didn't go in the calm, reasonable way you'd hoped."

Billy looked wonderful in abashment. That expression became his stolid peasant features. "No, sir. It was the same old story. Ronald'd grin and say something and I'd want—" He quickly realized his mistake. "But I didn't. I stayed calmer than other times. I tried to ignore him, to talk past him to Lorrie."

"According to Mr. Sims, you weren't calm when you and Ronald went out to the front porch."

"He started that. The yelling and pushing. It took me by surprise, because I'd never seen Ronald like that. Usually I was the mad one. What happened was, I started getting to Lorrie. She was listening more than usual. When she got mad, it was at him, not me. Once I said how closing the factory here would just devastate this town, and she said, 'I know, Billy. You're right.'

"Well, that just made Ronald furious. He suddenly went into the bedroom they were staying in and came back with a pistol."

"This pistol?" Clyde Wolverton said, lifting the State's exhibit from the shelf in front of the judge's bench.

"Yes, sir, that one."

Wolverton stole back to his seat, actually ducking his head as if to stay out of the spotlight aimed at Billy.

"He was waving it around and yelling and ordering me to get out of his house. I said it wasn't his house, which was stupid, to

argue with a man with a gun, but you know how you get, somebody yells at you and you yell back. He came over and was
getting the gun close to my head and I tried to take it away from
him. But with us fighting over the gun I could imagine it goin'
off, so I just pushed it away and stepped back and said I was
leaving. That's when we went out to the porch. Ronald was still
yelling and I yelled back, I admit it. But after Andy honked and
waved and I waved back to him, I came to my senses, I guess,
and realized what time it was.

"I got in my car and drove straight to Houston Intercontinental. On the way I called Morgan to say I'd had another stupid
fight with Ronald."

Billy paused for breath. What Morgan Fletcher had observed
about his brother was true, his face reddened easily. The emotions of his argument with Ronald Blystone had played clearly
across Billy's face as he talked. His face remained pink now, but
it made him look embarrassed rather than angry. The witness
stand is an embarrassing place, for the defendant.

"Did you hear anything as you were walking away from the
house?"

"I heard them yelling at each other. Ronald and Lorrie. It
sounded like the fight was getting hotter, I was glad I was out
of it."

"Did you catch your flight on time, Billy?"

"Yes, sir. Here's my boarding pass, stamped to show I
boarded."

Clyde Wolverton rose to take the ticket stub from his client.
"We'll offer this as defense exhibit number one, Your Honor."

He handed the little stub of stiff paper to Kelsey, who looked
at the date and time and flight number printed on one side, then
turned it over to where "Houston Intercontinental" had been
stamped on the opposite side, the letters forming a little circle.

"No objection," she said. The defense lawyer glanced at her
sharply.

Billy resumed his narrative without his lawyer's assistance.
"Ms. Blair was the only other person on my row of seats. That
Miss Fortescue was our stewardess."

"Billy," Clyde Wolverton said sternly, "did you pay that
woman for her testimony?"

Billy answered quietly. "Not for her testimony, no, sir. I paid her for her expenses, and her time and trouble."

"Why?"

"Because she insisted on it. She didn't at first, when we first found her a couple of months ago, but then she lost her job and she said she was looking all over the country for a new one, and if she was going to take time off from her job hunt, she had to be—'compensated' for it. That's the way she put it. It even sounded to me like she was saying she'd be gone when I needed her if I didn't pay her. So I did. You and Morgan said it would be all right."

Wolverton nodded confirmation. Morgan Fletcher sat behind the defense lawyer with his feet flat on the floor, his elbows on the arms of his chair, his fingers laced together. He was staring straight at his brother, and his face brimmed with sympathy, almost a visible wave pouring out of Morgan's eyes. Returning her attention to the witness stand, Kelsey saw that the brothers were sitting in the exact same pose, mirror images.

"Do you have anything else you think you need to say to this jury?"

Billy turned to the jurors as directed. "I did not kill those peo-
. ple," he said distinctly. The line sounded forced. He tried again, leaning toward the jurors. "I didn't. I have never hurt anybody in my life. And I certainly—certainly—wouldn't have done anything to that baby. That doesn't make any sense at all, I had no reason to take their baby. I didn't. I turned and walked away, and they were alive. I swear it."

"Where was the baby during your argument with Ronald, Billy?"

"Playing on the floor, on a little quilt. She wasn't much of a crawler, she pretty much stayed in one spot."

"Did she get upset by the loud voices?"

"No, sir, she seemed used to it."

Kelsey heard the defense lawyer's small sigh. "I pass the witness."

Kelsey sat brooding for a moment. Cross-examining the defendant was a prosecutor's golden opportunity. She felt the burden of that opportunity. She remembered the lessons she'd been taught in the Houston district attorney's office. She had two primary jobs in the next few minutes: she had to get Billy Fletcher mad and she had to put the murder weapon in his hand.

But the first tack she took surprised everyone. "Why didn't you pick up your rental car at the Raleigh-Durham airport, Mr. Fletcher?"

"What?" Billy looked baffled.

Kelsey walked to him. "Do you recognize this?"

"Looks like a rental car reservation, with my name on it."

"Do you remember making this?"

Billy sat silent for several seconds. Finally he shook his head. "I don't. Maybe my secretary made it and forgot to tell me. Or maybe I just forgot."

"At any rate you didn't pick up a car there in Raleigh, did you?"

"No."

"How did you get from the airport to your hotel?"

"Cab, I guess. I really don't remember."

"Do you have a receipt for that cab ride?"

"I don't hang on to things like that. Just a short ride, I don't even ask the company to reimburse me for little things like that."

"Yet you kept your boarding-pass stub." It wasn't a question and Billy didn't answer it. As Kelsey waited, he finally just shrugged.

"Why did you change your plans in Raleigh, Mr. Fletcher?"

"I just forgot. I had a lot on my mind, I was upset over my argument with Ronald, I just . . ."

"Still that upset, three and a half hours later? I thought you said these arguments were commonplace. Did they always upset you so much?"

"They kept getting worse," Billy said, his voice gaining a gravelly quality. He pushed one hand against the other. "Until that morning I— On the plane I kept going over what had happened, thinking there must have been something else I could have said."

"You said you told Lorrie Blystone that closing the factory would devastate this town, is that right?" Kelsey walked back toward her table but didn't resume her seat. She leaned back, watching Billy.

"Yes," he said emphatically. "It would."

"And no one would be more devastated than you, would they,

Mr. Fletcher? Who had the most to lose if Ronald Blystone prevailed in his argument to Mrs. Beaumont?"

"We all did. So many people depend—"

"But only one was the manager. Only one had the most at stake." Kelsey thought about asking Billy how many children he had to support, but decided not to bring up that part of his life. "Isn't that right?"

"I've still got my life. I can find another job. And I've got the farm." Billy roused himself. "If I had to be sacrificed for the factory to stay open, I'm willing to live with that."

"Sacrificed how?"

"By—" Billy struggled with the concept. "By losing my job. By taking the blame for this."

Kelsey abruptly changed tacks again. "Why weren't you wearing a suit when you had your dinner meeting with John Howard? Ms. Fortescue testified you were dressed in a suit on the airplane."

"Yes," Billy said quickly, as if glad of a question he could answer. "But it got rumpled on the plane, like they always do. As soon as I got to the hotel, I sent it out to be cleaned. They claimed they had a one-hour service, but of course it wasn't ready in time." He shrugged amiably.

"Had you talked to your brother, or to anyone in Galilee, by then?"

"Yes, there was a message from Morgan and I called him back. He told me there'd been some trouble, but they weren't sure what yet. It wasn't until later that night he called back and gave me the terrible news. I flew back first thing the next morning."

Kelsey had no way of checking on any of that, even the time of the phone calls. The hotel didn't keep a record of incoming calls. She didn't inquire further. "Why had you asked John Howard for a job?" she asked instead.

"It wasn't like that," Billy replied, again with a prepared answer. "It wasn't like I put in an application. I was just looking around, thinking I needed to look for some options in case the worst happened with the Smoothskins factory."

"Is that the reason you went to North Carolina?"

"No. I went to try to keep them off our backs. I went to try to convince them it would be ridiculous for them to expand their operations in Texas. I went to try to protect my people."

Kelsey felt this going nowhere. She thought Billy's answers sounded canned and false, but she didn't know how he was playing to the jury, who probably believed everything he said anyway. "Let's go back to the argument. It upset you badly, you said."

"Well, no more—"

"Enough that you were still brooding about it hours later."

"Well, yes." A little color crept into Billy's face, but not enough. Get him mad.

"Why?"

"Why?" Billy repeated, looking terribly uncertain.

"Why did this argument upset you more than the others?"

"I don't know. Just them going on so long, you get—to where you don't even want to talk to the guy any more."

"Wasn't this argument worse because Ronald Blystone said something new to you? Something he'd never said before?"

"What do you mean?" The puzzlement on Billy's face had deepened.

Kelsey said slowly, "I'm not testifying, Mr. Fletcher, I'm just asking questions. Don't you remember Ronald Blystone saying something new to you that morning in your employer's house? Something about your future, as distinct from the fate of the factory in general?"

Billy stared at her. "I don't know what you mean," he said, but his face said something different. A deep flush crept up the back of his neck, then into his cheeks. His blue eyes moved, looking more frightened than angry, but looking guilty nonetheless.

Kelsey walked toward him as if she were going to demand an answer, but instead she changed her line of questioning again. She picked up the gun, the murder weapon. "You said this argument grew so heated that Ronald waved this gun close to your face. Did he point it at you?"

"Not exactly. But I was in the line of fire if it had gone off."

"Show me, please. Would you demonstrate what Ronald did with the gun?"

She handed it toward him, butt first. But Billy Fletcher kept his hands folded together and shook his head. "No," he said clearly.

Kelsey looked surprised. "Mr. Fletcher, you're the only one alive who can show this jury what you meant by what you said. I promise you the gun's unloaded." She urged it on him again.

"No." Billy's face was adamant, even alarmed. "I hate guns," he said loudly.

He had been coached. Kelsey knew it. But they had come up with a good line for Billy. Its ardor echoed in the otherwise silent courtroom.

"Yes," Kelsey said. "They're dreadful things, aren't they?"

She dropped the pistol on the evidence shelf with a loud metallic clatter.

16

Judge Saunders said, "Call your next witness, Mr. Wolverton."

Billy was sitting beside his lawyer again. Wolverton put his hand on Billy's shoulder and in a voice ringing with righteousness said, "The defense rests, Your Honor."

Indifferent to the lawyer's noble tone, Judge Saunders turned to Kelsey. "Ms. Thatch, you have rebuttal witnesses?"

"Yes, Your Honor, two. They'll be brief."

Judge Saunders glanced at the clock high on the back wall. "After lunch, then." She turned to the jury. "This case will be coming to you soon, so come back from lunch prepared to put in a long afternoon. But do *not* begin discussing the case yet. You're excused."

As the jurors walked out, Judge Saunders said to the lawyers, "Let's prepare the charge."

Discussing the instructions Judge Saunders would give to the jury didn't take long because to their surprise and irritation, Kelsey and Clyde Wolverton found themselves in agreement on most issues. Lesser included offenses, for example: neither wanted to authorize the jury to convict Billy Fletcher for any crime less than murder.

"There was testimony about struggling over the gun," Judge Saunders suggested mildly. "That might arguably raise the issue of manslaughter rather than murder."

"But no testimony that the gun went off during that struggle," Kelsey quickly pointed out.

"I was going to say that," Wolverton said aggrievedly. "My

client totally denied shooting anyone, Your Honor. That doesn't entitle that jury to convict him of any lesser crime."

"So murder or nothing," Judge Saunders summarized.

"Exactly."

"Yes," Kelsey agreed. She and Wolverton glanced at each other. For a moment they were in collusion against the jury. Neither wanted to give the jurors the chance to compromise on the difficult case by voting to find Billy guilty of a lesser crime. Lawyers from both sides against the jury is not all that unusual a contest. For a moment the special prosecutor and the defense lawyer felt a sense of camaraderie. Neither liked the feeling.

"Please state your name and occupation."

"Efran Price. I'm a Texas Ranger, assigned as an investigator on this case."

And a damned poor investigator he'd been. Price had said so himself, over and over, as he'd apologized to Kelsey for the unfortunate timing of his daughter's birth. For Kelsey, the idea of a man's—a Texas Ranger, for God's sake—being so caught up in his family life that he neglected his duties was such a bizarre and admirable phenomenon that she'd fended off his apologies and asked him to do only one piece of investigation for her— and to testify about it today.

Price was painfully earnest on the stand. He had the Ranger jawline—tight, incisive. He answered Kelsey's questions straightforwardly and didn't embellish his answers.

"Ranger Price, as part of your investigation, did you go to Houston Intercontinental Airport?"

"Yes, I did."

"Did you have anything with you when you went to the airport?"

"Yes, ma'am. I had a plane ticket for a flight to Raleigh-Durham Airport."

Kelsey felt the unease at the table next to her. She knew when she glanced aside she would see puzzlement on Clyde Wolverton's face. Had his client left something incriminating at either airport this Ranger could have discovered? But Billy looked equally puzzled, not guilty.

"Was that ticket for the day you were at the airport, Ranger?"

"No, ma'am, it was for a flight that had been a few days earlier. I'd bought the ticket through a travel agent."

"Had you taken the flight to Raleigh?"

"No, I hadn't."

"So you still had your ticket when you went to Houston Intercontinental. What did you do with it?"

Price had the ticket in his hands. "I got the boarding pass part of it stamped," he said simply.

"May I see that, Ranger?" Kelsey took the stiff paper, glanced at the "Houston Intercontinental" stamped on the back, and casually handed it to the defense lawyer, who studied it closely. "How did you get it stamped?"

"I stood in line at the gate counter and handed it to the agent there. There was kind of a crowd, she didn't look at the date on my boarding pass. She just stamped it."

"Did you board that flight, Ranger Price?"

"No, ma'am."

"Was it difficult to get the boarding pass stamped?"

"I could have done it any number of ways. There's a stamp like that at every gate counter. They're not exactly under tight security. Anyone could walk up and stamp a ticket. There's no date on the stamp, it doesn't change from one day to the next."

"No, there's no date, is there, Ranger? Let me show you defense exhibit number one, another stamped boarding pass. Is that stamp identical to the one on your ticket?"

"Yes, they are," Price said after minimal examination.

"But even though you have a stamped boarding pass, you didn't get on that flight, did you, Officer?"

"No, ma'am, I didn't."

Kelsey let that information seep in while she sorted among the papers in front of her, before changing subjects.

"While you were at the airport, did you check on some flights that had left there on October twenty-first of last year?"

"Yes. I discovered there had been five other flights that had left at noon or later on October twenty-first that could have gotten someone to Raleigh—or close enough that a man could have rented a car and driven to Raleigh in plenty of time for a seven-o'clock meeting. The latest of those flights left at three o'clock in the afternoon Houston time."

"Thank you, Ranger. I pass the witness."

Wolverton sat as if he hadn't heard her hand the witness to him. He studied Efran Price, cleared his throat, and decided not to do himself any more damage. "No questions."

Judge Saunders's voice was painfully neutral. "Thank you, Ranger. Do you have another witness, Ms. Thatch?"

"Yes, Your Honor. The State's last witness is Mrs. Goldie Hatteras."

Aunt Goldie came forward slowly from the door at the back of the courtroom. The judge waited patiently to swear her in. Only after she was seated in the witness stand did the enormity of where she was sitting strike Mrs. Hatteras. She looked out at the packed courtroom. The front rows were taken up by reporters from around the state, informed that today would probably be the last day of trial. There was even a stringer from a network news show. Behind these out-of-towners were citizens of Galilee Aunt Goldie must have recognized, including her sister, all staring at her intently, wondering what Aunt Goldie could possibly know. She was an outsider in their midst, familiar by appearance but not close enough to anyone to have joined in the gossip after the crimes. Many a soul in the audience now wished she had made better friends with Goldie Hatteras.

Aunt Goldie glanced at the shifting, breathing crowd and looked down again hastily. She mumbled out her name, and Kelsey had to ask her to repeat it. By waiting quietly after the answer, Kelsey made her witness look up. Aunt Goldie looked directly at Kelsey and didn't move her eyes off the prosecutor's face.

"Mrs. Hatteras, were you in your sister Alice Beaumont's house the morning of October twenty-first?"

"Yes, I was. I was there to take care of Alice," the witness said quickly, as if she had to justify her intrusion.

"Who else was in the house that morning, say about nine or nine-thirty?"

"Alice was upstairs asleep." Aunt Goldie wore a navy blue cloth coat and a blue plastic hat so small it looked like an ill-fitting wig on top of her gray hair. Her cheeks were seamed but plump, almost concealing her eyes. "Downstairs were Lorrie and Ronald and little Taylor, and Helena and me."

"Helena Parker?"

"Yes."

Everyone tended to lump Aunt Goldie and the maid together. The older woman even did it herself. Kelsey was the only one who thought of them separately. She asked, "What was going on that morning around breakfast time, Mrs. Hatteras?"

Aunt Goldie looked down at her hands, where she held a little handkerchief. "Ronald and Lorrie were talking."

"Just talking, Mrs. Hatteras?"

"Well, discussing things."

"Did you hear Lorrie Blystone mention divorce?" Kelsey asked bluntly. She didn't like this hesitation. Aunt Goldie acted as if she were having family secrets pried out of her, though Kelsey had assured her she would have to say almost nothing that everyone in town hadn't already heard.

"Yes," Aunt Goldie muttered.

"So it wasn't a pleasant discussion Lorrie Blystone and her husband were having, was it?"

"No."

Kelsey let herself be satisfied with that. She didn't know if she could force the painfully polite older woman to say the word *argument*, let alone *fight*.

"Did you stay in the house all morning, Mrs. Hatteras?"

"No. I left soon after breakfast, about nine-thirty."

"Did Helena Parker stay in the house?"

"No, miss. She left, too, just ahead of me."

"What was it about the atmosphere of the house that morning that drove you both away?"

Aunt Goldie's blue eyes widened. "Oh, no, it wasn't like that. We just both had—errands."

Kelsey waited.

"And I guess we wanted to give Lorrie and Ronald some privacy," her witness added quietly.

"I know you weren't trying to eavesdrop, but before you left the house, did you hear the argument between Lorrie and Ronald continuing?"

"Yes," Aunt Goldie admitted softly.

"Did you hear Lorrie mention this man?" Kelsey pointed at Billy Fletcher. Pivoting further, she added, "Or this man?"

Kelsey's eyes lingered on Morgan Fletcher, though he didn't meet her gaze. Morgan was watching Aunt Goldie. He studied her as if he hadn't seen her before.

"Yes. I heard—I was trying not to listen, you understand, but I heard Lorrie say that Ronald should study Morgan to learn how—I'm not sure, to be a better husband or son-in-law."

"And what did Ronald reply?"

Aunt Goldie swallowed visibly. She didn't look anywhere as she said, "Ronald laughed and said he had studied Morgan."

Kelsey had more gossip in her bag. She looked up at Judge Linda Saunders. The judge was looking nowhere, out over the heads of the spectators. As Kelsey watched, Judge Saunders bit her lower lip. A spot on the lip could have been just the brightness of release, or could have been blood.

Aunt Goldie had told Kelsey everything she'd heard that morning, relaying in a horrified whisper the way Ronald Blystone had laughed nastily and said to his wife that Morgan Fletcher was no prizewinner as a husband, and that maybe Lorrie should drop by his office at the courthouse sometime to see for herself. Kelsey had a good idea, better than Aunt Goldie herself, what Ronald had been implying—but it was only nasty gossip that had nothing to do with this trial. Kelsey skipped ahead in the argument Goldie Hatteras had overheard, feeling a twinge of nobility as she did.

"And did you ever hear Ronald mention this defendant, Mrs. Hatteras? Mention Billy Fletcher?"

"Just before I went out." Goldie nodded. "He said—Ronald was still sort of laughing and he said maybe he could get to know Morgan better after he had his brother's job."

"After Ronald Blystone had Billy Fletcher's job?" Kelsey asked loudly over the rising murmur of voices. Aunt Goldie nodded. Judge Saunders leaned close to look at Mrs. Hatteras but didn't order her to speak up. Everyone understood.

"Did you hear anything else?"

"No, miss. I went out the door then."

Kelsey nodded. "Where did you go, Mrs. Hatteras?"

"To Houston. I drove home to Houston. Almost as soon as I

got there, I had a message from here about—what had happened, and I hurried back. I was back in Galilee by early afternoon."

Kelsey sat for another moment of silence, letting the jurors stare at the embarrassed old lady, so pained by what she had heard, even more pained by having to relay it in public. "I pass the witness," Kelsey said quietly.

Clyde Wolverton sat like a statue, staring at the witness, so thunderstruck his expression hadn't had time to change from stunned to horrified. Out of the corner of her eye Kelsey watched him, fascinated. Slowly the defense lawyer came unstuck. "Are you sure you heard Ronald correctly, Aunt Goldie?" he asked in a shaky voice.

Goldie looked up, eyes brightening as she saw a way out—maybe she had made a mistake. But before she could speak, memory reasserted itself. She shook her head and looked apologetically at Billy as she said, "Yes, sir, I'm sure."

"You heard Ronald say he expected to have Billy Fletcher's job?"

As the old woman nodded again, Wolverton realized he was emphasizing the evidence that hurt his client's cause. He cleared his throat and frowned. "Did Mr. Blystone say anything to justify such a ridiculous claim?"

"No, sir, not while I heard. I left right away."

"Do you have any idea why he would think such an absurd thing?"

"No, sir."

"Are you aware from talking to your sister that Billy Fletcher was the best manager Smoothskins ever had?"

"Objection," Kelsey said almost sympathetically. "Hearsay."

Clyde Wolverton's face was reddening steadily. He snapped, "Well, everyone heard her say it." And he violated one of a trial lawyer's fundamental rules: don't glare at the jury.

The judge and Kelsey glanced at each other like the only reasonable people in the room. Kelsey said, "I have no more questions."

"Mr. Wolverton?" Judge Saunders asked him gently. The defense lawyer shook his head grumpily. "Then do both sides rest and close?"

"Yes, Your Honor."

"Yes, Your Honor."

"Is there any reason why I shouldn't read the jury their written instructions and begin final arguments?"

Neither Kelsey nor Wolverton had an objection. The judge turned to the jury and began, "Ladies and gentlemen of the jury, you have heard all the evidence in this case. It is my duty to instruct you now on the law that applies. The defendant stands accused in the following three paragraphs: that on the twenty-first day of October of last year he did then and there intentionally and knowingly cause the death of Ronald Blystone, by shooting said Ronald Blystone with a deadly weapon . . ."

Kelsey sat looking calm to the point of inattention, but her heart was pounding. Her hands in her lap began to shake. All the trial was merely a preparation for final argument. For the past three days she had been putting on the evidence that would allow her now to show the jurors in a logical, coherent fashion why they had no choice but to find the defendant guilty of every charge against him. Kelsey tried to marshal those arguments.

Instead she thought about her failures. In cross-examining Billy Fletcher she'd gotten him red-faced, but she hadn't made him furious, she hadn't shown the jury how he looked when he was enraged. She hadn't managed to put the murder weapon in Billy Fletcher's hand. That had been crucial. Anything she could show the jurors, instead of asking them to imagine it, was a big part of her job done.

Kelsey remembered the weight of the gun, its insistence on being used creeping up her arm. She stole a glance at Billy Fletcher. He sat under the flow of the judge's words staring dead-eyed at his hands, turning them over, picking at his nails. Forget the jury. Did Kelsey believe this man had murdered an entire family?

Did she?

"Ms. Thatch?"

"Thank you, Your Honor." Without notes, Kelsey walked toward the jury. "I get to speak to you both first and last before you begin your deliberations. That is because I have the burden of proof. It was my job to present you with the evidence that would convince you that Billy Fletcher is guilty of the charges against him. For right now I just want to remind you of what those three separate charges are." She turned to a chart she'd prepared, on an easel standing near the jury box. "First, the murder of Ronald Blystone. I had to demonstrate these elements. That this man, Billy Fletcher, caused the death of Ronald Blystone by shooting him with a handgun on this certain date in this county.

"Second, the murder of Lorrie Blystone. Again, I had to prove to you that Billy Fletcher on October twenty-first caused Lorrie's death by shooting her with a handgun.

"And finally, kidnapping." This was where Kelsey wanted to give the jurors their most secret instruction. They watched her intently, hoping for a clue. "I had to prove that Billy Fletcher abducted Taylor Blystone, took her from the place she belonged without the consent of her guardians."

Kelsey stood as close as she could to the jurors. She felt hollow with the strain of the burdens she carried. Staring at each face in turn, she said, "What I want to emphasize is that these are three separate offenses. Three decisions you have to make. You are entitled to find the defendant guilty of one of these crimes, two of them, or all three. Or none of them. Please deliberate carefully.

"I will speak to you again after Mr. Wolverton has his turn."

Kelsey walked quickly to her seat. Clyde Wolverton looked momentarily startled at the sudden transition that had placed him onstage. Buttoning the jacket of his navy blue suit, he said, "Thank you, uh, Ms. Thatch. May it please the court. Ladies and gentlemen."

Then he stopped and spread his hands. He smiled sheepishly, unbuttoned his jacket again, and walked toward the jurors as if meeting them gladly on the street. "My friends."

It was the phoniest thing Kelsey had ever seen. But the jurors leaned toward the hometown lawyer and appeared to relax a little.

Paying minimal attention to Clyde Wolverton's performance, Kelsey thought instead about what she had to say to the jury. In her first brief argument she had told them as clearly as she could that they didn't have to buy her whole case. She knew the kidnapping was the weakest part of her case. She couldn't place the baby in Billy's car, and she hadn't been allowed to give the jury the evidence of the baby's gown found along the road Billy had taken. What she had been silently shouting at the jury was, *Discard the kidnapping if you want—but that doesn't make him innocent of everything.*

"The State hasn't much to prove to prove a murder was committed," Wolverton was saying. "Look at these few elements. Caused the death, used a handgun, the victim's identity. And Ms. Thatch proved what she could. The easy parts. The names we all knew. That they were dead. Well, of course. And then Ms. Thatch asks you to take a leap of faith with her and say Billy Fletcher caused those deaths. Because someone did. It's the prosecution's job to find someone to blame.

"But, ladies and gentlemen, the prosecutor has leaped to the wrong conclusion. For the simple reason that she doesn't know Billy Fletcher. Doesn't know the kind of man he is. She just plugged his name into the equation because she didn't know a thing about him.

"But we do, don't we? Now that you've heard the evidence," Wolverton added hastily. "We know Billy Fletcher as a good man, a man who never lifted his hand against anyone. A friend who always thought of others ahead of himself."

He turned toward Kelsey accusingly. "The prosecution asks you to believe that this good man abandoned all his principles and murdered three people because he was upset, because he got mad during an argument. But she can't even place Billy inside that house *when* the killings occurred. He was there, sure, earlier, he was even arguing with one of the victims. But that doesn't make him a murderer. The only murderer in this case is dead."

Obviously expecting to cause a stir with this pronouncement, Wolverton took a sort of victory turn around the small space in front of the jury box. He ran his hand through his hair.

"Let me paint you a different picture of what happened inside Alice Beaumont's house that October morning. Some of it you know for a fact. The rest you can figure out.

"The Blystones were having an argument. A common event in their marriage. But this one was worse than most. This time, for the first time, Lorrie Blystone mentioned divorce." Wolverton paused significantly, drawing himself up. "The atmosphere in the house was so bad it drove everyone else away. Aunt Goldie Hatteras, the maid Helena Parker—the only people who could leave did. And the argument continued.

"Think of Ronald Blystone's mental state, ladies and gentlemen. Think how much he had at stake if his wife carried through her threat of divorce. Because Ronald had been intent on worming his way even deeper into his wife's family. He didn't just want to win his arguments, he wanted his share of the family fortune. He wanted to run things."

Kelsey was startled at how quickly Wolverton had been able to incorporate into his final argument her evidence that Ronald had wanted Billy's job—evidence that had obviously shocked the defense lawyer when Aunt Goldie had said it this morning. She wouldn't have thought Wolverton that resourceful a thinker. Maybe it was in final argument that he shone. Maybe that was why he'd been hired.

Wolverton waved a long hand dismissively. "It was all a pipe dream, of course. Mrs. Alice Beaumont had no intention of hiring her son-in-law to run her factory. She was perfectly satisfied with Billy Fletcher.

"But Ronald didn't know that. He'd built up this fantasy for himself that he was going to take charge of the Beaumont family fortune and build it into a financial empire for himself. Remember what he told his friend at the college in Dallas? 'That's a gold mine there.' "

Wolverton put his hands on the jury rail and leaned far forward. "And then that morning of October twenty-first Ronald saw that pipe dream fading away. His wife was going to take it from him by kicking him out of the family.

"And that's when Billy Fletcher had the misfortune to come on the scene." Wolverton turned and made an introducing gesture at his client, as if urging him forward to address the crowd. Billy tried to present a picture of befuddled innocence. He was pretty good at it, except that his eyes shifted back and forth from the jurors to his lawyer, as if asking when he'd worn the expression long enough.

"Billy came to try to talk Ronald out of his position on what should be done with the factory, and unbeknownst to him he had picked the worst possible time. Because he stepped into Lorrie and Ronald's worst fight of their marriage. Soon Billy got drawn into that fight, too. And it was so bad that for the first time ever Ronald Blystone got out a gun and ordered Billy out of the house. Waved the gun so close to Billy's face Billy had to push it aside, thus—unfortunately again—leaving his fingerprint on that pistol."

Wolverton suddenly leaned toward the jury and held up one finger. *A point is about to be made,* Kelsey thought. She hated Clyde Wolverton's presentation. He was of the old school of jury argument, and there were good reasons why that school had been shut down years ago. This assuming of a dramatic personality made the defense lawyer's arguments reek of insincerity—in Kelsey's view. But she couldn't deny that he made some sense, or that the jurors watched him as intently as the faithful at a tent show revival, eager to learn the truth.

"And what was it that so infuriated Ronald Blystone that he went and got out this deadly weapon? Not something Billy Fletcher said. No. It was when his wife began to take Billy's side. It was when Lorrie said that Billy was right. That was when Ronald Blystone flew into such a black rage that he had to have a gun in his hand."

Wolverton subsided. "And Billy left," he said simply. "We know—we *know*—that Billy left that house immediately after Andrew Sims saw him on the front porch about ten o'clock. We know that because if he hadn't left then and driven as fast as he could to Houston, he would never have caught that airplane at eleven-ten.

"And he was on that plane, my friends." Now Wolverton looked shocked, as if someone had accused him. "We showed you his ticket, his stamped boarding pass, two eyewitnesses who saw him on board the aircraft, and the testimony of another witness who said Billy arrived in Raleigh, North Carolina, in time for his long-planned meeting."

Wolverton shrugged broadly. "The prosecution has cast doubt on that alibi. Of course. That is her job, and let me tell you she is very good at it." He was pointing at Kelsey, who sat stoically. "Ms. Thatch was sent here by the attorney general of Texas to prosecute this very high profile case, and you know he is going to send the very best he has."

If you only knew, Kelsey thought. She was used to having her skills praised by the opposition. Now when she rose to argue it should be part of her job to step into the spittoon, stumble over her words, and aw shucks a bit, to demonstrate that she was of no more than average competence. Kelsey felt she could play the role. She was brooding on her failures, the key places where with another witness, a little more investigation, she could have shored up her case.

"So of course she managed to poke a hole or two in Billy's alibi," Wolverton was continuing. "But look at the sheer weight of it, look at the numbers. Yes, we paid Ms. Jean Blair for her time, and that was a mistake, and it was *my* mistake. I said it was all right to do that, and I was wrong. But at the time it seemed necessary. Please, please don't blame my client for that. Blame me. Come up to me after your verdict and tell me, 'Clyde, you're a blundering old fool.' And I won't disagree with you. But don't blame it on my client because he took an old fool's advice.

"Where was I?" the defense lawyer addressed himself. Kelsey shook her head. "Oh, yes, Jean Blair. She may have been paid, but she told the truth. And so did the stewardess, Miss Fortescue. Maybe Billy didn't make himself stand out on that flight. Who does, normally? What does a man have to do?" Wolverton decided it was time to resume passion. He raised his arms and his voice. "Should Billy Fletcher have made a fool of himself on that airplane so everyone would remember him? Is he supposed to do that everywhere he goes in this world, on the off chance that someone behind him might have killed somebody? In this day and age does a man have to protect himself every minute of his life by establishing an ironclad alibi?"

Wolverton was glaring. The jurors stared at him. The defense lawyer lowered his voice.

"Meanwhile, back at the Beaumont house, the fight continued after Billy left. It got worse. And by now the gun was out. It was in Ronald's hand. We've heard how sharp-tongued Lorrie could be. She said the wrong thing that morning. She made her husband furious. Until he lifted the only thing at hand that could shut her up and he fired."

Wolverton slapped his hand on his chest. "And Lorrie Blystone died. And then what so often happens in these domestic tragedies happened again. Ronald Blystone realized he'd made a terrible mistake. He was overwhelmed by remorse. He was flooded by it. It swept his reason away. He wanted his wife back. He wanted to join her. There was only one way Ronald Blystone could do that. He took that path."

Wolverton pointed a finger at his own head. *Do it with the pistol,* Kelsey thought. She thought of trying the experiment herself, holding the murder weapon up to her head. She remembered the sinister compulsion to fire the thing, but didn't think that compulsion would assert itself when the gun was pointed at the holder's own head. She couldn't imagine someone who had just seen the horrible damage the gun could do pointing it at his own head and pulling the trigger. It happened every day, yes, but to people without recourse, with no hope left. Ronald Blystone had been a man with an argument always ready. Surely he could have argued himself out of suicide.

Besides, Clyde Wolverton's scenario had a major problem. He knew it himself.

"I know," he told the jury, holding out a restraining hand. "This leaves the last member of the Blystone family unaccounted for. What happened to Taylor Blystone? What happened to the baby?"

He painted bafflement on his face. "I don't know." He pointed at Kelsey. "She doesn't, either. But like Ms. Thatch told you at the very beginning, there are always mysteries left. This is a major one, I know, but neither side has solved it. Taylor Blystone may have sat there in that room with those two bodies for almost an hour before Morgan Fletcher came on the scene about eleven-thirty. Lots of time for someone else to come along. Who? Who knows? I hate to think about it. The drifter Mrs. Gottschalk had chased off her porch the day before, the evil-looking hobo who tried to break into her house? He was last seen headed in the direction of the Beaumont house. Isn't it a reasonable deduction that he came upon the scene, found the unprotected baby, and made off with her, thinking of ransom—then in the face of the huge search lost his nerve and just fled?

"Perhaps, to think kinder thoughts, someone took Taylor for

her own good. Aunt Goldie left town long enough to have taken her great-niece to safety. Helena Parker went to Houston and never came back. Why? What's she hiding?

"There are all kinds of possibilities," Wolverton said in a lowered, deepened voice. "But not Billy. Not Billy Fletcher. He was long gone from that house by the time the killings occurred. Why would he have taken the baby? What possible motive could he have?" Wolverton turned and pointed at Kelsey, who sat staring across the front of the courtroom. "She hasn't connected Taylor Blystone to Billy in any way. No trace of the blood that would have been on the baby's gown and hands in Billy's car. No one who saw him with a baby. No reason for him to take her.

"You know he didn't," the defense lawyer intoned, bending to look into the eyes of the jurors in the front row. "You know Billy Fletcher. You know he couldn't have done this thing."

Wolverton's strong finish to his jury argument was spoiled a bit by one cracked note. He seemed to be pleading for the sympathy that should have been his by right. "You know your verdict must be not guilty," he said, and walked slowly back to his seat.

Kelsey still sat without moving, eyes lifeless. Everyone watched her. She sat long enough that some began to wonder about her health. But neither the silence, nor an order from the judge, brought Kelsey to herself. It was a voice in her head, so clear she thought it audible. "Talk about the baby." It was the whisper of her training. She knew what a veteran prosecutor would do. Don't emphasize the killings of the sharp-tongued, sometimes venomous parents. Concentrate on the poor innocent baby, the natural source of sympathy.

"No," Kelsey said loudly. She looked at the jury. "Mr. Wolverton is right. The man you see here couldn't murder two people and steal a helpless baby. The affable, good-natured Billy Fletcher we all know couldn't have done that."

She stood.

"But the man he is today, the man he is on the job, in church on Sunday mornings, is not the man he was in Alice Beaumont's house on October twenty-first. You don't know that Billy Fletcher. A man driven to his absolute final extremity. Enraged, terrified. You know what an important person Billy is to this town. You know what a good life he has here. On October twenty-first, he was deathly afraid of losing that life. Two people were going to take it from him."

She grew quietly thoughtful as she approached the jury. "Ronald Blystone didn't kill himself. Mr. Wolverton told you how we know that. He knows the flaw in his theory. The baby. After her parents were murdered, someone was still there to take Taylor Blystone away." She turned suddenly fierce. "And it isn't good enough to say we don't know who. We don't know why. It was just one of those things. Can you possibly believe this was coincidence?

"No. Someone took that baby because he hated her. He feared her. Murder is a long moment of high intensity. Of off-the-track thinking, when there are no rules, and you aren't accountable to human standards any more. That's the state Billy Fletcher was in. Think of him. He's just murdered two people. Their screaming baby is on the floor, in her mother's blood. Billy is in his employer's house. His boss is asleep one flight up. Her infant granddaughter is screaming bloody murder, literally.

"So why wouldn't he just run away? Just get out of there, get out! Let the baby cry. That's what a normal-thinking person would do, maybe. But a person who's just committed murder is by definition not thinking normally."

Kelsey looked a little irrational herself. No one's eyes were straying from her face.

"Think what that baby represented to him. He came to talk her parents into letting him keep his life. But that had failed miserably and instead he'd killed them. Taken them out of the picture so they couldn't control his life any more.

"But the job wasn't finished. Billy would be safe when the only people left to make decisions were on his side: his brother, Morgan, and Morgan's wife, Katherine. When they were the only heirs to the Smoothskins fortune, Billy would be safe again. But there was one obstacle to that, wasn't there?

"In the meantime Taylor was crying. Screaming. Driving Billy even more frenzied. He put the baby in her crib while he tried to think. We know that from the bloodstains in the crib, that the baby was put back there after she'd crawled in her mother's blood. Maybe Billy thought that would calm her and she'd go to sleep. But it didn't work. Taylor kept screaming and screaming, like a little infant burglar alarm. Crying and crying. Telling people what he'd done. Calling to her grandmother. Calling Andrew Sims to come back, or anyone else driving by. The baby's screaming piercing his ears. Striking to his heart. He had to shut her up."

Kelsey saw jurors flinching, though she had raised her voice only marginally. She put her hands on the railing in front of the jury box and lowered her voice. "He couldn't leave that baby screaming. Piercing him with her accusation. Until he snatched the baby up, wrapped her up tightly to shut her up. Wrapped her so tightly the blood wouldn't seep out. Or found her carrier close at hand and put her in that. Then he ran out to his car and fled."

Kelsey breathed deeply. She stood quiet, letting her heartbeat slow. "And somewhere along the road to Houston," she said more quietly, "his mind began to reassert itself. He realized he'd made a mistake. He realized having the baby could only incriminate him. He realized he couldn't take her back.

"Somewhere along that highway he abandoned Taylor Blystone. Did away with her as he had her parents."

Kelsey wouldn't let herself cry. She stiffened her face and turned away. "Now that," came her voice loudly, "is a version of events that makes sense, in a twisted way. The defense's version could not have happened. Aunt Goldie took the baby? Helena did? The trouble with that is, the defendant himself refuted it with his testimony. No one else was in the house when he had his fight with Ronald and Lorrie, he said. Goldie Hatteras and Helena Parker were long gone by the time Billy arrived.

"Let's look at his conduct after the crimes." As Kelsey turned back to the jurors, she got a glimpse of Morgan Fletcher looking distressed, Billy Fletcher looking down, shaking his head continually, and Judge Saunders staring off into the distance.

"He did, in fact, get to North Carolina somehow. Whether he caught the flight he was supposed to catch is doubtful. Terry Fortescue's testimony I dismiss out of hand. She seemed like a nice young lady, she wanted to be helpful, maybe after the defense team had shown her Billy Fletcher enough times he did begin to look familiar to her, and she even began to believe what they told her about when and where she'd seen him. But for her to remember him on that precise flight after all the flights and passengers she's seen? No."

She saw pursed lips in the jury box and thought more than one of them agreed.

"That leaves Jean Blair's ten-thousand-dollar testimony. She has a remarkable memory for names and faces, she told you. She sure does. We've all flown, haven't we, or sat by a stranger in a theater or a restaurant? Would you be able to identify that person again a month later? How about an hour later? But Jean Blair is a lot better at remembering than you and I are. That's why she's so much better—compensated for it."

The defense team tried to look stoic and unaffected, but their looks were in directions other than the jury box. Except for Morgan Fletcher, who stared at the jurors with his lips tightened and his legs coiled beneath him, as if he were about to rise to give the final defense argument.

"Then Billy arrived in Raleigh. Somehow. He didn't get to his hotel as he'd originally planned, he didn't pick up his rental car. Maybe that's because he didn't want to leave a record that he'd come in on a later flight than he was supposed to. Maybe it was because he'd had to fly to another city and rent a car there to get to Raleigh. Something changed his plans.

"And then his big dinner meeting. The meeting he'd set up at least a week earlier. Where it was important to him to make a good impression." Kelsey walked slowly toward Billy. He wouldn't look up. "And how did he appear at that meeting? In a plain white shirt. He was having his suit cleaned. It was more important to him that that suit get cleaned than that he appear a good, solid businessman dressed in a suit for one of the most important meetings of his life.

"His brother had already called him by then," Kelsey said, looking past Billy at Morgan. Kelsey wished she could have heard that telephone conversation between the brothers. Morgan would have been restrained, quiet, and efficient. "If you're innocent," he would have told his brother, "don't do anything to destroy evidence. Don't get your shoes shined, don't get your suit cleaned." That's what a good lawyer would have told his client, leaving the client to figure out for himself what to do if he were not innocent.

"Billy knew his crimes had been discovered back in Galilee," Kelsey said to the jury. "He had stood close to Ronald Blystone when he shot him. He had carried that baby. Maybe the bloodstains were so slight they weren't noticeable on his brown suit. But Billy knew they were there. He sent the suit out to be cleaned.

"And he went to his meeting. What was that meeting all about?" Kelsey asked suddenly, as if the jurors might have an answer for her. "Saving the Smoothskins factory from competition? Could Billy really have thought he could dissuade a competitor from whatever it planned to do? That's not what John Howard seemed to think was the primary purpose of the meeting. He thought it was a job interview. Billy Fletcher was looking for a job.

"Which brings us back to another defense argument," she said, pacing. "Mr. Wolverton told you it was just a pipe dream of Ronald's to become manager of the factory. Alice Beaumont was satisfied with Billy's performance as manager. But had she ever told Billy that? Is she the kind of employer to praise someone who does good work for her?"

Now the hothouse nature of the small town worked to Kelsey's advantage. Everybody knew the answer. Alice Beaumont tell Billy what a swell job he was doing, that his position was secure? Not hardly. Alice Beaumont didn't keep people comforted, she kept them on edge. Kelsey sought her out in the audience. Mrs. Beaumont was a little island in the crowded seats. Even her daughter had drawn away from her. Alice Beaumont sat alone, face flinty, staring at her special prosecutor. Did she get it even yet—the primary role she had played in this tragedy?

"Something had happened that made Ronald happy," Kelsey said, still watching Mrs. Beaumont. "He had a new idea that morning that whether he could direct the future of the Smoothskins company or not, he could take over its factory. He could get a high-paying job out of the deal. He said it to his wife gleefully that morning. 'When I have Billy Fletcher's job . . .' Do you think, a few minutes later when Billy himself appeared, Ronald would have restrained himself and kept that news to himself, not torment Billy with it? Was he that kind of person?" She shook her head. "No. Ronald would have used it like a weapon, to goad Billy that much higher. And when he heard it, would Billy have believed it? Would he have said, 'Oh, no, my boss is much too happy with my work to fire me'? Could he possibly have thought that after the way Alice Beaumont treated him constantly?

"He believed it," Kelsey said firmly. "He'd seen her dump other managers. It would have sounded oh so natural to him that she was about to do the same to him, to put her much smarter son-in-law in his place. We know—one fact we know absolutely out of this whole tangle is that Billy Fletcher didn't feel secure in his job. That's why he planned his trip to North Carolina in the first place."

Kelsey looked at Billy. He stared sullenly toward the judge's bench. He tried to look pained, as if he were being unfairly maligned. The pain was real, but combined with the sullenness, it did not create an expression his lawyer would have chosen for him. Billy was beginning to look mad. Kelsey noted that fact distantly.

She stood before the jury. Kelsey had been afraid of these people ever since she'd let them become the jury. They were the people who would pour her out of court. Every obstacle she faced in Galilee sat represented in that jury box. Since the beginning of trial she had thought of them as her opponents. But that feeling had gradually faded, until now she was willing to stand close to the jurors, huddled with them against the spectators, the judge, and the defense team. She lowered her voice as if she could keep what she said just between her and the jury.

"So the scene was set that morning. Billy Fletcher arrived at the Beaumont house at a bad time, all right. If he had gotten there in time to see Goldie Hatteras and Helena Parker fleeing the scene, maybe he would have had the sense not to go in. Billy knew as well as anyone in this town that you didn't want to get in the way when Lorrie Beaumont was mad." The name fell easily off Kelsey's tongue. She didn't even realize that she had dropped Lorrie's married name and called her by the name everyone in town remembered her by. "Because Lorrie didn't confine herself to the primary target when her temper was roused. That's what Helena said. That's what Aunt Goldie hinted at by leaving the scene.

"So Billy arrived nervous, worried—no, scared. Scared of losing his whole life, his position, the respect he'd earned but never had. He came there to make a last-ditch argument, not knowing the only people there to hear him were in no mood to give him a fair hearing.

"They got into an argument. We know that. Billy was right in the thick of the fight. Andrew Sims saw Billy and Ronald yelling at each other so loudly they didn't even notice the first time Mr. Sims honked to get their attention. Nose to nose, he described them, screaming, furious.

"That's the end of the last witness testimony we have. The rest we have to puzzle out from the physical evidence. But we can. Ronald had his gun, we know that. We can presume that if he got it out, he displayed it. He gestured, he threatened.

"But both men handled that gun, we know that from the fingerprints.

"Picture it," Kelsey suddenly said sharply. The jurors were so focused on her they didn't change expressions at the heightened tension of her tone. "You're Billy Fletcher. You've been working at that factory all your life. You've finally worked your way up to manager, the best job in this town some might say, a position where people look up to you, seek your advice, treat you with respect. But even there you never feel secure. Your employer belittles you, she listens to idiotic advice from this outsider, this son-in-law. She gives you nothing but little grins when you ask her what she's going to do."

Kelsey had turned and aimed her voice at the defendant. Billy's gaze was on the table in front of him. His hands were locked together. His shoulders looked strained. Kelsey began to walk toward the defense table.

"Things are so desperate you've tried to look for another job. But John Howard has already told you they've hired someone else. You're going to go talk to him anyway, but you know how hopeless that is. You have nowhere to go.

"So you go that morning to try to reason with this bastard who stands in your way, and does he listen? Is he susceptible to logic at all? No. He laughs in your face and tells you things are worse even than you figured. That he's going to have your job.

"You scream at him," Kelsey said harshly. "You hate him

worse than anybody on earth. You appeal to his wife for help, but then she turns on you, too. You have no place to turn."

Kelsey reached the defense table. She leaned on it, talking down to Billy. He wouldn't look up at her. His shoulders knotted further.

Kelsey spat out, "And then this punk, this little twerp who plans to destroy you, brings out a gun. He's finally developed a little sense, Ronald sees that he's messing with the wrong guy. Why else would Ronald have gotten his gun?" Kelsey asked the jurors over her shoulder. "You arm yourself when you feel threatened. That's why Ronald Blystone went and got a gun, because he realized he was no physical match for Billy Fletcher, and he had goaded him too far. Ronald got the gun and he ordered Billy out of 'his' house.

"And that was a bad, bad mistake. Because Ronald *was* no match for Billy. It must have been a joyful moment for Billy Fletcher when he saw that the contest had turned physical. Because that was his turf. That was where he could best this little bastard easily. Billy has spent his life doing man's work, heavy work, hard, muscle-building exercise, while this little creep has spent his life in a chair.

"Billy snatched that gun from Ronald Blystone as easily as taking a toy from a child." Kelsey said it triumphantly, making a sweeping, grabbing gesture, then stood as if mesmerized by the power in her hand. Below her, Billy Fletcher had begun to shake his head again.

"And then one of two things happened. It may be that in a struggle over the gun, Ronald got shot. But I don't think so. When two men are struggling over a gun, I don't think one of them lets the gun get so close to his head that it's almost touching his head when the gun goes off.

"No, I think Billy turned his rage in the other direction. He has the gun. He has it. He doesn't have to take any more crap from anybody now. Ronald jumps back, terrified, the way he should look.

"But the other grown-up in the room isn't one to be intimidated by a gun or anything else. She's never had to curb her tongue. It's always been a better weapon than anything anybody else was holding.

"Lorrie Beaumont was across the room. She stepped forward and she said something." Kelsey was staring down at Billy Fletcher again. His hands were on the table. Kelsey made the last word, "something," sound as scathing as the worst insult imaginable. "Something contemptuous of this stupid man who thought a gun was going to end this argument. 'You stupid fool. You're too stupid to breathe, let alone manage anything. You have to hire someone to tell you when you need to go to the bathroom.'"

"*No!*" Billy Fletcher screamed. He leaped to his feet. His hands gripped the table's edge as if he would overturn it. He leaned toward Kelsey. She stood still, letting him get as close as he wanted. Billy's face looked like a match head. His teeth gleamed as he screamed again, spraying her with spittle.

Distantly Kelsey heard the bailiff jumping to his feet. She didn't move. She stood eye to eye with the defendant, his bulk surrounding her. Kelsey looked at him flatly, almost pityingly. Something twisted in Billy's eyes.

Clyde Wolverton was just staring up at him, openmouthed. It was Morgan Fletcher who stepped forward, put his hands on his brother's shoulders, and lowered him gently back into his chair. Morgan was looking at Kelsey. "You're wrong," he said quietly.

Kelsey said to the jury, "His brother wasn't there to restrain Billy that morning. Billy had the gun. This time, in this argument, he was going to have the last word. He fired." Kelsey thrust out her hand, snarling. "It may have been little more than an angry gesture. Snap! He fired. He shot Lorrie in the chest. He shut her up but good.

"Then he turned," Kelsey said forcefully, "and knew he couldn't leave her husband to tell what he'd done. Ronald backed up but Billy caught him. He put the gun right to Ronald's head. Ronald flung up his hands, but that was no use. One shot and Billy ended that menace forever."

Returning to the jury box, Kelsey said, "Meanwhile, across the room, Lorrie was still alive. She was down on her hands and knees, but she was moving. She was crawling. In her last minute of life she tried to reach the one thing in this life that mattered most to her. Her baby." Kelsey thought she heard the words echoed around the room. "Lorrie crawled toward her baby. Her life was pumping out through her chest. She had to crawl through her own blood. But she got there, she reached out, in the last moment she had, and touched her baby's hand."

Shakily, Kelsey said, "I'm not going to demean Lorrie's death by acting it out for you. I don't have to. You can see it for yourselves." She picked up one of the photographs that had been admitted in evidence, a picture from the crime scene. Lorrie Blystone's body was stretched along the floor, face down in the pool of her own blood, her right hand stretched out, reaching. The death scene was vibrant with horror. When Kelsey held up the picture, one woman in the front row of the jury began sobbing quietly. She wasn't alone in the courtroom.

"She wasn't a nice person, Lorrie," Kelsey said quietly. "She liked to say snide things to people. No one was safe around her. Finally she was too sharp for her own good. She made one cutting remark too many.

"But she was a person like any of us. She had a life. She had things she loved to do. She had a baby who was precious to her. When Lorrie woke up that morning, she had a life stretching decades ahead of her.

"Now she has nothing."

She pointed at Billy. "He took everything from her. The life she loved, the bad times ahead that would have tested her character. Her family. Watching her child grow up. He took her baby from her. He took everything.

"Because Lorrie said too much," Kelsey said bitterly. "Because she didn't know when to speak up and when to shut her mouth." Kelsey walked close to the jury. "But that wasn't up to Billy Fletcher to decide. She had a right. She could say whatever she wanted to anybody. You could hate her for it, you could snap back at her, but she had the right that all of us have to say what was on her mind. She had a right to say whatever she wanted without someone shooting her for it.

"She had a right to a life. He had no right to take it from her. Don't you dare excuse him for it."

Kelsey felt ice-cold. She couldn't look at the jurors any more. Only when she got back to her chair did Kelsey realize her face was wet.

The courtroom was deathly quiet.

17

"That was the finest closing argument I ever heard," one of the reporters from Houston said.

"Have you heard very many?" Kelsey asked.

The crowd laughed. There weren't many of them, no more than a dozen, but since they completely surrounded Kelsey, the reporters felt like a huge throng. Four microphones were within a foot of her head and two cameras were aimed at her.

Not nearly so many people were flocking around the defense lawyer.

"Did you think the jurors looked especially grim when they went out to begin deliberating?" a serious-faced TV reporter from Dallas asked her.

"I hope so. They've got a grim job."

Politeness made Kelsey walk slowly, but she kept moving. At the courtroom door she said, "I'm sorry, I still have work to do," and managed to get out the other side of the circle of people. They let her go. There wouldn't be real news to report until the verdict came, and that might be hours.

Peter Stiller fell into step beside her as she went up the courthouse stairs. After they passed the landing, they were alone. Peter wore jeans, a corduroy shirt, and a heavy jacket with its fluffy inside lining showing at the collar. "You did it just right," he said. "I was afraid you'd try to gloss over Lorrie and Ronald and make them seem like they were as likable as Billy. You were right to confront the problem head-on. They weren't great people, but they didn't deserve this."

He sniffed. Kelsey leaned against him and put her arm around his back. The solidity of his presence lifted the exhaustion she felt. It seemed like a long time since she'd touched another human being. Peter smelled fresh. Kelsey felt grimy.

"You gave me the idea," she said. "You made me see her."

By the time they reached her office they had silently agreed to stop talking about the deaths. Kelsey hung her black jacket on the coatrack and wanted to continue to undress: blouse, skirt, pantyhose. She wished she had a shower to step into.

Peter watched her. Kelsey's nervousness was centered in those twelve people in their little jury room one flight down, but Peter was watching Kelsey. Whatever happened, after the trial she'd be gone from Galilee for good.

"Maybe I'll take some vacation time after this," he said. Kelsey took his arm in both hands and leaned her forehead on his shoulder. "Please," she said softly. "Come to Austin."

They held each other for a long minute before the old courthouse around them reasserted itself. Peter drew a shaky breath. 'I'll get us some sandwiches."

Kelsey nodded. "I want to look over a few things here."

When Peter was gone, she opened the file she'd carried up. It didn't hold much: a few police reports, the photographs she hadn't offered into evidence; the jury had the others. Kelsey spread out what she had left, as if she could fit them together. For the hundredth time she tried to think of an alternative to the case she'd presented to the jury.

She didn't give herself the easy out of believing in the evil-hobo theory for even a second. The timing would have had to be too perfect. The drifter would have had to stumble on the scene just as Billy was driving away, then decide to go in and take the gun from Ronald and shoot both Blystones—but not steal anything except the baby. Nothing had been reported missing from the house. She couldn't picture a stranger taking Taylor. No. Someone had hated that baby, or feared her, as much as he'd hated and feared her parents.

She pulled toward her a picture taken by the police photographer that showed Katherine Fletcher heading up the stairs to check on her sick mother. Her dark coat was wrapped tightly around her; she'd just come in from outside. Morgan was in a corner of the photo, looking up at his wife.

They were family, they were the logical other suspects, but neither one was a possibility. Katherine may have hated her sister—she'd certainly resented her—and maybe by extension her sister's baby, as well, but Katherine hadn't left her house full of people until ten forty-five at the earliest. The bodies had already been cooling by then. More likely she hadn't left her house until a few minutes before the first police officer on the scene saw her arriving at her mother's house about eleven-thirty or eleven-forty. Much as it would make her feel like a keen psychological detective, Kelsey couldn't work Katherine into the picture of the murders and kidnapping.

Morgan was even less a workable suspect. He'd been in the courthouse until he'd left it a little before eleven-thirty. Several people remembered him saying he was going to go by his mother-in-law's house. Five minutes later he'd called police to report his grisly discovery. His sister- and brother-in-law had been dead for at least an hour by then.

No. Billy was the one. Kelsey held herself to an even harsher burden of proof than the terribly high one on which the jury had been instructed. She had to be sure. This was why she'd gotten out of criminal law. She couldn't stand the possibility of sending an innocent person to prison.

Billy was the murderer. She was sure of that; she had to be. But maybe he'd had an after-the-fact accomplice. Lydia had suggested that maybe there were no traces of Lorrie's blood in Billy's car because someone had given him a ride. But who would have wanted to help him? And who could have? She pulled toward her a picture of the outside of the Beaumont house taken during the initial investigation. There was the Blystones' car, with its baby carseat showing. Parked directly behind it was Morgan's Lincoln Continental. (He drove a nice car, for a prosecutor. It was the kind of detail that might get him investigated by some suspicious assistant AG, except that everyone knew the source of Morgan's extra money.) Parked beside the Blystones' car, filling the driveway side to side, was Katherine's Buick. All those cars had been in Galilee all morning. There hadn't been time for any of them to drive Billy to Houston and back. What other possibilities were there? Aunt Goldie? She'd gone to Houston and back. But why would she help Billy escape? Helena Parker? Her disappearance screamed that she was hiding something, but why on earth would she have helped Billy Fletcher steal the baby?

And if someone had tried to help Billy, someone else had tried to hurt him. Who had planted blood in his car, and why? As Peter had said, it was a frame-up attempt that couldn't possibly have succeeded, once the blood was tested. Had it been an impulsive act? An accident? Or done by someone with no grasp at all of forensic science?

Kelsey stared at the picture of the cars in the driveway. A family huddle of metal, such as crowded many an American driveway where the children are all grown, and all have cars when they come back to visit. The cars congregated dumbly, without conflicts.

Again she pulled toward her the picture that showed Katherine on the stairs and Morgan in the entryway below her, bystanders at the crime scene. The photographer must have been snapping photos like a mad thing to have gotten this pose. Kelsey hadn't offered it in evidence; it didn't prove anything.

She suddenly realized that the police photographer hadn't been on the scene yet when Katherine had arrived at Mrs. Beaumont's house and rushed up the stairs to check on her mother. This picture couldn't exist. Kelsey studied it more closely. Katherine wasn't going up the stairs. She was standing at the top, saying something. The collar of her blouse showed above her tightly buttoned coat. This was a later picture, taken after the photographer had arrived.

Katherine wasn't going up the stairs, she was coming down them, or standing at the top to call down to the investigators below. Her husband was listening to her.

Kelsey frowned.

The jury was out for hours. Phones rang around the courthouse, Galileans calling to ask if the jurors were back yet. The afternoon lengthened.

The courtroom was never empty. Billy and his lawyer had

gone away, so had the other Fletchers and Mrs. Beaumont, but people drifted in and out of the courtroom, hoping for news. A few faithful stayed planted in the pews. The reporters grew restless but couldn't go far. The cook and waitress and coffee drinkers at the café across the street got interviewed all over again.

Kelsey's final argument was the talk of the town. Those who had heard it relayed as best they could what she had said, and the best storytellers among them managed to convey the sense of it. Billy *had* been a desperate man, they said speculatively. Billy's support in the town was growing less solid. "I could see him shooting them," more than one person said. The jury deliberations were spreading all over town.

By four-thirty the day was darkening. When dusk fell in Galilee, it seemed that the piney woods edged closer to town. Even indoors, twilight held a sense of menace in Galilee. When Kelsey came downstairs, people in the courthouse halls looked at her with mixtures of admiration and fear. One man muttered to her as she passed, "You done a good job," then scowled as if he'd condemned her. Kelsey knew what he meant: she'd done a good job of doing a terrible, ugly job.

In the courtroom Kelsey found Mrs. Terwilliger, one of the ladies who'd been at Katherine Fletcher's bridge party at the time of the killings. Mrs. Terwilliger, Kelsey remembered, had thought Katherine had left the house about eleven, after the phone had rung. But she'd been caught up in the game and admitted she could have been half an hour off.

The lady was in her late fifties. She was right to dye her hair dark brown, because her plump face didn't look old enough to sport gray hair. She had lively eyes, but on this deadened day she looked at Kelsey and shook her head sadly.

Kelsey showed her the picture of Katherine on the stairs. Mrs. Terwilliger flinched momentarily as if Kelsey were carrying a bloody totem, but then she realized what she was seeing. "Oh, yes. That's how Katherine was dressed when she left the house. It wasn't really cold enough for that heavy coat, but . . ." She shrugged.

"What about the blouse?" Kelsey asked.

Mrs. Terwilliger squinted at the picture. Only a tiny portion of

Katherine's blouse could be seen in the photo, but Kelsey counted on the bridge club lady to have a memory for clothes. She wasn't disappointed. "Oh, yes," Mrs. Terwilliger said brightly. "That blouse with its little scalloped collar. Very simple. Elegant. Yes, that's what she was wearing at the party. It's a very subtle color, lime green, but so pale you'd— Well, you know. I think it's Katherine's favorite blouse."

Kelsey shook her head. "I haven't seen it."

She went outside and stood on the courthouse steps, eyes searching. Peter was leaning against a tree in the little square across the street. He looked up at once. Kelsey ran across the street.

"Let's walk," she said. He looked at her questioningly.

Forty minutes later they were returning, walking slowly back across the courthouse square, in the full nighttime darkness, when they saw people streaming into the courthouse.

"The jury's back," Peter said.

They looked at the defendant, but they didn't smile: a very mixed signal, according to Kelsey's training. Supposedly jurors who had just condemned a defendant wouldn't look at him; jurors who averted their eyes were a good sign for the prosecution. But if they looked at the defendant, meaning they'd acquitted him, the jurors were supposed to smile reassuringly. Most of these Galileans as they filed back into the jury box looked at their neighbor Billy Fletcher, but they didn't smile at him. Their expressions were curious, some of them grim, uniformly solemn.

"Have you reached a verdict?" Judge Saunders asked.

Morgan Fletcher stood beside his brother to receive the verdict. Kelsey thought she knew what he was thinking. Had all his maneuverings paid off? Morgan Fletcher had been as much the defense lawyer in this case as Clyde Wolverton had been. More: all the strategy, from the day he discovered the bodies, had been Morgan's.

The jury foreman was a man who could have been related to Billy. He was the same size, had the same ruddy complexion, had the arms that looked uncomfortable straining the sleeves of his suit coat. He stared at Billy Fletcher and said harshly, "We find the defendant guilty of the murder of Ronald Blystone."

Billy sat with a thud. He lost all color. Kelsey found her own ears ringing. The noise of her heart and the noise of the crowd almost made it impossible for her to hear as the jury foreman continued, but the man's voice was strong and implacable:

"We find the defendant guilty of the murder of Lorrie Blystone. And we find him guilty of the kidnapping of Taylor Blystone."

A woman on the back row of the jury started crying. The verdict form in the foreman's hand was trembling. The man looked on the verge of tears himself, but his face was red with anger. Of the rest of the jurors, most looked sad, but none looked ashamed. They stared at Billy Fletcher with pain-filled eyes.

Billy sat without moving or speaking, his mouth hanging open. He obviously didn't hear the sounds of the spectators sweeping over him, the opening and closing of the courtroom doors as reporters ran out to use their cellular phones in the hall. Beside him, Morgan remained standing, but he, too, was stunned. His lips moved slightly. Kelsey could see him trying to think how to undo this disaster, but his mind wouldn't help him.

Clyde Wolverton stared at the jurors as if he didn't understand what their foreman had said. The defense lawyer obviously had no plan for this contingency.

The foreman sat and transferred his gaze to Judge Saunders. The judge glanced out at the still-noisy courtroom, up at the clock, and said to the jurors, "It's late, and this is a Friday night. I'm going to let you retire briefly and tell me whether you want to go on to the punishment phase of trial tomorrow morning or wait until Monday."

The foreman barely glanced around at his fellow jurors before he rose again and said, "Your Honor, if it's all right, we'd like to continue right now."

Judge Saunders blinked in surprise. The judge, too, had paled beneath her makeup. The overhead lights of the courtroom seemed harsher now that night had fallen. Judge Saunders turned to Kelsey. "Is the State prepared to go forward now?" It sounded as if the judge hoped for a negative answer.

Kelsey didn't help her out. "I have no witnesses on punishment, Your Honor. The state reoffers the evidence from the guilt phase and rests."

The judge blinked again. "Mr. Wolverton? Are you prepared on punishment?"

Morgan Fletcher was shaking his head violently. He was right: give the jurors overnight at least to question their verdict, to develop dream doubts. But Wolverton didn't see the district attorney. He stood hastily, disoriented, and said, "Um, yes, certainly, Your Honor. The defense calls, uh, Irene Fletcher."

Punishment phase is a delicate business for the defense. The defense lawyer has to make the jurors think they've made a terrible mistake, convicted an innocent man, in the hope that the jury will respond with a low sentence, even probation. But the defense can't attack that guilty verdict directly. Guilt or innocence is no longer the issue, and one doesn't want to piss off the jury by telling them they were wrong.

To be an effective witness on punishment a defendant has to break down in tears, sob out his remorse, say he made a terrible mistake, and that he could never, never, never do such a thing again. But even this wouldn't work for a defendant who had pled not guilty and staunchly declared his innocence from the witness stand. If Billy Fletcher took the remorse route now, he risked the jurors thinking, *You bastard, you mean you were lying to us when you swore you didn't do it?* The defense doesn't want the jurors mad when they go in to decide what punishment fits the crime.

Clyde Wolverton obviously didn't think his client was up to the delicate task of reasserting his innocence while respecting the jury's verdict, and asking their forgiveness for something he still maintained he hadn't done. Billy might not have been able to speak, anyway. He looked like a man having a long, slow stroke.

So Wolverton called Billy's wife, who broke down in tears as she testified that her husband was a good man, that he'd never been convicted of anything before, that he'd be an ideal candidate for probation. Wolverton called a neighboring farmer, who testified he'd give Billy a job if he were released on probation. He called Morgan Fletcher, who leaned half out of the witness stand and told the jurors he could guarantee his brother's rehabilitation.

"I promise you," Morgan said almost wildly, staring along the rows of jurors. "It's an absolute certainty Billy will never hurt anyone else."

Kelsey watched the jurors during all the defense testimony. They shifted uncomfortably in their seats. They would not like, in the years to come, to sit in church with these witnesses. But the jurors did not look abashed.

Kelsey asked no questions of any of the defense witnesses.

Clyde Wolverton was at his best in his argument on punishment. He had gradually recovered himself as he'd questioned his own witnesses. By the time he rested, he was again patting Billy reassuringly. When Wolverton rose to address the jurors, he looked more than ever like an old preacher, an evangelist who had spent his life traveling the world saving souls. He stood tall under the harsh white courtroom lights. From the jurors' perspective the defense lawyer was backed by the windows of the far wall, which were black with night. There was something unearthly about being in this daytime place as ten o'clock at night approached, as if they had all broken in to perform some ancient but unlawful ritual. The room was more hushed even than it had been during the day.

"My friends," Clyde Wolverton said without irony, "you had a painful, very difficult job to perform, and I admire you for your courage. I disagree with the verdict you reached, but I respect your integrity. I know nothing entered into your deliberations except your very honest attempt to do the right thing. This was a very difficult case to decide. Judge Saunders will thank you for your service, and the defense thanks you, too. Yes, we do, for giving Billy Fletcher his day in court."

He came closer. "Now you have just as difficult a task. I want to make clear to you what that task is. You are to decide what punishment fits the crimes of which you've found Billy Fletcher guilty. Yes, but that is not your only job. You are also to decide what punishment fits this man."

He turned and gestured at his sunken client. As if that sight had been impressive, when Wolverton turned back to the jury, his tones became even rounder and fuller. "When Billy Fletcher argued with Ronald Blystone about what was to become of the Smoothskins factory, he wasn't just thinking of himself. Billy knew he represented this whole town. Yes. He was a sort of unofficial mayor of Galilee, a delegation of one sent to argue that this town should endure, should prosper. That was what made

Billy so angry at Ronald Blystone's facetious arguments. It wasn't a game to Billy. He knew how many people's lives were at stake. He felt responsible for those lives. He wasn't just the manager of the factory, he was a shepherd guarding his flock."

Kelsey winced. There was a saying to describe a lawyer addressing an audience already convinced of what the lawyer was arguing: preaching to the choir. If ever a defense lawyer were preaching to the choir, Clyde Wolverton was at that moment. Everyone in the room understood what he was saying, and most of them probably believed it implicitly.

Kelsey still felt weak and hollow-limbed. She stole a glance at Billy and saw that he had not yet begun to recover from the guilty verdict.

"When Billy Fletcher went to Alice Beaumont's house that October morning, he wasn't going just for himself. He went on your behalf, and yours." Wolverton was talking to individual jurors. Then he gestured to the packed courtroom. "On theirs. He went thinking of every man, woman, and child in this town.

"Maybe that's why his emotions got the better of him. That's why things got so wildly out of hand. But you look at Billy Fletcher. You look at the man he is, look at his whole life. And you know—for an absolute certainty, as his brother said—that Billy is a man who could never, never do anything remotely like this again. He is an absolutely perfect candidate for probation. He would never be a risk to anyone."

Wolverton lowered his voice and leaned forward. Tears were in his eyes. "You've rendered your judgment. Now show us you are also capable of understanding. And forgiveness. Show us you are capable of feeling some small portion of the great love Billy feels for his town.

"Please."

The defense lawyer straightened slowly and slowly slumped back to his seat. Kelsey waited, giving Wolverton the respect due not to a good performance, but to honest emotion. For the first time during trial, she had found the lawyer believable.

She felt a little light-headed when she stood. The air was thin in the courtroom. The heat had been turned down, it was growing cold. Kelsey walked slowly toward the jury box. She had nothing prepared to say. Then she looked down, saw each juror giving her his full attention, and realized she needed to say very little.

"I know, and I know you know, there's only one acceptable punishment for what Billy Fletcher did."

She turned toward the defense table. "Probation?" she asked wonderingly.

She turned back to the jurors, started to speak to them again, then only shook her head, sadly, and walked slowly back to her seat. Behind her back, two of the jurors nodded.

This time the jury was hardly out long enough for anyone to shift in their seats. No one left this time. Kelsey stood and looked over the spectators. Their murmurings had died down almost completely. The guilty verdict had been shocking, but not nearly as great a shock as it would have been a week ago. Kelsey had forced the citizens of Galilee to confront the possibility of evil in their midst, and the jury had come through, put aside their self-interest and decided someone had to pay for the horrors of the crimes.

Only one person came forward out of the spectator seats. Alice Beaumont sailed out of the center of the pew as if the people blocking her way had had their legs evaporated. She marched up to Kelsey and didn't lower her voice to make their conversation particularly private.

"I would have thought you'd have more to say about what they should do to him for what he did," Mrs. Beaumont sniffed.

"I will have."

Alice Beaumont didn't know what that meant and didn't care to inquire. Her manner softened. She even put out her hand to touch Kelsey's arm. "Well, dear, you did a good job. You did. I knew you would. That's why I recommended you."

Recommended was too mild a word. *You had me made up special,* Kelsey thought, *like a special dress waiting in the attic for an occasion that might never come.* Maybe Kelsey was thinking melodramatic thoughts. The nighttime courtroom inspired them.

Alice Beaumont looked at her with slight puzzlement. "Well, congratulations. You did a fine job."

You won't think so for long, Kelsey thought.

When Mrs. Beaumont turned away, Kelsey noticed that her

constant companion was missing. There seemed to be a palpable blank spot where Katherine Fletcher usually sat next to her mother.

Morgan Fletcher was gone, too. Clyde Wolverton leaned half over his client, as if trying to revive him, but Morgan wasn't part of the huddle. There was nothing more to be done in the courtroom, Morgan had realized that. Kelsey glanced up at the judge's empty bench, and the nearby door out which Judge Saunders had gone to her office. Morgan hadn't followed her, that would have been too obvious, but there was a roundabout way.

Kelsey walked to the back of the courtroom, feeling the mob's eyes on her. She looked straight ahead, not meeting anyone's eyes, until she came to the door. Peter was standing there.

"They went out together," he said.

"Morgan and Katherine? Where did they go?"

Peter opened the door and gestured with his head. "Up toward his office. Morgan was doing the talking. Planning something. I couldn't hear what."

"Planning something with his wife," Kelsey said curiously, and Peter looked at her, as bereft of answers as Kelsey felt.

The jury was out no more than fifteen minutes, only long enough for the jurors to look at each other and nod their agreement. Kelsey knew what their verdict would be. She had never felt so certain before. She had known it since the jury foreman had asked to finish the trial that night. That could only mean that the jurors had already decided on punishment at the same time they'd found Billy Fletcher guilty.

Everyone reassembled quickly when the jurors announced their readiness. Judge Saunders returned to the bench, her composure intact. She didn't look at anyone as she asked for the verdict.

The jury foreman stood slowly this time, having a little trouble straightening his back. The lateness of the hour seemed to have struck him. He unfolded the verdict form. This time the foreman sounded terribly sad as he read their judgment. "We sentence the defendant to life imprisonment," he said quietly. "Three times over."

18

The lights in the courtroom flickered, as if the building itself had blinked. There was one loud moan from the spectator seats at the pronouncement of the sentence. People hunched their shoulders. Family members put their arms around each other. Life was cold and lonely, with little protection from disaster. There was no general outcry. Accepting the jury's guilty verdicts, as people were beginning to do, meant Billy Fletcher had murdered two people and probably a third. No other punishment was possible. In the morning Galileans would say, "Well, that's that," and the most reflective among them would realize a sense of relief. At least it was solved. They could begin to put behind them the worst crime in the history of Defiance County.

Meanwhile, in the late-night courtroom the few small remnants of trial passed in a blur: the dismissal of the jury with the judge's hollow-sounding thanks for their service, the formal sentencing of Billy Fletcher to three life sentences, and his being handcuffed and taken away, casting one baffled, gaping look back into the courtroom. Then everyone stood or sat as if it couldn't possibly be over.

Kelsey was the first to recover. She managed to rush most of the way down the courtroom aisle before the reporters caught up to her. But catch her they did. The few reporters clustered in Galilee knew they represented many more of their kind in the outside world. What they could pick up now would be salable around the country. Kelsey Thatch was about to become a mini-celebrity.

"What are you going to do next, Ms. Thatch?" one called out, and they all waited for her answer.

"Finish the case." Kelsey wasn't wearing the appropriate expression for the victor over such tremendous odds. She looked more angry than exhilarated.

"What do you mean?" the TV reporter from Dallas asked, showing the surprise that also silenced his colleagues. "You mean the appeal?"

Kelsey laughed harshly, a short, sharp sound like choking, and escaped from them.

Kelsey sat looking out her window. The courthouse and its square across the street were well-lighted, but the lights only emphasized the blackness beyond. Kelsey felt how easy it would be to disappear. Drive into that night, no one would ever find you again.

Leaving was her specialty. She felt its attraction. Discard the problems, start a new life, become a new person. She could do that. She had the experience.

From where she sat she could see her lonely car parked at the curb. Only one reporter maintained the vigil at it. Others might have gone to her motel. Peter had said he'd drive by there and give her a call to let her know.

No one had thought of her remaining in the courthouse. Kelsey had used her tiny office so little, probably no one remembered she had it.

Except the man who had given it to her.

Kelsey heard the creak of a floorboard and the sound startled her. It was so loud in the silence that she wasn't sure if it had come from just outside her door or from the stairs. She looked out the window again. The last reporter was gone. So were the other cars. The courthouse was nearly empty. By this time Kelsey might be locked in.

It felt strange to be frightened sitting in a courthouse. Courthouses were places of sanctuary, where whatever horrible events had happened on the outside could be sorted out calmly. But Kelsey's breath grew short as she stood up from her desk and saw that her door was open, spilling its light in a dim wedge out into the dark hall. She put her hand on the phone, wishing it would ring.

Morgan Fletcher stepped into the light. He filled the doorway. Morgan looked like a different man, a used-up model of the one Kelsey had first met in Galilee. His tie was askew. His cheeks were stubbled, and the overhead lights threw such shadows that Kelsey couldn't see his dark eyes. She could smell his breath, though. Somewhere in the courthouse, Morgan kept a bottle.

For the first time in a long time, Kelsey was aware of his size. In the courtroom he had been diminished, shrunk to normal human dimensions as if out of courtesy. But now he almost filled her doorway side to side. Morgan was taller than his brother and had the same large hands.

He didn't speak for a long minute, and when he did, Kelsey understood why he hadn't used his voice on her. It, too, had changed. Morgan's smooth explanatory tones had turned guttural.

"Ms. Thatch—"

"I hope you're here to tell me that you're going to hire a better lawyer for your brother's motion for new trial."

"What?" When he raised his head, the light hit his eyes, which were wide with puzzlement.

"Never mind," Kelsey said briskly. "I'll do it myself. There's something I need from you, though."

"What's that?" Morgan walked toward her, growing larger. Kelsey remained aware of his hands.

"Your confession."

He stopped. His expression turned questioning, but it wasn't the look of puzzlement he'd had a moment before. Morgan was no stupid criminal, he wasn't going to blurt anything out. He waited for her to specify.

Kelsey said carefully, "Ronald implied to Lorrie that he'd come here to the courthouse and seen something. What he saw was you and Judge Saunders, wasn't it?"

Morgan looked stricken. Kelsey tried to make it easy for him. "I saw it myself, Morgan. Nothing erotic, nothing bad, just a private moment that made me know she cares for you."

"Well, of course she does," Morgan said with an edge of harshness. "We've known each other a long time, Linda and me. I helped her get elected. We work together. She's a kind person. Maybe she—shouldn't be as evident as she is sometimes. Someone with Ronald's nasty mind could have made something ugly out of some little touch he saw. But I swear"—he lifted his hand to make a small gesture of oath-taking—"there is nothing between Linda Saunders and me that anyone would think was wrong."

"I believe you." It was the first lie Kelsey had told in Galilee.

Two weeks later, the same courtroom, now bright with sunshine. February had arrived with a day of mock spring, a cloudless blue sky and a temperature in the fifties. It was a ruse of nature's, though. A cold front was bearing down on east Texas. It could arrive any time. People who listened to weather forecasts carried heavy coats, which made the spectator seats crowded. There weren't as many people as there had been for the trial. Those who'd asked lawyers had been told that hearings on motions for new trial were routine and nearly always ended with the request for a new trial being denied. Billy Fletcher still had his friends, though, and this was their best hope of the moment. His wife and four children were in the front row of spectator seats.

A few reporters were on hand, too, looking not so bored as they should have. Kelsey wondered if Morgan had alerted them.

The jury box was empty. Kelsey recognized three of the jurors from the trial scattered through the courtroom. She had told them all not to worry, no one was going to attack them or what they'd done in the jury room. But the former jurors retained watchful expressions. The verdict they had reached still frightened some of them, but it was theirs.

The door behind the judge's bench opened and Billy Fletcher was brought in, hands handcuffed in front of him. There was a uniform intake of breath from the spectator seats. Hardly anyone had seen Billy for the past two weeks. He had been incarcerated in isolation in the Defiance County Jail, refusing all visitors except his wife and brother. He looked as if he'd refused food, too. Billy wore a white jail coverall that might have fit him two weeks earlier, but now it hung on his arms, and his protruding stomach was gone; the coverall flapped loosely on him.

He had lost his color, too. His skin almost matched the white coverall. The color scheme was reflected in his hair, where Kelsey noticed for the first time gray hairs scattered all through Billy's reddish hair.

He looked around as if he had never been in this place before; as if, in fact, he'd been isolated so long he'd forgotten his past. The bailiff had to lead him to his seat at the defense table. Clyde Wolverton leaned over to whisper to him reassuringly.

That was to be the defense lawyer's main function at this hearing. When Judge Saunders, absolutely expressionless, took her seat and asked if the defense was ready to proceed on its motion, Wolverton stood, glanced at Morgan Fletcher on the other side of his client, and said without looking at Kelsey, "Your Honor, the defense is going to allow the State to present the evidence at this hearing."

The judge raised her eyebrows, which was acting: she'd been informed that the hearing was going to be unorthodox. "Unusual," she said loudly, for the benefit of the spectators. "But in the absence of an objection from either side—Ms. Thatch, you may proceed."

"I call Mrs. Alice Beaumont."

Mrs. Beaumont stood immediately from the spectator seats, as if she'd expected this call, though Kelsey hadn't said a word to her. Mrs. Beaumont came forward with her mouth set and her eyes snapping. She was an amazing woman. She had no idea what her function was in this hearing, but she came forward boldly, ready to take charge. She stopped in front of Kelsey. "Why are you calling me in this man's defense?" she demanded.

"Because you were the only witness in the house."

"But I didn't see anything."

"Let's see." Kelsey gestured at the witness stand. Suspiciously, Alice Beaumont took the oath and sat.

"Mrs. Beaumont, you were in your house the morning of October twenty-first, weren't you?"

"Yes, I was. I was upstairs in bed, very sick with the flu. I was there all morning. All day."

"Were you alert? Watching TV, reading?"

"Not hardly. I was out. I'd had codeine cough medicine, and pain reliever, and I was asleep."

"Yes, very deeply asleep, weren't you? But you did wake up sometime, didn't you?"

"Yes." Mrs. Beaumont remembered. And now she knew that her memory was important. She watched her prosecutor carefully. "One time I woke up, something woke me, I don't know what. Nobody was in the room with me. I don't remember whether I looked at the clock, but it was morning. Midmorning, I could tell by the light. It seemed strange—"

"Did you hear anything?"

Mrs. Beaumont frowned at the interruption. The frown turned into the concentration of memory. "I heard the baby crying. I wondered why nobody was seeing to her, and I thought I should. But I was so tired. I just lay there and listened to her. It seemed like a long time."

"Do you have any idea how long?"

"Fifteen minutes, at least. It seemed longer, because I was lying there helpless."

"Did you ever hear anything else?"

"Like what?" Mrs. Beaumont looked confused.

"Men's voices. That's what you told me." Kelsey was leading the witness, but no one objected. No one was opposing Kelsey. She could do entirely what she wanted with Alice Beaumont.

"Oh, yes. I did. Men's voices. They weren't loud enough for me to recognize them, but I could hear the tones, you know. It was men's voices, no doubt about that." She directed a glare at Billy Fletcher. But that was a dead target. Billy was so bereft of life and hope that he just stared at her expressionlessly.

"No woman's voice at all?"

Mrs. Beaumont searched her memory. "No."

"Did you hear anything else?"

"I was drifting off again, but then the shot woke me up."

"The shot?" Kelsey said mildly. "Now you're sure you heard a gunshot."

"Yes, dear." Alice Beaumont leaned forward eagerly. "Once you've heard that sound you don't forget it, and you don't mistake it for anything else. I was so groggy at the time I didn't know what I'd heard, but I've been thinking and thinking and now I'm sure—"

"One shot? That's what you heard?"

Alice Beaumont frowned. "Yes. I did hear it. I heard him murdering my baby. If I had realized then—" She glared at Billy Fletcher.

"And did you hear anything else after that?"

Alice looked off into space. It was hard to imagine her in bed, frail. Even in the distress she began to feel she looked like a force of nature only fleetingly confined to human form.

"I heard the baby crying." Her eyes began to fill. "I heard Taylor, crying and crying. I so wanted to get up. It went on and on, until I passed out trying to sit up."

"Do you have any idea how long you listened to the baby cry?" Kelsey asked, her tone going soft for the first time.

Mrs. Beaumont was determined to keep her face stiff, but her lips trembled. Tears were flowing down her cheeks. "Forever."

Kelsey coughed and looked away. "No more questions."

"Wait!" It seemed impossible that the command could have sprung from Alice Beaumont, who a moment earlier had looked on the verge of collapse. But in an instant her face was hard again, and her stare commanding. The tears still on her cheeks looked like inappropriate makeup. "Now do I get to speak?" she said peremptorily.

"No. You may listen if you like. No more witnesses on the motion, Your Honor."

"Argument?" Judge Saunders said, her tone declaring that argument was necessary. What Kelsey had just proven with her few fragments of testimony was far from clear.

"Yes, Your Honor. To remind the court briefly, the State's theory during trial, which the jury obviously found to be fact, was that Billy Fletcher argued with Ronald and Lorrie Blystone, became so enraged that he shot and killed them both, then abducted the baby, Taylor Blystone.

"That can't have happened."

Alice Beaumont still sat in the witness stand, as if Kelsey were arguing to two judges. The older woman gaped. Her stunned expression erased the look of anger she'd still been wearing a moment earlier at not getting to say what she wanted. Then her eyes narrowed. Willing belief did not overspread Mrs. Beaumont's features. What appeared there was a look of suspicion: who had gotten to her prosecutor?

Kelsey paced the small space between the judge's bench and the lawyers' tables, which gave her a momentary glimpse of Billy Fletcher. His face showed life for the first time that day. Morgan sat beside him, his hand on his brother's shoulder, watching Kelsey with a look of painful hope. Kelsey turned away from the brothers.

"Why couldn't it have happened that way?" Alice Beaumont said.

Kelsey ignored her, but the continuation of her argument was an answer. "Something woke Mrs. Beaumont that morning, she stayed awake for some time; finally after she fell asleep, she was awakened again by a gunshot. One shot. She hasn't realized it yet, but that was the second gunshot Mrs. Beaumont heard. What woke her the first time? She was very deeply asleep, she said, but something woke her. Not the sound of people arguing, it was a quick, very loud sound that was over by the time she was fully awake. A gunshot. Then the baby crying. Men's voices. I think it was probably *a* man's voice, a man talking to himself, reproaching himself, going crazy. Then sometime later another single gunshot."

Kelsey felt the stares on her back. She concentrated on her argument, picturing what she was saying. "This means the theory I presented at trial is wrong. There was one shot fired, which woke Mrs. Beaumont, then nothing, though she stayed awake listening for another fifteen minutes. She didn't hear a woman screaming, or a man shouting in rage. Just a single gunshot.

"If Billy Fletcher was the one who fired that one shot, committing the first murder, what would have happened next? Lorrie Blystone would have screamed. Her mother upstairs would have heard her. Or if Billy had shot Lorrie first, Ronald would have screamed in rage and attacked Billy; Billy would have had to kill him immediately, too. But Mrs. Beaumont didn't hear any of that. One isolated shot, then nothing. Mrs. Beaumont heard a long gap between the two shots."

Judge Saunders nodded thoughtfully, caught herself, and stopped giving clues to what she was thinking. It was Alice Beaumont who looked confused. Kelsey directed her next few sentences directly at Mrs. Beaumont.

"If Billy Fletcher had committed these two murders, he would have had to do them quickly, one hard on the heels of the other. He wouldn't have had the luxury of waiting. He wouldn't have had quiet time to contemplate what he'd done, and what he should do next. Billy would have killed Lorrie and Ronald the way I described at trial, quickly, in a rage. Mrs. Beaumont upstairs would have heard two gunshots close together. But she didn't. She was awakened by one and then long, long minutes later she heard another. Which means the State's theory of what happened was wrong.

"What makes more sense is what the defense argued at trial: Lorrie and Ronald continued their argument after Billy left. But now a gun was out, and when the argument grew too heated and Lorrie said something too cutting, Ronald shot her."

Mrs. Beaumont's faded blue eyes drifted away as she gave thought to the idea, and her eyes brimmed as Kelsey continued the description: "Ronald was probably horrified by what he'd done. He watched his wife crawl toward their baby, he watched her die, and he knew his life was over, too. His ambition, his freedom, they both died with Lorrie.

"He picked up Taylor out of her mother's blood and put her in her crib. She went on crying, like an accusation. Upstairs, Mrs. Beaumont heard her. And she heard a man's voice: Ronald talking to himself, rehearsing an excuse, but nothing was good enough. Finally he put the gun to his own head, and that was the next shot Mrs. Beaumont heard.

"If it was Ronald who shot Lorrie, he would have had leisure to think, to decide, to let those fifteen long minutes pass before he reached the decision to fire again. Billy Fletcher would not have had that luxury." Kelsey glanced once more at Billy Fletcher, saw him nodding, saw tears on his cheeks, and couldn't look at him again. "This is a theory that fits the evidence," she said loudly. "The prosecution theory doesn't."

Judge Saunders cleared her throat and spoke quietly. "If I recall correctly, Ms. Thatch, you shot down this very theory at trial. Rather convincingly, given the jury's verdicts."

"They didn't have the evidence of the spacing of the gunshots."

"No. But you haven't answered the question you asked at

trial." Quietly, the judge asked the question that was reflected on Alice Beaumont's face as well: "What about the baby?"

"I wish I could tell you." This was the hardest part, admitting she didn't have all the answers. "I can't prove what happened to Taylor Blystone. I do have a theory." She felt Mrs. Beaumont clutch her arm, but Kelsey pulled gently away. "Helena Parker."

Kelsey addressed the courtroom. "Helena returned from the store sometime after the murders, she must have, but then she left again and hasn't come back. Why? I suspect she returned after the Blystones were dead. She stumbled into the horrifying scene, didn't know who was responsible, and took the baby away for safekeeping. Took her to Houston." Kelsey talked directly to the reporters on the front row of the spectator seats. "Then she got scared, after she found out about the search for Taylor's 'kidnapper,' and now she's afraid to come out of hiding. I'd send her a message if I could. Come back, Helena. Bring Taylor home. No one's going to charge you with anything."

The reporters scribbled fiercely. Kelsey could almost see the message going out. Turning back to the bench, she said, "This would account for the inadmissible evidence, too, Your Honor." The padded envelope was back on Kelsey's table. She opened it, just enough for the gown to spill out visibly, and set it down again. "The baby gown that Peter Stiller found on the highway to Houston, stained with Lorrie Blystone's blood. Yes, it is, I've had it tested by now.

"But this isn't evidence against Billy Fletcher, Your Honor. This is evidence in his favor." Both women at the front of the room looked at her in surprise. "Because the gown was in a trash can from a rest stop. Picture Billy Fletcher as I described him, grabbing up Taylor Blystone, rushing with her away from the scene of his crimes, taking her with him on the highway, then gradually realizing he's made a mistake and he needs to discard the baby.

"So he stops with her at a busy rest stop at high noon, where he risks being seen by any number of witnesses, and changes the baby's clothes, throwing the bloodstained gown in a trash can? I don't think so. That's not the work of the desperate man I described.

"The other most compelling evidence that Billy didn't take Taylor came from this witness stand this morning, from the woman who still sits there." Kelsey walked back to Mrs. Beaumont, the woman who had seen Kelsey assigned to this case because she would do what she was told. "Because after the second gunshot was fired, you continued to hear Taylor crying. For a long time. 'Forever,' you said. Again, that means it doesn't make sense that Billy took her. He would have fled, Mrs. Beaumont. He would have run from that house as fast as he could. If you still heard Taylor crying in the house, after the gunshots, that means Billy didn't take her."

Mrs. Beaumont closed her eyes, took a deep breath, and lowered her head to her supporting hand. Kelsey continued, "In this state of the evidence, I can't accept a conviction." She looked dead at Judge Saunders. "Can you?"

Preaching to the choir, indeed. Kelsey was sure Judge Saunders had entered the hearing looking for a good excuse to grant Morgan Fletcher's brother a new trial. In fact, the judge had expected this to be the most difficult decision of her judicial career. But the prosecutor had made it easy. "No," Judge Saunders said after only a moment, "I can't. The motion for new trial is granted."

The reaction began from the spectator seats. Before it had time to crest, Kelsey presented prepared motions, dismissing the three indictments against the defendant. Suddenly, sitting at the defense table too frozen even to draw a breath, Billy Fletcher became, instead of a convicted murderer preparing to serve three life sentences, a free man. Clyde Wolverton was explaining in his ear, Morgan was hugging him, but Billy wasn't smiling yet. His recent life hadn't prepared him for good news. Kelsey thought fleetingly of adding her congratulations, but decided instead to stand back. She felt a hand on her arm again.

Alice Beaumont leaned her face very close to Kelsey's. Her stare was as intense as ever, but the expression in her face that demanded answers wasn't the imperiousness of authority, it was the beseeching of bereavement. "Are you sure?" she implored.

"Yes, ma'am. I'm very sure."

Mrs. Beaumont nodded. "You're right." Her own memory had convinced her.

Alice Beaumont stood. Kelsey accompanied her as the older woman made the long, painful walk to the defense table. Friends had gotten to Billy, pounding his back. Two of his children were hanging on his arms, his wife was crying behind him. Billy was finally grinning. Then he looked up and saw Kelsey.

She wanted to creep away, but in the next moment Billy was on his feet and lunging toward her. Before Kelsey could react, he had grabbed her hand and was pumping it. He babbled as he grinned. "Morgan said it'd be okay. He said just to wait, we'd—"

"Wait to do what?"

Billy blinked. "Wait for it to be all right," he concluded confusedly.

Then his employer compelled his attention. Billy grew soberer as Alice Beaumont stepped closer. The look in Billy's eyes was as if he'd just been told his trial was about to resume.

"I think," Alice Beaumont said haltingly, "I may have wronged you."

This was undoubtedly an unprecedented statement from the matriarch of Defiance County. Billy looked momentarily stunned, then he threw his heavy arms around his boss, almost over-whelming her. "I'm so sorry for you, Miz Beaumont," he mumbled into her neck. "I'm so sorry."

They were both crying. Kelsey turned away. She didn't get far. The courtroom had erupted in delight, and Kelsey was one of the centers of the emotion. The band of reporters was waiting for her. They looked familiar by now. Always in front was the handsome, well-groomed TV guy from Dallas, looking so serious it was obvious he was concentrating on his next question, paying no attention to whatever answer was forthcoming. It didn't matter: the camera would capture it.

There was a woman from Austin who'd gotten Kelsey's attention by always calling her by her first name and treating Kelsey as if the two of them were frequent lunch companions back in Austin. "Kelsey," she called now in the courtroom. "Just a word?"

"Sure, Eloise," Kelsey said intimately. There was no one around to get the joke.

Holding up an encapsulating hand, the reporter said, "Two weeks ago you won the biggest trial of your career. Why did you keep investigating the case?" She had the fake wide-eyed look of someone representing millions of ignorant people, while possessed of all the answers herself.

"Because I had to. I couldn't just let it lie, when I wasn't sure."

The reporter's quizzical look turned real. "So it was an ethics thing?" she asked, but her question was swamped in the wave of others.

A writer from *Texas Lawyer* who actually knew something about law said, "You said there are always mysteries left over after a trial. Why did you feel compelled to attack the guilty verdict you'd worked so hard to get in this case?"

"That's why." Kelsey waved a hand at Billy Fletcher. He was sitting again, smiling wearily like a child on Christmas night. His eyes were still wide. "There were too many mysteries in this one. I didn't believe that man belonged in prison."

"If you hadn't done such a good job, he'd have never been on his way there," the *Texas Lawyer* reporter muttered, but then she smiled at Kelsey. There wasn't going to be any hostile questioning from this crowd. Kelsey had not only proven herself a brilliant courtroom tactician, she had seized the high moral ground. She could almost see the stories writing themselves.

The last question sobered them all. "Do you think Taylor Blystone will turn up alive?" Silence fell. The Dallas TV guy had shocked even himself by saying it aloud.

"Please, God," Kelsey answered softly.

She had only her briefcase to carry. She hadn't rented a hotel room this time, she'd known she wouldn't be here that long. Her temporary office upstairs was a storeroom again. When the courtroom began to clear out, Kelsey looked around. Peter wasn't there.

She would call him later.

She left the courtroom, taking in its details of aged wood and plaster walls. Already the place felt old in her memory, like her high school.

She decided to pay a formal farewell to the judge. Her clerk was gone from the outer office. Kelsey knocked on the judge's door.

Morgan Fletcher opened it. He smiled broadly when he saw Kelsey, not the grin of triumph or relief displayed in the courtroom. This one had a shy but comradely quality. "Kelsey," he said warmly, and put his arms around her. Kelsey remained stiff, though she smiled. Over Morgan's shoulder, Linda Saunders smiled back at her.

"I came to sign off," Kelsey said rather formally. Then she turned to Morgan with earnest eagerness. "I do have some ideas, though, I'd like to discuss with you. Ideas about—"

"Kelsey," Morgan said gently. "You were only authorized to prosecute one person. Now that you've dismissed the charges . . ." He shrugged. Morgan was in charge again. "Don't worry," he said reassuringly. "We'll handle it."

"You knew he was innocent," Kelsey said suddenly.

"I felt sure he was. I know Billy."

"Why didn't you ever say that to me?"

Morgan looked surprised. "I didn't want to influence you. I wanted you to reach your own conclusions."

Kelsey studied him wonderingly. She didn't think she'd ever known anyone else with such a quivering moral sense.

Well, maybe one.

Judge Saunders came to her, took her hand, and said, "You do great work, Kelsey. If you ever need a recommendation . . ."

"You never know. I might."

It felt strange to drive away, out of Galilee forever probably. When she called Peter, she'd suggest he come to Austin. It would be too strange for Kelsey to walk the streets of Galilee again, though even now she felt the town pulling at her.

But the broad interstate highway made the back roads and small towns seem imaginary. Kelsey sighed, turning her thoughts ahead for a change. She didn't know if the attorney general would be pleased or not at the way she'd concluded the case. The worst that could happen was that she'd be looking for another job, and she found that prospect didn't bother her.

Kelsey was so preoccupied she didn't notice that she was being followed.

A car horn startled her. She glanced at her speedometer and saw she was only going forty. She moved over to the right lane and speeded up. But the weight continued to drag at her. The weight of responsibility. Somewhere on that road, it had descended on Kelsey again. She remembered her first day driving into Galilee, the feeling that she was there as the only defender of the murder victims. Now all that was left of them was their baby. Kelsey had failed all three of them.

A rest stop appeared on the right and Kelsey pulled into it. She passed the campers, the long-haul trucks, kids tumbling in the narrow strand of grass, the little brick bathroom building. Kelsey parked far down the line, away from everyone, and sat in her car.

"I needed a Deep Throat," she said aloud. Some Galilee insider to tell her the secrets, at least point her in the right direction. She'd never found such an informant, but she remembered the words of the original Deep Throat, who had advised Woodward and Bernstein when their Watergate investigation stalled. "Follow the money," Deep Throat had said.

"And the blood," Kelsey added.

Her mind swirling, she forgot where she was. She was back in the courthouse, in the midst of trial, confessing her ignorance. Then she flew headlong through that memory, the scene crumpling like paper, and she was in Mrs. Beaumont's dining room the morning of the murders. In her car Kelsey was completely silent, but her body was taut, her face stretched as if by a grating scream. She heard the shot, smelled the burnt gunpowder, and saw Lorrie Blystone fall.

Most of all, she heard the baby crying. Then she saw hands reaching for the baby.

She recognized the hands.

The knock on her window, right beside her head, made Kelsey gasp. Her vision disappeared, but not its fright. An anonymous male torso was standing beside her car door. Kelsey shot a glance to the right, thinking she might be surrounded. She reached for her door lock.

But the torso wasn't so anonymous after all. As she reached for her keys to start the car, she glanced at it again and recognized something: the carriage of the hips, the line of thigh, maybe, the way his thumbs were hooked in his side pockets.

She sprang out of the car, almost hitting Peter in the face with the door as he stooped to peer through the window. He jumped back, then stared at her aghast.

"No!" Kelsey screamed. She slammed the car door. "Damn it, damn it, damn it, *damn!*"

In fury, she slapped first her arms, then her head, in a forehead-bruising slam, down onto her car's roof. The impact took her sight for a moment. When her head cleared, Peter was holding her. "Oh, my God," Kelsey said. She was crying. She clutched his arm, then pulled away.

"What is it? My God, Kelsey—"

Her emotion was spent. She slumped against the car, dazed, but her eyes were still moving, seeing something in imagination. "Helena Parker didn't take Taylor," she said to no one.

"What?"

Kelsey looked up at him wonderingly. He seemed part of her vision. "Peter. What are you doing here?"

"You left without saying good-bye." His voice was mild, but he stepped closer to her with an expression of deep concern.

Kelsey looked at him with the earnestness of an impending declaration of love. But what she said was, "I've got to go back. But I've got no authority left. Will you help me?"

19

"What theory are we working on here?" Peter asked. Then as he heard voices, he ducked down between two parked cars. Kelsey joined him. They squatted like children playing hide-and-seek; their listening was just as intent.

After the danger passed, Kelsey answered, "It's not a theory, it's just groping in the dark. And I wish it were dark," she added ruefully.

Late on a Sunday morning, the sky was bright. Fluffy white clouds sailed majestically. On the horizon were some darker numbers, but none of them threatened the sun, which smiled down benevolently on the two trespassers in the church parking lot. Peter raised his head cautiously, Kelsey followed his example, and they went to the next row.

"I thought sure they'd be here," Kelsey said angrily, standing on tiptoes to stare around. It was a very democratic church, with members' cars ranging from old Chevrolets, pickup trucks of every age range, new American sedans, but no maroon Lincoln Continental.

"Maybe he got a new car to celebrate," Peter speculated.

"Uh-oh," Kelsey said, and they ducked again. Past the cars in the last row the Continental sailed through the parking lot. Its doors slammed. Peter went around one parked car, Kelsey another, trying to keep out of Morgan and Katherine Fletcher's way, following their progress by the sounds of their mild, habitual snapping at each other.

"No one would have seen a stain on your sleeve if you keep your coat on," Katherine said.

"If I hadn't had to wait for you, I wouldn't have had another cup and spilled it."

"So it's my fault you . . ."

Their voices passed on, toward the church. Kelsey slid out from under a pickup with a blessedly high undercarriage. Peter helped her up. They watched the Fletchers go into the church. "Listen to them," Kelsey said. "Nothing between them at all, after the way he pursued her."

"Morgan pursued Katherine?"

"He must have. When they were both in Houston. Katherine would have been too shy to go after him, and Morgan could have had anybody he wanted. Everybody says that. Don't you know?"

"Before my time, Kelsey."

She shook her head disgustedly. "My God, if I lived in this town, I'd know so much more about it than you do."

"If." They crept toward the Continental. "Hope he left it unlocked."

"You can get into a locked car, can't you? I brought a coat hanger." Kelsey pulled it out of her jacket. Peter looked at it skeptically.

But the car was unlocked. Morgan Fletcher probably felt invulnerable to Galilee thieves. Kelsey opened the driver's door and caught the plush smells of cologne and leather.

"Go," Peter said.

Kelsey pulled the spray bottle out of her jacket pocket. It sloshed with the liquid inside. Kelsey bent inside the car and began spraying. The Continental's seat and back, the gas and brake pedals, the carpet on the floor. Then Kelsey climbed into the back seat and closed the car door.

"Hurry."

Peter opened up the thick tarp he was carrying, spread it on the car's roof, and draped it around all the sides, cloaking the car so that Kelsey, inside, would be wrapped in darkness. He waited a moment, hearing nothing, then lifted a corner of the tarp.

Kelsey stared out. "Damn it."

"Nothing?"

"Not a glow. Not a glimmer."

"Are you sure you're doing it right?"

"You point it and press the button," Kelsey said irritably. "Lydia promised me it wasn't any more complicated than that. You want to try it?"

Peter declined. "Let's do the trunk," Kelsey said.

While Peter folded the heavy tarp, Kelsey popped the trunk open. The trunk was almost empty, just an old pair of tennis shoes on the carpeted floor. Kelsey sprayed all over the interior, then climbed in, and reluctantly, pulled the lid closed on herself. Immediately, the space was airless. And dark as hell.

The trunk opened. Peter could tell from her face the results she'd gotten. "Sure you've got the right spray bottle?" he asked his partner mildly.

"Let's test it. I'll punch you in the nose to draw some blood."

Peter held up his hands. "Sorry."

Kelsey sighed. "Me, too."

"I take it then this doesn't fit your theory?"

"I told you, I don't have a theory." But Kelsey's frown said otherwise. "Let's go to their house," she decided.

Peter sat comfortably in the passenger seat, looking around Galilee with his habitual proprietary air. Kelsey wondered how his work life was. When she'd asked him, Peter had said, "Just routine." But that's what he would say. Peter had been a better investigator for Kelsey than his bosses had intended. He might be paying for it now. She put her hand on his. He caught her little finger with his thumb.

"What makes you think the maid didn't take Taylor?"

Kelsey stiffened. It was the first time Peter had referred to her scene at the rest stop, as if he'd been afraid of setting off a psychotic reaction. Kelsey made a point of speaking analytically. But her subject was emotion.

"The last thing she said to me. I asked her why she hadn't been back to the house, and she got this faraway, frightened expression and asked me how anybody could stay there and hear that baby cry all the time." Kelsey let that sink in, then said what she'd subconsciously learned from the interview. "Helena Parker thinks Taylor is dead."

She expected Peter to say something quietly disparaging about women's intuition, or at least about lying suspects, but he only nodded, accepting her evidence at face value.

They had driven almost entirely through town, which was quiet and vacant on Sunday morning. "Are we going to check Mrs. Beaumont's?" Peter asked.

"If this doesn't work out. Although how anybody could have driven her car away, I can't figure. It was supposed to be in the garage the whole time. How could they even have . . . ?" Kelsey stopped, struck by a sudden thought.

"Good, she left it out," Peter said.

They had arrived at the Fletcher house. Kelsey had never seen it before. The low, wide, ranch-style house was ensconced on the same edge of the piney woods where Mrs. Beaumont's house dwelt, half a mile down the road. But while Mrs. Beaumont's Victorian-style pocket mansion was a bold proclamation, Morgan and Katherine's house was quietly watchful. The trees came up close behind and around it, as if the house had emerged from the forest and could withdraw back into it at any moment.

They stepped out of the car and heard what Kelsey, a lifelong city dweller, thought of as silence, meaning the only sounds were those of nature: a bird calling, pine needles rustling, the sighing of wind through grass. Even in February, the piney woods breathed.

Peter walked quickly to Katherine Fletcher's dark green Buick Riviera, tried each of the doors with increasing frustration, and stood at the last one glaring into the car's interior. Kelsey came up beside him and offered her coat hanger. Peter looked at it contemptuously, returned to her car, rummaged through the small case he'd brought, and returned with a long, flat piece of metal. It didn't look like much of an implement, but with a few gropings and tugs it had the passenger-side door open in less than a minute. "Now this is a truly illegal search," Peter pronounced.

"Doesn't matter," Kelsey said briskly. "If we find something, I'll follow it up with a legal one. If not, nobody needs to know I suspected Galilee's leading citizens."

She walked around the Buick and opened the driver's door. The air was brisk and energizing. But the interior of the car seemed stuffy, as if it were seldom used. "Here goes," Kelsey said, and began spraying. She leaned across the seat to spray the passenger side and its floorboard.

This time Peter climbed into the back seat of the car with her, letting the tarpaulin fall around the sides as he closed the door. In the darkness, they could feel each other's presence. They stared over the seat.

Here and there across the front seat of the car, and in a few small spots on the passenger-side floorboard, patches of a misty green glowed faintly. It didn't take much imagination to turn one of the patches, on the back of the passenger seat, into a baby's handprint.

"Oh, God," Kelsey breathed.

She leaned over the seat and sprayed the gas pedal.

Green.

Peter knew Judge Saunders's home address. It was another ranch-style brick house, its porch adorned with plants. The judged looked momentarily startled, then smiled widely and opened her screen door. "Why, Kelsey. How nice. Come on in."

The case over, they were now old friends. "I'd just as soon stay here on the porch," Kelsey said. "I've got a request for you."

She handed over her papers, the affidavit and request for search warrant. Linda Saunders's smile remained in place, but became compounded with polite puzzlement. "I thought we agreed your authority here in Defiance County was over."

"Actually an assistant AG can present a case to any grand jury in the state. And running a search warrant goes along with that."

The first sentence was true, the second Kelsey's personal legal intepretation. She waited, and the judge started reading the affidavit. After a moment she looked up. "Katherine?"

Kelsey wondered how awful Linda Saunders would really consider the arrest of Mrs. Morgan Fletcher. Kelsey looked for clues, but Judge Saunders's expression was conventionally horrified when she added, "Her own sister?"

Kelsey shrugged. The judge read on. She got to the bottom of the first page and saw there were several more. "Quite a summary. What's the bottom line? What are you looking for this time?"

"Clothes," Kelsey said. "Bloodstained clothes."

The judge frowned. "And where are you expecting to find these bloody clothes?"

"I'm not."

Peter was waiting around the corner, standing beside his own car. When Kelsey pulled up beside him, he raised his hands and his eyebrows. "She sign it?"

"I told her I knew I could get a federal judge to issue the search warrant, but that would seem discourteous to her."

"She signed it. Now who're you going to get to run it?"

"My own little self."

Peter frowned. "You know the judge is on the phone right now." Kelsey didn't deny that observation. "I'll go with you."

Kelsey shook her head. "Your job is to bring the cavalry."

On her way back to the Fletcher house Kelsey drove by Alice Beaumont's familiar Victorian home. It looked as if it had had a new paint job, a bright blue with the trim all in white, the scalloped shingles hanging like a sly eyelid over the dining room window.

Morgan's Continental was in the driveway, parked beside Alice's Cadillac so as not to block it. The two cars filled the driveway side to side. Kelsey wondered what had become of the Blystones' Toyota. It had been gotten decently out of sight, the same way the house had been painted, shoving the horrific events that much more quickly into the past.

Through the dining room window Kelsey got a glimpse of the table at the end of Sunday dinner. Alice and Morgan and Katherine sat on three different sides of the table, coffee cups in front of them. What was their gathering like? Subdued, from the look of it. Would these three survivors ever feel like a family again?

Not if Kelsey was successful at what she was about to do.

She drove away, so she missed Morgan rising from the table to go answer the phone in the kitchen.

Judge Saunders had wrestled with her conscience that long.

The Fletcher house looked the same as when Kelsey had left it a couple of hours earlier. The incriminating Buick still sat in the driveway. Kelsey tried the front door of the house, but predictably it was locked. The door was of solid dark wood, with no glass in it. Kelsey walked along the cement front porch, testing the low windows. They were locked as well. She wondered if Peter had an implement that would get her into the house. She could wait for the Fletchers to arrive home, but if possible she wanted a quick look through their closets without Katherine or Morgan present.

On the back of the house was a wide screened porch. Redwood patio furniture was scattered inside, but Kelsey couldn't imagine Morgan and Katherine sitting back here, talking quietly as they watched night spill out of the woods.

The screen door was locked, but someone had handled that problem in the past; the screen was torn beside the simple hook-and-eye latch. With a key Kelsey lifted the hook and opened the door, feeling triumphantly like a burglar. But her achievement was limited: the back door of the house was solidly locked.

Kelsey walked back around the house, deciding to wait but not liking the decision. On the side of the house by the driveway she looked up and saw a small window well above her head. As soon as she saw it, Kelsey knew what it was: a window over the kitchen sink, placed to allow a housewife to look out while she did the dishes. It was also the kind of window that would occasionally be opened during the summer then that everyone would forget to lock when it was lowered again, because it was so small and so high off the ground.

Kelsey looked around. There was still no sound but that country silence, but she could hear that now. The sounds of the woods were like something small or invisible creeping up on her from all sides. Without her realizing what caused it, the small sounds made her edgy.

But she had the crackle of officialdom in her jacket pocket. Kelsey hurried back to the screened porch and with difficulty lifted one of the small redwood drink tables. The table wasn't terribly heavy, but it was bulky and awkward, and getting it out the screen door took a bit of engineering. When she stood with the table under the high kitchen window, she was already annoyed by the effort she was suddenly sure was about to prove futile.

Shakily, she stood on the table. One of its legs sank deeper into a soft patch of ground, throwing Kelsey against the wall. She almost simplified her entry problem by putting her fist through the window as she scrabbled for a handhold. Balanced at last, she put her thumbs under the window's top sash and pushed.

She almost dislocated her thumbs.

But one side of the window gave upward. The window felt painted shut, not locked. Unwilling to be stopped now, Kelsey returned to the screened porch, looked around as if confronting an array of suspects, and found an old croquet set. She selected one of the stakes that served as a goal, and a mallet, and was aware of looking like a determined vampire killer as she returned to the small kitchen window.

She set the point of the stake under the center at the top of the window frame, right against the glass, and tapped against the opposite end of the stake with the mallet. The window groaned. Kelsey moved the stake to one corner of the frame, tapped, worked on the other corner, and finally when the window began lifting, returned the stake to the middle and hammered the window high in its frame.

But it was a small window. Open, it provided an access of little more than a foot, above Kelsey's head. She had to return yet again to the screened porch and drag out another table, which she set atop the first, in such a rickety structure that after she climbed it and stuck her head and shoulders through the window, as she pushed off the top table, it fell out from under her and thudded to the ground.

But Kelsey was half inside the house by then, her hips on the windowsill, her legs hanging outside. Inside the kitchen, she grabbed for handholds on the sink and pulled herself in, knocking down sponges and a small flower vase from the windowsill that luckily was made of pewter. Kelsey fell onto the linoleum floor.

Before setting out to explore the house, she closed and locked the window, unlocked the back door, and returned her equipment to the screened porch, tiptoing like a burglar in spite of the search warrant in her pocket.

Then the house was hers. It was a dim, gloomy acquisition. The

Fletchers hadn't left a light on, and the house needed lighting, even in the middle of the day. The interior was dark with paneling and carpet. A den at the back of the house featured heavy stuffed furniture; weaker, spindlier furniture was in the living room at the front of the house. The predominant color in both rooms was brown. The feminine touch was a guerrilla one, in candles here and there, crystal ornaments on the heavy dining-room table and mantelpiece, magazines on the coffee table in the den.

Kelsey passed quickly through, found a hallway, and discovered that Katherine and Morgan had separate bedrooms. To give them their presumption of conjugality, perhaps the middle bedroom was just where Morgan kept his clothes. The double bed in that room was plainly made with a simple spread, like a guest room, and no mementos were on the walls or the nightstand to proclaim this the room of the master of the house.

On the other hand, there was no evidence of Morgan in the master bedroom, either. The four-poster bed was neatly made with a ruffled bedspread and a bedskirt almost brushing the floor. The flowered lamps on either side of the bed had white shades, and though they were turned off, light through windows on two walls brightened the pale green wallpaper. Between two windows on the far wall were two framed silhouettes. A rag doll sat in a club chair upholstered in a flowered fabric. On the wall near the dresser, opposite the bed, was a painting of a young girl in a meadow, leading a horse. Through the half-open bathroom door on the far side of the dresser was a glimpse of a dressing table with its own fabric skirt. The decor was a little froufrou for Kelsey's taste, but this was far and away the most pleasant room of the house.

The long interior wall of the bedroom was nothing but closet, but the closet wasn't stuffed as Kelsey had expected. Apparently Katherine Fletcher was an unusual woman who kept her clothes collection well pruned. The far section of the closet held nothing but coats and sweaters. Hats sat neatly on the shelf above. Kelsey went quickly through the outerware and found nothing that interested her.

Another section held dresses, which Kelsey went through more slowly, finding the dress she had first seen Katherine wear in the

Busy Bee and again one day of trial; finding also the dress Katherine had worn to the country club evening.

Finally Kelsey investigated the last section of closet, looking closely at each blouse. Hanging below on a second rod were pants. Kelsey found the dark slacks Katherine had worn with two different blouses to trial; the dark slacks she'd apparently also been wearing in the photograph taken the day of the murders—the day of Katherine's bridge party, when Katherine had worn her favorite blouse, a simple pale green number Kelsey had never seen.

She didn't find the green blouse. Kelsey went through the closet three times. Katherine hadn't been wearing the blouse that morning to church, she'd worn a dress.

Kelsey turned from the closet toward the tall dresser, thinking Katherine might keep some of her blouses folded there. But as she turned, she almost screamed, as Morgan Fletcher stepped farther into the room. He was so quiet, arms folded, that Kelsey had the sudden conviction that he had been in the house almost as long as she had.

"Find anything?"

Kelsey's heart was pumping furiously, eager to live, making her legs quiver with the urge to run. She shook her head.

"And yet you had a look of satisfaction on your face," Morgan said quietly. "As if you didn't expect to find what you were looking for."

Judge Saunders had told him Kelsey's remark, she was sure. Kelsey didn't answer. Morgan asked point-blank, "What is it you were looking for?"

"A blouse. The one your wife was wearing the day of the murders."

Morgan frowned. "I don't remember it."

"It's not here." Kelsey was standing rigidly, while trying to keep her voice light. "And I haven't seen it, through all the days of the trial, though I'm told it was her favorite blouse."

Morgan's stern look turned sadly wise. "Mourning is a strange state, Kelsey. People do odd things. Some react by embracing the past, others want to destroy every trace of it, so they won't be reminded."

"Maybe you're right," Kelsey said, and tried to brush past him out of the room. Morgan leaned just enough to keep blocking her exit.

"But a missing blouse isn't all you discovered, is it?" He reached into his suit coat pocket. "You dropped your spray bottle under the kitchen window."

He examined the bottle. "I don't believe our law enforcement agencies have this technology yet, but I've seen it at conferences." He looked straight at Kelsey. "Did Katherine's car come up green?"

"That's what I want to talk to your mother-in-law about," Kelsey said, still striving for lightness in her tone. Her body was ordering her to push him as hard as she could and run like hell, but she knew the physical impulse was wrong. Again she tried casually to pass Morgan. "Maybe you'd like to come along."

He blocked her again. "No, I think we'll—"

"I'm here," Alice Beaumont said from the doorway.

Morgan stepped quickly aside. Alarm passed almost immediately from his face as he went through several gradations of concerned, questioning, solemn expressions in a matter of a second or two. "Mama Beaumont," he said, not like a boy caught, like a host in his home.

"I thought you said you were going to the courthouse, Morgan. So I brought Katherine home." Her daughter stood behind Alice, just outside the doorway, watching Kelsey rather than either of her family members.

Morgan said easily, "No, that call I got was from Judge Saunders, saying Ms. Thatch here was intent on searching my house. I didn't want to alarm you two."

"Uh-huh." Alice was in her element, surrounded by edgy people in a situation that needed explaining. Her eyes were bright with curiosity and anticipation. She walked into the bedroom, casually separating Morgan and Kelsey. Kelsey glanced at Katherine. The younger woman didn't take the opportunity to come through the doorway. She was still watching Kelsey with a flat stare that was growing hostile. Kelsey was an intruder in Katherine's bedroom.

"I'm sorry, Mrs. Fletcher. But I do have a warrant."

"Why?" Alice asked, drawing Kelsey's attention back to her. "I thought you said your work was over."

"But it wasn't. I didn't finish the case, did I?"

Mrs. Beaumont's eyes suddenly widened with hope, and she stepped forward and grabbed Kelsey's arm. "You've found Helena?"

"No, ma'am," Kelsey said gently. "But I don't need to right now. I know what happened to Taylor."

Mrs. Beaumont's grip tightened. Kelsey turned. "Ask Katherine."

Katherine Fletcher's expression didn't change. It was flat, angry, directed at no one now. Everyone looked at her as Kelsey said, "Katherine came to your house twice that morning."

"Katherine? Is that true? I don't remember."

"You were asleep the first time," Kelsey explained to Mrs. Beaumont. "After the gunfire was over and you said you'd passed out trying to get up to help the crying baby."

Mrs. Beaumont let go of Kelsey's wrist and moved around her closer to her daughter, but she directed her question at Kelsey. "Why did she come?"

"Because she got a phone call. That's what two of the bridge club ladies said, that Katherine left this house after getting a phone call about eleven o'clock. I thought they'd gotten the time wrong because it didn't fit, but now I think they were right."

"But who would have called her?" Mrs. Beaumont was watching her daughter as if she were an exhibit. Her strange detached tone and the way she asked questions about rather than of the daughter standing right in front of her made Katherine seem like a ghost, or a portrait.

"That's the question." Kelsey was no longer trembling. She felt very sure of herself, as if she were back in court. Alice Beaumont was the judge who mattered now. "Who called Katherine that early to tell her about the trouble at your house? Not Billy. He called his brother at the courthouse shortly after ten. We know that from the phone records. No, the call Katherine got was from her husband."

Morgan said mildly, "I was at the courthouse all morning, you may recall."

"You were when you received Billy's call," Kelsey said to him. "And you were about eleven-thirty when you announced to several people that you were going to your mother-in-law's house. Which was odd because it isn't like you. Your habit is to slip out without telling anyone. I know because I've looked for you a couple of times when everyone said you were in the building, but in fact you were returning from running some errand. When you're not in your office, your secretary assumes you're in court, and when you're not in the courtroom, they imagine you're in the judge's chambers or the sheriff's office or the clerk's, so in fact you can come and go pretty much as you please."

Morgan didn't answer. He waited to find out what Kelsey knew. She obliged him. "After you got Billy's call saying he'd had a fight with Ronald, you decided to go over to Mrs. Beaumont's house and play the peacemaker. But when you got there, things had gotten much worse. The fight had resumed between Ronald and Lorrie, it had turned much uglier, and just like I said at the motion for new trial hearing, Ronald had used the gun.

"Was Lorrie still alive when you got there? Had he shot her that recently?"

Morgan wouldn't fall for that. He was no stupid criminal. His lips remained set together, his eyes watchful.

"When you walked in, Ronald was on his knees, sobbing. He'd dropped the gun. It must have been a shock to come on the scene, but you quickly realized that this was the solution to all your problems. With Lorrie dead, Ronald in prison, your wife would be the only heiress to the Beaumont fortune, and you'd be in control of the factory's fate, which would assure your position in the community for the rest of your life.

"So Ronald would still be alive if he could have kept his mouth shut. But that wasn't his way. He begged you for help at first, didn't he? That's when Mrs. Beaumont heard men's voices. He asked before he threatened, didn't he?"

"It never happened," Morgan said.

One reason he kept his face so rigid was that his mother-in-law was staring at it. He shook his head adamantly. Alice Beaumont was studying him in an astonished way. The head shake had no effect on her study.

"Ronald thought you could help him. You're the district attorney. He asked you for help and then he used on you what he'd already used on you. Whatever ugly information he thought he had on you. Something about you and Linda Saunders, I imagine."

Kelsey saw Katherine's head jerk minutely. The words weren't shocking to her, they were just the painful twisting of a knife already in place. Hearing the words spoken aloud, realizing that someone else knew about her husband and another woman, was probably more painful to Katherine than the information itself.

From the tightening of Mrs. Beaumont's mouth as she stared at her son-in-law, this was news to her. Morgan said to Kelsey, "You watch yourself!" But his anger was feigned. He was still waiting.

To Mrs. Beaumont, Kelsey said, "You said yourself that Morgan had stopped opposing Ronald. He'd even sided with him a time or two in the ongoing family argument. That was because he and Ronald had already had a chat about what Ronald thought he'd discovered. That's what Ronald had implied to Lorrie that morning, that he had some leverage that was going to make Morgan support him or at least remain neutral when Ronald went after Billy's job."

Kelsey turned back to Morgan. "And if he said it to his wife, he'd damned sure say it to you, when he was desperate, when he was standing in the room with the wife he'd just murdered. 'Help me or I'll ruin you,' he said, or words to that effect. Knowing Ronald like you did, you knew he'd do it. He might go down, but he'd take you with him. Wreck your marriage so publicly Katherine would divorce you. You'd be out of the family, too. And without the Smoothskins money you'd be only one election away from being just another scrambling lawyer. That was unacceptable. So you picked up the gun. Did you use a handkerchief, or did you just know that you wouldn't leave prints on the gun if you handled it carefully? Ronald lunged toward you, reaching for the gun, and you let him come, until you could place the gun almost against his head when you fired.

"And then it was a perfect solution. Then it looked like murder-suicide, acceptable to everybody."

She hadn't hurt Morgan. He stood stoically, shaking his head, looking more annoyed than angry. "I don't know why you dreamed up this fable," he said, "but it's silly. You can't prove any of it, of course, since it didn't happen."

Kelsey heard the challenge. He still wanted to know just what she had. "I just have logical proof so far. Look at this picture."

It was the photograph taken the day of the murders, of the cars in the driveway at the Beaumont house. Kelsey showed it to Mrs. Beaumont, and Morgan leaned over his mother-in-law's shoulder. Kelsey could feel Katherine behind her, still in the doorway, not curious enough to come forward and join the huddle.

"This is after you'd reported the crimes, after police arrived. Ronald's car was parked in the driveway. Yours was parked behind his, your wife's beside Ronald's. But you were supposed to have been the first person on the scene, Morgan, the discoverer of the bodies. Why would you have parked behind Ronald, blocking him in, if you had thought he was alive inside and might want to leave? Anyone would have parked next to his car instead.

"So in this picture your car should be parked next to Ronald's. Why didn't you? I finally realized it must have been because another car was already parked beside Ronald's when you arrived. Katherine's car. And you knew Ronald wasn't going anywhere, because this was your second trip to the house, you knew Ronald was dead inside. So you parked behind him, blocking his car."

"You mean Katherine got here first?" Alice Beaumont asked.

"That time she did, yes. Morgan had already been here, he'd killed Ronald, then he did the only thing he could for the baby, he put her in her crib and hoped she'd fall asleep. That's why you kept hearing Taylor crying long after the second gunshot."

Mrs. Beaumont nodded. She had such a strange expression as she remembered hearing those cries, as if the memory pained her but it was the only thing she had to hold on to of her granddaughter.

"Then Morgan went back to the courthouse, made sure everyone thought he'd never left, made sure everyone knew he was around, and waited for the bodies to cool. But in the meantime, he called his wife."

Kelsey looked at Katherine. So did her mother. Katherine didn't bother with even a silent denial. She looked past the women at her husband.

Alice Beaumont said, looking at her daughter, "He called her to warn her to stay away. He was afraid she might come to check on me and become a suspect."

"Yes. And have the bodies discovered sooner than Morgan

wanted. So he called her and told her to stay away, but that alarmed Katherine. She rushed out of her party and hurried over here. She parked beside the Toyota and came inside and found her sister and brother-in-law dead and their baby alive in her crib.

"And Morgan was announcing to everyone at the courthouse that he was leaving to go to his mother-in-law's house. He made sure everyone remembered the time was about eleven-thirty, which he knew was an hour after the murders were committed. So he'd be in the clear when he pretended to discover the bodies. He figured Billy would be in the clear, too, since he was racing out of town toward a great alibi. So Morgan would be able to influence the investigation to make sure it was declared a murder-suicide, and everything would be swell."

"But the baby?" Alice asked helplessly.

"That's what screwed up his plans," Kelsey said. Morgan's jaw tightened. He saw Kelsey watching him. "His wife raced over here and she didn't just find the bodies, she found an opportunity. The only one left alive was her niece, and Katherine saw that her husband hadn't finished the job."

It took a long moment for Mrs. Beaumont to catch on, because she resisted the idea. The stages of acceptance played quickly across her face: understanding, denial. She looked at her daughter, and when Katherine didn't say anything, Alice knew Kelsey was right. But acceptance was horror. "No!" Alice said.

"She gathered up the baby, she took the baby away," Kelsey said relentlessly. She renewed her attack on Morgan. "You got back about then, before Katherine drove away. Was she still in the house when you got there, or was she already in her car? Did you realize what she was doing? Would you have stopped her if you could? Because that baby would have been in your way sooner or later, too. She was the only other heiress. Did you think your wife was doing the right thing?"

Morgan didn't answer. Behind Kelsey, Mrs. Beaumont walked toward her daughter. Her tone was determinedly gentle, but insistent. "Katherine? Aren't you going to answer her? Say something, Katherine. Tell her you didn't take Taylor."

Katherine didn't. The muscles were standing out along her jaws. Her eyes were fierce but frozen. Contradictory impulses held her immobile. Her arms were crossed, her fingers spread like twigs. Kelsey said, "But she did, Mrs. Beaumont. I can prove that absolutely. Her car is full of traces of blood. Her sister's blood. The baby already had that blood on her when Katherine wrapped her up and took her out to her car. The baby left the traces of that blood all over the seat.

"And not just the baby. Katherine, too. There are traces of blood on the gas pedal. From Katherine's shoes. That room was so covered with blood Katherine couldn't have walked across it to the crib without getting some on the soles of her shoes. Then she left those traces inside her car when she left with the baby. She should never have had that blood on her shoes because everyone at the scene of the investigation said she never went into the dining room. She went straight up the stairs to take care of you.

"But she'd already been here before then. Look at this other picture." Kelsey held out the photo of Katherine standing on the stairs in Mrs. Beaumont's house, looking down at her husband. "This was taken after Katherine had been in the house for a while, after the police photographer arrived. So why was her coat so tightly buttoned? It wasn't cold, everyone else had shed their coats. But Katherine couldn't, because then everyone would see her blouse, the blouse she'd gotten bloody when she picked up Taylor. No one has seen that blouse again. Katherine got rid of it. It was the evidence that she'd come to the house before anyone knew. That's when she took Taylor away and hid her, then came back, so she arrived again just as the first police were arriving. So she had witnesses to when she apparently arrived for the first time. But by then she'd already left the telltale traces of blood inside her car."

Katherine was looking at Kelsey flatly, with her head slightly lowered, avoiding her mother's stare of growing horror. There wasn't even hatred or anger in Katherine's expression, just an implacable intensity that was even more frightening; it was the flip side of the stubborn devotion Katherine had lavished on her mother all these years, futilely hoping to win her mother's affection. Kelsey continued, "Then after Aunt Goldie came back to stay with you, Katherine went out and supposedly joined in the search. She was gone all night, but no one ever saw her among the search teams. She was on her way to Houston, taking Taylor, getting rid of her."

Alice Beaumont spoke softly, not wanting to believe, still looking for a way out. "Why?"

"You know why, Mrs. Beaumont. Katherine hated the baby. She hated her sister. All Katherine's ever wanted is your love, and there's always been someone standing in the way. First Lorrie. Then Lorrie did something awful. She had a baby. You wouldn't let Katherine have a baby, but you let Lorrie, and you doted on that baby. Katherine knew in a flash that with Lorrie dead you'd transfer all your affection to Lorrie's daughter. She couldn't let someone else get in her way again.

"People told me Katherine never played with Taylor, never picked her up. And since the murders she's been destroying every trace of the baby's existence. She started by burning her own incriminating bloodstained blouse, but then she starting burning baby clothes that weren't evidence of anything except the baby's life. That sounds like obsession, to me."

Alice shook her head horrifiedly, staring at her still-stone-faced daughter. "That's not true. About me. About Katherine. It's not—"

Kelsey was tired of talking. She saw on the faces around her that she was right about everything. She wanted to scream. She did scream. She grabbed Alice Beaumont's arm, whirled her around, and shouted almost in her ear, pointing.

"Oh, Mrs. Beaumont, look around this room! It's a grown-up fantasy of a little girl's room. *Your* little girl! That's all Katherine ever wanted to be. She couldn't let another little girl take her place!"

Fierce wet heat spilled from Kelsey's eyes. Mrs. Beaumont put her hands on her own cheeks as if to hold herself together. She stared at the four-poster bed, the painting of the little girl in the meadow. The room looked like a horrible parody, something that belonged in an atrocity museum.

"Don't say a word," Morgan suddenly said. He was looking over Kelsey's and Mrs. Beaumont's heads. Kelsey whirled and saw that Katherine had finally come into the room. She was advancing on her mother.

"Don't," Morgan said again warningly. "She's just trying to goad you into saying something stupid, Katherine. That's how—"

Katherine wasn't listening. "That's not it," she said loudly. "It was you, Mama. I couldn't let you have that baby. You don't know what to do with babies, Mama. You ruin them, you use them. I wasn't going to let you have another one to ruin!"

Her words were accusing and her voice was loud, but Katherine was crying. Her head leaned so close to her mother's she was practically screaming in her face, but Katherine's own expression was anguished, not angry. She still yearned for her mother's approval, even while condemning her.

Alice Beaumont was utterly stunned. Her mouth was open but silent. She leaned back away from her daughter's emotion.

"I wouldn't let you have another baby girl to ruin," Katherine sobbed again.

Kelsey backed away from them. Suddenly she realized Morgan Fletcher was directly behind her. She whirled quickly. Morgan had closed his eyes wearily. He knew a dam breaking when he saw one, he'd seen a hundred codefendants break and turn on each other. That's how police and prosecutors make so many of their cases. If the conspirators would just have the sense to keep quiet . . .

His gaze turned on Kelsey. She didn't say a word. Morgan was ruined. A man stripped of everything was the most dangerous man in the world. Kelsey saw Morgan come to the same realization. He looked at her with hate. Then his expression turned more crafty.

It was all still a family matter, and he was still in the family. The only outsider who knew anything was standing right in front of him, a girl who'd been stupid enough to bring no backup.

He reached for Kelsey. Kelsey was mesmerized, fascinated at this flowering of utter amorality before her eyes. Maybe he was only reaching to hug her. Maybe he thought he could still manipulate her the way he had every other woman he'd ever wanted.

But his hand closed on her arm painfully. His other hand reached for her throat.

He drew her in. Kelsey let him. It was like being enfolded by the prince of darkness; horrifying but alluring. She lifted her face toward Morgan's.

And stepped down hard on his foot. Morgan choked out a short scream and Kelsey ripped free of his grip. She drove her fist as hard as she could right into his tie, just below the breastbone. Morgan whooshed out all his air and bent almost double. Kelsey brought her knee up into his face, with all the strength of years of running and the furious helplessness of her too-lateness. There was a crack and Morgan fell over backward, nose gushing blood.

Katherine and her mother were still so preoccupied with each other they didn't notice. The stir at the doorway wasn't them, it was Peter Stiller. Peter stopped just inside the doorway, staring at the tableau. The Texas Ranger Efran Price and a Department of Public Safety trooper in brown uniform jostled past him, but then looked reluctant either to come between the women or to aid the injured man.

"Well, I brought the cavalry," Peter said to Kelsey. He looked down. "Looks like we got here just in time to rescue the district attorney."

After the sorting out, after the handcuffing and the taking away of the prisoners, Kelsey was left oddly alone with Alice Beaumont. Even more oddly, Kelsey felt responsible for the older woman. Suddenly Mrs. Beaumont had nothing left, no one.

"Let's go out and lock up," Kelsey said, gently taking the lady's arm. Kelsey felt uncomfortable with this pity the sight of the bereft Alice Beaumont inspired in her, because it was revulsion she really felt. All this horror and tragedy sprang directly from this woman, the only one of the family who could now return to her home and resume some semblance of normal life.

Alice Beaumont must have been thinking along the same lines. She withdrew her arm from Kelsey, straightened her spine, and looked searchingly and with her old hauteur into the prosecutor's face.

"You think this is going to break me, don't you?" Alice's chin came up. "They'll all think that, but they're wrong. This won't break me."

"If it doesn't," Kelsey said, "then you're worse than I think you are."

20

The arrests of Morgan and Katherine Fletcher set the verdict-stunned town of Galilee back in motion. The media teams reassembled outside the Defiance County Jail. Sheriff Early, since he was one of the last people in town to learn about the arrests, had to act more knowing than any other cop in town. "We'd had our eye on Morgan for a long time," he said once, to no response except the rolling of eyes.

The best result of the publicizing of the arrests was a car traveling at moderate speed down the highway from Houston to Galilee. But no one knew about it yet.

"You promise me you got this one in jail for good?"

"It's a strong case, Helena," Kelsey said into the phone. "But you can make it a much better one."

"I didn't hear you say you promise," Helena Parker complained. There were a couple of beats of silence. "Suppose I come in and testify against him, and some Galilee jury believes him instead of me?" A touch of sarcasm showed how strongly she believed in this possibility.

"Then you'll have done your worst and still not hurt him. He wouldn't have any reason to try to get back at you."

"Hmmph. He's still the district attorney."

"Not for long." In fact, Kelsey was standing behind Morgan Fletcher's desk in the Defiance County Courthouse and was doing his job. As the only prosecutor in town who wasn't in custody, Kelsey had become the de facto district attorney of Defiance County. It was Linda Saunders herself who had said, "Just stay here, Kelsey. We need you."

Alone in Morgan's office, Kelsey looked out the window. It was a bitterly bright morning; the cold front had swept through Galilee during the night. Kelsey could see the jail next door. She wondered if Morgan was in a cell on this side, if he could look up at his old office window and see Kelsey's outline there.

Peter Stiller came in without knocking or being announced; the secretary had taken a sick day. Peter wasn't in uniform, but he was on duty. His boss the sheriff had put Peter in charge of the Fletcher investigation. Since Peter had been the only local officer on the scene of the arrests, the sheriff decided to pretend his deputy had been on official assignment at the time.

"Helena—," Kelsey said, both into the phone and to Peter, but the former maid interrupted her.

"I'd like to come home," she said softly, then the line went dead. Kelsey displayed the droning receiver.

"That's how every conversation ends. It's like a hostage negotiation."

Peter was bright and clean and alert, but in his sheep's-wool jacket he looked like a man on his way out of town. Kelsey walked close to him.

"The judge went home early," he said matter-of-factly.

"Probably to take a series of hot showers." Kelsey knew the urge. She could still feel Morgan Fletcher's hands on her shoulders. What was most insulting about the case was that Morgan had had some fuel to try to have Kelsey removed from the case— her supposed debt to Alice Beaumont—but hadn't. Kelsey had realized that was because Morgan had expected to manipulate Kelsey as he had everyone else. He almost had.

The imagined feel of hands on her shoulders became real. She covered Peter's hand with hers.

"Does Helena really know anything?" he asked.

Kelsey nodded. "She came back from the grocery store earlier than anyone knew, about ten-thirty. She saw Morgan's car in the driveway and she heard—well, she won't tell me what yet, but it scared her straight out of town. She was afraid Morgan had seen her, too. But just putting his car at the Beaumont house at that time helps the case against Morgan tremendously."

"We could use it. Katherine's said a little, enough to implicate Morgan, put his phone call to her at the right time. And she's as good as admitted taking Taylor. I don't think she'll ever tell us exactly what she did with her, though."

Kelsey gazed out beyond the buildings of the town into the woods, thinking of the long, futile search that had taken place three months ago. It wouldn't be resumed. No one would ever quite know . . .

"But Morgan's not saying a word," Peter continued wearily, almost admiringly. "He's sent for some hotshot lawyer from Houston."

Kelsey laughed harshly. "Clyde Wolverton's not good enough for Morgan, huh?" She sobered. Her laugh had been false and quick. "That was one of the things that made me suspicious. I could understand thinking Billy should have a local lawyer— make the prosecutor look like even more of a outsider—but Clyde Wolverton? Morgan's the district attorney, he'd know every lawyer in the area. He couldn't have thought Wolverton was the best. But he wouldn't have wanted some good, thorough, out-of-town lawyer handling his brother's defense. Morgan wanted someone he could control."

"You're sounding like the sheriff, now."

"I really was suspicious of Morgan, now and again. You know, one or two of the things that made Billy look guilty actually pointed at Morgan, too. Like Billy getting his suit cleaned. Morgan should have told him not to do that, he should have told him, preserve all the evidence, you want it to prove your innocence. But Morgan didn't want Billy cleared too quickly. If you cops had discarded Billy as a suspect right away, the investigation would have continued. Morgan didn't want that. He wanted the case against his brother to go at least to indictment. I give him credit for not trying to let Billy take the fall, but Morgan didn't want him off too early, either. He knows that once there's been an indictment, the case is closed, as far as cops are concerned. No matter what happened after that, they wouldn't have reopened the investigation. Morgan would have been clear. He was playing a risky game. Remember what Billy said at the end of the hearing? 'Morgan said to wait.' Hold back their best evidence of Billy's innocence until later in the process. He almost held it too long.

"That's why he kept me from seeing the initial report of the search of Billy's car, the one that showed no blood in it. Then it must have been Morgan who planted some blood—maybe his own, wouldn't that be nice?—in Billy's car before you and I seized it." Peter hadn't been the only one who'd known she planned to do that. She'd remembered that Morgan had walked into her office, to invite her to the country club, just as she was announcing her intention of searching Billy's car. Kelsey also remembered, after the shouting confrontation with Wolverton and Billy in the courthouse hallway, how Morgan had stood behind her with his hands on her shoulders and told her to follow her conscience—almost pointing her into the grand jury room. Between Morgan and his unwitting mother-in-law, they had pushed Kelsey into seeking the indictment too soon, before the result of the blood test was in.

"It was perfect. I'd get the evidence of blood in Billy's car, that would be enough for me to get him indicted, then when the blood got tested and found not to be Lorrie's, I'd have to dismiss. I don't think Morgan counted on my going to trial anyway."

"He didn't understand your stubbornness?" Peter asked innocently.

Kelsey butted his arm lightly. "There must be a more flattering way to put that."

Peter smiled. "What happens now?"

Kelsey gave him a quick glance, but Peter wasn't getting personal, not yet. "I don't know. They'll be tough cases to prove. I'd just as soon not be the one appointed to do it."

He gave her a knowing look. Kelsey's gaze returned to the window. A car was pulling into one of the parking spaces in front of the courthouse. The car was several years old, with rust growing along the chrome line at the edge of the roof. For some reason, the car drew almost immediate attention from the few Galileans passing on the sidewalk. Stranger in town, Kelsey thought, recalling the experience.

"If I can talk Helena in from hiding," she said quietly, belying her assertion that she wanted nothing to do with prosecuting Morgan Fletcher, "that would do it, I think. Assuming it's even possible in this town to get a conviction against—"

"I think you know it is."

A man got out of the old car in front of the courthouse. A white man, in an inadequate jacket. Kelsey turned away from the window.

She and Peter were still talking a few minutes later when they heard the outer door open. Peter stepped to the still-ajar door of the office to intercept the visitors. A man came in hesitantly. Peter looked past him, out into the secretary's office. The visitor was the stranger from the car outside. He turned out to be a young man with insistently blond hair that stood up at the back of his head, and earnest features he twisted a little as he said, "We're looking for the district attorney."

"Oh, my God," Peter said at the door. A young woman came past him, looking shy. She wore a heavy coat and had a bundle pressed tightly against her chest.

"The district attorney—," Kelsey began explaining, then stopped, staring.

"No, we mean you," the young man said. "She's the one, isn't she, honey, we saw in the paper?"

Kelsey didn't hear him. She was walking toward the young woman, slowly as if not to frighten a deer, or make a mirage vanish.

The young woman didn't smile. She nodded. She pulled back the blanket and displayed the face of the baby she was carrying.

Kelsey found that her hand was outstretched. Her fingers touched the blanket, touched the baby's hair. Just as she did, the baby cried out, as if in recognition.

They didn't call anyone and they moved fast, but the small-town vibrations had already begun when the strangers had gone up the courthouse steps carrying a baby. Already heads were popping out of offices inside the courthouse as Peter and Kelsey rushed the young couple down the stairs. Kelsey had much to ask them, but she wanted to get to the jail right away, so they talked on the fly.

"Kathy brought her to us. Mrs. Fletcher—she was a volunteer at the adoption agency, we met her when we applied."

"Family-planning clinic," Peter had called the place where Katherine volunteered time in Houston, and Kelsey had thought only of abortions. But such places did arrange adoptions, too. She stared at Peter.

"We checked," Peter said. "Houston cops checked all those places, looking for babies left on their doorsteps."

"They wouldn't have found us," the young woman said. "We didn't even keep our application up-to-date. We knew we were so far down the list we'd probably never get to the top. Kathy seemed to feel sorry for us. She kept in touch." The young woman had smooth, pale skin, a nose that was barely a bump on her face, and chapped lips. Kelsey had hardly glanced at her. She kept staring at the baby. Three months works great changes in a five-month-old baby, but this was Taylor Blystone, no question. She had her mother's green eyes and her aunt's dark brows. Her little jaw was too small to clench impressively; it was hard to say whether the baby bore much resemblance to her grandmother. The baby kept staring at Kelsey questioningly and kept a grip on Kelsey's index finger as the little group walked together, all huddled around the miraculous child.

"Kathy came to our house that night," the young man said, taking up the narrative. "She said she'd found a baby for us but it was all unofficial. If we said anything to anybody, they'd take her away from us."

"But didn't you—," Peter began.

"Oh, we knew," the young man said quickly. "The next day when we read about the murders and the kidnapping, we knew whose baby we had. But we were scared—not for us, for the baby. We didn't know who had killed her parents, we didn't know if the murderer still wanted to find Taylor."

"We've been calling her Kristin," the young woman added suddenly, holding the baby closer to her. She stared down at Taylor, eyes filling. A tear fell onto the baby's hand. Taylor grinned and reached for the young woman's face. "But we know her real name," the young woman sniffed harshly.

"We felt terrible for these people here," the young man hurried on. "But Kathy called us, she said she was the only one who really cared about the baby, and as long as she knew she was safe, it was okay. She said Kri—Taylor would never be safe here, they'd arrested the wrong man. She said she was ours to keep. She knew how much we'd wanted a baby. We—well—"

The young woman said, "After you let that man go, we even let ourselves think maybe Kathy was right, maybe we could keep her forever. But when we heard Kathy'd been arrested for kidnapping her—"

"We just read about it this morning, we came right away."

The little group went out the courthouse doors. A crowd waited for them, a few reporters, but mostly townspeople. "Is that—?" the cries began, and after a couple of people got close enough to see the baby, there were screams of astonishment. Voices called to each other across the small crowd. The reporters couldn't make themselves heard.

The young couple looked frightened. Peter was creating a path for them, insistently moving people aside. Instinctively, Kelsey took the baby from the young woman. Taylor nestled into Kelsey's arms at once. Kelsey gazed down at her, astonished in the throng. The baby looked at her with wide eyes, about to cry or to smile. Kelsey held her breath waiting, not hearing any other sound.

Somehow they reached the jail next door to the courthouse. They hurried through the public lobby past the counter, in among the desks. Startled deputies ran to hold back the crowd. Peter rushed away. Kelsey stood with the young couple, the three of them surrounding the baby. Kelsey handed her back to the young woman but touched Taylor's cheek, then held the baby's hand so her little fingers curled around Kelsey's. She wasn't a tiny baby, she was eight months old. She had a recognizable face. Her eyes continued to look around curiously. She made sounds that were almost speech. Kelsey leaned forward to listen. The young couple smiled at each other over Kelsey's reactions. "We did this for a month," the young man said. "Just stared at her." The young woman sniffed again, but smiled at her baby.

"What? What is it?" a frightened voice said.

Katherine Fletcher stood there in a white jail coverall. She looked thin to the point of boniness. Her cheekbones stood out. Her dark eyes looked larger than Kelsey had ever seen them.

Peter stood behind her, in the doorway through which he'd just brought Katherine from the back of the building. He was arguing with another deputy.

Kelsey stepped forward. "Deputy," she said, getting the other man's attention. "I'm dismissing the charge against this woman. You know who I am, you know I'm the one who had her arrested in the first place? Get the sheriff, I'll take responsibility."

"Miss, I know you, but you're not my boss, you don't—"

"Get your boss," Kelsey said, but the argument was interrupted by a scream.

"*No!*" Katherine Fletcher was shouting. She had finally caught sight of the young couple. Even as she flung herself toward them, she said it again. "No, no, no! I told you to stay away. Keep her away forever. Oh, why did you—"

Kelsey put out her arms to keep Peter and the other deputy from intervening. Katherine reached the young couple and stopped. They each put an arm around her. There were murmurs among them. It was obvious they were friends.

"We couldn't let you . . . ," Kelsey heard both the woman and man saying. Katherine was shaking her head. She reached out, and Peter went toward her again, but Katherine took the baby gently, looked down at her sadly, and lifted her to her face. The baby's hands took her aunt's hair.

Katherine was sobbing. "I told you she'd never be safe here," she said quietly. But she smiled as she held the baby close to her face.

I wonder if I was right, Kelsey thought. Did Katherine steal this baby in order to kill her? But Katherine hadn't been able to do it. Looking at Katherine, at the joy and pain mingled on her face, Kelsey remembered the abortion her parents had forced on the teenaged Katherine. As she fled with this baby the day of the murders, the living, crying baby must have become mingled in Katherine's mind with the baby she had never had. She couldn't have harmed her.

"I asked you to stay away." Katherine's tears had stopped falling. "I didn't want her back here. I wanted her away forever."

But she laughed quietly as she stared down at the baby and the baby reached for her face.

The large room was silent. Even the reporters only stared. Katherine Fletcher was coming alive before their eyes. When she'd stepped through the door from the cells, she'd been a stick figure, devoid of life—the mode she'd been willing to assume for the long years until her heart stopped beating. Now her face moved expressively, the few murmured syllables she exchanged with her two friends were lively, her eyes played over her niece's face as if Katherine could absorb the baby into her. People in the crowd who'd known Katherine her whole life realized they had never seen her before today.

Then the outer door slammed open, and the specter appeared at the feast. Mrs. Beaumont stood dramatically in the open door, dressed as well as ever, but a light like insanity illuminating her face. "Where is she?" she shouted.

No one thought she meant her daughter. A path opened, through citizens and cops alike, and Mrs. Beaumont went sailing up this human corridor to where her daughter stood at its end. Katherine didn't look up until her mother was right in front of her. That was when one alert news photographer took a picture that would appear on front pages of newspapers around the country the next day: Mrs. Beaumont in her mink reaching to take her recovered granddaughter, not even looking at her daughter in her white jail coverall. In the instant of the photographing the baby was caught between the two women. But there was no struggle. Katherine released her hold and let her mother take Taylor from her.

"Oh, my baby, my baby," Mrs. Beaumont declaimed, lowering her face to the baby's. Kelsey, standing back, couldn't help hearing a theatrical component in the woman's simpering.

The baby began crying. The young woman reached for her, but Katherine was quicker. "That's enough, Mama. You're scratching her." She deftly extracted Taylor from her mother. The same soft smile came over Katherine's face again when the baby was in her arms.

Mrs. Beaumont dabbed at her cheeks with a handkerchief, removed a heavy bracelet from her gloved wrist, then put out her arms. "Here, Katherine," she said peremptorily.

"No, Mama." That was another good picture, Katherine smiling down at the baby, not even glancing at her reaching mother. "I'm going to take care of her."

Katherine looked back over her shoulder. Her eyes found Kelsey's. Immobile, Katherine's face changed. She hadn't forgotten Kelsey's charges against her, nor that Kelsey had uncovered her worst secrets. She flashed momentary anger, then she forgave, acknowledged her complicity, acknowledged much more than that, the years of silent rage and hopelessness, then thanked Kelsey, reaching out for her; she needed a friend. It was all in Katherine's eyes. She'd spent so many years as an undercover agent in her own life that her body and her face wouldn't radiate her emotions. But Katherine's eyes expressed everything. Her dark eyes were prisoners stepping free.

Kelsey nodded. "You're free to go."

The little group turned away.

"Now, just a minute." Alice Beaumont drew herself up and stared at Kelsey both questioningly and commandingly. Kelsey made no reply, until Mrs. Beaumont snapped, "Aren't you going to do something?"

"Mrs. Beaumont, it'll take some time to sort out custody. Fighting over her would be the worst possible thing for the baby."

"Hmmph." Mrs. Beaumont gave Kelsey's opinion all the consideration she had ever given anyone's advice. She turned the imperious look across the room, looking for someone else who would behave normally and take an order.

Everyone turned away from her.

It wasn't coordinated, it wasn't obvious. Deputies who had a moment earlier been standing around remembered their tasks. They returned to their desks or picked up phones. One appeared with a coat and put it over Katherine Fletcher's shoulders as she went out past the counter. The people out there gathered around Katherine, the young couple, and the baby they mutually sheltered. It was the politest crowd Kelsey had ever seen. They congregated but they parted, letting the group pass on. People leaned their heads close enough to see the baby, smiled, and stepped back. The reporters weren't part of the politeness, of course, their jobs didn't permit it, but when their questions were ignored, they subsided, content to take footage and snap pictures. The writers among them could compose captions.

Mrs. Beaumont gathered herself together and walked, didn't run, after the departing group. Her shoulders were back. She had a look in her eye as if she had an infinite store of ploys, and allies no one had suspected. After all, it was only her daughter walking out, whom Alice Beaumont had spent a confident lifetime cowing.

The press of people followed the group out. Once again Kelsey and Peter were left alone, standing in the penetrating glare of the overhead lights in the sheriff's office. They began walking slowly toward a side exit Peter knew.

"Do you really think Katherine's strong enough to fight off her mother to raise the baby?" Peter asked skeptically.

"She was going to go to prison rather than let anybody know where Taylor was. I think she may be stronger than anyone's suspected."

"She's let everybody in the world ride roughshod over her. Her mother, Morgan—"

"She never had anything worth fighting for." Kelsey felt Peter's sidelong glance. "Katherine changed on that highway to Houston. How many miles out of town was that rest stop where she stopped and changed her out of the bloody gown? That was a gesture of caring. It didn't take Taylor long to win Katherine over, once they were alone together."

They were walking down a narrow, hard-floored corridor, clattering with artificial light. At the end of the hall Peter opened a nondescript white door that opened like magic onto the outdoors. A gust of crisp air enveloped them. The doorway framed a scene of a side street of Galilee, shops lining the street on both sides, a few cars moving, parking available at the curb. Far down the street the buildings ended and the scenery began to rise. As always, Kelsey's eyes were drawn upward, to the greenness of the pines. The trees looked even taller in the bright winter air.

Peter laid a hand lightly on her shoulder. "When're you heading back?"

Kelsey discerned the falsity in his casualness. *Austin*, she thought, looking at the scenery and the houses and the few pedestrians, some of them still heading toward the courthouse.

Maybe some of them were looking for her, with stories to tell. *Why is it I live in Austin?*

"Maybe never," she said, startling herself. She tried to cover with a light, mild joke. "But jobs are so hard to come by in these little bitty towns."

Peter smiled his slow, true smile. "I think I know of an opening," he said.